THE SARDANA DANCERS

Robin Jenkins (1912–2005) studied at Glasgow University and worked for the Forestry Commission and in the teaching profession. He travelled widely and worked in Spain, Afghanistan and Borneo before finally settling in his beloved Argyll. His first novel, *So Gaily Sings the Lark*, was published in 1951 and its publication was followed by more than thirty works of fiction, including the acclaimed *The Cone-gatherers* (1955), *Fergus Lamont* (1979) and *Childish Things* (2001). In 2002 he received the Saltire Society's prestigious Andrew Fletcher of Saltoun Award for his outstanding contribution to Scottish life.

ROBIN JENKINS

THE SARDANA DANCERS

Polygon

First published by Jonathan Cape in 1964.
This edition published in Great Britain in 2006
by Polygon, an imprint of Birlinn Ltd

West Newington House
10 Newington Road
Edinburgh
EH9 1QS

9 8 7 6 5 4 3 2 1

www.birlinn.co.uk

ISBN 10: 1 904598 88 9
ISBN 13: 978 1 904598 88 6

British Library Cataloguing-in-Publication Data
A catalogue record for this book is
available on request from the British Library

The publisher acknowledges subsidy from

 Scottish
Arts Council

towards the publication of this volume

Typeset by Hewer Text UK Ltd, Edinburgh
Printed and bound by CPD (Wales) Ltd

One

The horned cloud on the horizon now drooped. He poked at it with his forefinger. The moment of truth.

He said it aloud: 'I have as few creative impulses in my head as this Mediterranean has seagulls, and they do not have a vast blue exhilaration to soar into, but crawl in and out of the dark narrow lobes of my brain, like earwigs in a stump of rotten wood.'

Pleased with the similitude, in spite of the annihilating confession it embodied, he repeated it, with fond lips.

'At this moment of surrender I am already four years older than Alexander the Macedonian when he set out on his conquest of the world, and Jane Austen when she wrote *Pride and Prejudice*.'

The six gulls swirled inland, up over the pink and white cubes of houses, the superb and arrogant hotel amidst the pines, over the decaying church so useful to painters, and over the dusty stunted olives on the dry terraces, until they had as their background again the immense hot blueness of the sky, and the American radar temple on the crest of the hill.

'Because of my mouth that remains – sweet? demure? humane? – despite all the pursings and poutings of disillusionment, and because of my smooth cheeks, large blue eyes, wide calm sunburnt brow, high earnest voice, and fair hair that I like to stroke for its silkiness I am accused of homosexuality. If it were true I might find opportunity for suffering. If I could suffer then I might sympathize, and if I

had sympathy I should perhaps be able to understand why
the characters in my thrice-written twenty-seven-times-
rejected novel convince no one, and also why Maddy, after
a glum-faced winter of bad unfinished paintings, has decided
to become beautiful and gay again, for no better reason
apparently than that Norman has written to say he is coming
to visit us, although last summer their love for each other, at
first as exciting as a pool of tropical fish, in the end turned
into a mysterious dismal mess, like a squid unsold by
evening.'

If not in love where else to find escape? In drink? But
drunkenness that made Terence O'Donnell more charming
and persuasive than ever made him bilious and inane. In
misanthropy, for which in this Belsen of a century there was
so much justification? Hatred of an appropriate magnitude
and intensity was beyond him. Perhaps of course he ought
not to want to escape at all. As Isabel had said, with the
shrewish relevance of a pregnant woman: there were other
responsibilities besides those owed to art. He could spend
the annuity left him by his Aunt Edith, not on prolonging
this deception of himself as a writer of genius, but on
relieving misery and combating cruelty. Yes, but were there
not so many worthwhile urgent causes that to try and choose
among them would only produce a paralysis of philan-
thropy?

About to scurry back into his shell, he lifted the binoculars
and again scanned the bay for his sister. Soon he saw her,
conspicuous among the water-skiers, not so much because
of her skill and daring as because of her happiness and her
talent for sharing it. The very wake she left spelled it out; all
the blue sky, every white yacht, the clouds, reflected it.
People watching her found it the best moment of their
holidays. All were laughing; some clapped.

He laughed and clapped himself.

Yet there was a doubt. That letter had struck him as odd,

even ominous, though he could not quite say why. Not only was it the first for almost a year, it seemed also to have been written in one of those fits of gloomy earnestness that had interspersed Norman's guitar-strumming crew-cut nonchalance. Maddy had taken its high-flown queerly moralizing tone as a joke. Its obscure commending her to sweet Jesus Christ she had laughingly interpreted as a more or less witty reference to the fact that their house stood in the Calle de los dos Angeles, the Street of the Two Angels. She could of course be right, but Jonathan had no reason to trust her, or for that matter, any woman's intuition; his own was usually sounder. Like most people in love, Maddy betrayed a simpleness and trust that her brother found disconcerting and pathetic. She confided in everyone, in Ampara the maid, Pedro, Ampara's Guardia Civil boy-friend, the cartero who had brought the letter, the boy from the bodega. Long ago she had cheerfully admitted she had no real talent as a painter; her level, if she was lucky, would be illustrating women's magazines. Love was her compensation.

Perhaps it was to be Norman's too. In his travels about Europe since last summer he also might have encountered apocalypse. If anything he was a more arid writer than Jonathan, in spite of a persevering eroticism in his themes. Revelation when it came must be for him bleak indeed.

Ceasing to smile, and opening his eyes, Jonathan watched Maddy skim towards the beach. The café with its striped sunshades came into view. Under the arch leading out to the promontory a donkey rested in the shade a yard or two from a painter crouched at his easel, painting the church above. At least six others could be counted painting it from different angles. On the pebbles lay the sun-soakers, among them several in justly illegal bikinis. A Guardia Civil, gun over his shoulder, stood watching from the road; his patent-leather tricorn hat glistened like lechery. When Jonathan had challenged Pedro with not doing his duty and arresting all repulsive bikini-wearers, he had shrugged his burly shoulders, spat on the ground, and then squinted cryptically at the spittle. Jonathan had not quite understood.

Among the great red whale-like boulders beneath the pines three couples embraced; two he judged by their oblivion of the discomfort – and possibly of the stink, for that corner was a latrine – to be French; the other, ill at ease, must be English or Swiss. Children played near by. A bald man, gross with fat, wearing scarlet trunks, strode master-fully towards the sea and hurled himself belly-first upon it.

Suddenly Jonathan remembered something. Their own outboard engine being out of order once more, Maddy must have got someone else's to tow her. He searched through the binoculars again and came upon her seated at a café table on the terrace; just beyond gleamed a magnificent speed-boat, no doubt owned by one of the near-millionaires from the hotel. He looked to see if its owner was now Maddy's host, but found his view obscured by an enormous woman in a yellow bathing costume and a huge straw hat. Maddy could be seen, laughing and talking eagerly; but instead of her companion was this big yellow rear. Jonathan smiled, appreciating another of fate's little ironic touches; his novel was full of such, or rather of attempted imitations. Yet he was anxious too. He in theory, she in practice, believed sex to be a means of liberating one's self. When in Paris studying she had had more affairs than he cared to think about; here, in Spain, there had been so far three, including Norman. Isabel, respectably married – if either word could be applied to an alliance with David Reeves, that critical Savonarola – had declared herself scandalized. She had demanded that Jonathan take his duties as a brother, a twin at that, more responsibly. He had conceded he should.

At last the fat obscurer waddled off, waving like a lover to a bald fellow on the beach. Jonathan was therefore a little irritated before he saw who Maddy's companion was: Spanish, middle-aged, tall, handsome, and obviously rich. Probably he was married to the daughter or sister of some high Falange official. Let Maddy be involved in scandal with such a man, and the price would be the instant withdrawal of her *residencia*, and of Jonathan's too. They would be deservedly expelled from Spain.

But surely even Maddy could take a drink with a courteous stranger without disrupting her own life or her brother's? After all, the vivacity which the Spaniard was admiring was caused by her expecting Norman in a day or two. Love by its nature was bound to be a little grotesque, but it need not be destructive.

All this time Ampara's singing below in the kitchen, jolly and raucous, had been disturbing him. Now it began to ascend, accompanied by her clumping footsteps. Then in the narrow doorway leading on to the roof appeared her red-cheeked, dark-eyed, lively face. For a few seconds he had to suffer her admiring grin. Herself black as a raven, she boasted to other servants about Maddy's hair, and his.

'Well, what is it you want?' he asked, in his stilted Spanish.

'The wine's finished, señor. I don't think there's enough for lunch.'

She came out on to the roof. A Galician peasant-girl, thirty years old, she was physically tougher and stronger than he, though she hardly came up to his shoulder. She thrust out her chest, to show off her new brassière with foam-rubber inlays. In his opinion she was foolish not to be grateful for the blessing of small neat breasts.

It was not the first time she had flaunted her sex at him. On one occasion, indeed, a flicker of temptation had been kindled in him. Coming home unexpectedly he had surprised her using his shower. She had scampered to her own quarters, holding a towel big enough to have quite concealed her had she wished it to. As lonely as Crusoe, he had

stared at her damp footprints on the tiles. How gruesome –
no, how piteous – her buttocks so muscular, her feet so
horny. She had reappeared in a minute or two, wearing only
a thin cotton dress, and with her hair as wet as Aphrodite's.
Reeking of Maddy's scent, and of every woman's duplicity,
she had explained that her own shower being out of order
she had had to use his: he had guests coming that evening,
and it was necessary for her to be fresh.

Afterwards, of course, it had meant he was immune to her,
and a little more so to women in general. On her part,
however, her campaign of giggles, oglings, and bottom-
wagglings had been intensified. Other men would have got
rid of her. Unfortunately since to give the true reason would
have been indelicate he would have had to proffer some
other, such as her pilfering of Maddy's cosmetics or her
clumsiness with dishes. Such a lie would damage his inmost
core, his profoundest manhood.

He had written a short story about the situation. It had
been rejected by several magazines, British and American.
After one such rejection he had thought, in despair, of
actually cohabiting with, or even of marrying, Ampara,
and so by violence altering his whole inadequate nature
and the course of his life. Thus only might he be convulsed
into writing acceptable stories. As his wife, as the mother of
his children, she could hurl him into a way of life utterly
different from that which he had so far abortively led. For a
minute or two he had gazed in fascination into that vortex of
paternity: a wife brawnier than he, niños that prattled their
conceit in Spanish, and swarms of garlicky in-laws with soil
under their finger-nails.

From the moment of that glimpse, their relationship had
never been simply that of employer and maid. In a lunatic
but inescapable way, he frequently felt he was her husband.

'Then go and buy some,' he said.

'You'll have to give me money.'

Every morning he doled out to her from his purse exactly enough for the day's purchases. It could not help becoming, in that Spanish ambience, a sort of man and wife arrangement. Besides, it was almost impossible to avoid unintentional intimacies when conducting a conversation in a language one used imperfectly.

She was laughing. He himself frowned. The burden of people's amorous absurdities was intolerable enough without having to shoulder also their childish risibility. All his life he had distrusted laughter, especially if female. Sometimes, as at the market in the mornings, it burst into guffaws behind his back. His sandals might provoke it, especially if, in the course of some experiment in reorientation, he had stained his toe-nails; or his shorts, lilac or green; or his fastidiousness worn like a scent; or his very chivalrous forbearance in the face of their biological rudeness.

He should have shouted to her to go about her business. But in issuing orders he could not trust himself not to sound like a strict, fond, Spanish husband. To speak as a master was in his nature, certainly; but it would have distressed his principles. Abhorring politics, and worshipping art, he tried to see every human being, not as a soul, for he abhorred religion too, but as an inspirer or suggester of beauty.

He counted out forty pesetas for the wine.

'Is your tall sister arriving tomorrow?' she asked.

Su hermana alta, his tall sister, was Isabel, the eldest and most practical of the Broxmeads. Trained as a secretary, she had been expected to grab some well-to-do executive; instead, to everyone's astonishment, she had married David Reeves, the art critic.

He nodded.

'With the niña?'

'I suppose so.'

Of course they were bringing the brat, in spite of his hints that her presence might be inconvenient. Neither he nor

Maddy had yet seen their niece, born eight months ago in England. He had had an obscure but powerful feeling that a baby in the house would end once and for all his pretensions to be a creative artist. Coming from a manuscript or canvas where all had gone well to a chuckling or even a howling infant, one would be able to show that excess of human optimism expressed by tickling tiny toes or by prattling the gibberish that had stood for speech before language was invented. How different, though, when novel or painting was a perpetration, not a creation at all; then a baby, even if one's own, must seem a perpetration too.

Ampara of course was delighted; had the child been male she would have been in raptures. The Spaniards were ridiculously fond of children, and their glaring bias in favour of boys was surely pagan rather than Christian.

'I'm afraid it'll mean more work for you,' he said, spitefully.

Isabel had asked him to engage a nursemaid for the four or five weeks; he had done nothing about it.

'I don't mind,' cried Ampara. 'I love babies. Do you know what I would like most in the world?'

He gazed at her distrustfully.

'A baby,' she cried. 'Un niño.' And then she added boldly: 'Un niño rubio.' A boy with fair hair.

She ran downstairs singing her wish.

In spite of the sunshine, the blue sea, the scarlet flowers, laughter in the street, and Ampara's singing, he felt surrounded by sinister forces, or, what was worse, by their innocent agents.

Two

Maddy brought in a letter, handed to her by the postman in the street; and also, pressed upon her by one of her fishermen friends at the quay, a large triangular fish, whose glazed eyes emphasized the brilliance of hers. Whether or not in the dark depths of the sea it had ever known love, Jonathan could not tell; nor could he imagine how, if it had, it had expressed it. Maddy, ablaze with emotion, was almost as mysterious. She was also, what no fish could ever have been, unscrupulous. Every smile, every lilt of her foot, every swift turn of her head, every gleam of her eyes, commanded you to share her joy and admire her loveliness. If not, she would not hesitate to torment you with them. Postmen, fishermen, and wealthy speedboat owners would obey with gladness and alacrity; a brother, particularly a twin, and a chaperon to boot, could not. He wished she would not wear such gaudy slacks, so bespangled with sequins, and so tight in the bottom. Her hair could have stood almost any other eccentricity of arrangement, but not this Highland cow frill effect. Half the time she squinted at you through it.

She came up the stairs singing. Ampara from the kitchen sang more loudly in response.

'From Terence, I think,' cried Maddy, tickling him under the chin with the letter.

He snatched it from her. 'Nothing from Isabel and David?'

'Surely you didn't expect them to write once they'd set

out? Isn't it hot? Isn't it glorious? I could do with a beer. What about you?'

As she spoke she went dancing into the kitchen, where Ampara greeted her with raucous '*Olés*'.

'No, thank you,' he cried, rather peevishly. 'I consider it most inconsiderate of them. After all, it's only decent to let people know when you propose descending upon them.'

She called from the kitchen: 'But you aren't people. You're Uncle Jonathan. Tio Jonathan.' The Spanish was added for Ampara's benefit. Both of them laughed.

Upon a small table stood a melancholy Quixote carved in wood. Jonathan tapped him on the helmet with the envelope.

Yes, it was true, this child had altered his status in the universe. It was certainly one of those innocent agents.

Maddy came from the kitchen and went out on to the terrace where the table was set for lunch. She drank her beer gratefully.

'I may as well tell you now,' he said.

'Tell me what?'

'I have finally faced it.'

'Faced what?'

'The truth.'

She giggled, and then apologized. 'It's the beer, it's so cold.'

'Do you take me for a child? You're laughing at me.'

'Well, for heaven's sake, Jonathan, how does anyone face the truth? Where is it, to face it?'

'I have decided to give up writing.'

More than half her attention was elsewhere, probably on the rich speed-boat owner.

'I have no creative ability,' he said. 'It has been obvious for years. At last I have faced it.'

'But I thought you said few novelists under thirty ever write anything worthwhile?'

'Yes. But there must be glimmers at least of the coming maturity.'

'Up to now you've had nothing to say. Some day you will have.'

'What day?'

'The day you yield to temptation. But what's Terence got to say? I hope he and Bridie aren't proposing to descend upon us. Yes, Jonathan, like the rest of us you lack vision; but, unlike us, you persistently resist temptation.'

He knew she meant the temptation of love, or rather, to put it more frankly and crudely, of sex.

'I noticed you yielding to it rather flagrantly,' he said.

'Did you?' she cried eagerly. 'Were you watching? Isn't he marvellously handsome?'

'He seemed to me quite old enough to be your father.'

'Maturity, Jonathan.'

'I was under the impression you were in love with Norman.'

She stared at her empty beer glass.

'Just what do you mean by the expression, being in love?' he asked.

'You don't know that, do you, Jonathan?'

'I have my own ideas. It's yours that puzzle me.'

'You think it's not possible to be in love with two men at the same time?'

'God forbid I should call anything impossible in that distempered kingdom. But it would be irregular, at least.'

She just smiled.

He felt excluded. She too was an agent, though not so innocent. Perhaps Terence was also, through this letter.

With trembling fingers he opened the envelope. Few men in the world could be at the same time both charming and tactless like Terence. Who else would have dared to take away the typescript of *Journey to a Life* for eleven weeks, ignore entreaties, commands, and threats, and then blandly return it without a page read? He and his wife, Bridget Mary, taught English at an eccentric language school in Barcelona. Often they owed rent, sometimes they were hungry; but at their flat, where you might have to sit on the floor, you would meet interesting people like poets and toreros. Terence not only wrote poetry himself, he also got it published, in journals like the *Spectator* and *New Statesman*, which meant of course that they were as ephemeral as the editorial vapourings. Still, he had his moments of vision, blurred deliberately by too much whisky, if he could get it, or too much cheap red wine. He could not bear to see, with crucifying clarity, his maimed ambitions.

The letter was written on a piece torn apparently from some pupil's jotter. Before Jonathan could unfold it the telephone rang in the hall.

'I'll get it,' cried Maddy, jumping up and rushing out.

Jonathan frowned and shook his head. Likely she had given that fellow at the hotel her number. Colour she flung recklessly on to her canvases, and into her life too: green for Norman's jealousy, red for his ardency, and silvery-grey for the Spaniard's middle-aged smoothness.

He read the letter.

Dear Jonathan boyo,

As you can see from the notepaper I have been correcting some hideous exercises. My soul's destroyed. It's hot and sticky here in Barcelona, so I do it in the nude. Bridie says it's a form of perversion, because you see some of these exercises have been done by chic and shapely señoritas. But this you will, with Tolstoyan purity of mind, condemn as vulgar. Bridie and I feel it's time we escaped from this oven, and where are breezes fresher and welcomes more cordial than in the Street of the Two Angels? Expect us shortly.

We met a friend of Maddy's the other day, Ramon Tapiolas; he paints grey abstracts, with bits of string imbedded. Bridie thought they were mice's tails. Lord, I think she's given him an idea. How is darling Maddy? Give her our love.

By the way, dear boy, I hope you won't object if we bring a friend with us for a day or two. It's not quite settled yet, but I should warn you it's on the cards. Hush, in the meantime. If she does come, you'll enjoy meeting her. Bridie and I think she's the most beautiful woman we've met here, and as you know it's a city of beautiful women.

How's the second novel coming along? Out of the ashes of the first, the second will arise, every word an iridescence, to dazzle the world.

Fuller explanations when we meet, very soon, I trust.

Through the thunder and lightning of humiliation Jonathan heard Maddy talking to Isabel on the telephone. Now she was calling him. He did not want to go; nowhere in the undazzled world was pleasant. He did not want to speak to Isabel, or to anyone. Pale with bitterness, he stood beside Quixote. He felt himself within disintegrate and turn cold; only from these ashes would rise no phoenix but some ludicrous parrot. How diabolical of those forces to use Terence's prattle to deliver such an atomizing blow.

'Jonathan!' called Maddy, for the fourth time.

He walked into the hall.

'Here he is now,' said Maddy. She spoke to him. 'Isabel says David's got something to tell you.'

'What?'

'I don't know. She wouldn't tell me. They expect to arrive tonight. They're at Perpignan. What's Terence saying?' As she handed over the telephone she took the letter from him. Life, the gesture said, goes on; and said it so cheerfully.

'Hello, Isabel,' he said. 'Jonathan speaking.'

She burst out laughing. 'Why so doleful?'

He tried hard to be cordial. 'Sorry. How are you, Isabel?'

'We're all very well, thank you, except for poor little Linda.'

'Why, what's the matter with her?'

'She's had diarrhoea for three days.'

'Haven't you seen a doctor? It might be dysentery.'

Why did she have to laugh at his solicitude? 'Yes, that's what we were afraid of. Luckily it wasn't. She's almost better now, thank goodness, but it's given her an awful shake. I did so want her Uncle Jonathan to see her at her best.'

'I'm sure he will, in due course.'

'Is there anything the matter, Jonathan?'

Had she been his mother, and he sixteen years younger, he might have confessed to her that he had just realized he was not the genius he had dreamed himself to be. As it was, he merely said: 'No, nothing's the matter.'

'What about Maddy? Is she all right?'

He glanced round to see if Maddy was listening. She was seated out on the terrace reading Terence's letter.

'She seems to be preparing her usual summer fireworks,' he said.

'That's what I thought. So he's coming after all?'

'I'm afraid so.'

'But I thought we agreed he should be kept away from her?'

'We did, Isabel; but she didn't.'

She sighed. 'Yes, I suppose so. Well, here's David. He wants to tell you something. See you tonight then.'

As the telephone in the Perpignan bar changed hands he heard a baby wail. Soon it would be wailing here in his home, his sanctuary. Not only Norman should have been prohibited. Now that art had cast him out to be at the mercy of life, how subtle once again of fate to send, as life's first inquisitor, this crawling little creature with its ceaseless onslaught on his unprotected human nature.

David's voice was, as always, tense and dramatic; so it was when asking for the salt to be passed, or when explaining why someone's painting or novel was imitative, false, sterile, and without vision. Someone seemed to be always tugging cruelly at his beard. He was so tall too, six feet six, and quite fanatically skinny.

'Hello, Jonathan,' he said, 'how are things?'

'Pretty much as usual, David.'

David's giggle was a formidable rather than effeminate noise. 'Do you expect me to be sorry for you, wallowing in sunshine all winter?'

'It did rain sometimes. Have you had a good trip?'

'Yes, not bad. Isabel's probably warned you we expect to arrive tonight. The joy of our lives has had a dose of the skitters, and the car's got a dozen rattles I can't trace. Apart from those, I don't see why we shouldn't be able to make it, provided we don't roll over a cliff. We're taking the coast road. How's Maddy?'

'Very well.'

David ruminated. Last summer he had threatened to horsewhip Norman. It had been a scene of ridiculous melodrama. In the end of course everyone, except Jonathan, had got hilariously tight; even Isabel, seven months pregnant. David had sung bawdy songs, to Norman's accompaniment on the guitar.

'Will he be there?' asked David.

'I think so.'

'Pity. There's something I'd like to put to you, Jonathan, as early as possible.'

As Jonathan waited he forbore to speculate. Even people one liked and respected needed all the surprise one could afford them; otherwise, dullness and ordinariness took them prisoner. It applied to him too.

'I've taken the liberty of inviting someone to visit you, Jonathan.'

For the first time Jonathan was reminded of Terence's outrageous proposal to bring a woman, with that puerile bait of her beauty. 'Of course, David,' he replied, rather haughtily. 'Any friend of yours will be welcome.'

'But I can't honestly call him a friend. I've only met him once. I'll tell you what I think he is, in one word: a genius.'

Here was fate striking again, savagely this time. Of all the words he wished to avoid at present, genius was foremost. How cosy and reassuring it had been, under yesterday's dispensation, with all his illusions rosy as wine, to read some novel acclaimed by reviewers, and find it no better than his own, not by a comma's amount. In a mediocre world one might admit one's own mediocrity without too numbing a humiliation. But among the gelded and tethered oxen no lion must pounce.

'Not old Pablo himself, David? Or Salvador, with a flower in his ear?'

'Somebody few people have heard of so far.'

'A Frenchman?'

'No.'

'Spaniard?'

'No.'

'Not an Englishman surely?'

'A Scot.'

'A Scot!' Jonathan's voice rose as high in incredulity as David's had sunk in diffidence.

'Yes. Why not?'

Jonathan had never been to Scotland, had met few Scotsmen, and, so far as he knew, harboured no prejudice against the country. Whenever he had thought of them it had been as a rather uncongenial mass of dour porridge-eaters, religious bigots, football fanatics, bare-kneed buffoons, and dedicated shipbuilders. As artists he would have put the Eskimos in front of them. The spark from heaven knew better than to alight on that soaked wilderness.

'Well,' he said, indulgent rather than hostile to a nation so inveterately mediocre, 'if you'd asked me to guess where the vision was going to come from to light up all our darknesses, I'm afraid Scotland would never have occurred to me.'

'They did produce Raeburn and Mactaggart.'

'Raeburn I have heard of. Was Mactaggart a football-player?'

'He was a very fine painter.'

'And where, in Scotland, does your genius hail from?' Edinburgh, after all, must be allowed some distinction.

David hesitated. 'Glasgow.'

Jonathan laughed. This was really too absurd. David could hardly be joking, for his sense of humour had long ago been jettisoned as a danger to his swift and resolute faith.

'I don't quite understand your incredulity, Jonathan. I'd have thought myself that if we were ever going to produce men of vision for our own times, it would be our big industrial cities they'd come from. You don't expect modern painters to paint buttercups, do you?'

'David, are you trying to convince me, or yourself?'

David answered with a strange eagerness. 'I'm not relying entirely on my own judgment. In fact I can't claim to have discovered him. Maybe he's well enough known in Scotland; though I doubt it. You've heard me speak of Jacques Dumont? He's one of the shrewdest judges in Europe. When in Paris I always visit his gallery. While we were chatting, out of the blue he asked me what I thought of John Lynedoch. I had to say I'd never heard of him. He was surprised; but he said nothing, just walked me to a painting. Jonathan, I've never been more impressed by a picture by an unknown painter.'

'But you art critics are a crowd of charlatans, David. If we tell you a picture's by Vermeer, you acclaim it; then if we tell you it was really by Van Meegeren, you say it's not really much good after all.'

'Fair enough. I often say myself that few of us would have approved of Rembrandt had we been his contemporaries. All the same, I'd stake my reputation on this one picture. Apparently Lynedoch called it "Gathering Mushrooms".'

'How trite. Not the H-bomb, for heaven's sake?'

'No. Just children in a field gathering mushrooms. But all the threat in the world's in it, and all the faith too. Truly marvellous. I took Isabel to see it. Ask her. She was bowled over.'

Jonathan felt almost desperate. Having just set down his own ambition, like a dung-beetle its load, he was in no mood yet to appreciate another man's burden of glory.

'Does one good picture constitute genius?' he asked.

'Jacques showed me another two, just as good. It seems Lynedoch's been coming to Paris every summer for the past three or four years, with a couple of paintings to sell. Jacques would buy a hundred if he could get them, but it seems Lynedoch's not greatly interested in money. Which is odd, for all his life he's been what you and I would call desperately poor.'

'You say you met him?'

'Yes. Once.'

'Does he look the part? Of the still unacknowledged genius, I mean?'

'How would you expect a genius to look?'

Like myself, he would have said yesterday. Now he thought: so supereminently superior that envy was unnecessary. He hid behind jesting. 'Wild eyes and long honeyed beard, like John the Baptist; hypnotist's hands; demoniacal energy; paint-splashed shirt; unwashed sinewy feet.'

David's laughter was high-pitched but menacing.

'Well, how far am I out?' asked Jonathan.

'His father was a bricklayer's labourer. His mother died when he was fourteen; he's fended for himself ever since.'

'What age is he?'

'About thirty, I should think. By the way, if he does happen to come, you needn't worry about accommodation for him. He's got an old shooting-brake, with a bed in it.'

'He sounds most self-sufficient. Does he cook for himself too?'

'Yes. And he can handle a baby better than most women.'

If ever there was an accomplishment Jonathan did not envy, that was it. 'Is he married then?' he asked.

'I don't think so. But Isabel's beckoning, and this has already cost me a fortune in francs. Expect us this evening. In the meantime give Maddy our regards; and Ampara too. By the way, how's the writing going? I'm looking forward to hearing all your plans, and of course to reading that new novel you promised to write. Till this evening then; between eight and nine, I hope.'

Putting the telephone down Jonathan walked straight out on to the terrace, sat down at table, and began to crumble a roll. He could have wept, so bullied did he feel, and so helpless to strike back. Once he had seen in a bull's eyes rheum like tears as, its back gleaming with blood and the red and yellow bandilleras, it stood, its great head drooped, waiting for the sword to be plunged into its heart. Thus now he pictured himself: Isabel and her baby, David and his genius from the slums, Terence and his interloper, Maddy and Norman; all were equally the preparers of the sword, it did not matter who thrust it home. They represented forces that could not be resisted or bought off or even assuaged by surrender.

As he supped his octopus soup, specially made according to his own recipe, he felt his soul being strangled by tentacles black as the sea's foot, and as slimy as unappeasable desire.

Yet here on this terrace, in the silky shade, with the warm-hearted sun shouting hurrah everywhere, was as delightful a spot as anyone could wish. The garden, though unkempt, was bright with roses and flowering shrubs. Beyond the wall, itself topped with scarlet flowers, was the dusty road, and the little pebble beach immediately beneath, with its rows of vividly painted boats. To the right lay the human village, with its white and pink houses, cool narrow streets, wide tree-shaded plaza, cheerful casino, companionable cafés, and open-air sardanas. To the left lay the wild and lonely haunts of the sea.

Here, if anywhere, peace amounting at least to under-standing ought to be achieved.

Maddy's voice, the most familiar and usually the dearest sound in all nature, now irritated curiously as she tried to prise from him information about David's Scotsman. How unbearably naive were her enthusiasm, her anticipation, and her declaration that if David had really unearthed a genius they should be getting ready to sing hosannahs. Thus she cried aloud whenever some large strange yacht sailed into the bay, or when some waterskier displayed unusual tricks, or when she visited some new museum. She bought no insurance against that disappointment which follows upon uncontrolled expectation. That she was able to turn dis-appointment itself into a kind of defiant pleasure was perhaps the truest indication of superficiality.

Or of her ability to love. It evidently did not matter whether love made for confusion, misery, and fright; it also added some other dimension which appeared to exalt.

'What do you think of Terence's cheek?' she asked.

'I refuse to think about it.'

'But you'll have to do something about it, Jonathan; otherwise, you know Terence, he'll dump her upon us.'

'I shall take steps.'

'She'll be that Catalan poetess he was raving about.'

Jonathan thought not. He had seen a picture of the poetess in a magazine. Not even the most gallantly mendacious of Irishmen could have called her beautiful.

He wondered if his lack of creative talent had been preordained at the beginning of the world, as the Calvinists believed; or whether his too hasty flight into the womby warmth of Spain had shrivelled the small talent he had been given. If he had gone north to Lynedoch's Glasgow instead, would the cold, murk, and inspissated philistinism have tormented him too into vision? Genius was shaped by suffering. He had never suffered. Those wincings of pride provoked at school by mentions of his father's books, and then that horrified realization at Oxford, had not been his own agony but his father's.

Recalling again the obituaries, with their perfunctory commiserations and their elegant euphemisms for rubbish, he could have wept in pity for his father and in scorn at himself. Now for the first time his mother's attempts to dissuade him from becoming a writer were seen to have been wise and compassionate, not spiteful as he had thought. She had known that the son of a bad novelist ought to have gone in for accountancy or advertising or even teaching; anything, in fact, but novel-writing. She had died with the advice still in her eyes. Across the mountains at Lourdes they were not so simple-minded as he had been; there they prayed hard for their miracles, he had crassly assumed one would happen.

Maddy was speaking. 'Really, I mean it, Jonathan. Have fun. I was telling Isabel you've become far too solemn. Have an affair. Heaven knows you get chances enough.'

He stared at her for a long calculating minute. 'Don't be ridiculous,' he said at last, with a smile.

Three

Hitherto it had always seemed to Jonathan vulgar to examine, even in the privacy of his own mind, the reasons why he, young, handsome, eligible, and entire, should be prejudiced against women. That evening, however, seated at a café table in the plaza under a dusty fairy-lit orange tree, waiting for the car to arrive with Isabel and David, and appraising the women of various nationalities who strolled up and down, he unaccountably found a part of himself demanding from some other part an explanation as to why Maddy's suggestion of an affair should have been dismissed as ridiculous. The previous excuse, that all his energies must be concentrated on his writing, was no longer valid; nor were high-minded lies, or Lawrentian fantasies, such as the one in which he saw himself as a young swift unblemished stallion thundering with flying mane across a sunny prairie.

He owed himself the truth. Well then – he took a sip of cognac – his least commendable grudge against them was that in so many ways they were superior to him, in water-skiing, for instance, or driving a car, or writing novels. Another was their rapacious curiosity; still another the vulgarity of their laughter; but what he found most unforgivable was their lack of sexual pride. Love might exalt, yes; but lust, its flourishing rival, degraded. Even now, in this busy plaza, those faults were being paraded. Look how those three girls kept eyeing him; listen to that other group at the *bunoleria*, flirting with the blond Germans in the silly shorts and sillier hats; and had he not noticed, on his way down from the house, girls submitting like animals in heat among the boats on the beach?

If I do have an affair, he vowed, let it be with dignity and wit.

Then he caught sight of Maddy, lovely in a blue dress, strolling by the side of the tall middle-aged Spaniard. Jonathan turned his head away so as not to be seen. He heard his sister laugh; merrily yes, but a little vulgarly too; yet it was the vulgarity rather than the merriment that wrenched his heart with affection. The Spaniard, handsome and distinguished, received from almost every woman that stare of sexual homage with which Jonathan himself was quite familiar. It was conceivable that Maddy might fall in love with such a man, and it would not matter to her, as it had not mattered to her mother, that he was married, with children. But was she not already in love with Norman, and did not love shut out love, as one pregnancy precluded another?

I do not ask satirically, he murmured to himself; I ask frankly, not now as a writer ambitious to extend my knowledge of human nature, but simply as a young man exposed to certain risks. It might be dangerous to venture into an affair without some previous knowledge, however academic.

Then, perhaps because of his sympathy for his sister, it struck him that there must be a sadness in all human love. His mother's tears had not altogether been selfish and hypocritical.

These thoughts were reverberating in his mind when, suddenly, to his alarm his table was noisily surrounded by those very three girls whom he had noticed gazing and laughing at him from all over the plaza. They brought with them perfume and swirls of colour, for each wore a wide skirt like a rainbow; but alas, through their heavy man-catching make-up of lipstick, eye-shadow, and powder,

could be seen the coarseness of spirit and impudent inquisi-
tiveness, in their cases aggravated by being plebeian.

He leapt up, ready to flee.

To his astonishment their speech proved them as Scottish
as porridge.

'D'you mind if we join you?' asked the tallest, a pale girl
with lemur eyes and a neck as bony as Rosinante's haunch.
Round it she wore a galaxy of cheap jewellery. 'Our feet are
killing us,' she added.

They flounced down, with squeals and jingles of relief,
and kicked off their high-heeled glittering sandals.

Fascinated, he sat down too.

'You must be thinking we're awful forward,' said the
smallest, dark-haired and shrewd. Round her shoulders
was a scarf illustrated with Spanish churches, including
the Sagrada Familia of Barcelona. But her eyes were Calvinist. 'You see, we just arrived yesterday, and do you know
something? there doesn't seem to be another single British
person here, except yourself and your sister. Lots of French
and Germans and Swedes. Wait till we get back to that
travel agency. They said June would be quieter, but they
didn't say there would be nobody to talk to at all.'

The third, a plump-cheeked dimpled giggler, apologized.
'I can see you think we've got an awful cheek, accosting you
like this; but the wee man in the post office, who speaks a
wee drop English, he told us you and your sister were
British.'

She had, he noticed, flecks of caries in her teeth. All their
breaths reeked of cheap wine, consumed, he felt sure, with
ogles of debauchery. None of them was older than twenty-
two or twenty-three. He tried to be indulgent.

'Maybe it would be more polite if we introduced ourselves,' said the small one. 'This,' indicating bony-neck, 'is
Teresa. And this Katie. I'm Peggy.'

They waited for him to tell his name.

'You *are* English?' asked Teresa, anxiously.

'He couldn't be Spanish with that hair,' said Katie.

'No, but he could be German.'

Again they waited.

He nodded.

'You *are* English?' they cried.

'Yes.'

'And may we be so bold,' asked Peggy, 'as to inquire what your name is?'

He could not withhold it. Their eyes gleamed like pins; he felt like a winkle in its shell.

'Jonathan,' he said.

Their plucked brows went up. They looked at one another. They laughed. They thought it funny, but did not hold it against him. Some day they might have sons, to whom in fondness they would give equally foolish names.

Again he attempted to escape.

'No, no,' they cried. 'Sit where you are, Jonathan. We're just getting acquainted.'

'Don't worry,' said Teresa, 'the drinks are on us.'

He became slowly aware that the insinuation of meanness was jocular.

Katie was still a little conscience-stricken. 'You see, we're from Glasgow, and we've never been abroad before.'

'Blackpool was the furthest we'd got,' said Teresa.

'Glasgow folk get the name of being very friendly,' went on Katie. 'Sometimes I think we try a bit too hard to show it.'

So it was among people like these that Lynedoch had found universal vision? How fantastic!

'To tell you the truth,' said Katie, 'we're still a bit scared. You should have heard the stories we were told by the other girls where we work; about these passionate Spaniards, you know.'

Something was wrong. Why was he finding it so difficult

to be his usual aloof misogynistic self? Females ten times more attractive had been easier to repulse. Suddenly he realized they reminded him of Ampara: the same plebeian frankness, the same ability to recognize what was spurious and accept without fuss what was genuine. He felt obliged to be as sincere as he could.

'Know what we are?' asked Peggy. 'You'd never guess. Nymphs of Midas.'

They squealed with laughter at his wonder.

'That's what a reporter once called us. We work with Littlewood's pools; you know, checking coupons.'

'But Jonathan never tries the pools,' said Teresa.

She was right. How could he have thought of himself as a man of his time?

'You'd be surprised,' said Peggy. 'It's a professional secret, but we can tell you lots of unlikely folk try them: ministers of religion, for instance; sirs and lords; and even MPs.'

'What's your sister's name?' asked Teresa.

'Madeleine.'

They looked at one another again, and shook their heads. 'We tried to guess it,' said Teresa, 'but none of us was right.'

'We should have been,' said Katie. 'I think Madeleine's perfect for her. She's beautiful.'

'Is she your twin?' asked Peggy. 'That's what we were told, but we would have known. As my dad says, you're as alike as two sausages.'

'She's beautiful,' repeated Katie.

'She can fairly ski on the water,' said Teresa. 'We'd like to learn that, but we'd be scared.'

'Speak for yourself, Teresa,' said Peggy. 'Is it true you live here all the time?'

'Don't be nosy, Peg,' said Teresa. 'Do you know something, we haven't got our drinks yet.'

'I beg your pardons,' said Jonathan, and beckoned the waiter.

'Mind now,' said Peggy, 'if you think we're nuisances—'

'Forward hussies,' giggled Teresa.

'Just say the word,' went on Peggy, 'and—'

'She's warning you,' said Katie, 'that there's no getting rid of us. She says just say the word, but the word was never invented to convince Glasgow folk they aren't welcome.'

The waiter came over. It was painful for Jonathan to see the glare of astonishment in the man's eyes; interpreted, it said, how in God's name does it come about that these jolly natural girls are associating with this cold-eyed hider behind conventions?

He tried to be jovial. 'Well, girls, what's it to be?'

'Cokes, just,' said Peggy firmly. 'We made a vow not to try any of these new-fangled drinks just because they're cheap.'

As Jonathan ordered three Coca-Colas and another cognac for himself he was becoming dimly aware that in his companions' remarks, naive and trite though they were, there was something that redeemed them and made them quite as fruitful as his own so much more sophisticated and pertinent observations. For instance, when two elegant French girls passed, they assessed their predatory qualities with a shrewdness and tolerance that amazed him. They might have been criticizing blood cousins.

Perhaps it was this same instinct of kinship and involvement that illumined the paintings of their fellow Glaswegian, Lynedoch.

None of them of course would do for him to have an affair with. Shrewd in his turn, he suspected that each girl, separated from her friends, would lapse into a bashfulness that would completely frustrate this rare gift of participation. She would be revealed as dull and gauche, ignorant of the arts, and sexually uneducated. Together, they represented a zest for humanity that made him, with a curious inward itchiness as of growth, feel human too.

He found himself recklessly inviting them to tea.

Their reaction disconcerted him.

'No, thanks all the same, but we couldn't think of it,' cried little Peggy.

Her friends supported her with head-shaking firmness. 'Thanks all the same,' they said.

They were like children playing a game, they looked so solemn.

'It's awful kind of you,' added Teresa, 'but we just couldn't.'

'Nothing personal, of course,' said Katie.

Gravely they sipped their Coca-Cola.

They weren't just being coy. They obviously meant it. It must be surely another custom of the tribe.

Peggy explained, as if to a puzzled anthropologist, 'It's like this, you see. We really had no right to speak to you tonight. But we just thought you looked so lonely sitting here by yourself among all these foreigners. That's all. It should go no further.'

Had he really been looking lonely and woebegone? No doubt. From now on he would always look lonely. All those imaginary people who were to inhabit his future novels had this morning, pallid and weary, been returned to the limbo from which he had so despairingly summoned them.

'One thing we never do,' said Katie, 'and that is to impose ourselves.'

The two others nodded amens.

'But if we see you about the beach or in the plaza here or in the shops,' said Teresa, 'we'll be glad to say hello.'

What he must never do was to think their way of life superior to his own; that would be not just treacherous, but so sentimental as to be insulting. He had studied the proletariat novels and plays then in vogue. Their crudity had disgusted him, and he could not see how it was atoned for by their vigour. To be crude violently was worse than to

be crude feebly. Adultery after fish and chips in front of the
kitchen sink was rather less attractive than adultery under
a chandelier after champagne. Coarse language did not
necessarily mean poetic or illuminating language, no more
than mincing refinement did. Judging by the newspapers
with millions of readers the working class's chief interests
were murder, sex, football, and royal gossip.

Unfortunately his knowledge of that class was derived
entirely from reading and aloof observation. He had lived
in England for over twenty years like an officer in an army of
occupation for all the contact he had ever achieved, or wished
to achieve, with the masses. At prep school he had obeyed the
rules and kept well away from the workers' children with their
big boots and unintelligible accents. At public school he had
begun to learn why such avoidance was advisable. At Oxford
he had met a few students from working-class backgrounds,
but they had been even more anxious than himself not to talk
about their relatives, especially if these worked in mines or
factories or anywhere where hands got dirty. He had escaped
National Service owing to a slight deformity in a bone in his
left foot which no sculptor would have noticed, though a drill
sergeant would. Nothing, and certainly not the missed
opportunities to rub hairy khaki shoulders with the sons
and daughters of colliers and boilermakers, had ever made
him regret that particular rejection.

These three girls were the first of their tribe he had ever
spoken to on anything like terms of social equality. Something – he could not as yet see what – was to his credit in
their willingness to accost him; and so he strove hard,
toppling over prejudices, in order to be able to see that it
was to their credit too. Thus he saw their vulgar curiosity as
a zest for humanity, and their unintentional rudeness as
warmth of heart.

All the same, to make love with one of them would be a
kind of miscegenation. Only a liar would deny that there was

such a thing as a class bar, not so spectacular as a colour bar, but just as instinctive.

Yet he could not help reflecting, a little wistfully, that he had no means of knowing what they were really thinking of him. He would have said they were considerably impressed, by his appearance, his accent, his poise, the all-over smoothness of him, skin, voice, and mind; but all the time there were about them certain little alarming signs, the quickest of winks exchanged, sly fingerings of false jewels, and even sudden smiles of apparent good-natured satire. It was not out of the question that they considered him a well-bred jackass, and later that night in their hotel bedroom would mimic him, with termagant and vindictive mirth.

He was about in agitation to order another round of Coca-Colas when into the plaza came two dusty cars, the first with an upside-down pram tied to its roof, and the other a decrepit shooting-brake. Both had British number plates. Isabel and David had arrived, and it looked as if they had brought Lynedoch with them.

He jumped up. 'Excuse me,' he cried, and rushed into the road, waving and shouting.

The leading car stopped. He ran up to it.

Seated beside David, Isabel held the baby on her lap. Spectacles and black hair brushed hard back gave her an air too efficient somehow to be motherly; but the smile she gave him, though partly a yawn, was warm with affection. He felt a great fondness for her too, so much so that he bent down and kissed her. There might have been, he conceded deep within, a trace of self-pity in that kiss. Also it could have been because he saw in her an immediate and welcome proof of the superiority of their class. Tired and travel-stained though she was, she had an authority and urbanity that made the three Scots girls in the café appear unfinished by comparison, as if they were at a much earlier evolutionary stage.

The baby was restless, hot, smelly, cross, and dominating.
'Kiss Linda too,' said Isabel.

Eyes closed, he kissed the infant's damp forehead.

'Look at her. Who is she like?'

Like himself and Maddy, he supposed; yes, the same fair hair, wide brow, smallish chin, sweet mouth. It was terrifying to see oneself, or rather another attempt at oneself, back at the starting-post, even although the race was half over and totally lost.

'There's nothing to sigh about,' said Isabel. 'She's lovely, and the very image of you and Maddy at the same age.'

It was a relief to look across at the red-eyed, bearded father.

'Hello, David,' he said.

'Hello, Jonathan.'

As they shook hands Jonathan thought that with such a beard one could, if no cloth was handy, wipe the windscreen. It was a panicky thought, likely to cause a stampede into folly of all his thoughts, and so he crushed it. 'Is that Lynedoch's car behind you?' he asked.

'Yes. We ran into him over the hill at Puerto de la Selva. He was getting ready to move on, so I suggested he should come with us. You'll find him no bother.'

Isabel was eyeing the girls in the café. 'Who are the girl-friends?' she demanded.

But he was staring at the shooting-brake, or rather at its driver who had come out and was standing beside it, smoking, as indistinguishable as any mechanic from any garage in Europe. Yet Jonathan's heart kept giving dolphin leaps.

'I'd better introduce you,' said David.

'Can't you wait till we get to the house?' asked Isabel, sharply. 'You know Linda's got to be attended to.'

Nevertheless David got out and unfolded himself. He gazed up prophetically at the stars above the plaza lights, and took deep breaths. 'Yes, the spirit gets a chance here to refresh itself,' he said.

Or to discover, with cruellest clarity, its limitations.

Heedless of Isabel's protests, they walked towards the shooting-brake.

'Don't jump to conclusions,' muttered David. 'Wait till you see his work. Who would have looked twice at Turner?'

'Isabel doesn't seem altogether fascinated.'

'She's absorbed in Linda.'

'You're still convinced he's a genius?'

'Let me put it this way. I said to Isabel I'd give up her, Linda, Mother, everything, if in return I could paint as he does.'

'Isabel would be charmed to hear you say that, David.'

David snapped his fingers testily. 'She wasn't, much. But you understand what I mean, Jonathan. You and I, who can recognize what's supreme, have to suffer in ourselves what at best is only second-rate. The greatest achievement in life, as well as the greatest joy, is in creating a masterpiece.'

The remark nettled Jonathan; its priggishness was so naked that he could not help seeing it was like his own. He could have retorted that surely in his child David must feel he had created something more miraculous and more valuable than any painting or book; but that would have been priggish too.

Besides, there was the meeting within seconds of Lynedoch to prepare too.

Had he been supereminently superior, with an appearance of grandeur and mystery, it would have been easy to look on him, and shake hands with him, with more awe and admiration than envy. Had he been, indeed, at least the equal, as far as outward distinction went, of Jonathan and David, then envy might have been appeased by having something to feed on. But no, he was so commonplace as to constitute fate's subtlest and final stroke: the almost loving thrusting home of the sword; well, not quite home, this being left to the moment not far off when Jonathan was shown a painting and had to admit its excellence.

To begin with, beside Jonathan and David he looked puny, with thin shoulders and narrow chest. He was neither handsome nor ugly, but drearily in between; even his complexion had the common coarseness of his class, with no carbuncular oddities of its own. He had no beard, only a small moustache that was like a sad attempt to make look masculine what was really neuter. Even his hair was dull, being short, tidy, and dark brown. Only his eyes hinted at anything beyond the humdrum. They were bright blue, and had instants of concentrated scrutiny, though these could have been produced by myopia; at all other times, though not shifty or humble, they were veiled by a reserve that appeared to have its origins in social inferiority. Altogether it was the kind of face you would expect the repairer of your ice-box to have.

His voice, though, was a surprise. Quieter and calmer than diffidence, it did actually suggest the self-sufficiency of a creative artist. The accent was Glaswegian, but not as aggressively so as that of the girls. Indeed, it was pleasant, and almost captivating, to listen to. It made Jonathan look at the hands, and in them he thought he saw the mastery the voice hinted at. Restful and confident they were, far too sensitive for an ice-box repairer however competent, and never at a loss where to be. Yes, though the right now held a cigarette with all the common gestures, it was possible to imagine it wielding a paintbrush impressively.

Two other painters passed, macaws beside this sparrow.

'They all paint the church,' said Jonathan.

Lynedoch turned to stare at the floodlit tower.

'Shall you?'

'Maybe.'

'Could a Calvinist do it justice?'

'Why not? Fear and hate illuminate as well as love and faith. But I'm not a Calvinist.'

'I thought all Scots were.'

'I'm a painter.'

Jonathan's blood ran cold. Had the man exposed himself, he could not have felt more embarrassed. It was worse than embarrassment, it was the same kind of feeling he had got at the Abbey of Montserrat in the shop where plaster legs, arms, torsos, or even kidneys were on sale to people who, with those parts diseased, wished to pray to some saint for a cure. Jonathan had felt in the presence of a mystery, with enough sinisterness in it to freeze his blood.

In the car in front Isabel sounded the horn.

'You'll follow on behind, John,' said David.

'Very good.'

'It's only a hundred yards or so,' said Jonathan.

As they walked back, Jonathan said: 'I notice he kept referring to you as Mr Reeves.'

'What should he have referred to me as?'

'You called him John.'

David snorted.

'Sorry,' said Isabel, 'but Linda needs to be changed, washed, fed, and put to bed. So do I. Who are those girls, Jonathan? They keep staring. Should I know them?'

'No. I see you've got no room.' The back of the car was crammed with baby's paraphernalia. 'I'll walk.'

'Lynedoch will give you a lift,' said David.

'Where's Maddy?' asked Isabel, for at least the sixth time.

'Somewhere around. She was here half an hour ago. Probably she's gone to the house to wait for you.'

The truth no doubt was that she was being caressed somewhere in the fishy dark among the boats by that tall Spaniard. The latter would try, but there were stages in the game of love, especially when played out of doors, when dignity was bound to fail. He could have beaten on the roof of the car in a rage that would have astounded everyone, and which he could never have explained. To have said he was trying to protect in advance his own embraces with the woman he loved would have been laughed at as prudish, by himself as well as by others. Yet far away on the uplands of his mind the purity of that idealistic love-making forever shone.

He decided not to mention the Spaniard. 'Lynedoch is patient,' he said, laughing.

'If you had eternity in your hands,' said David angrily, 'you'd be patient too. Look here, Jonathan, if you'd rather he didn't come to your place just say so, and I'll tell him. He's not the clot you evidently take him for. He's a bloody fine painter. Ask Isabel.'

'I'd rather be asked if Linda was in bed, asleep,' said Isabel.

'But isn't he good?'

'Oh, wonderful.'

'I mean it, Isabel. Isn't he good?' The question was almost shouted.

'I like what I've seen of his painting, though I've seen very little. But please remember I've liked other paintings you thought were rubbish.'

Scowling, David started the car and drove up the road towards the house.

As Lynedoch came up Jonathan stopped him. 'D'you mind giving me a lift?' he asked.

'Of course not, Mr Broxmead.'

'Thank you.'

Jonathan got in. He felt nervous, and what was worse, shy. 'David was saying how much he admired your work.'

Lynedoch did not even smile.

'I suppose you'll know he has quite a reputation as a critic?'

'I'd heard of him.'

'You'll know then that a favourable notice from him is worth a great deal.'

Lynedoch raised his brows.

'I suppose you'll have been painting for years, Mr Lynedoch?'

'Aye.'

'Where did you study?'

'Glasgow School of Art, evening classes.'

'I understood you had studied in Paris?' As a sneer it failed. Most such sneers would obviously fail. He tried sincerity. 'My ambition was to be a novelist.'

'Isn't it still?'

'No.'

Lynedoch smiled now. 'You've given it up?'

'Yes.'

'Just like that?'

'The finger of God touches, just like that, does it not?'

'Does it?'

'And is removed, just like that.'

'Well.'

Jonathan's voice rose. 'I am of course speaking figuratively.'

'I thought ye were.'

'We never discuss religion here, or politics; especially politics.'

'Do I turn in here?'

They had reached the gate. Just inside it, caught in the headlights, Maddy was kissing her Spaniard under a tree. It was goodbye for, a moment after, she turned and fled up the drive towards the house. The Spaniard's face was for Jonathan both hateful and curiously dear; on it could be read a marvellous fondness for his sister. He recalled Hamlet's wild cry:

> I loved Ophelia. Forty thousand brothers
> Could not, with all their quantity of love,
> Make up my sum.

'Have we disturbed the maid saying farewell to her boy-friend?' asked Lynedoch, very Scottish.

'That was my sister, Mr Lynedoch.'

Not in the least put out, he murmured: 'Madeleine?'

In front of the house, making a fuss of Isabel and the baby, she was at her most brilliant; even the baby was outshone. She was insisting on carrying her niece, now howling in Isabel's arms, into the house. Ampara too kept stretching out greedy arms.

Isabel refused them both. 'Jonathan's going to carry her,' she cried.

'No, no,' he protested.

'Yes. I promised myself that months ago.'

'But, good Lord, Isabel, I've never carried a baby before. I'd let her fall.'

About to persist in his refusal, he noticed she was actually in tears.

'Very well, Isabel. Show me how.'

As cautiously as if she was a glassful of wine he took the baby. For some reason she stopped crying as soon as he had her safely in his arms. Isabel and Ampara were ravished by this little miracle. Maddy too laughed in a peculiar calm delight.

He thought he noticed Lynedoch in the background smirking.

'Now you know, Jonathan,' cried Isabel. 'Doesn't he, David?'

'Know what?' asked Jonathan.

'That you're one of us.'

He was taken aback. Moreover, the baby began then to crow and chuckle and make overtures with her tiny hands; and at the same moment down in the village the band for the sardana dancing blared out its first triumphant blast. Those were for him moments of heart-rending perplexity. Did Isabel mean he was now one of the dancers, the dance being life itself, and formed a single link of the circle of humanity? Surely she must, for she had never believed that he was one of the elect, a creator of beauty and explorer of truth. As in the dance now jigging sedately in the village, to the blarings of trumpets, men's fingers clung to women's, so, symbolically, his niece's seized his.

He looked to see how the others were reacting to his agonies of initiation. Ampara found them funny, but also so entrancing that she seemed about to embrace and kiss him. Maddy nodded encouragingly. Despite beard and skeleton thinness, David beamed like any other proud father. Only Lynedoch was doubtful: it could have been that as a stranger he felt he had no right to participate, but it could also have been that he was not interested in so common a sight as an uncle nursing a niece.

Ampara, laden with suitcases heavier than three babies, dashed into the house ahead of him, singing in his honour. Had he been her husband, and this their fair-haired first-born, she could hardly have been more excited and gleeful. She was at the very heart of the human family to which, according to Isabel, he now belonged, willy-nilly. So were the three coupon-checkers, the contemptuous waiter, the untalented fierce-faced artists, the sun-baskers, thieves, murderers, adulterers, priests, politicians, policemen, big-fisted guffawing market-women, and old shrivelled women, black-clad, who every day crept up the steep street to pray in the twilight of the church.

Most eligible because of his appearance, Lynedoch might not be a member. If he had genius, if God's finger was upon him, if he looked on glories, he would not, could not, be admitted.

Sombre with these thoughts, Jonathan carried the child up to David and Isabel's room and laid her on the bed. At once Ampara flew upon and mother-birded her, with clucks and fondles. He wondered if he should allow such menial love. Maddy, more temperately, sat on the bed and tickled the small pink legs.

At first he thought this was not the place for upbraiding her about her contemplated adultery, and then he thought no place could be better. They were in the presence of innocence; moreover it had their own shape, and blood.

'I saw you,' he whispered, 'at the gate. Why do you do it?'

She gave him a smile that might have been for the infant. 'Because I love him,' she whispered back.

'Love!'

What English Ampara understood was never certain. He hoped she was too concerned with the baby to heed. Then from below Isabel called impatiently, wanting Ampara to go down and help David to carry up the cot.

He told her. Since it was in the baby's service, she rushed off at once.

Maddy and he were alone, with their chuckling niece.

'I'm afraid it isn't good enough just to say you love him,' he said.

'What more can I say? Love includes everything.'

'Don't be flippant, please.'

She laughed. 'No, I don't think you're quite one of us yet.'

'I simply meant you're hardly in a position to talk about love, in relation to this stranger.'

She was silent.

'Have you found out if he's married? Or doesn't that matter?'

'No, not to me.'

'It should then. Surely it should. I would have thought a certain example would have restrained you.'

'Leave Mother out of it.'

'I shall have to tell Isabel.'

'It's none of her business, or of yours.'

Yet he and she had lain side by side in the same womb. Later certainly that womb had betrayed them. But perhaps

Maddy was right in saying their mother ought to be left out of it. Death was hardly a satisfactory way of settling accounts, but it had to be accepted.

'What about Norman?' he asked. 'Haven't you been rejoicing, this past week, because he's coming?'

'I let you think that, Jonathan. I'm sorry. He's not coming. He and I were finished last summer. I don't want to see him again, ever.'

'But he wrote to say he was coming.'

'I wrote to tell him not to come.'

'When did you write? You didn't tell me.'

'No. These are matters too deep for you, Jonathan.'

'I'm not laughing, Maddy. I'm serious. How long have you known this Spaniard?'

'Ten days.' She spoke with a gladness that even her stroking of the baby could not express.

'But I thought he'd just arrived. Why haven't I met him? Why all the secrecy?'

'When you fall in love, Jonathan, I suppose you'll shout it from the hill-tops.'

Suddenly the baby began to laugh so heartily he thought it must have taken hysterics.

'I'm going away with him,' said Maddy.

The music changed, became quicker, and he could picture the dancers begin their energetic skipping, with only the calculation of the steps to trouble them. But when the dance stopped, and the trumpet-players wiped away the saliva, everyone would become an individual again, enduring in loneliness the sorrows of love granted on conditions or denied altogether.

Ampara and David staggered in, carrying the dismantled cot. Behind them marched Isabel with a pile of the baby's belongings.

'Get a move on, you twins,' she cried. 'She may be the most important, but she's not your only guest, you know.

Maddy, how would you like to help me get Linda ready?
Jonathan, you can help David put up the cot. Ampara's got
dinner to attend to, and a hundred other things too, I
suppose.'

'There's no need to worry about Lynedoch,' said David
sarcastically. 'He's setting up his bed in his car.'

'Well,' murmured his wife, 'isn't that how he prefers it?'

'It can't be very comfortable.'

Jonathan intervened. 'Maddy's just told me Norman
won't be coming after all. So there will be a room for
Lynedoch, if he wishes.'

As Isabel kissed Maddy in a kind of congratulation, David
hurried downstairs to tell Lynedoch.

Jonathan crouched, pondering how to put up the cot.

Four

This early morning sunshine, this being able to lie in peace, warm to the marrow of his bones, with all his senses growing more and more alert, was a luxury which could never be stale to him, accustomed to Glasgow's cold gloom and dour distrust of idleness. He watched the soaring in a sunbeam of thousands of motes that reminded him, in this Catholic land, of souls in ecstasy rising to heaven; which in their turn reminded him of his host, the tall fair-haired Englishman with the high-pitched lah-de-dah voice, and a soul like a nestling that, too ambitious for its powers, had toppled out and lay piping in the grass, for some hawk to swoop and rend. Aye, green was the colour against which to see him; and there must be some sad shrillnesses of yellow.

He thought of the other members of the family: Madeleine the twin, beautiful and unscrupulous; Isabel virtuous, efficient protectress of class, so reasonably pointing out to her brother and sister that Ampara the maid must tactfully be let know that she was not to make so much fuss of Linda, lest, it appeared, the baby was corrupted in some way left undefined; and her husband Reeves the critic, for all his *avant-garde* pretensions barren with middle-class assumptions about art that Rembrandt for one would have laughed at.

The processes of history had made them his enemies. They would be hospitable, courteous, and charitable, provided their superiority was recognized; if not, they would be – never offensive, which would be vulgar, thus lowering them to the enemy's level – but coldly indifferent. He thought of his mother, for instance, in that household. She would have been the woman who came in twice a week to help with the heavy scrubbing, spoken to in a friendly enough way, but regarded instinctively as an inferior, so that her being on her knees serving them, though she was twice their age, would never have occurred to them as in the least shameful. Old Granny Adamson, too, with whom he had lodged after his mother's death, would have been to them pathetic and grotesque, with her thirty-odd crucifixes that she had cleaned by spitting on and rubbing with her sleeve. Tom Gilliespie, the joiner, with his big warty nose and massive hands, would have amused them by his eagerness to express himself in paint, with imitations of Sir John Millais. There were others, dozens, hundreds of them, all, as far as the Broxmeads were concerned, characters in a book written, in rather a pedestrian style, by a deity not quite so inventive or comic as Dickens but twice as vulgar and twenty times as dull.

How many times had Margaret warned him not to become bitter and obsessed, pointing out that he really did not know how such people felt and thought? Aye, true enough; but what would these Broxmeads have thought of her, a shopgirl, her father a plasterer's mate, her sister a bus conductress, her home a council house amid hundreds of other council houses identical even to the knobs on the front doors, her education the statutory limit, her accent uncultured, her grave still adorned with artificial lilies under sooty glass globes?

For a minute or two he lay touching in his mind the hideous half-healed loss; then he got up and unwrapped the painting of her. Before looking at it he glanced out of the window and saw a robin hopping with exhilarating grace among the purple flowers of a shrub in the garden. Comforted, he was reminded of Ampara, the small red-cheeked energetic maid. Of the women in this household he much preferred her.

He gazed at the painting, as he had done every day, often several times a day, since her death. It was not only, to be truthful not primarily, to keep his memories of her fresh, but to renew and strengthen his faith in himself as a painter. He would say that it was for her sake he must never lose that faith, but it was not quite true, it was simply for his painting's sake. It was a fine painting, though the few who had so far seen it, Margaret's family for instance, had disliked it; but then they had disapproved of him for never keeping a steady job, and also they had placed those lilies on her grave. They could not be judges. But let the whole world say otherwise, he would still know it to be good, and he knew too he would do even better.

Now, looking at it again, he saw beyond Margaret, vivid and loving though she was, to the seeking and the finding that had given her this life in paint, this immortality. Aye, it was good all right, but he must do better: not to strike back at the Broxmeads and their kind, not to win a place among them, not even to portray his mother's kind as they deserved to be portrayed, with their staunch and enterprising humanity; no, simply for the long patient satisfaction of achieving what he felt himself capable of.

Wrapping up the painting again, he went along to the bathroom quietly but confidently, found the door shut, knocked twice and then boldly turned the handle and entered. As bathrooms went it was ornate enough, with its green and white tiles, its black bath, fluorescent lighting, and button to push instead of plug to pull, but he refused to feel nervous in it, and winked at himself in the mirror as he remembered the black iron sinks in the kitchens where he had been used to wash, and the lavatories on the stairheads with their chains mended with string, or with their handles missing. He washed and shaved as tidily and quickly as he could, kept the door closed until the noise of the flushing had lessened, and then returned to his room.

No one else seemed to be astir, except the baby, whom he could hear talking and whimpering to herself.

A few minutes later he ventured downstairs to the dining-room. Only Ampara was there, watering the plants on the terrace. As she busied herself putting his breakfast before him, he could see she was puzzled. All other Broxmead guests would speak and act in the same well-bred assured manner as they did themselves. He, reared in a Glasgow working-class district and educated there, spoke more crudely and showed his lack of social self-confidence even in the tearing apart of a croissant.

Another thing about him puzzled her still more. He had been introduced to her, by Madeleine, rather facetiously, as a painter; yet, compared with the beards and gorgeous blouses she often saw in the village, he was meek-chinned and drab. Suddenly, refusing any longer to take him ser-iously as a guest and superior, she began to stroke her chin with witty fingers, then to daub the air with imaginary brush, and finally to point at him with incredulous shakes of her head.

In spite of what others had said, he could take a joke as well as anybody; but not about his painting. Moreover, she was just a servant; not for his own sake, but out of loyalty to his host, he ought not to condone this rather insulting familiarity; otherwise it would get worse and make his position in the house intolerable.

Then she was laughing, and trying to appease him, as if he was a child whose feelings had been hurt. In a rage he leapt up, gestured to her to wait, rushed to his room, and hurried back with the painting of Margaret.

As he unwrapped it, confidence was stripped from him: by no means because he dreaded her ignorant and philistine disapproval, but because he was seeing in her that crudity which Margaret too, for all her gentleness and sincerity, had had traces of, and which was honestly revealed in the portrait. Washed from birth with the scented soap of privilege, Madeleine Broxmead was quite free of it, sexual adventuress though she might be.

Ampara took the painting from him and held it up in the sunshine. When she saw it was a portrait of a young woman, her attitude changed. For some reason she at once assumed Margaret was related to him, and therefore this likeness, though scarcely photographic, must be praised as such, not as a work of art at all. She would have been better pleased with a coloured photograph, but out of sympathy discounted those strokes of originality which of course were the painting's strength.

'Su esposa?' she asked, touching her wedding-ring finger.

He shook his head.

'Su hermana?'

He did not understand.

'Señorita Madeleine es las hermana de Señor Jonathan,' she explained.

Irritably he shook his head. His love for Margaret was expressed in the portrait; whatever its nature, it had not been brotherly.

'Su novia?'

Reluctantly he nodded. From her rather lecherous snigger, it must mean sweetheart. Well, Margaret had certainly been that: this painting proclaimed it, too sensually perhaps. Small wonder Margaret's douce people had been offended. In speech, paint, or music, or on paper, the Scots distrusted too fervent a show of love. Only drunk ought a Scot ever to attempt that, so that the result would be obscured by incoherency.

Why then should he be so reluctant to admit it now to this red-cheeked simpleton of a maid? Was it shame, because his love had never been whole-hearted? Margaret more than once had remarked, laughing, that she only got what was left over from his painting; but, she had added, it was enough for her. He had been secretly alarmed. Nothing ought to be left over from his painting; if anything was, because of her, then to that extent she was a handicap. Yet, as surely this painting so triumphantly stated, he had loved her.

'Pero donde ella está?' cried Ampara. 'Porqué no está aqui? No le gusto venir a la España?'

Madeleine walked in, wearing a red silken dressing-gown over knee-length pyjamas.

She translated: ' "Did she or he not want to come to Spain?" '

He turned nervous. Love and grief, especially when flawed, could easily enough be made to appear unrefined and inferior. Quickly he took the painting from Ampara and propped it in a corner, back outward.

Madeleine watched him with amusement. A glance dismissed Ampara to the kitchen.

'You're an early bird,' she said. 'I hope Ampara's not the worm you hoped to catch. Her boy-friend is a civil guard, a policeman.'

He blushed. 'I want to visit the church.'

'Oh. Are you a Catholic?' Twice she had glanced round at the painting.

'No.'

She sipped her coffee. 'I'm afraid I have to apologize for Ampara,' she said. 'While Jonathan and I are here alone, during the winter, we tend to treat her as one of us.'

He did not believe her.

'She'll ask the most impertinent questions, if you're soft enough to let her.' Then coolly she asked one herself. 'Was she inquiring about Mrs Lynedoch?'

At first he thought she meant his mother.

'You are married, aren't you?'

'No.'

'I was sure Jonathan said David had mentioned you were.'

He was sure she was lying, but he did not know why.

'Tell me, Mr Lynedoch – but shouldn't I be calling you Willie or Alistair or whatever it is?'

'It's John.'

She was delighted by his dourness. 'Tell me, John, how old are you?'

'Twenty-eight.'

She studied his face. 'Yes, you do look older. David said he thought you'd be about thirty. I'm twenty-six. Yes, Ampara's so awfully inquisitive and frank; especially about paintings. I'm a painter myself, you know.'

'Aye, Mr Reeves said so.'

She laughed. 'I wonder in what terms. I'm a damn bad one, and I'll never be any good, if I keep trying till I'm a hundred. Same with Jonathan and his writing. He may, with the air of one about to challenge you to a duel, demand that you read his novel and give your honest opinion. If he does, decline.'

'Would that be polite, Miss Broxmead, seeing I'm his guest?'

'If you're John, then I'm Madeleine, surely. Very well, read it if you wish; but at least make sure you're reasonably drunk first. Do you get drunk, John?'

'No.'

'You know how it is when we're asked to give our opinion of a painting. We must tell the truth, but being civilized we usually try to soften the blow with a little woolliness. Ampara, bless her, just swipes out.'

'I prefer swiping out.'

She paused. 'You do?'

'Aye, of course.'

Suddenly she pushed back her chair, jumped up, and fairly pounced on his painting. Before she could look at it they heard the baby begin to howl, most disturbingly.

She laughed. 'Well, that's a noise should do brother Jonathan a world of good. Didn't you find him a trifle priggish, John?'

It struck him she was being so confiding because to her his opinions just did not matter. Her brother, priggish enough, at least felt obliged to show, and by showing attempt to justify, his class superiority.

'Now for God's sake don't be coy,' she said, smiling. 'David says you're next door to a genius, but I'll never believe it if you're coy. First you want to be polite, then you tell me you never get drunk, and now you're acting coy. I don't know what all that adds up to, but I shouldn't think genius. Isn't your job to help us to see ourselves as we really are, and to find joy in the world around us? By the way, John, what is your attitude to temptation?'

She waited for an answer. The baby howled.

'There are different kinds of temptation,' he said.

'Right. Let's restrict it to one: sexual temptation. It must have come your way; after all, you are twenty-eight. Did you yield or resist? I'm inclined to yield, but my brother always resists. I think you do, too.'

He remembered her passionate kissing of the man at the gate last night.

'Perhaps I'll find the answer here,' she said, turning the painting.

And as he watched he saw, to his dismay, that she had.

Before she could say so, in on red moccasins shuffled her brother, red-eyed as if from want of sleep. The baby whom they heard still crying might have been his, keeping him awake half the night.

'Good morning,' he said.

'Why aren't you comforting your niece, Jonathan?' asked his sister.

He refused to answer, his mouth sulky as any baby's. How he would have had his soul roasted out of him in any factory where girls worked; and how perhaps a humbler and more useful one might have been forcibly installed.

'John's been showing off his paintings to Ampara,' said Madeleine.

'Indeed.'

Again Lynedoch found himself blushing. What made him so susceptible was the knowledge that she did not like his painting.

Jonathan decided to smile. 'What is conceit in those without talent,' he said, 'is merely generosity in those with it.'

'What do you think, Jonathan?' she asked, and held the painting in front of him.

At the same time she stared at Lynedoch with what seemed to him animosity mixed with contempt. Though he smiled back patiently, inwardly he was shouting resentment that she, little better than a whore, should despise his portrayal of poor Margaret.

Meanwhile her brother was giving as much attention to the painting as could be spared from his breakfast.

As Lynedoch gazed at it himself, for the ten thousandth time, wave after warm wave of reassurance surged through him. Whatever Madeleine Broxmead or anyone else might say or think, here was the face of a Scottish working-class girl; the ignorance, shoddiness, conformity, and materialism which had blemished her from birth, and previous generations, were honestly portrayed; but so too were the triumphant bravery, tenderness, hope, and humour. Almost in tears, he remembered Margaret's own verdict: 'Judging from her photos, John, and from what you've told me, it's more like what your mother must have been like at my age.'

'Has David Reeves seen this?' asked Jonathan at last. 'Or Jacques Dumont?'

'No.'

'Or any reputable art critic or dealer?'

'No.'

'What do you think, Maddy?'

'I don't like it.'

He seemed relieved. 'I must confess there's something in it I find off-putting. Perhaps portraiture isn't your true line, Lynedoch? But it's very powerful.'

'It makes me shudder,' said Madeleine.

'As usual you exaggerate, Madeleine. Don't mind her, Lynedoch.'

Lynedoch stood up, pale and furious. 'And what exactly is it that makes you shudder, Miss Broxmead?'

Pale too, she stared at him. 'I thought you preferred swiping out?'

'I do. I'm just asking you what it is that makes you shudder.'

'Perhaps this is one of your earlier works?' suggested Jonathan.

'I am prepared to have my worth as a painter judged from this one painting, Mr Broxmead.'

'Still, often the creative artist, whether painter or novelist, isn't the best judge of his own work.'

'I'm waiting, Miss Broxmead,' said Lynedoch.

'It's very clever,' she said. 'It's a hundred times better than I could do myself. I'm sure David's right, you're a fine painter.'

Rather gloomily her brother looked at the portrait again and nodded.

'What I don't like about this one,' said Madeleine, 'is the contempt you seemed to have had for the girl, whoever she was.'

'Contempt?' Astonishment made him almost inaudible.

'Yes. All right, you've given her good qualities, she's pretty, she's kind-hearted, but she's so stupid.'

'Stupid?'

Broxmead laughed. 'Well, she may have been some factory-girl,' he said.

Both of them ignored him.

Madeleine became quite bitter. 'Yes, and you meant her to be. You worked hard at it. Shifty, too. Were you trying to get your own back? Were you and she lovers at one time?'

He had to sit down. Had her blows been physical he could not have felt more sickened and discouraged.

'Now, Maddy,' remonstrated her brother, 'aren't these rather impertinent questions?'

'No, they are not. In any case, I'm not the one asking them.'

'Then for heaven's sake who is?'

She pointed to the painting. 'You wouldn't notice them, Jonathan, not if you were to look for a hundred years.'

He laughed, peevishly. 'May I ask why I should be so obtuse?'

'Because you've never been in love. Because you've never slept with a woman, and had her weeping.'

He winced, but again managed to laugh. 'Am I to believe then that frequent and unsuccessful fornication brings insight and compassion?'

Lynedoch picked up the painting.

'Were you lovers?' asked Madeleine.

'She was my fiancée.' He meant to say it with dignity, but failed. It was a lie, doubly so, because not only had he never mentioned marriage to her but he did not think he ever would have. At the time she had been a great help to him as an artist; but afterwards she could have become as great a hindrance.

Both brother and sister had noticed his use of the past tense.

With as simple and quiet a dignity as he could carefully achieve, he added: 'She died last February; in a couple of days, of meningitis. So I hardly think, Miss Broxmead, your interpretation can be quite right.'

But as he left the room, carrying the painting, he thought he heard her mutter: 'Yes, I am right, all the same.'

Her brother called after him: 'We're awfully sorry, Lynedoch. I'm afraid these things will happen, if we're unwise enough to empty our hearts in paint or on paper.'

Five

Later that morning, with Lynedoch off to reconnoitre the church and Ampara to shop, Jonathan found an opportunity to challenge Maddy's threat to run off with the Spaniard. After her attack on poor Lynedoch she had flashed into one of her most splendid but also most dangerous moods. As she patted her yellow hair her finger-nails glittered like bloodstained claws; and when she swooped and snatched up off the floor little Linda crawling disconsolately about, it seemed to him more like an act of carnage than of affection, especially as her cries were fierce and inarticulate. The infant seemed terrified by that brilliant embrace.

It was obvious that Maddy, about to go roaming in the jungle of immorality, was preparing to be the prowler and not the prey.

Unfortunately, while he was still chiselling out his opening sentence, Isabel herself launched forth. Red-eyed, bitter, and frequently stifling yawns, she too was out for blood; his, more than Maddy's.

'I suppose you're aware we didn't get much sleep last night,' she began.

He nodded, and glanced at Linda, the slaughterer of sleep, still looking as if Maddy's caresses were punishment rather than reward. He decided better not to say his own sleep had been disturbed. All the same, if Isabel made too much of this, he'd find it hard not to be cross too. After all, he had urged that the child be left at home.

'Weeks ago,' went on Isabel, 'I wrote asking you to hire a nursemaid.'

David, stork-like in white shirt and yellow trunks, stood by the window gazing down at the blue sea. 'Can't this wait, Isabel?' he asked.

'No, it can't,' she yelled.

'But I want to go swimming, for God's sake.'

'Don't I too?' She pulled up her skirt to show her bathing costume on beneath.

'Then let's go and talk about this nursemaid business afterwards.'

'And who, pray, is going to look after Linda if we go swimming?'

'Well, I thought Ampara could, just for one morning.'

'Is that all you think of your child, David? You'd hand her over to anyone at all, so long as you weren't inconvenienced.'

'Ampara isn't anyone at all. She's been with Jonathan and Maddy for three years.'

'And don't forget,' remarked Maddy, 'she was almost your sister-in-law.'

'Now, Maddy!' protested Jonathan.

'For a whole day you contemplated it.'

He shuddered. 'I was never serious.'

'I should hope not,' cried Isabel, 'though you're so irresponsible and incompetent, Jonathan, and Maddy's so utterly selfish, that I wouldn't be at all surprised to hear you'd done something idiotic of the kind.'

Such misreading of his character, by his own sister too, astonished him. Surely his fault was an excess of responsibleness and competence. Who else in this sunny amorous atmosphere would have warded off those Scots girls, with sociological barge-poles, as it were? And what other male at the age of twenty-six had made it his business to know the prices of commodities down to the last centimo?

'You replied,' resumed Isabel, 'that you would hire a girl in good time. Where is she?'

'I apologize, Isabel. I must have been under the misapprehension that you were not bringing the child.'

'The child, as you call her, happens to be your niece.'

'She also happens to be your daughter, Isabel dear,' said Maddy, dumping the infant in her sister's lap. 'You wrote other letters, if you remember, in which you described the supreme joys of motherhood.'

'And what exactly do you mean by that, Maddy?' screamed Isabel.

Linda began to howl, in an ominous way: if I wish, she seemed to hint, I could go on like this for hours.

David shouted: 'Oh, for God's sake!'

Jonathan tut-tutted.

Maddy bristled but smiled.

'I'm waiting for an answer, Maddy,' yelled Isabel.

Suddenly Maddy was contrite; she dropped on her knees beside Isabel, and took Linda's hands. 'I'm sorry, Isabel,' she said.

Isabel had to make an effort of forgiveness that convulsed her, face and body. 'Well you might be,' she said. 'It's hardly for you to sneer at us.'

'I'm not sneering at the baby, Isabel.'

'Are you sure? Anyway, by us I meant women with children. You have the fun, Maddy, without the pain, and the life-long consequences.'

Jonathan now intervened. 'It's my fault really,' he said. 'I should have done something about hiring a girl. I'll get Ampara this very afternoon to make inquiries.'

'Not one of her cronies, please,' cried Isabel.

'What have you got against her, Isabel?' asked Maddy.

'She's far too rough and common.'

Maddy smiled and pressed the baby's hands. Linda too was now quiet, as if listening.

'Some fisherman's wife might take it on,' suggested Jonathan. As Isabel shook her head he had to add: 'Well, for goodness' sake, Isabel, who else is likely to take it on for a few weeks at this time of the year?'

'If you had advertised in a Barcelona newspaper, as I wanted, you'd have found someone. Isn't the country poor? Didn't you tell me university professors have to take on other jobs to have a decent standard of living? Well, there are bound to be dozens of Spanish girls of decent family who would have been only too eager to earn a few extra pesetas.'

'Where would we have put her up?' asked Maddy.

'Especially as you brought Lynedoch with you,' added Jonathan.

'No, thank you; don't blame me for that,' said Isabel sharply. 'That was none of my doing.'

'It was mine,' said David, without turning. 'None of you has got it into your head yet that he's going to be world-famous, that one day we'll boast of having known him. Now that we're on the subject—'

'But we aren't,' said his wife. 'We are on the subject of a nursemaid for Linda.'

He tugged his beard. 'Who was it that insulted him this morning?'

Isabel screamed: 'I said we were discussing a nursemaid for Linda.'

He had to be silent, but he turned briefly and glared at both Jonathan and Maddy.

'We'll get one, Isabel,' said Maddy, soothingly.

'Where?'

'Locally, if we can. Or perhaps Terence could send us one from Barcelona in a day or two.'

'And in the meantime?'

'Surely the four of us can look after the little darling?'

'Which would mean me. You forget, Maddy, I'm exhausted and have come here for a rest.'

'We'll see you get it. Won't we, Jonathan?'

He nodded, not too cordially, because of course Maddy might very well have sneaked off by the evening, in a turquoise Mercedes-Benz.

'Maddy,' said David, 'will you look after Linda until we come back from swimming?'

'Why not take her with us?' asked Maddy.

'You forget,' snapped Isabel, 'that she has just recovered from diarrhoea.'

'But she has recovered.'

'Not entirely. Hot sunshine could easily bring it on again.'

'God forbid,' muttered David.

'We've got the shelter up on the beach,' said Jonathan, helpfully.

David laughed. 'Won't it have been usurped by some French family as hard to shift as limpets?'

'If they are occupying our shelter, they'll be shifted.'

'Of course,' said Isabel, 'all we need to complete a delightful first morning is a squabble in French on the beach. However, far be it from me to spoil your pleasure.' She jumped up and rushed out, carrying Linda.

David slunk after, summoned by an imperious and petulant yelp.

Maddy and Jonathan were alone. He had not the energy or goodwill left to say anything about her absconding. She smiled, as if things were normal, the volcano still dormant. He was amazed, for it seemed to him to have begun to erupt; already the many-turreted tower of self-satisfaction he had built up in his mind was toppling.

'Isabel seems so excessively resentful,' he murmured. 'What do you think's the matter with her?'

'I don't know, but I thought perhaps she's pregnant again.'

'Good heavens!' And from then on, all the way down to

the beach, and during the altercation with the large stubborn French family in possession of his sun-shelter, he was wondering why the human species, capable only of imperfect love for one another, should nevertheless continue to reproduce so extravagantly. It all seemed some kind of horrid, universal, incestuous mistake.

Six

About an hour later, with his forefinger clutched in Linda's chubby little paw, he was lying on his stomach under the straw-roofed shelter, trying to resist her determined, apparently deliberate efforts to dispel his cynicism about the species. She chuckled, laughed, flashed her eyes, twinkled her toes, pouted her lips, blew bubbles, and submerged her tiny nose, all in a coquetry he could not help finding charming, and basically innocent. Nor was he, rather to his surprise, greatly embarrassed by the attention paid by the women round about, some of whom indeed crept forward over the hot pebbles on naked knees and rotund bellies, their bosoms visible and their buttocks oozing out, in order to pay homage to the small, blonde, white-hatted charmer. Though careful not to show it, he was pleased that Linda took little notice of these intruders, but continued her persuading of him. More than one assumed he was the father; this he was obliged to deny, but not as curtly as he might have done a day or two ago. He even explained, gratuitously, in three languages, that he was the child's uncle; it was almost a boast.

All the same, it was not possible to refrain from reflecting that even this pink morsel of femininity, so delighted with life, and perfectly fashioned to the nail on her little finger, ran the risk of growing up to become like these French, German and Spanish mothers, good-natured enough, with maternal love to spare for tiny strangers, but gross in body and dull in mind.

Of course there were younger, slimmer female bodies strewn around. From more than one he had got glances that, though obscured by sun-glasses, were clear enough in their intent. As Maddy had said, he never lacked opportunities. It was not, he now confided to Linda, that he was indifferent; no, his interest was in abeyance, that was all. If love had to be made, let it not be on these hot, hard, anchorite stones, let it not be with oily bodies, nor with minds dazed and darkened by sun lust. Above all, let it not be ordinary. If it could not be heroic, then at least let it be grand.

He jumped as cold water splashed on his back. It was Maddy fresh from the sea, shaking herself like a dog. As she flopped down beside him, he reflected that even if her white blue-dotted bikini was exiguous, still her body was so slender and tanned that even naked it should arouse delight rather than disgust.

'What are you chuckling at?' she asked.

He thought she was talking to Linda.

'You, I mean.'

'Me? I was not chuckling.'

'Yes, you were; louder than Linda. Wasn't he, Linda?'

But Linda coolly ignored her, and treated Jonathan to a particularly hearty series of chuckles.

'Why, Jonathan,' said Maddy, 'she's taken a fancy to you. You've got a girl-friend at last.'

He responded with wit: 'And one that's innocent.'

Maddy laughed inordinately. Was it the laughter of the adulteress committed to flight with her partner in sin? He did not think so; it was by no means as innocent as Linda's, but it was not depraved either. Yet it was quite possible that she was an adulteress.

Linda kept tugging his finger to remind him that he had been talking to her before Maddy had interloped. He had therefore to gurgle to her now and then, while he whispered with solemnity to Maddy.

'Now, Maddy,' he said, 'face to face with this child, let's hear the truth.'

She stretched forward and put her face so close to Linda's that the baby clutched her hair. 'About what?' she asked.

'You know very well about what.'

'It's finished. All over. Last night was goodbye.'

He believed her. Last night there had been a sad bewilderment of love on the tall Spaniard's face. 'But, Maddy, last night you told me you were going to run away with him.'

'So I did. Don't talk about it.'

'But I must, Maddy. As you know, I love Spain and its people; I intend to live here all my life, if they will have me. The regime does not interfere with me. I see little signs of it interfering with my Spanish neighbours. Therefore I certainly have no intention of interfering with it.'

She adjusted Linda's sunbonnet.

'They are a puritanic people,' he went on. 'I suppose that is one of the reasons why I like them.'

'You mean I haven't to misbehave and get you kicked out?' she asked.

'Precisely.'

Instead of being scornful at his timidity and prudishness, she whispered into Linda's ear: 'Tell him, Linda.'

'Tell me what?'

'Tell him I've decided to get married.'

The baby pulled her hair; he felt like pulling it too, much harder.

'What do you mean, Maddy? Please don't you start being difficult. Isabel, heaven knows, is trying enough.'

'But I thought that's what you wanted, Jonathan.'

'Yes, but doesn't it depend on whom you marry? You don't mean Norman, do you?'

'No.'

'Anybody I know?'

'Yes.'

He mentioned two or three names. She shook her head contemptuously at each. He was relieved. Yet her choice might well be worse than any of these. The fisherman, for instance, who had given her the fish.

'Who then?'

'John Lynedoch.'

A bucket of water, tossed over him by a revengeful French child, could not have caused in him a greater shiver; astonishment was in it, anger, incredulity, and alarm. As she lay smiling, almost as close to him as they had been in the womb, she had that air of resolution that, though delicate like the rest of her, was also formidable.

He felt as alarmed for Lynedoch's sake as for his own.

'As a joke, Maddy,' he said, awkwardly, 'surely that's in rather bad taste. Admitted he's pretty gauche and uncouth; but hasn't his background contributed to that? Still, thanks to David, he happens to be our guest. Not for long, I hope; but while he's with us shouldn't we show him as much consideration as we would, had he been, to speak frankly, one of our own class?'

She addressed Linda: 'Isn't your Uncle Jonathan the most pompous prig in the whole wide world?'

That was a stone often cast, but never before had it struck him so painfully, after ricocheting, as it were, off the baby so trustfully holding his finger.

'And the most barren-minded snob,' added Maddy.

He was hurt. From Isabel, yes, he expected obloquy, she'd been born years before him, and had always looked on him as a usurper, especially since Aunt Edith had left him most of her money.

'Tell him,' went on Maddy remorselessly, 'that John Lynedoch has a great talent.'

He stared at her, so familiar, so dear, so exquisite, so unpredictable, and so traitorous.

'And *he* has none.'

Had he been primitive in his emotions, he would have struck her. Being civilized, he laughed and stroked her hair. 'I've already admitted I have none,' he said, 'but his having some, great or little, has still to be proved.'

'Not to me.'

'But you've seen only one of his pictures, and you detested it.'

'Did I?'

'Well, you certainly sounded as if you did. You convinced me, not to mention poor Lynedoch himself.'

She spoke to Linda again: 'Now he's pitying him.'

'Well, good heavens, Maddy, his father was a bricklayer's labourer.'

'Your grandfather, darling, was an alcoholic writer of dreary novels.'

'Don't bring the child into this, Maddy.'

'You are in, aren't you, darling? Everybody human is in. Uncle Jonathan isn't human, so he's not in, in spite of what your mother said last night.'

But surely his sadness and spite, as he wondered what Lynedoch's mother had been, were human enough? His own had been a kind-hearted, rather stupid, adulteress.

Then they were hallo'd at from the sea. It was Isabel standing up and pointing to the road. 'Ampara seems to be looking for you,' she cried, and then lay down and floated blissfully on her back.

More stork-like than ever, David crouched on a raft a hundred yards off shore.

Ampara, in her maid's uniform, was standing between two of the boats drawn up on the beach. She would not come down among the shameless bikini-wearers. Now that she saw Jonathan and Maddy staring towards her she waved. Something was in her hand; it looked like a telegram.

'I suppose I'd better see what it is,' he said.

'Don't you know? It'll be to say Terence and Bridie are on their way.'

'I hardly think so. I made it plain.'

'Nothing is ever plain to Terence; that's his charm.'

'Charm indeed!' Gently withdrawing his finger from Linda's grasp, he rose up. At once the baby began to cry. He took a step or two away. She howled still louder. He kept on. She set about being heard across the bay.

'You'd better take her with you,' called Maddy.

Women smiled. Men laughed. They applauded. Confused, he turned back. Maddy was already up, with the baby, still howling, ready to hand over. He took her. Instantly she was pacified and began to laugh. Yet real tears were in her eyes. Separation even for moments from someone loved was pain. Would he some day find such tears in his own eyes? Painful though they might be, and not quite so transitory as the infant's, he hoped so.

Ampara stared at the ground. She could not bear to look at him, so scantily dressed; not even the baby in his arms redeemed his public indecency.

She handed him the telegram.

He was about to ask her to take Linda while he opened the envelope, but he recalled in time Isabel's hysterical objections to her, not any more ignoble, perhaps, than his to Lynedoch. Sweating with a peculiar guiltiness, he was about to read the telegram when Linda snatched it out of his hand, crumpled it in her tiny fist, refused to yield it, and made to put it in her mouth. He had to grab it back, making her cry.

It was not from Terence at all, but from Norman. He said he was arriving that evening at Figueras by the seven o'clock train. The last four words, apart from his name, were as supererogatory as any Jonathan had ever seen on a telegram: God bless you all. Whatever bitterness Maddy had put into her letter to him, this surely was the strangest rejoinder. It struck Jonathan as blasphemous.

Ampara still stared dourly at the ground. 'Good news, señor?'

'Señor Norman is arriving tonight.'

For her it was good news. She beamed. Norman had left her a handsome tip, and had often sat in her kitchen learning Spanish songs from her as she peeled potatoes or prepared paella.

For Maddy, though, it would be the worst of news. He exulted as he thought how this would destroy her designs on Lynedoch. True, neither had Norman any talent; but he had been at Harvard, his people were rich, and when he liked he could be very gentlemanly. As a brother-in-law he would be far from ideal, but in every way superior to the Scot. Norman was the kind that safely extinguished volcanoes and turned the searing red lava to cool grey ash. Lynedoch, with even a little genius, could blow up one's whole settled, cosy, third-rate universe.

He almost ran back down the beach to Maddy. Linda, thinking the hurry was for her benefit, bounced in his arms with glee.

Seven

As usual, by instinct almost, he let himself as a person suffer, to try and protect the artist so vulnerable in him; and in suffering, as in everything else, he showed to the world the face of ordinariness. Only in that way could he hope to preserve what in him he believed to be rare and valuable. Therefore, as he came out of the gate that morning, no one, and certainly not Madeleine Broxmead watching him from the terrace, could have suspected that inwardly he was writhing with humiliation and hatred of her who had caused it; or that he felt so morally and spiritually crippled and broken that he did not want to go anywhere or do anything. So it had been in childhood when a patch or hole in his trousers had been laughed at, or his crayon drawing had not been thought worthy to be among those pinned up on the classroom wall.

He wanted just to sit down on this dusty bank among the spiky-leaved blue flowers and brood over his humiliation, hatching it into fantastic schemes of revenge. All he did, though, was casually stoop, pluck one of the flowers, and walk on with dozens of the tiny spikes imbedded in his palm. Anyone looking – and he could still be seen from the terrace – would have thought he was clutching a holiday handful of sunshine or playfully frightening a butterfly.

His hand stung, but still he kept crushing the flower, seeing in its blueness not the beneficence of the sky but the unprovoked insolence of Madeleine Broxmead's eyes. Aye, unprovoked; because even if it were true that he had made use of Margaret, as he had made use of others, for his painting's sake, still it was no business of hers. If Margaret had not minded, what right had she?

In the village he sat down on a wall above the sea, to pick the spikes out of his hand and let his rage burn out. What he must do of course was to leave their house at once; he ought to go back now and drive the car over the hill to some other village along the coast. If he stayed on here, it would be because he was too cowardly or too boorish to take his leave. Humiliations would multiply, until very soon he would become so self-contemptuous that even his faith in himself as a painter, needing to be sustained daily, no hourly, would be incurably contaminated.

To keep telling himself that he was as good as the Broxmeads; to seek, more and more desperately, in Margaret's portrait and in his other pictures, for evidences or promises of talent; to remember his mother and the many women like her, the best representatives of his class, with their courage and their humanity as warm and consoling as this sunshine; to repeat praises of his work, by Reeves and other experts: all that would do little good. He would never be able to convince himself. For in so many ways the Broxmeads and their class were superior. But for them there would be no painting worth looking at, no literature, no music. Did not Broxmead, pompous and futile though he was, possess all the volumes of Proust in French, records of Bach's music, and an original drawing by Graham Sutherland as well as fine reproductions of works by Cézanne, Matisse, and Picasso? Besides being the sustainers of art, people of their class had a smoothness of social intercourse, of physical movement, of skin, and of speech, not altogether inherited, but produced by living from birth in spacious and comfortable homes, by eating good and interesting food, by taking a bath and changing their underclothes daily, and above all by being able to take for granted that these amenities would be always available. Not even the lucky possession of artistic talent could quite make up for the lifelong lack of all these.

In women, more than in men, those refinements were important. In many working-class girls could be seen the dismaying contrast between their external appearance, on which much expense and care had been lavished, and the rankness of their minds, from the first word they spoke. In Margaret herself that contrast, softened by her sweetness of temperament, had sometimes troubled him.

Such thoughts were disloyal, treacherous, and per-niciously snobbish; aye, but they were honest, too, and inevitable. If Madeleine Broxmead was to be his enemy, as she had apparently chosen to be, it was necessary for him to know the weapons she would use against him, and his own vulnerabilities. She was more dangerous than most because she was very bonny, vivacious, clear-sighted, clever, and cruelly fair-minded. She had instantly divined the real nature of his diffidence, and was prepared not to pity it, as her brother was inclined to, or despise it, as her sister did, but rather to attack it. Her sister would act the haughty lady towards him – even with a fretful diarrhoeal baby on her lap she had tried it – but no intimate damage could be done to him by such an attitude; as a boy delivering groceries to Pollokshields villas he had learned how to counter it. Madeleine despised in him what really deserved to be despised; she might in the end do him good, but the treatment would be much too agonizing. Far wiser, there-fore, to slip off this afternoon.

As he rose from the wall and made for the arch through which lay the street up to the church, he was passed by an old bowed woman, in black from the lace net on her white hair to the heels of her shoes. He caught a glimpse of her glazed blue-veined hands clasped calmly in front of her, and of her face wrinkled and swarthy with more than seventy years of sun. On her breast Christ was crucified.

His heart miraculously lightening, he remembered Granny Adamson's crucifixes and bleeding hearts, and remembered too how, as a boy of seven or eight, he had stood outside the Catholic chapel in the gloomy Glasgow side street, staring at the people going in, the Papes, who had looked so like other people, yet, according to the stories he had heard about them, they ought to have been different in some terrible way he dared not even guess at. He had believed that of the two Gods, his own gigantic in orange and the Papish in green, the latter must be the more potent and awful. Not long before a boy had secretly shown him a Catholic book in which were illustrations of victims in hell being speared by devils with tails, and bitten by big-fanged snakes.

Now, watching the old Spanish women, for others followed the first, he felt liberated not only from those terrors of childhood but also from his childish hatred of Madeleine Broxmead. She, too, might one day be trudging to church, to kneel and pray, perhaps for a husband and children dead, or for a grandchild ill, or for forgiveness for sins committed long ago and forgotten by everybody but herself.

Beyond the arch the street, cobbled, narrow, and winding, gave exhilarating glimpses of serene cloud, white houses, curved tiles, coloured screens, and red flowers trailing down from ironwork balconies. It was easy to put aside his hatred and envy of Madeleine Broxmead. Here in this small ordinary street was what it meant to be human; here what depraved or belittled or wearied the soul had been taken into account, and then left out; here a great deal of joy and peace remained; here, made plain, was the essence to be captured in painting.

Though he was going to leave that afternoon, and might never walk up this street again or look down on the village from this spacious terrace in front of the church, he felt, like an urgency in his blood, the need to paint it all. He would too, if not here then in another village, further down the coast, or even back in Scotland, in his studio in the top flat of the condemned tenement, from where the view was of factory chimney stacks, smoky backyards, and dismal grey streets, in any one of which you would be sure to find chalked on a wall the bitter snarl: KICK THE POPE.

In a few minutes he would go into the church and sit in its cool quiet refreshing shadows, not praying, like the old women in front of the huge ornate altar, but in a state of mind more fruitful surely than prayer. Later in his painting of the village he would try to show why people prayed, with what hope, and with what resignation. Already his fingers were nervous, as ideas grew in his mind, of shapes and colours; but he knew how fertilizing patience could be, and how problems difficult and discouraging would in a week or month or year be found to be splendidly solved. It was this knowledge that gave him the curiously modest feeling of being entrusted with a treasure which he had to guard with the camouflage of anonymity, or if that failed with deceit, hypocrisy, and callousness.

Suddenly he became aware that three girls whom he had watched coming up the steep street and who were now loudly admiring the view, were talking English, or rather that defiant, corrupt version spoken in those parts of Glasgow with which he was familiar. His reaction was quickly to turn his back and try to overhear no more. Judged by their bright clothes, they might have been the equals of Madeleine Broxmead, if not her betters, for she was casual in dress whereas they were ambitious. But their speech, their laughter, and the coarseness of their features proclaimed not only their inferiority but his too. In spite of his cautioned tongue, at which he had seen Madeleine smile, he spoke like them. His mind was marred by the same influences, going back generations. For himself as John Lynedoch, errand boy, factory hand, hospital janitor, house-painter, it didn't matter at all; but for the artist in him it could be fatal. The enemy most likely to despoil his treasure was within.

What was it old Sam Brownstead of the Iona Gallery in Glasgow had said two years ago, after looking at some of his paintings? 'You've got strength, Lynedoch, but you've got subtlety too; aye, and rarer than those, especially for a Scot, a sense of pity that rarely goes maudlin. But, Lord help you, son, there's something you lack, and you'll aye lack it, I'm thinking. How should you no'? You were brought up to lack it. What is it, son? It's hard to gie a name to it, but I'll try. Grace. Aye, that's as near as I'd ever get to it in one word; and one word's a' I'm allowing myself for it's no' for me to discourage as original a talent as has come my way for many a year. Grace. No, I'm no' saying it's impossible to acquire it even if as a bairn you were brought up in an atmosphere entirely hostile to it. Nothing's hopeless to a gift like yours. Don't think, though, you'll be able to pick it up in the kind of polite society that your painting will lift you into, the minute you want. Hae I no' offered to introduce you myself? There's any number already curious to meet you. My advice would be to find some lass brought up to it so that it's in her as natural as her breathing; if you can, let her smit you wi' it.'

One of the girls had produced a flimsy scarf and put it on, slowly tying it under her chin in a pious knot. Then she made for the church, her right hand ready to dip into the holy water.

Her companions, obviously Protestant, watched her solicitously, almost with pity. The smaller let out a sigh or snort audible to him twenty yards off. Her friend laughed nervously, and waved her hand in front of her plump, pink face in a gesture that might have been to banish flies or Catholic devils. Then, the crisis over, they leant their elbows on the hot stones of the parapet and again admired the village. Now and then they glanced quickly along at Lynedoch.

He had intended to go into the church and soak himself in its atmosphere; but now it was made impossible by these girls. Though only four or five years his juniors, they had brought with them all the stultifying confusion, dreary bigotry, and petty arrogance of their country and class; above all, they demonstrated so brashly how like a kind of spiritual malnutrition was gracelessness.

He was about to go away when the smaller girl suddenly, heedless of her friend's embarrassed expostulations, made straight for him, her heels clanking with purpose. Against the wall, he could retreat no further, at least in body; in spirit he tried to flee, into the brightness and tranquillity of the scene below.

He had to turn and look into eyes that he had been seeing all his life: blue, inquisitive, appraising, materialistic and graceless; eyes that had never once looked on a work of art, or if they had then with suspicion and distrust; to him eyes of accusation and threat, which he had travelled a thousand miles to escape.

The voice went with the eyes, and the smile with the voice. This Mediterranean seascape and village, this Spanish chanting from the church, this warmth in which oranges and creative ideas grew, were all nullified, and he might have been standing at any street corner in Glasgow. You are what you were brought up to be, eyes, voice, and smile said; it is in your blood, and in the remotest crannies of your brain; you cannot get rid of it. Go home, give up this feckless dream of becoming a notable painter, take a steady job, paint if you must in your spare time as a hobby, all the better if it brings you a few extra guineas. Admit that your practice of working for a few months and then painting more or less in poverty for the rest of the year is not only unmanly but also unpatriotic. What self-respecting woman do you think you could get to share such a life? All right, you have had some success; paintings of yours have been bought in

Glasgow, Edinburgh, and even Paris. Well, perseverance does deserve to succeed up to a point, but please never forget that the bearded, gaudy, shiftless life of an artist is one no Scotsman worthy of his country would lead. First things first is our motto, and only a fool with sun in his eyes would put painting first.

So much she said without uttering a word, without knowing she was saying it.

What she did say was, pertly: 'Excuse me for speaking to you like this, but aren't you a friend of Mr Broxmead's?'

He wondered by what grotesque aberration they had come to know Jonathan.

'Aye, I thought so,' she said. 'See, Katie, I was right. We saw you arrive last night, with the other lady and gentleman with the baby. As a matter of fact we were having a drink in the open-air café with Mr Broxmead at the time. Isn't that so, Katie?'

Katie wanted to be quiet, but couldn't help saying, with a giggle: 'We would have kent you were British. D'you know why? Because of how wide your trousers are at the bottoms.'

'It's true,' said her friend.

'Every time,' cried Katie. 'If they were waving Union Jacks you couldn't tell any better.'

'Katie, please remember where you are, standing in front of a church. We came up with Teresa. She's our friend. The three of us work together in Glasgow. She's a Catholic.'

'It's funny to see old women cross themselves going on a bus or crossing the road,' said Katie.

'It's funny, but we know better than to laugh. Do you know Miss Broxmead? Madeleine?'

So far he hadn't uttered a word. He was afraid to. They must not discover he was from Glasgow too. He might be able to achieve an imitation of English English that would take in a Spaniard; but these acute Glasgow ears would be quite undeceivable.

Therefore he nodded again.

Katie was now aware he was showing no pleasure in the conversation. Blushing, she whispered to her friend, calling her Peggy.

Peggy stared at him.

He looked past her at the cross on top of the church.

'Mr Broxmead invited us to tea,' said Peggy coldly, 'but we declined.'

Desperately Katie tugged at her friend's blouse.

Peggy rose higher than her five foot nothing, raised her head, and spoke in that very kind of voice which he had been afraid to imitate: 'So sorry, Mr What's-your-name, that we've troubled you with our idle conversation. We come from scruffy Glasgow, don't you know? There everybody has the foolish belief that everybody's got a right to speak to everybody else.'

Katie's face sweated with mortification. As she walked away she whispered: 'You've no right to, Peggy. People don't have to talk to us if they don't want to. Maybe there's a reason for it.'

'Sure there's a reason for it,' said Peggy clearly. 'Conceit. Stuckupness.' Then she turned and proudly clanked away.

As they went down the street into the village he noticed Katie trying to explain, sympathize, and console. It seemed to him that the encounter, so unexpected, trivial, and ludicrous, was really his long-contemplated farewell to Scotland: he would not return there again, not for a long time.

Eight

The most frustrating thing in the world was selfishness, one's own, yes, but also that of others. Small wonder the mystics called it the barrier to God.

Thus Jonathan reflected as he drove alone that evening over the twisting hill road to Figueras, to meet Norman's train and try to prevent him from coming to Cabo Creus. First Madeleine, and then Isabel and David had refused to accompany him. To make it worse, Madeleine's refusal had been neither humble nor conscience-stricken; on the contrary, it had been light-hearted, as if Norman was merely some tedious acquaintance and not her last summer's lover.

All afternoon she had talked with Lynedoch in the garden, looking at the two dozen or so pictures he had, at her coaxing, unearthed from the junk in his car. So enthusiastic had she been that she had called Jonathan down to see them. He had found the garden decked out like an exhibition: paintings hung from tree, bush, and wall; and he had had to admit that amidst the colours and shapes of nature they more than held their own. Their variety, power, and eloquence had astonished him. It was incredible they could have been created by so nondescript a person as Lynedoch, a year or two older than Jonathan, but in many ways so much more juvenile.

With Linda in her arms Madeleine had gone from painting to painting, encouraging the infant to share her enthusiasm; Lynedoch had stood by, more like a husband and father than an artist. As if in an inspiration, Madeleine had decided to hold an exhibition of the pictures in the house. Every painter on the coast would be invited, as well as critics and dealers from Barcelona. What displeased Jonathan more than her quite wifely enterprise on Lynedoch's behalf was the latter's far too meek acceptance. As always he had said very little, giving nothing away, but his eyes had followed Madeleine everywhere, with calculation in them. Jonathan, given Linda to hold for a spell, had been bothered into agreeing to the exhibition; and when David came in later, and saw the paintings, he had been almost insanely keen on it.

Even Isabel, freed from Linda, had been eulogistic; but then, since she and David had arranged to go to a dance that evening at the big hotel, she was in a mood to be indulgent; she had consented to let Ampara look after Linda.

Madeleine had decided too to take Lynedoch out in a boat. She wanted him to see the village from the water in the moonlight. She wanted him, heaven knew, to possess the moon. Yet Jonathan could have sworn that that morning, leaving the house to visit the church, Lynedoch had been determined not to stay with them a day longer. Why had he changed his mind? Had he on his knees sought guidance? Any man might do that – had not Jonathan himself tried it once? But surely any reasonable deity with an equal duty towards others would just as soon have advised him to move on as to remain and become a complication if Norman, as Jonathan feared, refused to keep away. The trouble was, every man, praying in earnestness, knew what he wanted, and was so childishly determined to get it that God, out of paternal benevolence or timidity or spite, usually sanctioned it as a course of action at any rate, without, however, guaranteeing it success. Indeed, as Jonathan himself would have done in His place He in the end frequently inflicted a discomfiting failure, or appeared to do so.

Unfortunately others, including Jonathan, might be

involved in Lynedoch's particular discomfiture. Suppose, for instance, the exhibition on which Madeleine and David were so set turned out to be a fiasco. It needed only two or three critics to pronounce the paintings as bad, or still worse as mediocre, for Lynedoch to be cast down to Jonathan's own self-discovered level. David had been proved wrong before. Besides, had not Jonathan remarked to Madeleine that he found in almost every one of Lynedoch's paintings a lack, of refinement, he would have said, had that quality not been artistically out of favour in an age that extolled Epstein's gross Adam, Moore's enormous bronze contortions, and Picasso's two-faced balloon-bosomed women.

Never an expert driver, he found himself weaving rather worse than usual, to the indignation of motorists approaching and coming behind. On the whole, he was relieved to have to concentrate on driving; wheels could be made to reach a conclusion, thought seldom could.

The platform at Figueras was crowded with people waiting. Jonathan strolled among those patient Catalans, enjoying their remarks to one another, and not minding at all the grins that he, the tall fair-haired Englishman in the mauve shorts, provoked. When a small boy chased by his brother bumped into him and clawed at his bare knee, he patted the child's head and said: 'Guapo!' as any child-loving Spaniard would. Nor was he unaware that a group of girls, not beautiful, with cheap scent, but movingly Spanish for all that, were discussing him with some hilarity. Their laughter was satirical as any women's would be when directed against an inaccessible solitary male, but it had admiration in it too. They recognized in him qualities that it was high time others gave him credit for. He had been honest enough to acknowledge his lack of creative ability; surely in fairness he ought with equal frankness to declare his assets, physical and intellectual. It would be dangerous, he said – to himself, he thought, but really aloud – to perform so severe an operation as excising the swollen tumour of unjustified ambition, and thereafter to allow no period of convalescent flattery, even if self-administered. That way might give rise to spiritual and moral anaemia.

As he walked up and down, more and more quickly, he smiled as well as muttered aloud. Not only women, but men, some with berets like onion-sellers, laughed. Elbows nudged elbows, brown eyes winked. He saw it all and loved it for its Spanish jolliness. Confidence upsurged. Let him get to know these people well, and who knew what significant themes he might yet discover to write about? He had been too drastic and precipitate in condemning himself as sterile. Many a woman, childless for years, suddenly conceived. The spark from heaven, like the fertilizing seed, was a mystery. How strange, for instance, that it should apparently have fallen on Lynedoch who, in any crowd, Scots, English, French, or Spanish, would never have been noticed, and not on Jonathan himself, outstanding in any company, as was at that very moment being proved.

He was so carried away by these buoyant reflections that he was startled to hear a train approaching, but from the wrong direction. Hastily inquiring, he learned it was the train from Barcelona; that from Port Bou for which he was waiting was late. He stood back to watch the passengers alight. Without surprise, but with much indignation, he saw among them Terence and Bridie O'Donnell; and yes, behind them, another woman. He had no time to get a good look at this last, as he had to move lest Terence, a flamingo among geese, should catch sight of him. Retreating along the platform he watched from round the thick bole of a plane tree.

Quite a number of people had got off and were racing one another, lugging luggage, towards the buses outside, one of which at least was for Cabo Creus. Terence rose high among them, his head bare, and his long auburn hair curlier than Linda's, despite all Isabel's efforts with pegs, ribbons, and cream. Bridie, small and quick, hurried on ahead to book their seats in the bus; in her, Irish charm never clogged self-interest, as it so often did with her husband. Jonathan, his indignation growing, saw her push her way on to the bus, and reserve three seats. Terence stooped a little under the weight of a large suitcase which seemed to belong to the other woman. She could of course be some acquaintance they had met on the train. Jonathan still had not got a satisfactory look at her. She was dark-haired; wore a pink dress; was not fat, and above average height for a Spaniard; conducted herself with little fuss.

Terence waited in the queue at the hut where tickets were sold. When he had got his he went into the bus and sat down, his composure lordlier than ever, smoking a cigarette in a holder almost a foot long.

Ten minutes later, as the train from Port Bou could be heard approaching, the bus moved off. It had to stand at the level crossing till the train passed. Jonathan shook his fist at it; he was furious. He remembered, with scorn, Terence's typically mendacious attribution of beauty to his female friend. When it suited Terence, a rhinoceros was beautiful.

Then the Port Bou express thundered into the station, whistling plaintively, as well it might, bringing still another problem in Norman. Jonathan had planned to catch him either before he got off or immediately after so that he could be pushed back on again. Unfortunately the train was very long, with mostly third-class carriages. From one of these Norman would alight, for he liked to be thrifty in order to afford his fits of extravagance. Moreover, Jonathan was on the lookout for someone clad in jeans and checked shirt, with crew-cut hair, guitar, sandals, and luggage in a scruffy hold-all. Therefore, though not many people got off, he missed Norman completely and at first thought, with joy, that he hadn't come. He was congratulating himself and Norman too, on that intelligent decision, when he saw striding towards him along the platform a young man in a very smart light grey suit, with wide-brimmed hat to match, mahogany shoes, and white shirt, carrying in one hand a fat briefcase of tan pigskin and in the other a black book that looked like an elegant expensive Bible.

It was Norman. His face was thinner and paler, as if he had been ill; and though his eyes shone with their old friendliness there was at their centre a glitter of dedication that shocked Jonathan as much and as quickly as the tie did; this, of pink silk, had inscribed on it, below the knot, in tiny fancy yellow characters, over and over again: GOD IS LOVE.

It must surely be a practical joke, in grotesquely bad taste. Jonathan was aware his sense of humour could be sluggish at times, especially where he himself was involved. Frequently at school practical and other jokes had failed when practised on him because even when they were over he had not been completely aware of them.

Norman took his hand and stared into his eyes, with a peculiarly rude effect; it was as if he was stripping off the usual deceptions that civilized people meeting find it necessary to adopt. His drawl, too, though recognizable, had a thickness of unction in it, as nauseating as warm treacle.

'Still the same old Jonathan,' he said. Looking round, he added: 'I don't see Maddy.'

The train was about to pull out again.

'She's not here, Norman,' gasped Jonathan, pushing him towards the train. 'Didn't you get her letter warning you not to come? The truth is, she's getting married.'

Norman resisted the lie as easily as he did the push. 'Sure, she's getting married,' he said. 'To me.'

The train moved off, snorting and screaming with derision.

'Got your car outside?' asked Norman.

'Yes, but really, Norman, I'm serious. There's little point in your coming with me. It isn't simply that I'm not in a position to offer you hospitality; it's just that Maddy doesn't want you. I'm sorry, old man, but that's it.'

Norman laughed. 'Say no more, Jonathan.' He led the way out of the station. 'I'm not the man she doesn't want. He's been discarded, and rightly so. Still the same old jalopy?'

He meant the car. It was Jonathan's chance. 'Norman,' he said, 'what game is this you're playing?'

Norman laughed, showing his fine teeth, and disconcertingly looked very like his old self, the singer of bawdy folk songs, the teaser of Ampara and, alas, the lover of Maddy.

'That's simple, Jonathan,' he said. 'I can answer that in one word. God's game.'

Jonathan winced. 'I say!' was all he could manage.

'The most important game there is; the only one worth playing. But I'm not playing it right yet. If I drop the ball and make a fumble now and then, blame me, not the game itself. Shall we get in? I'm truly anxious to see Maddy.'

Jonathan was almost convinced it must be a leg-pull; either that or Norman was mentally ill. That awful tie could be explained only in terms of sarcastic jest or idiocy.

'You are seeking an explanation?' asked Norman, laughing still more heartily.

'Well rather.'

Norman laid a hand on his shoulder. 'Again I can give it in one word,' he said. 'Or two. Frank Redhall.'

Jonathan's blood froze, his soul squirmed, and his lips writhed.

'The most wonderful guy in the world,' said Norman piously.

Redhall was a famous American evangelist who went about the world holding mammoth conventicles in football or boxing stadiums, at which droves of people rushed forward, like the Gadarene swine, claiming on the contrary to have been saved. In print Redhall's exhortations were as trite and uninspiring as Hitler's had been; but, it seemed, uttered in his fervent Tennessee drawl, and supported by his gold-linked cuffs rattling at heaven, they were as rousing and irresistible as the Austrian house-painter's had been.

'You may smile, Jonathan. I smiled myself. When he came to Geneva months ago I went along just for the laughs. And do you know what happened?'

'You were saved?' Seldom had words more offended the tongue that they tumbled feebly off.

'Sure I was saved. I thought myself as immune an egotist as yourself, Jonathan, but it happened. In one searing flash, sin and pride were all burnt away. God pressed on my shoulder and I just had to go down on my knees.'

A genuine mystic was another thing altogether: on his way to God he thought and felt profoundly, wrestled with carnality, endured infinite loneliness, and suffered as greatly as any Belsen victim. Therefore he had to be respected, even if his utterances were incomprehensible and his example impossible.

'I'm afraid I must say,' said Jonathan coldly, 'that I'm completely out of sympathy.'

Neophyte though he was, Norman knew how to ignore disbelief. 'Frank thinks I could become a Voice,' he said. 'That's what we call our preachers. But, for obvious reasons, they must be married. When I told Frank about Maddy he was very enthusiastic. You see, his own wife Phyllis is one of the most beautiful women you ever saw. Laugh if you like, Jonathan, but in your heart you must know that the world's got to be mastered with its own weapons. We want to redeem it, so first we must interest it. It's my hope Maddy will share my vocation with me.'

It was all too ludicrous for smiles or tears or visible protest. Maddy, thank God, was merciless to humbug.

Jonathan at last got into the car. Norman settled beside him.

'Don't you agree, Jonathan, that God is love?'

The tone of voice reminded Jonathan of Isabel in her most maudlin maternal mood, say, when bathing Linda with the baby's hair cherubic with scented soap suds.

'Don't you, Jonathan?'

It was like being invited to perform publicly an act of perversion or obscenity.

'Well, don't you, Jonathan?'

The voice was soapier and more scented than ever; yet the face was recognizable as that which last summer, on the moonlit terrace, had with whiskied earnestness read aloud a story that had struck Jonathan, with his own tepid manuscript on his knee, as quite pornographic. The hair at the back of his neck had bristled in icy revulsion, as it was doing now.

'Well, Jonathan?'

He had to answer. 'In view of the H-bomb, venereal disease, famine, and archiepiscopal smugness, I do not,' he said.

'Isn't it a terrible catalogue, Jonathan? Yet you have left out the worst of the lot.'

'And what is that?'

'International atheistic communism.'

'To which, if I remember rightly, you seemed rather attracted no longer ago than last summer. Some of us thought you pretty ingenuous in your views, Norman. I doubt if anything that's happened is going to cause us to change our opinion. However, before we set off, I must warn you again that you will have to put up at a hotel, if you can find one with an empty room.'

Jonathan trembled with rage as he thought of Terence, Bridie, and their friend; these would probably not be able to afford to go to a hotel. They would make beds about the house.

'As a matter of fact, Jonathan, I have a room reserved at the Miramar.'

'The Miramar!' This was the big hotel, where a cheap room cost three pounds a day. 'You can't be expecting to stay for long.'

'As long as is necessary.'

Jonathan started the engine. 'As her brother, her twin, I know Maddy better than anyone else does. Nobody in the world loathes humbug more. If you insist on coming, and on pursuing this new career, then the consequences are on your own head.'

'Like a crown of thorns?'

Nine

'Never,' whispered Madeleine, 'undervalue yourself.'

Lying in her arms, with an oar or part of the boat pressing painfully into his right haunch, and afraid a little of capsizing, though the bay was as calm as Madeleine herself, Lynedoch uttered a gasp of acknowledgment. Beyond her profile and moon-fringed hair he could see the sky, moon-possessed as she was attempting, with similar serenity and brilliance, to possess his mind. Though one ear was folded over against her cheek he could hear the small waves gurgle, slyly, around the boat, and further away raucous music from the cafés.

If I'm to put a proper value on myself, he thought, in regard to yourself, Miss Broxmead, what value would you say that was?

'Remember you've got a gift a king would envy,' she said. 'Never undervalue yourself, in eating an olive, in saying thanks, in drinking wine, or in making love.'

She added that last because of Norman Ashton. In an act where a man ought surely to have felt triumphant he had kept sobbing that he wasn't worthy. As a result he certainly hadn't been. To make it worse, he had tried to explain afterwards. But she had come to learn that his feeling of unworthiness had been fundamental. Had he been at home, in the States, he would have been under a psychiatrist. On his knees he had begged her to help him find faith in himself. She might have tried, had she loved him, or had she thought him valuable enough, as a writer, say; but she did not think she or any woman could have succeeded, so deep and ancestral was his feeling of insufficiency. With John Lynedoch, on the other hand, it was on the surface, not very prepossessing, but shallow and removable. Underneath she suspected a belief in himself as hard and muscular as his thin body. He was the most exciting proposition she had ever considered taking on; with her to torment and inspire him he might well become a great painter.

He thought, moving a little to ease his behind, that he could never become fond of this beautiful, subtle, confident woman, as he had been of poor Margaret, or as he could be of Ampara the maid. Her gaiety, frankness, and above all her superb self-confidence fascinated but also intimidated him. He foresaw her urging him on to paint better than he had ever done before; he could even foresee himself marrying her, but never loving her. Perhaps it was because, in a way hard to define, she kept reminding him of her brother. Indeed, there were moments when Lynedoch felt, with reverberations of dismay, that it really was Jonathan he was embracing, or more truthfully being encouraged to embrace.

'Your brother,' he murmured.

'What about him?' she asked, after a pause.

'He doesn't approve of me.'

She laughed. 'Poor Jonathan, he doesn't much approve of himself.'

'Is he a writer?'

'He tries to be. Being Scots, you'll have read the novels of Sir Walter Scott?'

'Not recently.'

'Only schoolkids have ever read them recently. Don't you remember how the heroes and especially the heroines are marble statues, without guts or sex? Julia Mannering, for instance. Well, all Jonathan's characters are like her. It's impossible to tell the difference between his men and his women.'

Lynedoch wondered, not for the first time, if her brother was really a homosexual.

'Has he ever had a girl-friend?' he asked.

'You mean,' she said, with provocative coarseness, 'has he ever slept with a woman? I don't think so. He's got some absurd thing about purity. Perhaps he feels he's got to compensate for me.'

He simply had to take his hip off that projection, whatever it was. He was sure there must be a dent in him that would last for days. Besides, he had a ridiculous but compelling feeling that he ought not to be making so free with Madeleine (though not so free as she seemed to wish), without her brother's sanction. Jonathan might be a hermaphroditic snob, as marmoreally pompous as the characters in his book; but he had also a curious potentiality that Lynedoch could never have described in words; in paint, though, he thought he could. Broxmead had a magnificent head; crowned, it could have been a Renaissance prince's.

He rose up, trying not to dig his elbow into her breast. Was it her middle-class upbringing, or her natural aptitude for love-making, that made her able to appear so composed and comfortable in this inadequate space? Or had she dents too which she was too well-bred to complain about?

'This Ashton fellow,' he said, 'he's an American, isn't he?'

'John, you're so damned Scotch.'

The moonlight was blue on her hair; it sparkled on the sequins in her slacks.

'"This Ashton fellow,"' she repeated, mimicking him, '"he's an American, isn't he?"'

Another boat chugged discreetly past.

'Buenas noches,' she called, deliberately indiscreet.

After a pause, a young man's voice, Spanish, pleasantly satirical, responded: 'Buenas noches, Señorita Broxmead.'

'Do you know him?' whispered Lynedoch.

'Well, he knows me.'

Far too many knew her. He could not help feeling appalled and affronted. Though he would without a qualm paint what would have outraged his mother and her fore-bears, in his own person he shared their puritanic standards. It wasn't that they regarded chastity as beautiful or moral or preferred by God; no, it was just that sexual relations between men and women were, of all utilitarian activities, the least respectable; to look for joy in them was deservedly punished by none being found. Thus believed many in Scotland even today. No one brought up there could be altogether uninfected by the belief.

'What was he like?' he asked.

'Who?'

'Ashton. He's a writer, isn't he?'

She took his hand. 'Are you interested in him merely as a topic of conversation, to pass a few tedious minutes, or as your predecessor?'

She waited for an answer, and got it.

'As my predecessor, of course.'

She laughed. 'In that case there's only one thing about him you need to know; and being a Scot you ought to know it. Normally he was as pagan as I am. He shocked Ampara by singing bawdy sacrilegious songs to her in Spanish. He shocked Jonathan by writing stories that could only be called filthy. But there were certain moments, rather intimate moments, when he turned, most inopportunely, very pious, sacerdotal in fact. I don't know whether you understand, though I suspect you're a lot quicker on the uptake than you let on; but whether you do or not that's the last word about him. Now do we head for shore, or do we sit here, or do we go voyaging round the headland?'

'What's round there?'

'A little bay, with beds of pine needles; and perhaps some lovers.'

'But I thought you wanted to introduce me to sardana-dancing.'

She stared at him in the moonlight. 'Aye, you're very Scotch,' she said. 'All right. To the sardanas. Look out, while I start the engine.'

'Why are you laughing?'

'At the picture of you in the sardana ring.'

'I don't mind looking silly.'

'Good for you.'

'Your brother, though, I should think he would hate it.'

The boat was now gliding over moonlit ripples towards the lights and music of the village.

'Come and sit beside me,' she said.

Cautiously he did so, not to embrace or kiss, but to begin telling her, in a quiet flat voice, about the old black-clad women he had seen that morning on their way to the church, and then about his experience as a child outside the Catholic chapel in fiercely bigoted Glasgow.

She could have sung for joy, not because the sky above the hills was so splendid, or because the village was so cheerful to be sailing home to, but because she was going to be in this strange man's life when he began to express in paint these impressions and recollections that even as described in the sparse colourless words were so much beyond what she herself was capable of, in richness of feeling and sense of human unity. Whatever the effect on herself in the end, she must see to it that the lack of grace which the shrewd old Glasgow art dealer, and Jonathan too, had detected in his work would not impair this, the first to be painted under her guardianship.

Ten

It was dark before they reached Cabo Creus. Never had Jonathan been so glad to see the lights of the village below as the car groaned up over the skyline and began its spiralling descent. All during the hour's journey Norman had hardly stopped talking, about himself saved, and about 'that wonderful guy, Frank, the H-bomb of God's grace, from whom the fall-out of salvation would eventually reach more than half the world's population'. He spoke in atrocious quotations like that, from a book he was writing, 'about real people, not the phonies I used to write about, and you still do, I guess. Case histories of how they came to Jesus, after hearing Frank. Our files are like Midas's treasure-house. It'll sell a million copies, too; sell, I truly mean, because don't think they'll be hand-outs, gratis. No, sell, at four ninety-five a copy. And what's most glorious of all, it'll be real folk who'll buy and read it, not sharks like reviewers, and the deadbeats of the literary world.'

So he rhapsodically drivelled, not even noticing when Jonathan, usually old-maidish about overtaking, shot recklessly past the bus from which singing came, and in which a glimpse was got of Terence, still smoking, sultanically relaxed, though the bus was as unhygienically crowded with bodies as a seraglio. In the crush nothing could be seen of Bridie, or of their Spanish companion. The bus usually detoured into Rosas, set down passengers, picked up a few, and then returned to climb up over the hill and down to Cabo Creus. It would arrive there at least half an hour after the car, giving Jonathan time to carry out preparations for inhospitality, if he could think of any. In those thirty minutes he must find some means of impressing upon these intruders the enormity of destroying his privacy, or rather of coming to mock at him shivering in its ruins. For of course it had already been shattered by Isabel and David, embittered by this second pregnancy coming so haughtily upon the pink heels of the first; by Maddy practising her courtesan's wiles on Lynedoch; and by Lynedoch himself, sent so pat from slumdom to rub salt into Jonathan's raw, bleeding, and incurable wound of confessed mediocrity.

It did strike him, once or twice, as remarkable that Norman never once asked about his rival, the man who, as Jonathan had lied, was going to marry Maddy. Most men, including even Jonathan himself, would have been inquisitive about their usurper. It was as if Norman had a guarantee in his brief-case, signed by God, and undersigned by Frank. Well, Maddy would very soon jolly well tear it up.

'I'll drop you at the hotel,' he said.

'You know, I've been thinking how nice it would be to say hello to Maddy.'

'She won't be at home. She was going out in a boat.'

Norman gazed down at the moonlit bay, and grunted piously. If anyone knew what being in a boat with Maddy meant, it was he. He seemed disturbed, fingered his tie, closed his eyes, prayed.

'She got her sister with her?' he asked hopefully.

'No. David and Isabel are at a dance, at the Miramar, as a matter of fact.'

'So she's alone? She used to like going out in a boat alone.'

'She's not alone.'

'Some girl-friend maybe, some sister artist?'

'Her companion is male. I told you she intends marrying him.'

Norman became petulant. 'I'm not going to say it ain't my business, for it is, in my own eyes, and in God's.'

Jonathan frowned: not so much at the impertinence, as at the pronunciation of God as Gad; blasphemy, already puerile, could scarcely stand the addition of vulgarity.

'Do you think you ought to have allowed it, Jonathan?'

'I am not responsible for what Maddy does.'

'Ain't we all responsible for one another?'

'No, thank God.'

'Sure we are, Jonathan; but a man's more deeply responsible for his sister, especially his twin sister.'

'If I remember rightly,' said Jonathan, 'last summer when I attempted to exercise my duty of brotherly responsibility, did you not encourage Maddy to tell me to mind my own business? Who was in the boat with her then?'

'Sure, you failed in your duty towards me too. You ought not to have allowed it.'

'Ought I to have used force? Look here, Norman, if your conscience is just back from the launderer, whiter than white, do not blame me for its erstwhile filthiness.'

'But, Jonathan, the rest of us looked up to you. We still must do. You have raised yourself above the lusts of the flesh.'

It was the third-rate shoddiness of the phrase rather than the imputation of frigidity that it conveyed which nettled Jonathan. 'Have I?'

'Sure you have. Everybody knows it. Some have misinterpreted it; I used to myself.'

'Did you really?'

'Yeah, but I was wrong. All honour to you. Frank was terribly impressed.'

'You mean to say you discussed me, in those terms, with Mr Redhall?'

'I discussed everything. Frank has the most widely ranging mind in the whole world, I guess. He cares for you, Jonathan, as he does for his own children.'

'How many of those does he have?'

'Five; and a sixth expected.'

'It would appear then he himself is not quite above those lusts of the flesh.' With what luscious contempt his tongue lingered over the beastly phrase!

Norman was not provoked; far more exasperatingly, he pitied Jonathan for his spitefulness.

'There is the same difference,' he said, 'between mere carnal concupiscence and the love of a man for his wife, as there is between hell and heaven.'

While he was perpetrating that mess of begged question and sanctimonious lie they drove in through the gates of the hotel and up its winding avenue among olives and pines. With the sea everywhere below, it was like an ocean liner, vividly white, and brilliantly lit. Dance music whined and yearned from the ballroom, and dancers could be seen through the open windows; some pairs had danced out into the open air on to the wide terrace. Among these Jonathan caught sight of Isabel and David; she was wearing a sleeveless red dress scandalously low at front; it was as well her breasts were so flat.

'Ain't it good to see folks enjoying themselves?' asked Norman.

'I thought Mr Redhall would condemn dancing as a thing of the devil.'

'Oh, Frank's no kill-joy. A lot of folk have that notion; they're one hundred per cent wrong. Catholic though it is, Spain's a happy country. That's what comes of making sure that the communists are where they ought to be, rotting in jail.'

Jonathan found this vindictiveness distasteful, especially from one who boasted of being with Christ. 'I prefer not to discuss politics,' he said, coldly.

'Wake up, for civilization's sake. Communism ain't just politics; it's anti-Christ, it's a universal poison, it's death to the soul of man.'

'Whatever it is, I prefer not to discuss it. Now, Norman, I'm afraid I must repeat my warning. Come and visit us, by all means, but do not pester Maddy.'

'As sure as Christ is my judge, I've come to marry her, not pester her.'

'I shall tell her you are here. If she wishes to see you, then either she or I will let you know. Until then, I must repeat, do not pester her. Good night.'

As he drove towards the village he stopped at an out-of-the-way but popular café to have a glass of cognac. Norman had left a bad taste. Amidst the thick cigarette smoke, and the cheerful racket of guitars, watching the flamenco dancers, the women skinny in red dresses and the men in black like small pale masterful eunuchs, he found himself trembling, so much so that he could scarcely hold the glass. Norman's religiosity might be spurious and even sinister, but at least it was an interest through which he became involved, however futilely, with other people. Jonathan's own isolation must be ended soon while he was still young, or else he would all too quickly find himself marooned in middle and old age, unsuccessful and unconsoled. Rather than seek to preserve his privacy, and hate those who ravished it, ought he not to abandon it altogether, for a period at least, live in the crowd, wallow in humanity, and emerge if not richer in spirit at any rate thicker in skin?

On his way through the village he stopped for a minute or two to watch the sardana-dancing under the trees in the plaza. He noticed the Scots girls watching too, and was on the point of calling to them, when the friendly impulse just shrivelled in him, he did not know why. A moment later he was considering getting out of the car and taking part in the dancing, but that rather wilder desire shrivelled too, just as mysteriously. Then, causing him to make at once for home, he saw, in the ring of dancers, Maddy and Lynedoch, the latter performing rather less elegantly than Jonathan himself would have done, but far more wholeheartedly.

Ampara met him on the doorstep almost, her finger sternly at her lips. He was not to make a noise, she warned, as the baby was at last asleep after crying for over an hour. The advice seemed sensible enough, and he went on tiptoe in accordance with it, but it ought surely to have been given not to him subdued with loneliness, but to whoever – Terence and company, he supposed – was in the sitting-room, listening to Beethoven's Violin Concerto and no doubt drinking Jonathan's whisky and gin. When he pointed this out to her, in the discreetest of whispers, she agreed with rolling eyes. The tall red-haired Irishman had been cautioned half a dozen times, and every time had promised to turn the music down, but had never done so. She thought he wasn't really listening to it. No, there were no women with him, not even his wife; he was alone, and since he'd been drinking before he'd arrived, and had been drinking steadily since, he was now quite drunk.

So he was, but with it so seigneurial in his bright yellow shirt, so benevolent in his gestures, and so cordially im-pervious to rebuffs, that Jonathan could do nothing but smile and sigh, turn down the music a little, shake the large soft hand so royally offered, accept his own cognac poured out so profusely, and then sit down when invited, in the chair Terence knew to be his favourite.

Then for almost a minute they sat and stared at each other, over and round their glasses, with Beethoven's music delighting them. Faintly in the background sounded the crying of an awakened baby.

Terence's full red warm lips glistened, with whisky and also with what he evidently was going to tell Jonathan, but in his own time. Jonathan was sure it would have to do with a request for accommodation, but he decided to be unco-operative from the very beginning, and say nothing.

Suddenly, as if glad the diversion had occurred to him, Terence turned to point his glass towards the wall where Maddy had hung one of Lynedoch's pictures. 'I would like to congratulate you on your new acquisition, Jonathan. I've been admiring it. Remarkably good. There aren't many paintings that can hold their own with Beethoven. This can. Is it by someone big? Did David bring it? By the way, how are Isabel and he? Ampara was telling me they haven't found a nursemaid yet.'

As if upon a cue Ampara opened the door and looked in, a flushed and fretful Linda in her arms. Before she could upbraid, Terence rose and taking the baby from her began to dandle her, and sing what sounded like a lullaby in Erse. Linda howled louder. He finished his song before surrendering her, bawling with temper, to Ampara who rushed off with her.

'How like her mother!' murmured Terence, returning to his chair.

'You think so, Terence?'

'Well, she hasn't got a beard like her father.'

'Feeble jest. The consensus of opinion is that she is very like Maddy and me.'

'Ah yes, of course; the blonde hair and wide open brow of the Broxmeads. How is my darling Maddy?'

'Very well, thank you.'

Terence looked at the painting again; he even got up to squint at it closely. 'It is damnably good. I like it, I like it a lot. J.L. is it? Well, whoever J.L. is he can paint. Who is he?'

'A fellow called Lynedoch.'

'Lynedoch? Never heard of him. Sounds Scottish.'

'He is.'

'A protégé of David's, I suppose?'

'You might call him that.'

'Well, he can paint. Now who would have thought of making that tree yellow? Yet it's the perfect colour for it.'

He turned and looked at Jonathan. 'How do you feel, Jonathan, when confronted by something really good, as good as this, so far above what you know yourself to be capable of? Myself, I feel like – like taking another drink. May I?'

Jonathan nodded, though he thought it would have been braver and kinder to refuse.

Terence poured himself another generous whisky and soda. 'I wouldn't mind meeting the man who painted that.'

Jonathan decided not to mention Lynedoch was at that moment trying to dance the sardana in the plaza.

Terence made himself comfortable again; his socks were the same bright yellow as his shirt. 'Have you heard from Norman Ashton lately?'

'Yes.'

'Has he gone back to the States, or is he still in Geneva? I must say I could never see what Maddy saw in him. Did I ever tell you that once, when he was drunk, rather drunker than I am now, he took me to task for being a Catholic; and when I explained I was lapsed, he got into quite a temper and gave me a lecture a village priest couldn't have bettered, except that it had rather more four-letter words than his reverence would have felt permissible.'

'You didn't come here to talk about Norman, did you, Terence?'

Craftily Terence listened to the music, for almost a minute. 'Who's looking after the baby?' he asked.

'We're looking for a nanny. They just arrived a day or so ago.'

'In a letter some weeks ago, Jonathan, you mentioned something about Isabel wanting a nursemaid while she was on holiday here.'

'Yes. Like myself, you forgot all about it.'

Terence held up a long finger. 'No, I did not. Trust Terence of the tenacious memory. I've had it in mind all the time. To prove it, I've brought the very woman you want.'

'It's Isabel who wants her. But what do you mean? Aren't you alone?'

'Bridie's sitting in the casino at this moment; and Montserrat is with her.'

'Montserrat?'

'Señorita Montserrat Puig, student of Barcelona University, speaker of English, daughter of deceased lawyer, lover of children, little Linda's new nursemaid.'

Jonathan nodded. The woman's credentials sounded just right. Isabel would be delighted. Miss Puig could sleep in Ampara's room, where the beds were in a two-tier arrangement. The whole thing seemed suitable. He almost felt grateful.

'Of course she would have to satisfy Isabel,' he said.

Terence emptied his glass quickly, and then slowly refilled it. 'Bridie and I aren't staying.'

Jonathan tried to show neither true relief nor false disappointment.

'We're returning to Barcelona tomorrow. As a matter of fact, we're flying to Ireland on Friday night. Bridie's people sent us the tickets. Her grandmother, aged eighty-two, is expected to pop off any day. It's up to us to say goodbye to the old lady, particularly as she's very likely going to leave Bridie a handsome legacy.'

It struck Jonathan as just too remarkably obliging of them to come all the way from Barcelona to deliver this woman Puig when they had to prepare so soon for their journey to Ireland. There must be a catch in it. Was Terence going to borrow money again? As if to justify this suspicion he now got up, tiptoed to the door, opened it, listened, heard Ampara singing to the baby, sang a note or two himself, and then slouched back to his chair.

He spoke slowly: 'Whatever else they may say about you, Jonathan, at least they've got to admit you try to be a man of your time.'

Flattery so reluctant was worse than insult. 'What do you mean, Terence?' demanded Jonathan.

Terence gulped down his drink and stretched forward for another.

'Aren't you drinking too much, Terence?'

'From whose point of view, old man? From yours, as the owner of this exorbitantly expensive whisky, yes; but from mine, with something to communicate that may well shock your pompous little soul, by no means.'

'What is it, Terence? Out with it, for heaven's sake, and don't skulk behind insults.'

Terence glared at him and spoke very thickly: 'So you've deduced at last, you perspicacious bastard, that I am finding it hard to tell you something? Well, if I am, more shame to you. If you were the kind of man you think you are, upright, fearless, above intrigue, humane, idealistic, and above all chivalrous, then I would not find it so hard, would I? No, I should be able to blab it out easily, with relief, like a girl informing her ma her virginity's been safely disposed of.'

Drunken men were so prone to lewdness: even the urbane Terence. It had been galling too to have that catalogue of unclaimed virtues paraded before one. As for the term 'perspicacious bastard', in Terence's warm brogue it could be endearment almost, but somehow not tonight.

'What is it, Terence?'

'I'll tell you, I'll bloody soon tell you, Mr Superior Wash-my-hands Broxmead.'

With drunken tears in his eyes he slipped off his chair and crawled across the tiled floor to Jonathan. It was not entirely an act of entreaty or submission; it had menace in it too. He thrust his puffy flushed face, reeking of whisky, so close to Jonathan's that their noses collided.

'Yes, I'll tell you, because I see no alternative, though Bridie, and something in my own guts, warns me I oughtn't to. Listen to this, Mr Pontius Pilate Broxmead.'

'You'll have to speak more articulately if I'm to listen to it, whatever it is; and really, Terence, these gratuitous insults are rather wearisome. You've taken too much whisky to have any control over your sense of humour.'

'Gratuitous, is it?' He had difficulty in pronouncing the word. 'Gratuitous? Prove them gratuitous, me boyo. Now I'm watching you, to the depths of what, God help us, in the absence of better you call your soul. Are you listening?'

'Yes, Terence, I'm listening.'

'Last week Jordi Puig, Catalan patriot, was arrested. At this very moment he's in a military prison, suffering God knows what beatings up. The bishop's been trying to intercede, but without success. In two, three, four months' time Jordi'll be tried, and sentenced to eight, ten, twelve years' imprisonment. Go to Barcelona this minute, and what will you see chalked up on every wall? The name Jordi Puig. Can you tell me why? No, you can't. I shall tell you. Because, Mr Pass-on-the-other-side Broxmead, he's what you and I will never be, a hero of our own times.'

Jonathan did not quite understand. In any country a man could be arrested for many reasons. 'Why was he arrested? Besides, what has it got to do with me?'

'He's Montsy's brother.'

'Montsy? You mean, Miss Puig? But he wouldn't be arrested for that, surely?'

Terence scowled at the witticism, and crawled back in some kind of disgust to his chair.

Yes, there were so many reasons, of different degrees of turpitude: theft, drunken driving, fraud, rape, homosexual practices, murder; the list was endless.

'I'm sorry,' said Jonathan. 'Of course Miss Puig is not to blame for what her brother has done. Still, I must point out that if Isabel was to hear that he'd been arrested for, say, theft, she might not be so keen to employ his sister to look after her baby. Illogical and unjust, I agree; but very feminine, not to say maternal.'

Terence was finding it difficult to keep awake. Scorn in one eye, contempt in the other, were insufficient props to keep them open. 'Not theft,' he muttered. 'Political offence; in possession of pamphlets hostile to the regime.'

Jonathan remembered Norman. 'Is he a communist?' he cried, his voice shrill with a horror that was largely borrowed.

'Why the hell should he be a communist? He's a Spanish patriot, a lover of liberty.'

'Communists assume strange disguises.'

'A lover of liberty. What do you love, Mr Lick-me-own-arse Broxmead?'

Shocked, Jonathan cried: 'These heroes of our own times, as you called them, let them be heroic in suffering the consequences, one of which inevitably is the incrimination of their own families. I'm beginning to understand, Terence. Is Miss Puig a revolutionary too? Is she in trouble with the authorities? Have you smuggled her here, not to oblige us, but in the hope that we might be tricked into sheltering her? Terence, you have been guilty in your day of some colossal irresponsibilities, but really this is by far the worst.'

Terence opened the eye with scorn in it. 'It would be only for a week at most.'

'And what's to happen then? Are we to be arrested along with her?'

Now it was the turn of the eye with contempt in it. 'Some friends in Barcelona are arranging to get her over the border. She's got relatives in Perpignan.'

'Terence, you have put me in a very difficult position. As a foreigner, a grateful guest, isn't it my duty to inform the authorities?'

Both eyes opened. 'It would be your duty, as a lousy yellow bastard; and it would be mine to drown you in the bay.'

'Terence, wake up and be serious.'

With an effort Terence kept his eyes open. 'For Christ's sake, forget your piddling little self for a moment. For twenty years you've never had it out of your thoughts, not for as long as it takes a fly to cross its legs. So you're due a brief holiday. Think of Montsy. Think of her position. Her brother's been arrested, she'll not see him again for years; her mother was ill before it, she's worse now; her father died years ago. She's in trouble; she needs help. I thought, when Ampara told me Isabel wanted a nursemaid, that the good Lord Himself had arranged it to help Montserrat.'

'According to my information, the good Lord goes out of His way to foil communists, not to help them.'

'She's not a communist.'

'Merely a lover of liberty, I suppose?'

'No, not merely that; also a lover of God. There isn't a devouter Catholic in the land.'

'Terence, you were always too willing to be deceived. I suppose she wears a crucifix round her neck? Of course, I'm sorry for Miss Puig, though no doubt she went into this business with her eyes open. But why, of all the hundreds of thousands in Catalonia, choose me?'

'Because I knew you, because the opportunity was here. Bridie said you would be too yellow, as well as too selfish. As usual, she was right. As you said, I've always been too willing to be deceived. All right. Let's say no more.' He shut his eyes and began to snore.

'I suppose you'll take her back to Barcelona?'

'Mr Broxmead, you've washed your hands of us; have the goodness not to show a pharisaic interest.'

'I am interested for your sake, Terence, and Bridie's. Aren't you my friends?'

'Your friends, Jonathan?' It was said sleepily, with a long yawn of derision. 'Maybe I might forgive you, but

Bridie never. You have no friends, Jonathan. Name one person, outside your family, for whom you would put your pinkie out of joint. I'm a bastard without much principle myself, so I'll drink your whisky and accept your hospitality, but I'll be damned if I let you call me your friend.'

'Obviously you're drunk, Terence, so I'm not going to heed these insults. Don't you think you should go now and help Bridie to find accommodation for the night?'

'We can sleep on the beach.'

'The police might be inquisitive if you did.'

'Well, it's a bloody churlish way of offering it, Jonathan, but we accept.'

'What do you mean? I'm afraid there isn't room here. You know Isabel and David are here; and John Lynedoch.'

'Lynedoch? The painter?'

'Yes.'

'You didn't say he was here.'

'We weren't discussing him.'

Again the eyes, bleary and baleful, opened. 'Yes, we were. I see what it is, Jonathan. You're jealous. I heard it in your voice when I was praising the man's picture. He's got talent, masses of it. You haven't a grain. So you're miserable with jealousy. You've even been jealous of me, and my meagre poetry.'

'This is beside the point. The fact is the house is full.'

'Where there's a will there's a way.'

'If you like I'll telephone some of the hotels.' Jonathan rose as he spoke, and without waiting for Terence's agreement went out into the hall.

He telephoned six hotels or pensions, including the Miramar; none had an empty room.

Crossly he returned to the sitting-room, to find Terence asleep in his chair, snoring imbecilely; a glass in his hand dribbled whisky on to the floor. He shook him. 'Terence, wake up. Every hotel's full. I'm afraid we'll have to try and squeeze you in somehow. Wake up, for heaven's sake.'

Terence just snored.

Jonathan shook more roughly. He shouted: 'You'll have to go to the casino and tell Bridie. Don't be a fool, Terence.'

It was no use. Terence snored and slobbered. As a picture of a man making a daring sacrifice for a friend in danger he was not impressive. His fly buttons were not properly fastened.

Jonathan thought of telephoning to the casino, and asking to speak to the fair-haired Irishwoman, but decided it might be unwise, in that it would bring attention upon Miss Puig. For the same reason he dared not send Ampara. It looked as if he would have to go himself, and he very much did not want to.

When he met Miss Puig he would try hard to be courteous and hospitable, but he felt he had the right, if an opportunity occurred, to point out to her the peril and inconvenience she put people into, so wantonly. He might even hint that in his opinion prostitution was a less ignoble occupation for a woman than subversive politics.

On his way to the casino, at the heart of the village, he walked slowly, amidst the laughter and music, trying to subdue the bitter and rebellious reflections that Terence had let loose in his mind. He could not; they growled, devoured, and were unapproachable. Very well, he whispered: perhaps I deserve this savaging; perhaps I am selfish, jealous, and cowardly; but please, all of you, and especially you, Señorita Montserrat Puig, let me work out my own salvation.

The sardana dancers were still at it, but Catalans only now, experts, in their dedicated jigging ring, according to their intense faces counting the steps not only to the proper end of the dance but to the day when Catalonia again would be a separate independent country. Indulgent before, as to children believing in fairies, he could not bear to look at them then. Childish and ruinous their ambition, he himself had none. Towards their ideal they danced, though solemnly; to attain hers Miss Puig distributed seditious pamphlets that few people wanted to read. If they were to be condemned, it ought not to be by him.

A few yards from the casino, on the bridge where the local youths sat and admired the free parade every morning of bosom, buttock, and thigh, he was stopped by the three Scots girls. They would not let him pass. Their mood seemed to be one of grim repentance, though their dresses were flamboyant.

'We won't keep you a minute, Mr Broxmead,' said Peggy, the small dark-haired competent one. 'We want to apologize to you.'

'Whatever for?'

'This morning, up at the church, we met a guest of yours.'

For a moment he wondered who it could have been, and then he remembered Lynedoch. 'It must have been Mr Lynedoch,' he said.

'He didn't give his name. I lost my temper. He was so stuck-up, taking us for dirt. There are many like him, who think people like us have no right to come to places like this for our holidays; the Isle of Man and Blackpool are good enough for us. We spoil the romance, or something. We work in factories, you see, or check football coupons. Well, nobody's going to show me to my face he despises me. So I told him so.'

Bewildered, he noticed she was almost in tears. 'I'm afraid I don't understand,' he said. 'Mr Lynedoch didn't say anything about it, at least not to me.'

Perhaps he and Maddy had had a good laugh over it in the boat.

'Oh, he wouldn't. It would be no more important to him than a fly landing on his nose.'

Curious she should use a fly as illustration, so soon after Terence had.

'Still, as Katie and Teresa have been busy reminding me, it's not your fault, Mr Broxmead, but we think I should apologize to you for being rude to one of your guests. You see, there was no need for me to speak to him at all. In a manner of speaking, I was the aggressor.'

'Are you saying Mr Lynedoch was rude to you?'

'You could call it that. Aye, Katie, it was,' she added, turning on her friend who was shaking her head. 'If somebody's spoken to you politely, isn't it rude if you won't even open your mouth to answer?'

'Well, you know what I've said, Peggy.'

'Katie thinks maybe he's got a lisp or has teeth missing. But I was nearer; I saw his eyes.'

'But he's from Glasgow himself,' said Jonathan.

They yelped in astonishment and glared at one another. 'I can't understand why he didn't reply to you.'

Was it possible these girls had reminded him paralysingly of his dead Margaret? She would not have been any more beautiful, and would speak like them. Had he been afraid he might weep? That he had been trying to dance that evening did not mean his tongue-tied grief in the morning had been insincere.

'We know now,' said Peggy.

Her friends nodded.

'Your own kind, they're the worst. We're from Cowcaddens, he'll be from Kelvinside, a toff as we call them. Does he talk like this?' She spoke the question in what could have been a sarcastic take-off of Jonathan himself.

'He speaks like you. He's very Scottish.'

'Like us?'

'He's a painter.'

'Withoot a beard?' asked Katie, giggling.

'Withoot a tongue,' said Peggy, still grim.

'But no' withoot legs,' added Teresa. 'We saw him dancing with your sister.'

'What happened at the church must have been a mis-understanding,' said Jonathan. 'Why not come and have tea, and demand an explanation?'

With glowers, pouts, nods, shakings, and winks, they consulted. He thought the decision was again to decline, but he was wrong.

'Thank you very much,' said Peggy. 'Maybe it will clear it up. When, please?'

'Tomorrow afternoon?'

'Remember Perpignan, Peggy,' said Katie.

'We're hoping to go on a coach excursion to Perpignan in France tomorrow. It's no' fixed yet.'

'Then the following afternoon?'

'We'll be very pleased to keep that free, Mr Broxmead.'

He was about to move on when it occurred to him that perhaps they could take in Miss Puig for the night. To ask them was shameful, but to avoid having to entertain Miss Puig he would do anything. He was afraid of her, not as a person, but as a symbol of his own weaknesses; yes, of her as a person too.

'By the way,' he said, high-pitched with nervousness, 'we find ourselves inundated with unexpected guests. We've tried to find them accommodation at several hotels, without success. We may be able to squeeze two of them in. I wonder if there is room at your place for the other. She's a Spanish girl.'

They shook their heads, genuinely sorry they could not help. 'We're awful sorry. Our place is packed out. We were talking to the girl at the desk just this evening. We've only got one room ourselves, and it's so crowded with beds we've to walk sideways.'

Shame drove him away from them towards the casino.

'At what time, please?' they called after him.

'Five o'clock?'

'That will suit nicely, thank you.'

They waved farewell as if they'd known and liked him for years. Could it be that their eyes, almost child-like in sharpness of insight, saw in him qualities deserving of affection, which Terence, bleared with worldliness, never could, and which, to be truthful, he himself had not been able to find after many excavations?

Eleven

Bridie's grandmother, now dying in Dublin, had been a more fanatical underground fighter against the tyrannical English than Montserrat ever would be against Franco; but then, like Bridie herself, she had been small and plain, and so sexually undistinguished that, as she had once put it, she could have shimmied past a batch of drunken English soldiers in her shift, carrying a gun, without drawing a single look either of suspicion or of lechery. It was very different with Montsy. Not only had she a figure just short of voluptuous, but she had also a native fondness for bright clothes, like her present pink dress. Her face, austere one minute, could be merry the next; her hair was the glossiest, and her eyes the brownest, in all Spain. She had a nature, too, so friendly that after half an hour in this seedy casino, to which she had insisted on coming in preference to more fashionable bars, the waiters and customers, mostly fishermen and artisans of the village, kept turning to make sure she was still there. To be able to give pleasure simply by your presence was a marvellous gift, for anybody but a refugee.

And of course if you were female, and looked to Jonathan Broxmead to help you at some inconvenience to himself, far better to have breasts like flounders, legs like poles, and eyes as glazed and sexless as a dead cod's.

From their corner they could hear the sardana music, with its sudden victorious blasts. Montsy's fingers danced in time amidst the blue yachts on the oilcloth. Not once did she express impatience or fear though Terence had been away over an hour. Bridie herself kept wondering aloud what could be keeping him, but inwardly she was sure she knew. For all his blarney he would not be able to persuade Jonathan to see Montsy as a woman of his own age, with warm breasts, lovely eyes, dancing fingers, and an unhappy heart. Jonathan would prefer to see her as a bundle of dangerous and inconvenient opinions, in one word a nuisance. In that high-pitched indignant voice he would demand why she should be dumped on his doorstep, and not on someone else's. As Terence had said: 'Prepare for the worst, Bridie. Jonathan is one of the few bastards I can think of, capable of an absolute no.'

Glancing away from the tiny gold crucifix round Montsy's neck, Bridie prayed, to the stern Father and not to the meek Son. She asked, not very suppliantly, that He take Jonathan by the scruff of his puny soul and shake him; otherwise Montsy ran a great risk of being betrayed, not because of her politics, but because of her womanhood.

Opening her eyes, she said grimly: 'We should have gone straight to the house.'

Montserrat shook her head. 'Mr Broxmead has a right to be forewarned.'

They spoke in Spanish, cautiously.

'You're too scrupulous, Montsy. All he has a right to know is whether you've had experience with children. My hope is that Isabel's still looking for a nursemaid for her baby. She'll let him know that either he lets you look after it, or he looks after it himself.'

'Perhaps he would prefer that, Bridie.'

'Being what he is, he might.'

'But a man willing to look after a very small baby cannot be the selfish creature you have described him as.'

'Well, you know what Terence said: there's a good man lost in Jonathan somewhere, so deep no one's ever likely to

find him, especially as all over his mind are No Tres-
passing notices. Everybody's selfish, we know that; but his
is so nebulous you can't ever catch hold of it and wring its
neck. Now take his sister Maddy. She's a selfish bitch, if
ever there was one; but she's so honest about it, and so
willing to do battle with everybody else's selfishness, that
you can't help liking her. God help the woman Jonathan
marries.'

'Yes,' murmured Montserrat, staring towards the door, 'I
think I see what you mean.'

Bridie turned quickly. Yes, there he stood, his nose high
and twitching, like a deer ready to race off. If either she or
Montsy made a loud sudden female noise, away he would
go, neighing with fright.

'Don't laugh, for God's sake,' she whispered. 'Let me
speak to him first.'

She hurried to the door and pulled him outside. 'Where's
Terry?'

'He fell asleep.'

'And I told Montsy not to laugh,' she muttered.

Both of them looked at her through the open door.
Brief though his glance was, it must have shown him
that seated there in the corner with courageous patience,
was one of the loveliest, most desirable women he had
ever seen. Most men would have been on fire instantly
to help and cherish her. He visibly grew colder; he even
shivered.

'I hope to God he explained everything to you first,' she
said.

'He did.'

'Remember, Jonathan, it will only be for a week.'

'I'm afraid not, Bridie. I'm prepared to offer Miss Puig
accommodation for tonight, but no longer.'

Bridie could have reached up and clawed the sullen,
haughty resolution from his face.

'I'll explain to Miss Puig myself,' he said.

'You know she's in danger of arrest? Her brother's in jail? Her mother's ill?'

'Terence was quite contemptuously eloquent. I must say, though, Bridie, she doesn't look as tragic as all that, does she?'

Montsy was smiling.

'Do you expect her to sit and weep? It's possible to suffer bravely, you know. We don't all moan at the moon.'

He glanced up at the moon, and envied its serenity.

'Just one week, Jonathan,' she whispered. 'You'd be running no risk to speak of. They don't know she's here. She's got an identity card made out in the name of Carmen Ripoll.'

'Bridie, I'm not going to be entangled in lies and deceptions.'

'Even if they do get her, which God forbid, they could do nothing to you. All you'd have to do was swear you'd employed her in good faith, without knowing anything about her.'

'More lies and deception.'

'She wouldn't give you away, if that's what you're afraid of; she'd suffer the tortures of hell first.'

'Really this is quite irrelevant, Bridie.'

Bridie felt sick. She wanted to cry, to fall on her knees, to attack him with her nails. Holidaymakers strolled past, laughing. She tried to smile.

'If I was to tell you I'm going to despise you for the rest of my life, would that be irrelevant too, Jonathan?'

He did not answer.

'What am I to say to her, for God's sake?'

'I shall explain to her myself.'

'And pour insult over injury? No, Jonathan, I can't let you do that.'

'You must certainly despise me, Bridie.'

She clutched at him, with sudden hope. 'I don't want to, Jonathan. I think you don't understand; not with your imagination. This isn't a game, you know. Don't think because Terence is mixed up with it, and has got drunk as usual, that it's all a joke. Her brother Jordi's in prison at this moment, so beaten up, they say, that his mother wouldn't recognize him, if she could get to seeing him, which of course she won't. Jordi's a lawyer, like his father before him; he's not a fanatic, he's popular, and respectable. But he'll be jailed for ten years. It could happen to Montsy, too. They're after her. This past week she's been hounded from hiding-place to hiding-place. Her friends hope to get her over the border to Perpignan, where her aunt lives. What we're asking you to do is to give her that chance.'

After a long pause he said: 'I suppose she was aware of what the consequences might be.'

His voice seemed dry with shame, but all the shame in the world could not mitigate so despicable a remark.

'I happen to believe,' he added, hoarser than ever, 'that meddling in subversive politics is ignoble in a woman.'

'Christ Almighty,' she breathed, in angry prayer. 'Is it because she's a woman?'

'Bridie, I don't want to argue with you. I've come to offer you hospitality for the night, and to drive you into Figueras tomorrow morning if you wish.'

'Jonathan, Terry and I didn't want to tell you a thing about Montserrat, except that she has had some experience in looking after children. It was she who insisted that you must be told. She hates lies and deceptions more than you do. She's a devout Catholic.'

A minute later, while he was gazing at the bay with the pain of utter unawareness on his face, Montserrat came out of the casino and joined them.

As she introduced them Bridie could not help thinking

what a striking couple they made, Montserrat with her black hair and vivacious eyes, he so blonde, blue-eyed, and bleak. Though Montserrat must have realized, from the haggle in the doorway and from his bitterly blank expression, that he was unwilling to help, she smiled and shook his hand with characteristic friendliness and humour. Indeed, Bridie wished she wouldn't show quite so frankly that she found his imitation of a tragic hero so silly.

They stood for a few moments in silence.

'Well, what now?' asked Bridie.

Montserrat put up her brows in a query.

'I suggest we go to the house,' said Jonathan hoarsely.

'I think we should, Montsy.'

'Of course, Bridie.'

'On the way I shall try to explain,' he added. He glanced back. 'Don't you have any baggage?'

'Terry took it up to the house,' said Bridie.

'I see.'

They walked on. Bridie saw to it he was in the middle. She noticed how his right arm, that now and then brushed against Montserrat's, winced as if broken.

They crossed the plaza. Acquaintances nodded, waved, called to him, and were ignored. He looked as if he was being led away to be shot. Beyond the lights of the village they came into the zone of lovers; the air was perfumed and murmurous with these. Concertina music, interrupted by yells of rut, was heard from an open window.

Bridie could bear it no longer. 'I had better warn you, Montsy,' she said. 'He refuses to help.'

'He has the right, Bridie.'

Montserrat was very calm. But she stopped. They could hear her breathing deeply. She sighed once; it might have been at the cowardice of the world now represented by him. 'Then why do we go to the house?' she asked.

'Mr Broxmead says we can stay there for the night.'

Mr Broxmead stood like a wax dummy.

'If Mr Broxmead does not want that I go to his house, then I do not go.'

'That's how I feel myself, Montsy. But where will we sleep? It's getting late, and the hotels are all full.'

'We would not die among the olive trees.'

'No, but we wouldn't be very comfortable either. There's tomorrow too. What will you do then?'

'Return to Barcelona. I think it was a mistake to come here.'

'It's too dangerous there, Montsy. You know what Francisco said. Here you're half-way to the border.'

'My mother is ill.' She said it in Spanish, in a voice to melt wax.

Melted a little, he whispered: 'Even if I were in England, I would take no part in politics. If there was an election I wouldn't vote. Here in Spain, where I'm a foreigner, I have an even better reason for not meddling.'

Montserrat turned on him with a fierceness that took him aback. 'Why are you in Spain, señor?'

'I happen to love Spain.'

'And the Spaniards, you love them too?'

'Yes, I do.'

'I think not.' She went on, with passion, as if making a declaration of love, 'You love our sunshine, our blue skies, our warm seas, our low prices, our cheap servants, our churches which are so nice to paint. These you love. But us Spaniards, how can you love us if you do not know us? You should return to England, Señor Broxmead. You have enjoyed your holiday; it is time to go home. You do not know that our best young people live in despair, with nothing to believe in, nothing to be proud of? They see that Spain contributes nothing to the world but shame; therefore they despair. If the best despair, what should the others do? Things to make them forget.'

'Miss Puig, you must not persuade me to take sides.'

'I do not persuade you. I am not interested to persuade you. I tell you the truth. Bridie,' she added, in quick angry Spanish, 'I cannot go with him. I am sorry.'

She turned and walked back towards the village.

'Run after her, for God's sake,' cried Bridie, giving him an angry push.

It did not seem to be necessary, so eagerly did he go, stumbling in the dark and calling: 'Just a minute, please.'

Bridie, listening, heard him make up on Montserrat, ask her to stop and then apparently compel her to, by seizing hold of her. There was a sort of scuffle. Then he spoke earnestly, at some length. Montserrat was silent. Eventually he was silent too. They seemed prepared to wait for long enough, like lovers on the verge of reconciliation. Bridie, her feet tired, went to sit on the wall at the edge of the road. Below her the sea had far more patience than she. Beyond the two standing so strangely in the road she saw the moonlit tower of the church.

They came slowly back, still in silence, with yards between them.

'Well?' asked Bridie.

'I have told Señorita Puig she is welcome to stay for as long as is necessary,' he said.

'Thank God!'

'She has not so far accepted.'

'Of course she accepts. Don't you, Montsy?'

'Si.'

With no more talk they walked on, and were through the gate, close to the house, when Montserrat went rigid and stopped. On a seat near the door, under some bushes, Ampara was allowing her sweetheart Pedro, in his policeman's uniform, the liberty of holding her hand. His gun stood between them like a chaperon, with his tricorn hat hung over its muzzle.

It should have been a scene for laughter, rather than fear; and Bridie did laugh, hoping Montserrat would too.

'It's just Ampara's boy-friend,' she whispered, 'he's harmless.'

So, no doubt, alone with their sweethearts or wives, were those of his colleagues who had beaten up Jordi in prison. Would Pedro, who enjoyed bikinis too much to reprimand their wearers, punch and kick a helpless man if ordered to, or if he believed promotion lay in such brutality? After all, like the rest of the world, he could always close his eyes.

Jonathan said: 'It's all right. No need to be afraid.' If he sounded afraid himself, it was surely on Montserrat's account rather than his own.

By the time they reached the door Ampara had it open for them, and Pedro, hat and gun on again, was slinking off muttering: 'Buenas noches, señores.'

'Buenas noches,' replied Bridie.

Jonathan gave no greeting, and when he addressed Ampara it was in a voice so strange and harsh that she was instantly surprised and hurt, and for some reason blamed Montserrat, at whom she glowered.

'We have two more guests,' he said, 'Señora O'Donnell, and Señorita Ripoll.'

Ampara gave Bridie a smile, but continued to glare at Montserrat. Bridie guessed why. Montserrat was unmarried, good-looking, and Spanish: a rival therefore. It had never ceased to be a joke between Terry and Bridie, this campaign of Ampara's to seduce her prudish and snobbish master. Terry, indeed, was sure she had managed to insinuate herself into his bed, but thought that might have been the extent of it. Bridie, though ravished by this picture of arrested seduction, couldn't believe it.

At the same time, for Ampara to be jealous of Montserrat, however farcically, might lead to danger.

Twelve

About an hour later, with Terence revived, and Jonathan in a peculiar garrulous excitement, they were having supper when Maddy and Lynedoch returned, she gaily and defiantly tipsy, he morosely. They were heard for minutes before they were seen, Maddy dancing round the garden singing what sounded like a caricature of the Scottish song 'Highland Lad', with Lynedoch pursuing and protesting. When they burst into the house they were holding hands, or rather she was dragging him by his. Unabashed at seeing the visitors, she went straight to the painting on the wall, and with her other hand beckoned to Terence. 'Come and see this painting, Terence,' she cried.

Lynedoch scowled at the floor.

'I've already seen and admired it, Maddy,' said Terence.

'Come and admire it again. It's worth admiring a hundred times.'

'Don't be a fool,' muttered Lynedoch.

Jonathan put his hand on Montserrat's on the table. 'My sister Madeleine,' he explained, 'and John Lynedoch, a painter.'

She smiled but pulled her hand from under his. He left his for a few moments where hers had been.

Maddy grew imperious. 'Come on, Terence,' she cried. 'You too, Bridie. And you, whoever you are.' That was to Montserrat.

'What about me, Maddy?' asked Jonathan, laughing. 'Am I excused?'

'Not excused, Jonathan; prohibited. You must cultivate a little humility before you are welcome.'

'As far as I'm concerned, they're all excused or prohibited or whatever you like to call it,' said Lynedoch.

'That's my gracious Pict,' said Maddy, ruffling his hair and shaking out of it a few pine needles.

Terence, seeing Bridie's thumb, got up and strolled across. Bridie followed; she knew Maddy in this mood could be a bitch if not humoured. She felt sorry for the Scotsman, who seemed defenceless.

It was then that Lynedoch noticed how beautiful the Spanish stranger was. Hair on end, he gaped at her, frankly and utterly impressed; so much so that Jonathan sprang up in a temper.

'Really, Maddy,' he cried, 'this is inexcusable. In the first place, there's a baby asleep upstairs.'

Maddy too was staring at Montserrat, with smiling animosity. 'And in the second place, Jonathan?' she asked.

'In the second place, as you can see, we have guests. Bridie and Terence you know. I would like you to meet Señorita Montserrat Ripoll, from Barcelona.'

'Puig,' murmured Terence, and would have repeated it had not Bridie's elbow prodded him in his yellow shirt. He did not notice Jonathan staring at him in horror, as at a betrayer. Drink, thought Bridie, betrayed as often as hate.

Maddy and Montserrat had shaken hands.

'And this is John Lynedoch,' said Jonathan, as cordially as he could.

'Pleased to meet you,' said the Scotsman, and looked it, to Maddy's further annoyance.

'And what are you doing here, señorita?' she asked.

Jonathan turned pink. 'Maddy, please. Miss Ripoll's going to look after Linda.'

'You mean she's going to live here, in the house?'

'Well, it wouldn't be convenient, would it, if she lived outside?'

'I suppose she can share Ampara's room.'

'That has still to be arranged,' said Jonathan, curtly.

'Are you a lover of art, Miss Ripoll?' asked Maddy.

'I am not an expert, but I have friends who are painters.'

'I'm sure you have. Well, here's warning you this painter isn't available. Shall I show you why?' She picked pine needles from her own hair and then, despite his protests, from Lynedoch's. She held them out in her palm to let Montserrat see them.

Jonathan was furious and anguished too. 'Maddy, for heaven's sake,' he cried. 'Miss Ripoll is our guest.'

'Guest, Jonathan? I thought you said servant? Just keep her off my painter, that's all.'

With a dignity that passed through absurdity back into dignity again, he approached Montserrat. 'I apologize, señorita,' he said. 'As is very evident, my sister has had more to drink than is good for her.'

'Do you know where we had it, Jonathan?' she cried. 'We've been up the hill, through the pine wood, to see old Higginbotham. He's the worst painter in the world but the most hospitable. He's painting a Christ, with a beard all carrots and feet like claws.' As she spoke she was staring at Montserrat's crucifix. 'He's coming to see John's exhibition. I've already invited over a dozen.'

Bridie again poked Terence.

'What exhibition is this, Maddy?' he asked.

'Of John's paintings. He brought twenty-nine, and to-morrow he's starting on another. Look, Terence, isn't it a wonderful painting?'

'I liked it the moment I saw it. It's got vision.'

'You hear, Jonathan?' she cried. 'Vision. What you and I

and Terence and Bridie and Isabel and David and Miss Ripoll have never had and never will.'

Jonathan stared at Lynedoch, possessor of vision. What in those blessed moments did this Scotsman, so frequently commonplace, and at present almost moronic with his drunken scowlings, see that was miraculously different from what the spiritually purblind such as Jonathan himself were doomed to see every moment of their lives? Did having vision mean the ability to see other human beings as they truly were, not obscured and diminished by the indestructible screen of one's own self? As, surely, Jonathan had seen Montserrat Puig on the moonlit road, an hour or so ago, and as he had been striving to see her again ever since.

Maddy of course did not count. She was loved and hated, admired and despised, flattered and baited, as if she was his own self.

He baited her now. 'I notice you left out Norman.'

She remembered. 'So you managed to get rid of him?'

'I did not. He's at the Miramar.'

'The Miramar!' She laughed. 'Has his father died at last and left him that half-million dollars he was always talking about?'

Jonathan paused. Somehow the question, because it had not occurred to him, revealed his own lack of sympathy. 'He didn't say,' he replied. 'But I wouldn't be surprised.' He almost added, how neat it was, and how conducive to a happy and prosperous salvation, if one's earthly father left one riches at the same time that one's heavenly father offered His favour. He could not have said what kind of shame it was that kept him from saying it aloud. Montserrat's presence had something to do with it, although for the past few minutes she had been more interested in Lynedoch and his painting than in himself.

'Half a million dollars!' repeated Lynedoch. Incredulity, resentment, alarm, awe, and envy were all in his voice.

'That's my thrifty Scot!' cried Madeleine.

Affection as well as irony was in her cry. Jonathan was surprised; Lynedoch was too. The latter stared at her, reconsidering, as well as his murky wits allowed, her interest in him. That his paintings, particularly those still to be done, were preferable to twice half a million dollars he knew; but it was profoundly startling to learn that she knew it too.

She put her face close to his. 'Didn't I tell you,' she whispered, 'there's no need for you to be jealous of Norman? It would be as silly as me being jealous of Margaret.'

'But Margaret's dead,' he muttered, with a sob.

She stroked his face. 'So is Norman dead, as far as I'm concerned. In any case, if there were a thousand Normans, you mustn't be jealous. Jealousy degrades, my dear; worse, much much worse, it destroys vision. What I want is to see through your eyes, through your paintings; that seems to me far more exciting than having all the dollars in the world to spend.'

Extravagant, over-generous, and too optimistic, as she had been so frequently before, she was nevertheless sincere.

Jonathan was put into a quandary. About to tell of Norman, with wit and malice, he now hesitated, seeing Montserrat gaze with such strange sympathy at Lynedoch, and Lynedoch despite Maddy's fervour return it, like one outcast to another. It might not be advisable to depreciate Norman, at any rate in Miss Puig's presence. Genuinely religious herself, she might be moved to pity rather than derision, and her opinion of Jonathan would not rise.

His quarry should be Lynedoch.

'By the way, Lynedoch,' he said, as if in hostly banter, 'I believe you offended some countrywomen of yours up at the church this morning.'

'I did not intend to offend them,' replied Lynedoch, dourly. 'I did not,' he repeated, apparently addressing Miss Puig.

'You recall the occasion then?'

'Of course I recall it. I recall it very well.'

'According to my information, one of them spoke to you, and you absolutely refused to answer. By the way,' he added, for the others' benefit, 'they're young, not much more than twenty.'

'I should hope you did refuse to answer,' cried Maddy. 'Soliciting in front of the church! Did you know that it's been done inside?'

That was authenticated, but why mention it now? Jonathan could not quite understand why Maddy had taken so immediate and active a spite against the Spanish girl. True, as she had said herself, jealousy degraded; but where in this situation so far was there cause for anyone to be jealous of anyone else? That Lynedoch and Miss Puig kept exchanging glances of sympathy wasn't surprising, since they were the only strangers present. Everything was at the beginning; there was no knowing what might develop, for him as well as for the others. He felt as if standing in front of a door about to open.

'I meant nothing personal,' said Lynedoch, intensely. 'They should ha' seen that. It was just that they reminded me.'

'Of Margaret, do you mean?' asked Maddy, as if humouring a child.

'No. No, I wouldna say that. No' of her personally. I don't want to give you all my complaints, but it has never been easy for me to keep on with my painting. Not just because I've always been poor, but mostly because I was born and brought up in surroundings no' just indifferent, but hostile. I've had to contend wi' a lot of ignorant opposition and bigoted discouragement. That's what they reminded me of. I've been told my paintings lack grace. It's true, though I'd find it hard to explain to you just what I mean by grace.' He looked round at them all. 'Miss Ripoll's got it.'

There was a silence.

'Have I got it?' asked Maddy.

He nodded. 'Aye. But they havena, through no fault of their own. They belang to a race that lacks it. How could it exist in the tenements of Glasgow, or the villas of Edinburgh? It was stupid and wrang of me to blame them. Are they no' here in Spain, like myself, seeking it?'

'I doubt that,' said Jonathan. 'They told me their job at home is checking football coupons, whatever that means.'

'So I made up my mind,' muttered Lynedoch, 'that I'm not going back, not for a long time. That's what I meant by saying nothing.'

'What you need,' said Maddy, 'is your bed. You're half asleep. Today's been too much for you.'

'Which reminds me,' said Jonathan. 'What are the sleeping arrangements?'

'Bridie can share with me, Terence with you, and Miss Ripoll of course can go in with Ampara.'

That left Lynedoch sleeping alone; it meant he was being favoured. Besides, Jonathan objected to Miss Puig's being put in with Ampara. Luckily he could offer a reason that would satisfy Maddy, and himself too in the meantime.

'But, Maddy, if Miss Ripoll's to look after Linda, won't she have to sleep in the same room with the baby? Isabel will insist on that.'

'Well?'

'They can hardly sleep in Ampara's room. It's much too small, for one thing; and for another, Isabel wouldn't hear of it.'

'I am not giving up my room, Jonathan.'

'No one expects you to, Maddy.'

'And I shall certainly not allow John to give his up.'

Lynedoch, brooding over his graceless country, became aware of what the argument was about.

'I've got a bed in my car,' he said. 'I'll sleep there.'

'No, you will not.' Maddy couldn't have been more determined on his behalf if they had been married. Jonathan wondered why she didn't brazenly suggest having Lynedoch sleep with her. It would come to that before long. Why not now in the beginning when it was convenient to all?

Terence had fallen asleep again in a chair. Bridie felt tired and cross. Never good-looking, nor with a seductive figure, she had had to rely on sharp commonsense; very often it distinguished her more than beauty would have done, stupidity being on the whole commoner than ugliness.

'The baby comes first, doesn't she?' she demanded.

None dared deny it.

'All right. I suggest Mr Lynedoch share with Jonathan, or Jonathan share with Mr Lynedoch; it depends on whose room is the bigger, for the baby's sake. After all, it'll only be for a week. Terence will do where he is.'

'Why a week?' asked Maddy. 'Isabel intends to stay for five at least.'

'I meant just for a short time; a week or a month, what's the difference? Stop being a lot of children, for God's sake.'

She was angry at her own blunder, but angrier still at Jonathan's hypocritical horror.

It was not altogether hypocritical. It had two causes, the first and lesser, her indiscretion; the second and far the greater, her suggestion that he sleep with Lynedoch. No man could have been less of a homosexual than Jonathan, despite what many had suspected. For as long as he could remember he had been pathologically shy about contact with other bodies, particularly male. At school he had suffered agonies of shame. It would have been a better reason than his malformed ankle bone for his rejection by the army. Therefore Bridie's suggestion, that he should share his bed with Lynedoch, strange, male, talented, and proletarian, contained in it an infinity of physical and psychological torments; even Maddy's, that he should share with Terence, was intolerable, as she well knew. Really her cherishing of Lynedoch was already a nuisance; had he been a genius in glorious flower instead of in doubtful bud it would still have been excessive.

'Linda may have my room,' he said. 'I shall sleep on the roof.'

'Thank you, Jonathan,' said Bridie. 'It's very kind of you.'

'It is very kind,' said Montserrat uneasily. 'But I do not wish—'

'No, Montsy,' said Bridie. 'Don't raise difficulties. It's after midnight. I'm tired. You're tired yourself. Terence is sound asleep. Mr Lynedoch is sleepy too. Let's all go to bed.'

Suddenly glad, Jonathan became a man of action. He summoned Ampara, and asked her to take Montserrat's suitcase up to his room. The result astonished him. She said nothing, but turned and rushed back into the kitchen where she picked up something breakable and flung it to the tiled floor.

'What's the matter with her?' he asked.

'You don't know?' cried Maddy.

'If I did, would I ask?'

'You couldn't have insulted her more. She's been in love with you for months.'

'Oh, please hold your tongue, Maddy.'

'How unfeeling of you, Jonathan, to ask her to instal another woman in your room, in your bed in fact.'

His blush grew warmer. He could have slapped her. A knot of frustration tightened in his belly. Maddy was delib-

erately insulting both him and Miss Puig, not to mention
Ampara, whose temper was more likely to be caused by her
being asked to undertake so much unexpected extra work.
He could scarcely look Miss Puig in the face. When he did
risk a glance at her he found that her reaction was merely
that of a well-bred guest accepting the arrangements made
by her host. He should have approved, but somehow did
not; he experienced what could hardly be disappointment,
and yet was so like it as to be indistinguishable. He could not
have said what reaction on her part would have pleased him.

He hurried out to carry up her suitcase himself. First he
had to find it, as Terence had hidden it under bushes. While
searching, he was joined by Montserrat.

'Please don't be offended at anything my sister has said,'
he murmured. 'She isn't herself tonight.'

He had a great desire to take her hand. In the moonlight
he saw again what had struck him at the casino door: that
part of her breast visible above the pink dress seemed
curiously fragile, with blue veins, and skin like transparent
silk. He found himself wondering, surely with innocence, if
the rest of her body's surface was similarly delicate.

It was she who found the suitcase. She wanted to carry it
herself. He protested. Their hands met. His held hers
prisoner. She gave him a glance from which alarm and
suspicion quickly yielded to, yes, to amusement. Nothing
could have dismayed him more: let her despise him, detest
him, ignore him even, but not laugh at him.

He tried to explain. 'I'm rather confused, I'm afraid. To
tell you the truth, I'm awfully ashamed. I thought of you as
some grim controversial woman. Instead I find you altogether different, so quiet and lovely.'

It was far less than he felt like saying, but rather more than
he ought to have said.

She said nothing.

A minute passed. He felt a joy greater than any in his life

before. Sweetness overflowed his mind. He could not
recognize it as his own.

'Well, shall we go in?' he asked.

She went before him, in every movement, of head,
shoulders, hands, body and feet, so graceful that, had her
suitcase been ten times heavier, he would still have carried it
with gladness and pride.

Upstairs they found Bridie and Ampara between them
carrying the cot, with Linda still asleep, into his room. Fresh
sheets were of course wanted for the bed, but he preferred
not to ask Ampara to fetch them, he would rather do it
himself. Leaving Bridie and Montserrat, he went downstairs
with Ampara. She was still sullen. At the kitchen door she
suddenly turned, and tugging at an imaginary crucifix round
her sturdy neck, said in fast angry Spanish: 'So you're like
the rest of men? You think that if a woman wears Our Lord
round her neck, for everybody to see, that she's virtuous?
Crucifixes are cheap. Whores wear them.'

Then she stormed into the kitchen. He waited for another
crash, and also for that suspicion she'd flung into his mind to
fall too. It was more than likely that a woman so twentieth-
century as to be hunted by a dictatorial government for
distributing seditious pamphlets would be similarly modern
in her sexual morality. No doubt one at least of her political
comrades had been her lover. Yes, despite her quietness,
beauty, gracefulness, and devoutness, she had suffered some
other man, out of love, to touch tenderly, with hand or lips,
her breast.

Within the kitchen the crash at last came, or tinkle rather,
for it seemed as if a spoon this time had been banged to the
floor; but within his mind the suspicion fell and reverber-
ated, like thunder. What he wanted could never be had: not
her only, but her utterly pure, with a purity that no one, not
even he, could ever sully. Already, long ago, by innumerable
and inevitable points of contact with the corrupt world, she

had lost the spotlessness that he had always, to Maddy's pitying amusement, dreamed of in the woman with whom one day he would fall in love. Now he thought that woman had come to him, and to his amazement, because of her imperfections she seemed all the dearer.

Thirteen

Bridie sat on the bed. 'Well, Montsy, can you stick it for a week?'

Montserrat turned from the cot to the door. There was a key in the lock. She tried it; it turned. With resolute fist she made sure the door was locked. Only then did she reply: 'I think so.'

Bridie watched in rueful amusement. Montsy was quite as prudish as Jonathan, though in her case it could honourably be called chastity; in his, unnatural aversion, perhaps. But against whom had the door to be locked? Hardly against Lynedoch, whom Maddy had in chains; nor Terence, drunk and asleep.

Radiant and vibrant with indignation, Montserrat came and crouched beside her. 'Bridie, he sleeps with the maid,' she whispered.

So it was locked against Jonathan. Bridie had to smile as, lovingly, she stroked her friend's hair.

'Don't be silly, Montsy. He does nothing of the kind.' Better for him if he did, she added, but to herself.

'And he thinks I shall take her place.'

'Of course he doesn't.'

'If I do not he will bring the police.'

'You can't really believe that, Montsy?' To Bridie herself nothing seemed more ludicrous or unlikely. Not because Jonathan was too virtuous, though to be fair she thought he was, but rather because he was much too frigid and conventional. This fullness of breast, softness of body, silkiness of hair, and daintiness of ear would conjure up for him the ignominy of a prison cell rather than the delights of a bed of venery. She supposed it was, on balance, to his discredit.

Montsy shuddered. It indicated a revulsion from far more important things than Jonathan's improbable lust.

'What is it, Montsy?' asked Bridie, gently. Despite Jonathan's role in it, it was not a joke after all. The girl was in danger and, whatever his shortcomings, Jonathan had her at his mercy.

Another great shudder. 'He keeps trying to touch me.'

From the horror and disgust in her voice, it must have amounted surely to indecent assault. They had been alone in the garden for at least ten minutes. Had Jonathan's bundle of inhibitions been held together by a single string, which suddenly had snapped? It had always seemed to Bridie there had been a complexity of strings, with more, tighter than ever, being added all the time.

'What do you mean? What did he do?'

'My hand; he touched my hand, twice, deliberately.'

Such loathing was in the quiet voice that Bridie felt sorry for Jonathan. He was being made to represent every sexual insult Montsy had ever suffered in her cause, and every brutal blow Jordi was bleeding from in prison.

'He's emotionally puerile,' she said. 'He'd be trying to make up for his churlishness.'

Montserrat sat on the bed and made an effort to compose herself.

'When I think of Jordi and the others in prison,' she whispered, 'I despise him.'

'But he's not to blame for that, Montsy.'

'Yes, he is. It's because of men like him, so false and selfish, that there is injustice and cruelty in the world.'

Such zeal and idealism in any other woman would have irritated Bridie; in Montserrat it saddened and frightened her. She knew herself to be among the false and selfish; her indifference to the world's sufferings might not be so glacier-like as Jonathan's, but it added to the total.

'We in Spain are beasts in a sunny cage,' went on Montserrat. 'He looks at us through the bars. If we lie in the sun or play games, like the flamenco, he is pleased with us; but if we try to jump out of the cage he is displeased and afraid. So he gives our keepers whips to drive us back in. Every bruise, every cut, every burn, on Jordi and the others, was done by Mr Broxmead and his like.'

Bridie, with her arm round her friend, felt her trembling.

'All right,' she whispered, 'but he's not worth getting upset over. It's you I'm worried about. Keep the door locked if you like. But whatever happens wait till Francisco gets in touch with you. Stay in the house or garden as much as you can. Keep back from Ampara, the maid. She's good-hearted enough, but she's so stupid and jealous and inquisitive that she could be dangerous. So could Madeleine, I'm sorry to say.'

'She does not like me.'

'Well, she was half drunk, and you were so unwise as to smile at her latest acquisition.'

'I liked him.'

'I'm not sure I did. He sounded far too sorry for himself.'

'He is unhappy because his country, like mine, has become sterile.'

Even in Spanish, such large statements bored Bridie. 'Well anyway,' she said, 'Maddy's claimed him.'

'Who was Margaret?'

'Margaret?'

'He said she is dead.'

'Oh, some friend, I suppose. You know what artists are. To be fair to Maddy, she's madly serious about painting, and she evidently thinks he's good. She can be the sweetest creature in the world, but she can also be the bitchiest. She put her mark on him tonight, in that pine wood. He'll not get away from her now until she's tired of him, which might not be for the rest of his life, if he turns out to be as good a painter as she thinks.'

Montserrat's eyes were closed. 'What do you mean, about the pine wood?'

Like Jonathan, Montsy too could do with being made to face certain facts.

'I mean, they made love.'

'She agreed to it, so soon?'

'She insisted on it, I would say.'

'But she could have a child!'

'There are ways of preventing that.'

How many revolutionaries, wondered Bridie, had to be reminded of contraception, and were aghast? Perhaps Jonathan was right to this extent: unless one was prepared for ruthlessness of all kinds, whether preventing birth or hastening death, one ought to live privately at home and leave all to God.

Then they heard him approach the door and turn the handle. There was a pause when he found it locked. Bridie pictured his face: according to Montsy's belief it would be convulsed with baffled lust; according to her own, supercilious with displeasure at a precaution unseemly in guest or servant.

'Miss Puig,' he called softly, 'I have brought the sheets.'

Bridie could have laughed, but Montserrat jumped up and stood in front of the door with an expression of disdain curiously contorting and puffing up her face. According to Terence's prophecy, at forty she would be just another fat middle-aged Spanish woman.

She unlocked the door, but left it to him to open; this he did, with a little coughing caution, as if he half expected her to be undressed. That she wasn't appeared to be a great relief. So much, thought Bridie, for Montsy's fantastic suspicion that he was a wolf slavering with lust.

Her blush of disdain, so evidently for him, made her beauty for him too; nothing she could do or say, now or later, could prevent that; if, tomorrow, she went away and he never saw her again, it would still be his, for the rest of his life.

As he came in, shyly, she retreated towards the cot, and turned her back on him. He noticed a ring on her right hand, and wondered if it had been given her by a sweetheart, now in prison perhaps with her brother. He noticed too how the backs of her ankles were slightly calloused where her shoes rubbed against them, and he envied those shoes, and felt his heart crack at the thought of her walking without him, along pavements, over grass, across streets, and into shops.

The baby whimpered. She soothed it in a low intense voice that grieved for her brother and at the same time condemned his persecutors, among whom Jonathan was included.

His blood turned to ice: the distance between them was too great for him ever to reach her: an Arctic waste of misunderstanding, prejudice, and incompatibility.

Bridie, a shadowy creature of that bleak desert, got up from the bed, took the sheets from him, and dropped them on a chair.

'Montsy will put them on,' she whispered. 'We'd better leave.'

'Yes, of course.' Yet he did not want to go; he wanted to stay there, more than anything else; and it seemed to him, confused by the familiarity of the room, and by that sense of Montserrat's belonging to him in spite of the impassable wilderness between, that he had a right to stay.

'I'd better take my pyjamas,' he said.

Bridie took them from under his pillow. Montserrat, still comforting the baby, kept her back turned. He saw, without apparently looking, how dimpled was the back of her knees, and how in her, and only in her, the plumpness of buttocks was beautiful, without being lascivious.

Bridie had to pull him with her to the door. His reluctance seemed to her hardly that of a baulked rapist, but rather of a huffy child sent off before the party was over. 'We're disturbing the baby,' she said. 'Good night, Montsy. I'll see you in the morning.'

Montserrat turned and smiled. 'Good night, Bridie.'

'Good night, Miss Puig,' he said, and would have said more, would have tried to explain the inexplicable, and might even have begun to tell her how necessary to his future existence was her presence, whether scornful or no, had Bridie not pushed him out.

'Good night, Mr Broxmead,' murmured Montserrat, at last.

He found himself outside, the door shut, Bridie's back to it, his pyjamas in his hand.

'You've got to remember, Jonathan, she's been through a great deal lately. You've no idea. I've told you her mother's ill.'

'Who is looking after her mother, Bridie?'

The question surprised Bridie. 'An aunt, I think.'

'Is there anything we can do to help? Money, for instance?'

Surprise gave way to suspicion. 'You'll be helping enough if you let her stay till her friends get in touch with her. It's not a game, Jonathan.' She had to add that, sharply. His interest, out of typical perfunctory politeness, was in this case intolerable.

'These friends, Bridie, who are they?'

'You'd better not ask that, Jonathan. You don't want to get involved. I may as well tell you I don't approve of

Montsy being mixed up in this wretched business of slipping pamphlets under doors and chalking on walls.'

'Does she chalk on walls?'

'I believe so.'

'What does she chalk?'

'Oh, I don't know. Nonsense like: Arriba España. Arriba Libertad.'

'I notice you call her Montsy.'

How fatuous well-bred indifference could be! 'If things go well,' she said, angrily, 'someone will come in a few days with a passport for her, and take her across the border.'

He became melodramatically hoarse. It was an aspect of his character she hadn't suspected. So he too liked to imagine himself a Galahad in gilded cardboard armour.

'And what,' he asked, 'if things do not go well?'

'Then she'll have to try to get across herself.'

'Will that be easy?'

'No, but it can be done, I suppose.'

'These activities, chalking walls and distributing pamphlets, however foolish, are scarcely criminal. If she is arrested, what will happen to her?'

'She'll be thrown into jail, for two or three years.'

He gripped her shoulder painfully. His eyes were fierce and haggard, his mouth tough. 'We mustn't let that happen, Bridie,' he said.

Disgusted by his play-acting, she pulled herself free. 'I'm going to bed, Jonathan. But let me tell you this: if she – well, shrinks from people – you'll understand it's because she's a lot more nervous than she'll admit. Better to leave her alone; and of course don't tell anyone about her, not even Maddy.'

She hurried away, not giving him time to stir out of his role of swashbuckling deliverer.

Maddy was already in bed, smoking, and staring at the

portrait of a girl, hung, not very straight, on the wall opposite.

'Tell me, Bridie,' she asked suddenly, as Bridie was on one foot drawing on her pyjamas, 'what's the mystery about Miss Ripoll or Puig?'

Bridie almost toppled over. She hid behind Irishness. 'Mystery? Why should there be a mystery? Isn't she an indigent student looking for a summer job with the rich foreigners?'

'Then why is Jonathan creeping about like a cat that's lost her kittens?'

'Is he indeed? I never noticed.' He had seemed to Bridie like a cat all right, but one that sat grinning out at the world, knowing a saucer of milk and half a fish awaited it in the parlour.

'She isn't by any chance a tart, like me? If so, I agree it's wise to conceal it, for dear Isabel is of the opinion that only a madonna's fit to look after her child. The crucifix is a good idea.'

Bridie got into bed. Maddy, she discovered, was naked. Along the passage Montserrat, alone with a baby of nine months, female at that, would have on a night-dress of white lawn, up to her throat and down to her ankles.

'Apart from the fact that she's got smouldering eyes, I've nothing against her,' said Maddy. 'But please advise her either to stick to her duties or to try out her charms on Norman.'

'She'll stick to her duties. The crucifix isn't just a good idea.'

'She believes in it?'

'Devoutly.'

Maddy smiled, but said nothing. All time she kept gazing at the portrait. Now she pointed to it with her cigarette. 'What do you think of her, Bridie?'

Bridie was careful. 'Was she the girl John Lynedoch mentioned?'

'Aye, that's Margaret.'

'But if she's dead, Maddy, what is there to say?'

'Do you think, painted like that, she'll ever be dead?'

It was true. The original, seen by casual eyes, wouldn't have stood out in any group of factory or shop girls. But in this vivid and, yes, violent painting, she became more and more impressive the longer you looked. In the end Bridie felt she was the one being judged, with kindness and honesty, but not, somehow, with much intelligence.

'She worked in a sweetie shop. Look at her hands. What help could she have given him? He says it himself, doesn't he? None; at least, not any more. He's ruthless, Bridie, though you'd think to look at him he'd run away and cry if you spoke unkindly. I doubt whether she was ever any good in bed; look at that mouth. Am I a bitch, Bridie, jealous of her like this, when she's dead? You Catholics pray for the dead, don't you? Pray for her, will you?'

'I'll give her a mention.'

Maddy laughed. 'Well, shall I put out the light?'

'Yes, if you wish.'

In the darkness, after a pause during which Bridie couldn't be sure whether Maddy was sobbing or chuckling, the latter said: 'I hope Terence doesn't snore like that all night.'

He had been snoring loudly when Lynedoch and Bridie had got him to bed.

Bridie did not know herself whether to laugh or weep. In Maddy's remark was surely all the concentrated pettiness of the species. She thought that when she was dead herself, in limbo, she would find relief from the tribulations there by recalling the pettiness of what was done on earth, in the names of Love, Faith, and Patriotism.

'Because if he does,' added Maddy, 'then I don't see John getting much sleep.'

Bridie lay grinning. What sleep was Jordi Puig getting this night, or Montsy, or any one of the millions all over the world, sick or maimed or hungry or lonely or bereaved? Even Jonathan up on the roof might find the rain or the stars or the shakiness of the legs of the bed hindering his slumbers.

Jonathan was alone in the sitting-room, as happy as a cat that had found her kittens, when David and Isabel returned. In a humour to love them not merely as his relations but as members of the same species as Montserrat, he was disappointed to find them in an ill temper with each other.

Isabel particularly was quite vicious. Jonathan's purrs of loving-kindness infuriated her, even when he broke the good news that if Linda was fretful that night she, Isabel, would not be disturbed.

'You're such an old woman, Jonathan,' she said. 'For Christ's sake, what are you snivelling about?'

David, hand under beard, leg over arm of chair, sat in a corner. 'It's no joke, Jonathan,' he said, high-minded but peevish.

In spite of them Jonathan could not announce it without stammers of joy: 'We've engaged a nursemaid.'

'I warned you, I'll allow no smelly fisherman's wife near my child.'

'She's a student of Barcelona University. A lawyer's daughter. Really a charming girl. Terence and Bridie brought her. I'm sure you'll find her very suitable.'

Isabel laughed vulgarly. 'If you find her charming, dear brother, I distrust her immediately, as a nappy-changer, I mean. What does she know about babies?'

His joy could not be subdued. 'Isabel, aren't the Spanish philoprogenitive to a man, or should I say a woman?'

'Oh, shut up, Jonathan. Keep your big words for your small novels. I asked if she knew anything about babies, about feeding them, changing them, washing them, keeping them quiet.'

'Particularly that last,' drawled David.

She shouted at him: 'You keep out of it.'

'I fervently wish I could, my dear Isabel; but you would be the very first to drag me back as close to the well-beloved cacophony as you could.'

'Wouldn't I just! And by the beard, too. Isn't she yours as well as mine?'

Without doubt, thought Jonathan, Maddy's diagnosis must be correct: an overdose of parenthood was causing this marital squabble. About to pass judgment, he felt himself curbed. Instead, he was saddened by this failure of human love, at its profoundest source.

'I think you will find Miss Ripoll competent,' he said.

'Charming and competent,' sneered Isabel. 'She seems to have taken your fancy all right. Well, let me tell you this, I'm not going to stand by and watch my child being looked after by some creature with whom you're having an affair. Maddy thinks it's high time you got rid of your precious virginity. Perhaps she's right; but I refuse to have Linda mixed up in it.'

He blushed, and wanted to rush across and slap her.

David laughed like a camel, his head held high.

'I'll be the judge of her competence,' said Isabel. 'Where is she now?'

'In bed.'

A moment too late, he saw the word would be misinterpreted.

Isabel joined David in camel-like laughter.

'I can't see what's so lewdly amusing about that,' he said, when of course he should have kept quiet.

'You sounded so sadly excluded, Jonathan,' said Isabel.

'The door slammed in your face!' cried David.

'I suppose she's in with Ampara?' asked Isabel.

'No. I hardly think she should be regarded as on the same footing as Ampara.'

'Why not? She's a servant, isn't she? She'll be looking for wages, won't she?'

'How much per month?' demanded David.

'It was not discussed.'

'I should say it's at least as important as her competence as a nappy-changer,' said David.

'She'll have to wash them too,' added Isabel. 'Did you make that clear?'

'Hardly.'

'There are times, Jonathan, when you talk as if you aren't much beyond the stage of nappies yourself. Well, I'll certainly make it clear to her. I don't want any elegant señorita. If she's not in with Ampara, where is she?'

'Isabel, Linda had to be considered.'

'I should hope so. Well?'

'I take it too you expect Miss Ripoll to look after her during the night as well as during the day?'

'Christ, what else?'

'Really, Isabel, there's no need to be blasphemous or hysterical. You seem to be prejudiced against Miss Ripoll before you've even seen her.'

'Aren't you aware that the smarmy way you've been talking about her would prejudice anyone against her? Well?'

He sighed. 'She had to have a room she could share with the baby.'

'So you threw Lynedoch out?' Isabel was delighted. 'I should say so.'

'At least I hope,' said David, loftily, 'it was put to him as a suggestion, not an order. The man's a guest, after all.'

'Isn't Linda?' cried Isabel.

'Miss Ripoll, and Linda, are in my room,' said Jonathan. He hurried on: 'For the time being. And please, since I'm old enough to make my own decisions – in spite of your pleasantry, Isabel – I'd be obliged if you'd accept them. And to forestall any further pleasantry, let me inform you I shall be sleeping on the roof. I usually do during the summer.'

'But it's going to rain,' cried David, in glee.

Jonathan too had seen the clouds lowering. 'It may not,' he said, rather weakly.

Isabel got up, trailing her white stole behind her. 'I may as well have a word with her.'

Jonathan went stiff. 'At this time? She'll be asleep. Not to mention Linda.'

'I've got to see she understands about the baby's feed at seven.'

'I believe she discussed it with Ampara.'

'What does Ampara know about it?'

He stood up. 'Isabel.'

'Well?'

'I'd rather you left her alone tonight. But if you must disturb her, please do not be unpleasant about it.'

'I like that. Am I in the habit of being unpleasant?'

'Recently, yes, I'm sorry to say. Among us it doesn't matter so much; but I see no reason why Miss Ripoll should suffer from it.'

'Miss Ripoll, Miss Ripoll. Are you sure this is the first time you've met her? The name comes off your tongue much too smugly. What kind of a freak can she be to have taken your fancy so much?'

He turned pale. 'You must not insult her, Isabel. Insult me as much as you like, but not her, not her at all.'

She burst into tears. 'Oh Christ, I wish I was dead,' she cried, clutching at her flat bosom; then she rushed out.

Jonathan had to sit down; his legs had gone weak. But he

listened as she went sobbing upstairs. She went straight to her own room.

'What is the matter with her, David?' he asked. 'One would think she's ill.'

His brother-in-law, celebrated intellectual, was jeering and picking his nose. 'You know, Jonathan, I've been watching you. At times you've looked quite human. This Miss Ripoll seems to be having a quite miraculous effect on you.'

'Is it true Isabel's pregnant again?' asked Jonathan.

'And what bloody business is it of yours whether she is or not?'

'She's my sister.'

'Then ask her.' The finger picking the nose desisted, lost its arrogance, crept down, and hid in the black beard. 'Christ, yes, it's true. And she absolutely refuses to see anyone.'

'You mean, she won't have an abortion?'

'Yes. And she doesn't want the child either. So what does one do? It's not as though she has religious scruples.'

'What kind of scruples does she have?'

'God knows.'

'Two children hardly constitute a tribe.' Jonathan himself, for the first time in his life, thought of the children he might have: dark-haired and brown-eyed, there would surely be more than two of them.

'Jonathan, tell me, if you like, we're a pair of improvident, lustful fools; I'll hang my head, I'll give you a handful of repentant beard. But do not, please, come the fig-leaved sham Apollo; that I just couldn't stomach. However, I've had enough of the subject for one night; let's drop it. So you didn't succeed in warding Norman off, after all?'

'No.'

'We met him at the hotel. What's come over him? He's so dapper now, and he used to be like a tramp, with his jeans and checked shirts. He's almost pious; but then that kind of voice, the warm drawl, always sounds like piety, doesn't it? Knowing you've got half a million dollars ahead of you is bound in the end to make you see the light. As men of the world, Jonathan, oughtn't we to persuade Maddy to take him back into favour? Most blandly he assured us he was here to marry her and carry her off with him to the States, to receive his patrimony. Between ourselves, she was fond enough of him last summer; much too fond for your brotherly liking, and much much too fond for Isabel's. All we've got against him is that he's a shockingly bad writer; but then, in any generation, only half a dozen books are likely to be remembered; out of many thousands.'

Jonathan was scarcely listening. It had already occurred to him that if Maddy did take up with Norman again it would mean that Lynedoch would be released, as it were, to win some other woman's favour and support; Montserrat Puig's, for instance. Hadn't she praised his painting? Didn't she believe that as a Catalan she had a kinship with him as a Scot, each of them seeking independence from foreign domination? Each of them too was a kind of exile.

'Besides,' said David, rising with a yawn, 'I'd like to see her leave Lynedoch alone.' He stretched up his long arms till they almost reached the ceiling. 'By the way, Jonathan, when am I to see that new novel?'

'What new novel, David?'

'I thought you'd started another? Remember, about the fisherman and the ballet dancer?'

'I gave it up.'

David laughed. 'Never mind. It didn't sound like your line of country. Don't worry. There are depths in you, my lad. It may be this Miss What's-her-name will plumb them. Well, good night. Hope the rain holds off.' He went out, laughing.

Alone again, Jonathan sat with his hands clasped, picturing Linda in her cot and Montserrat in his bed. The one roused as little lust as the other, and as much tenderness.

Surely he must have fallen in love. For proof, he began to worry more about her mother, who was ill and whom he had never met, than he had ever done about his own, whom he had watched dying.

Fourteen

'Now, Norman boy, would we ask you to describe the flavour of a peach?' Thus had Frank assured him, in a voice aswim with peach-like juices, when he had tried, in words, to prove his conversion genuine. 'I guess the grace of the good Lord is truly indescribable. We feel it here' – Frank had pressed his well-manicured sweetly smelling hand against his broad lapel of high-class flannel, with the dark red rose on it – 'and if that's good enough for Him, surely it ought to be good enough for us, whatever the ungodly may say.'

It had not been quite good enough for Norman himself, however. This extraordinary clarity in the mind, like sunshine on white rocks, and this intoxication, this sense of being unable to do, say, feel, or think anything wrong, had somehow to be defined to his own satisfaction before they could be believed in or taken advantage of. His best definition was necessarily vague: it was like, he thought, freewheeling on a bicycle down a never-ending not too steep hill, with fields of grass and flowers on either hand, blue sky above, and singing birds.

He had realized that Frank was right in this, as in so many other aspects of the business. In a corner of the sunny clarity there persisted a tiny motionless shadow, its origin and purpose unknown, and at the foot of that hill, if ever reached, would be a bottomless black hole. Shadow and hole must surely represent doubt. Frank, cautiously consulted, had laughed. The sincerest conversions were always a trifle clouded at the beginning, he had said. The remedy was steadfast prayer; in a day or a year or in fifty years – what did time matter to the Lord? – one suddenly was aware that the sky of one's soul was at last wholly serene. Meanwhile, it was one's holy duty to enjoy the clarity of mind and motive, revel in the free-wheeling, and forget the shadow and the hole.

Therefore every night Norman prayed, on his knees by his bedside; but he preferred his pre-breakfast prayers, in the sunshine, when he was shaved, dressed, and physically peckish. Somehow it was easier then to slip in little personal requests without their selfishness looking too gross. This morning, for example, as, on a yellow cushion on the red-tiled floor of his luxurious bedroom, he knelt, neatly, chin resting on bow-tie bright as a bluebird, hands not too greedily clasped, he felt able with gay humility and over-whelming confidence to ask God's help in his mission to reclaim Madeleine Broxmead by marrying her.

After a night of rain the sun was refreshingly warm on the back of his neck. A peep to the left out of the window revealed yachts on the tranquil sea; a wriggle of his left hip reminded him of his wallet there, containing the five hun-dred dollars sent by his father, if not in answer to prayer, then why? Memory, never altogether at rest, whispered to him with a wink that the maids in this hotel, judging by what he had seen of them last night, must have been chosen for their shapeliness, accentuated by uniforms of tight silky black.

When life was at its most auspicious, prayer was most likely to be efficacious. If a man felt miserable as he prayed what right had he to expect the Lord to rejoice? The poor in spirit had been promised that they would see God; but, as Frank had said, if the whiners and the moaners and the grumblers thought it meant them, then they were in for the biggest shock of their lives.

Norman was careful, in accordance with Frank's advice, always to include in his prayers a reminder to the Lord that since international communism was contrary to His interests, He ought not to let it even appear to be winning, anywhere in the world. In this instance His customary tactic of letting the Devil build up a leading score, to terrify the slothful and stimulate the godly, was just too risky.

At breakfast he was able to indulge in that most exquisite of pleasures, nibbling at temptation, licking and tasting it, while all the time knowing he would in the end spit it out in virtuous disgust. Not only the waitress attending him, but at least three others, not to mention two anyway of the lady guests, were, as one of the junior Voices had put it, worthy of King David in his lusty prime.

How delightful it was to watch bottoms swaying and twitching in their black silk, their libidinousness rendered innocent by the truly Christian quality of his admiration. These flowers on the table were no more, and no less creations of God. Exempt from sin, he could trust himself to pat those bottoms with the same pure pleasure that he would find in stroking flowers. This was the prodigious difference between those granted the Lord's exemption, and those who out of stubbornness refused to take it. The latter, never sure of the nature of sin, and therefore never sure of happiness, snatched at it where they could, too often guiltily; the former knew it was theirs for the taking. Yes, he thought he could even take one of those waitresses to bed, without sin. The privileges of the saved were comprehensive and beyond the logic of worldliness. Not of course that he had any intention or desire to sleep with a maid; but it was the most comforting feeling in the world to know that whatever he did he would not forfeit the Lord's goodwill.

'Nothing matters any more,' Frank had said, 'once the Lord's got you tightly by the hand.'

It was perhaps more accurately put like this: the Lord's hand was always there when you felt like putting your own into it. Yes, sir, you might be skin-diving at the bottom of the sea, or orbiting the earth in a capsule, or presiding over a board meeting, or addressing a congregation of one hundred thousand souls, or lying in bed with a pretty complaisant woman who might or might not be your wife: if you felt that terrifying loneliness of self about to surround you, you did not have any longer to cower in fear or cringe or rant or scribble down obscenities; all you had to do now was to place your hand in the Lord's. In no mere metaphorical sense, either: the firmness and warmth of that Fatherly grip could actually be felt.

As Frank had said it was like going into battle wearing an armour of invisibility. You could not help feeling sorry for your foes who grew weary and discouraged as they saw their fiercest, proudest blows having no effect. Norman had only to think of Jonathan Broxmead to realize how right Frank was again. As a spiritual enemy Jonathan was utterly insignificant. His peevish refusal to admit that God was love was typical. Godless and loveless both, how could he have admitted it? When Norman had mentioned Jonathan's case to Frank, the latter had said it was quite familiar: the intellectual with neck as stiff as his knees, who regarded prayer as perversion, and whose consorting with prostitutes was at heart a kind of devil worship. When Norman had pointed out that he didn't think Jonathan did much of that consorting, Frank had reminded him that the most profligate restricted it to the imagination. Even that had seemed improbable in Jonathan's case, but who, except the Lord, could be sure what went on in a man's soul?

In white slacks, white blue-dotted shirt, and sapphire tie, he went down to the beach by the hotel's private steps, and thence proceeded by way of the skimpiest bikinis towards the *plaza mayor*, from which at his leisure he could make for the Street of the Two Angels.

He had reached the plaza when he saw a car approaching slowly. Driving it was David Reeves, with his wife Isabel beside him. Behind sat those two Irish debtors, Terence and Bridie O'Donnell, who owed him two thousand pesetas.

He was not sure whether he should hail it.

Isabel he particularly distrusted. Last summer she had banged him, not in fun, over the head with his own guitar. Afterwards, true, she had apologized, but in a way even more wounding than the assault. Though he was now as different a man as change of ownership from the Devil to the Lord could make him, he had felt last night at the hotel that she was still inclined to see him simply as one of the men only too willing to accompany her sister among the pines or on to the hard boards of a dinghy. In a sense he ought to have been grateful to her: without knowing it she had been, too stridently and violently perhaps, the agent of the Lord. But she would never recognize his conversion. She would see in it only a new approach, a change of manoeuvre. As godless as her brother, she would consider herself personally insulted if Norman told her the simple truth, that he had come back at the Lord's behest. Jonathan, after all, being male had an imagination of sorts, however debauched with secret lustings. Isabel had none.

What she did have, though, was an intelligent attitude to money. Prayer, and faith in prayer, she would regard as presumptuous in a poor man; in a rich man she would be prepared to accept it, and whatever went with it, as a distasteful but tolerable way of giving thanks. Worse than atheist or agnostic, she looked on religion as a phenomenon among many others, to be used if possible to her advantage, but otherwise to be ignored.

Had the car not stopped at the petrol pump he might have let it pass. That it did stop, he took to be a sign. With the Lord's hand in his, he went forward.

Little Bridie too was a danger. Bony-faced, bony-buttocked, and bony-minded, she was into the bargain a

Catholic, not so lapsed as her husband, with the result that she was likely to share her Church's opinion of instantaneous conversions. To become a Catholic was a long slow wearisome ritual, with tests to pass, whereas to become one of the saved was over like a flash of wings. The followers of Rome had been forbidden to attend Frank's great rallies.

Terence saw him first. 'Good God Almighty,' he cried, 'it's Norman himself, bejabbers, transmogrified!'

They all came out of the car to greet him. David gave him a friendly enough wave. Terence looked sleepy and dissolute, but amiable, as well he might, considering those two thousand pesetas. Bridie, wary and impatient, was also prudent. Isabel was curiously diffident.

'And what have you been doing with yourself?' asked Bridie.

'Ah, Bridie, wonderful things!'

They misinterpreted his wink, and laughed.

'You're far thinner,' she said. 'Have you been ill?'

That was what most pre-salvation acquaintances supposed.

'I have never felt better in my life,' he said, piously.

He knew they would laugh again. He laughed with them.

'How are your parents, Norman?' asked Isabel.

'Very well, Isabel, thank you.'

'How long is it since you've seen them?'

'Three years. But I'm going back to the States next month.'

He felt that excess, as Frank called it, coming on; the downhill glide was too intoxicating, the clarity so intense that afar off he saw the glittering towers of heaven itself. Count ten, Frank had advised; sit down, and thrust your head between your knees; if this isn't possible, owing to company being present, put your hand in your pocket and pinch your thigh as painfully as you can bear. Excess was a sign of overflowing grace, too readily misunderstood by the uninitiated. Properly controlled, it could inspire fifty thousand souls to rush to Jesus within a week.

He pinched his thigh. 'It's my hope and prayer to take Maddy back with me,' he said.

There was a stink of petrol, but it wasn't that which made their noses go squirmy.

'I've written my people,' he went on. 'They're delighted. They're awful keen to meet her. They wrote back she sounds marvellous. She is marvellous, too. Do you know what I want to do right now? I want to run all over this plaza shouting to everyone how marvellous she is.'

The others smiled uneasily, but Isabel frowned.

'I wouldn't build up my hopes too high, if I were you, Norman,' she said.

Discretion, sure; but don't ever let it get to the point where you won't talk about the Lord because you're ashamed of Him. So Frank had counselled; so it was written in the new commandments.

'Didn't she write telling you not to come?' asked Isabel. 'As far as she's concerned, it's over.'

'She's found a painter, Norman,' said Terence.

'And do you know who I've found, Terence?'

'Well, apart from a natty tailor, I'm afraid I can't say.'

'Christ.' He pronounced it, for devilment, as if it was a blasphemous exclamation. Then he repeated it, in meekness and love. 'Yes, friends, I am eternally glad to be able to tell you that I have found my Lord.'

A guffaw died stillborn in David's beard. Bridie and Terence exchanged Irish and Catholic glances, subtle in their derision. Only Isabel was displeased.

'If this is a joke, Norman,' she said severely, 'I'm afraid I find it in very bad taste.'

'It is the most glorious joke in all the universe,' he assured her, laughing in his joy. 'Yes, friends, the Lord must have the most wonderful sense of humour. Aren't we the oddest, most comical creatures on His earth? Yet he loves us all.'

Another guffaw from David; this one, though not quite stillborn, died prematurely.

'What sort of gag is this, Norman?' he mumbled, horribly embarrassed.

Norman pitied him, and his thick-souled, middle-class Englishness. He would have been less shocked had Norman exposed his person here in public; sexual maladjustment, though unfortunate, was respectable by comparison with religious frankness.

'No gag, David,' he said, with sympathy. 'All I am doing is standing here, in the sunshine, in this public place, in front of my good friends, announcing that since I saw them last I have given myself to Christ, humbly and gladly.'

Then, after a pause, he added, in joyous impishness: 'It would give me the greatest happiness, David, if I could persuade you to come to Christ also.'

He took David's hand.

With a shudder David withdrew it as if from the face of a corpse. He scarcely knew where to put it; good manners kept him from rubbing it against his trousers. 'For God's sake,' he mumbled.

'That's it, David, for God's sake.'

'No, what I mean to say is that we're on our way to Ampurias, to have a look at the Roman remains, you know. But first we've to drop Bridie and Terence at Figueras. They've got to catch a train.'

Isabel stepped forward. Behind her spectacles her eyes were hard and hostile, but also curious. 'What good do you think this is going to do you?' she demanded. 'If it's intended to impress Maddy let me assure you it will have the opposite effect.'

They all agreed.

'You couldn't have thought of a worse tactic,' said Bridie.

'I don't know whether there's anything to see through,' remarked Terence, 'but if there is she will.'

'We ought to be pushing on,' said David.

'I suppose you'll tell us you pray?' said Isabel.

'Regularly, Isabel.'

'On your knees?'

'On my knees.'

She looked at his sleek, uncrumpled pants.

'And what do you pray for?'

'Isabel, for God's sake!' muttered her husband.

She ignored him: 'I don't mean for the starving millions in China, or anything like that,' she said to Norman. 'I mean what proof have you that your prayers are ever heeded?'

'I could give you a dozen instances.'

'One will do.'

'And even at that, we'll miss the train,' said David.

Norman chose the one most likely to impress Isabel.

'Laugh if you like,' he said, laughing himself, 'but once when I needed money I prayed, and ten days later a cheque arrived from my father for five hundred dollars.'

'Had you written to him for it?' asked Terence, interested.

'I had not.'

'It could have been a coincidence,' said Bridie, with bony sarcasm.

'You really believe,' said Isabel, 'that if you hadn't prayed for it the cheque wouldn't have come?'

'Yes, Isabel, I certainly do.'

He had not expected her to be his likeliest convert. It was obvious she wanted a favour of God very badly. He wondered what it could be. Somehow he did not think it was money. She would not stoop to ask for it, even from the Lord.

Suddenly she turned away and went into the car. Her husband and the O'Donnells followed her. They all gazed out at him with a kind of melancholy shame on their faces; on Isabel's there was also a sneer of speculation.

He stepped forward. 'I expect to be here only a few days,' he said. 'Will you be coming back, Terence?'

'Not this summer. We're off to Ireland on Friday. Don't think,' he added, his voice smooth as velvet, 'I've forgotten about that little matter.'

Norman pretended not to know. 'What little matter?'

'That thousand pesetas.'

'I remember two thousand, Terence.'

'Two, was it? Yes, you're right. Well, it's not forgotten. Leave Jonathan your address.'

'No need, Terence. If ever you feel able to repay, send the money to any charity you like.'

'I'll do that.' Terence was admirably calm.

'See that he does, Bridie.'

She smiled. 'Depend on me, Norman.'

They waved to him as the car drove away.

He stood gazing after it. Already they were discussing him, with laughter, contempt, anger, and also envy. They would not be able to forget that he had more money in store than they, but what they would never suspect was that he had resources enabling him, to take an extreme example, to indulge in those reveries about the waitress in his bed. Did they not realize, the fools, that the meek could inherit the earth, without any spectacular possession of it? The Lord did not turn rocks into gold. His gifts were more modest. He would not make Norman a writer as great as Shakespeare, but He would give him Madeleine Broxmead as his wife.

As he walked slowly across the plaza, making for the house, he wondered again what it could be that Isabel wanted so much that she was almost prepared to pray for it. Nothing had been said about their child. Had it been born an imbecile?

Now and then he stopped. Places as unromantic as this spot on the beach where brick and tile rubble was dumped, and this other with the heaps of clay on which grew the blue flowers, reminded him so poignantly of Maddy that, hands clasped, on the verge of tears, he had to thank God for having brought him back to her, able this time to love her as she deserved and as he desired. His old self, with its sulky face and spoiled child's rages, was no longer here by the rubbish and the flowers.

The iron gate was closed. When he put his hand on it to push it open, rust came off as it had done last year. He was reminded that people too had not changed; the Lord had not been at work in them, and, if not appealed to, would never be, all their unleavened lives. Baffled self-seeking in Jonathan, decaying charm in Terence, unavailing vigilance in Bridie, barren intellectuality in David, all were unchanged; and if Isabel's thoughts had been turned towards God because of some infirmity in her baby that she wanted Him to cure, ought that to be called change, was it not merely her old resolute selfishness entering upon new ground?

Ampara would not have changed either, no more than these stunted olives. He took out of his pocket the necklace he had brought as a present for her, and smiled as he imagined the mixture of suspiciousness and cheerful gratitude with which she would accept it. Last summer, catching her alone in the house one evening, he had thought it would pass an amusing half-hour pretending to seduce her. It had been funny enough, but not in the way he had supposed. In rebuffing his caresses she could not have been more haughtily indignant had she been a marquesa sparkling with diamonds, nor more virtuous than a nun. What had given her dignity and chasteness had been her loyalty to, and love for, Jonathan. Everybody had known she was fond of Jonathan; it was a household joke; but no one had guessed her fondness was so deep and sexual. Disconcerted, ashamed, and a little jealous, Norman had kept the discovery to himself.

As he stood among the bushes in the large wild garden he heard from round the side of the house a baby crying, and a woman comforting it in Spanish. Keeping out of sight, he came to the corner of the house and saw, on the small lawn of thin grass he remembered being there, a pram, with a handsome young Spanish-looking woman bending over it, dressed in a white skirt and sleeveless red blouse. He did not notice Jonathan until the latter, who had been reading in a deck-chair in the shade of the carib tree, suddenly got up, with the book still in his hand, and approached the girl from behind, so silently in his moccasins that she did not hear him. What happened then Norman was not sure. Whether Jonathan had merely bent down to look at his niece and so had accidentally touched the girl on the hip, or whether he had deliberately stroked her there, he could not honestly have told. But she was in no doubt. In a fury of insulted modesty she whirled round and up and struck Jonathan such a wholehearted slap on the side of his head that his sunglasses bounced off and fell on the grass. He recoiled, dropped the book, put out a hand to plead or ward off the second blow which looked like coming all the time, stammered something, and then turned and fled into the house, his face a picture of horror and remorse, so exaggerated as to be both comic and moving.

She stood gazing after him, with loud gasps, her fine bosom heaving, and her lovely face twisted with a disgust that surely must be exaggerated too. As Norman watched, thrilled, she covered her face with her hands. Shudder after shudder passed over her whole body. When at last she took her hands away, the grief on her face seemed wholly genuine.

For three long delicious minutes Norman crouched

among the bushes and watched her. He heard Ampara sing within the house, and saw the girl pick up the sun-glasses and book and take them to the deck-chair where Jonathan had been sitting. She held them in her hand for a few unnecessary seconds before dropping them. Then she returned to the pram and stood beside it, half her mind on soothing the baby, and half, probably, on her striking of Jonathan.

Norman's approach startled her rather more than he thought reasonable, especially as he came so softly.

'Good morning,' he said. 'My name's Ashton, Norman Ashton. Is Jonathan, Mr Broxmead, at home?'

She blushed very faintly, and nodded.

'You understand English, I hope? I can read and listen to Spanish pretty good, but I'm awful slow at speaking it.'

'I understand.'

'I don't think I've ever seen you around before.'

'I am looking after the baby.'

'I see. What the English call a nanny.' He peeped into the pram, not knowing what to expect, and was taken aback to find the baby not only quite normal but also very like Maddy. 'Isabel's baby, I take it?'

'Yes, Mrs Reeves's.'

Suddenly his hands sweated. He felt abandoned. Maddy, as the others had said, would laugh at him and his saved soul. She mustn't, for impenetrable and everlasting darkness waited beyond. It was the crucifix round this girl's neck that was doing it. He felt viciously that Jonathan ought not to have taken that blow so meekly, but should have struck back.

She was looking at him with pity.

'Miss Broxmead's not at home,' she said.

'You mean Maddy?'

'Yes. She has gone out with Mr Lynedoch.'

'I guess I don't know the gentleman. Is he a visitor?'

'Yes. He is a painter, from Scotland.'

'A painter, eh? I guess this whole coast is lousy with them. Has Maddy been doing any painting herself lately?'

'I arrived only yesterday.'

And yet she was beating Jonathan off already. There was something about her Norman didn't like or trust. It wasn't simply the crucifix. It must be that she was one of those rabidly virginal Spanish girls who, by seeing all men as potential rapists, insulted the Lord who had been proud to assume the shape and passions of a man. He had heard it called the madonna complex. They wanted babies to mother without the indignity and fuss of love. Trust Jonathan, that sexual simpleton, to pick on one of these for his first attempt at a seduction. He wouldn't mind having a go himself, not for pleasure, but to teach her some female humility.

He came nearer.

'They wouldn't say where they were going?' he asked.

'Yes. To the church.'

'To pray, d'you think?'

'Mr Lynedoch is going to paint it.'

'So he's one of those? I guess that poor old church must be heartily tired of all these guys painting it. You talk as if he's kind of old.'

She shook her head and smiled. 'He's like you, and me.'

'You make him sound old. Are you a professional nurse-maid, or are you doing it as a vacation job?'

'I am a student.'

He could not understand why he disliked and feared her. It wasn't because he was afraid the depth and complexity of her faith showed up the shallowness and simpleness of his; he saw no reason why the way to God, at any rate to his God, should be through a labyrinth of mumbo-jumbo, rites, and rigmarole.

'A student of what?' he asked.

'Philosophy and languages.'

'That's a mouthful. Well, I guess I'd better go in and pay my respects to the boss.'

He stared at her with candid lechery. You have a fine figure now, his eyes said, but in ten years or less, you'll have a belly that no corsetting will be able to contain, and these breasts, ripe enough to have incited even Jonathan to want to taste, will have become flabby and sour. You'll be lucky then if even a joe-soap like Jonathan gives you a fumble.

As if she understood she blushed and turned to attend to the baby. Laughing, he strolled across to the deck-chair to see what book Jonathan had been reading. It was a paperback edition of *Un Amour de Swann*, by Proust.

Jonathan was in the sitting-room, seated at a desk in a corner, writing furiously, with his left hand thumping hard on his knee.

Norman tiptoed in. 'Morning, Jonathan.'

Jonathan looked up wildly. Horror and remorse still clouded his brow and misshaped his mouth. 'What do you want?' he cried, covering what he had written with his hand.

'Why, Jonathan, just to see you, and Maddy.'

'She doesn't want to see you, Norman. She left instructions that if you came this morning you were to be told that. It would be better for everyone if you went away.'

Norman sat down. 'Is this poetry you're writing, Jonathan?' he asked.

'No.'

'If you'll pardon me saying so, you have the look of a poet in the frenzies of tragic composition. Fine-looking piece, the nanny.'

Jonathan went very still. 'If you are referring to Miss Ripoll,' he said, quietly, 'I should be obliged if you would speak of her with more respect.'

'I was giving the lady a compliment, Jonathan. She's a beauty.'

'I'd rather you did not speak about her; and Norman, I must ask you to keep away from her. I am not questioning the genuineness of your conversion. It is a peculiarity of certain religions to allow a substantial degree of licentiousness to its adherents. Yours, I should fancy, is such a one.'

Norman couldn't help being surprised and impressed by such a stroke of percipience. Had he not himself held four aces, he might have been bluffed into getting up and slinking out.

'Still using the big words, Jonathan?' he asked. 'There's a small word for it, greatly in vogue these days.' He uttered that word, twice; and then, as Jonathan's prudish disgust was gathering he went on: 'For a woman with such a small hand, Jonathan, she can give a hefty slap, can't she?'

Jonathan trembled; he even groaned. 'You saw it then?' he whispered, in profoundest shame.

Norman laughed. 'Sure I saw it. Do you know what you did wrong?'

Jonathan groaned again.

'You should have stood your ground. They say the hardest hitters make the most passionate lovers.'

To his astonishment and fright, Jonathan sprang up and rushing across seized him, clumsily, by the bow-tie and tore it off.

'Please leave,' shouted Jonathan.

He was almost in tears. Were they of ridiculous high-minded dudgeon? Or of puerile contrition? Or of repulsed lust? Or simply of love?

Norman got up, with dignity, and took his tie from Jonathan's shaking hand. He too saw no humour in the situation.

'I'll overlook this, Jonathan,' he said. 'Obviously you're not yourself. After all, it wasn't I who caressed the girl's behind.'

Jonathan struck him on the side of the head. Then,

appalled by his act of violence, he rushed back to his desk where he sat with his face hidden in his hands.

'I'll overlook that too,' said Norman. 'As a follower of Christ, I must; but also as your friend.'

'You see,' murmured Jonathan, in anguish, 'I love her.'

'But I understand she arrived yesterday. Did you know her before that?'

'No.'

Staring about, not knowing yet what kind of joy it was he was feeling, Norman caught sight of a painting on the wall that he did not remember having seen last summer. It was a mass of violent greens and oranges and saffrons, and he was about to dismiss it as another of the multitude of feeble imitations of imitations turned out daily throughout the world when he noticed the signature at the bottom, modest but legible; it was John Lynedoch. With that extra reason for despising it he looked again at the painting and found it beautiful, not as a representation of God's creation, but an interpretation conceived undoubtedly by an original, devout, and powerful mind.

He remembered what Maddy had once cried to the moon, that she was not interested in wealth or position or a home or children or even happiness; what she was looking for was a painter of genius, whose slave she would be for the privilege of helping him to produce his masterpieces. Norman had thought at the time and in the place – it had been on the bay in the moonlight – that she was being fanciful and juvenile. He had pointed out such painters were hardly as common as oranges. Now it looked as if, with incredible luck, she had found one.

Again he felt abandoned. It wasn't that Christ had left him and gone away; no, He was still there, in that room, as close as Jonathan. Indeed, He had become Jonathan. It was not the first time this had happened, and Norman knew its purpose. What better way to warn him not to depend entirely on prayer and favouritism than to have Christ Himself assume human shape again and be in need of help?

He sat down and stared gloomily at Jonathan. 'In love?' he muttered. 'How do you know? What are your criteria? What symptoms are you going by? If you find you can't keep your hands off her, that ain't necessarily love.'

'I had no right to say it,' said Jonathan sadly. 'Please forget I did.'

'I don't see that. Who says you had no right? Humility's good in its place, but where it ain't called for it's a stone round your neck. She's only a woman, ain't she? In need of money, too. And don't think a slap on the face is always meant as discouragement. Is she going to be here long?'

'About four or five weeks.'

'Well, with all that time to work in, why act as if you'd only a couple of days? I saw she's wearing a crucifix. Naturally some of them in this country wear it as a habit started damn near at birth; but a few, I guess, wear it because it means a lot to them. She could be one of these; mind, I said could be. I'm not convinced. But if she was, you'd have to be willing to kneel beside her in church. Didn't you once tell me you're allergic to incense? Either that, or you'd have to rouse her an awful lot. I doubt, Jonathan, if you could do that, even in five weeks. You just haven't got what it takes. But with the right coaching you could make some headway; I couldn't say how much. There's no excitement about your appearance. If tomorrow was to be the end of the world you'd be so darned cool and polite. Well, if you're really in love, and she don't love you back, tomorrow is the end of the world. In a certain kind of way you're a good-looking guy. Lots of women would be impressed by that wavy fair hair, that noble brow, and that pretty mouth. Not this one, though; she's got too much fire in her blood.'

But Jonathan had not been listening. He was engrossed in

writing what must indeed be a poem, so many scoring-outs, additions, pauses, and sighs being necessary.

Norman rose and crept over. 'Help me with Maddy,' he whispered, 'and I'll help you with the señorita.'

Jonathan became aware of him, and at once covered what he had written. 'I'm sorry I lost my temper, Norman,' he said.

Norman's jaw ached. 'I understand Maddy's out with this guy Lynedoch?'

'Yes.'

'He painted this?'

'Yes.'

'Does she think it's any good?'

'Yes.'

'Does David?'

'Yes.'

'Do you?'

'I think so.'

'So do I. What's he like anyway? Beard like David's, I suppose; but eyes like a hungry tiger's, not like a stuffed bear's; and hands ready to grasp all creation.'

'Not really. Actually, he's only got a silly little moustache, and his eyes, I would say, are more like an anxious Pekinese's.'

'Then how come he could paint like that?'

'I believe that's what Maddy's so excited about finding out.'

'So she's excited?'

'I've never seen her more so.'

Norman crawled back to his chair. He hid his face behind his hands and after a minute or two began to sob.

From Jonathan came a long silence, of sympathy, Norman thought; but when he peeped between his fingers he saw his host had returned to his writing.

Being abandoned by Christ was awful, but a kind of

honour; being abandoned by this tall, fair-haired, conceited imitator was nothing but ignominy.

To make it worse Jonathan turned to stare at him, in concern and pity. 'I don't think you're well, Norman,' he said; 'spiritually well, I mean. This fellow Redhall, isn't he a dangerous charlatan?'

'You're saying I'm crazy?'

'Not any more than I am myself, alas.'

It was that alas that did it. Norman's confidence and pride surged back. He jumped up and took from his pocket the necklace of red and blue beads.

'I brought this as a present for Ampara,' he said. 'Do I have your permission to go and give it to her?'

'By all means. She's upstairs, I believe.' Then Jonathan concentrated on his writing again.

Ampara was in Jonathan's room, or rather on the small terrace outside its window. Norman was astonished to see the cot, and on the bed a woman's pink dress. For a few moments, thoroughly confused, he wondered if Jonathan and the Spanish girl were already married, and the infant was theirs, not Isabel's. That blow in the garden could have had its origin in marital bitterness.

He went out on to the terrace. Ampara turned, was pleased to see him, put her finger to her lips, and pointed downwards. Miss Ripoll was walking up and down with the baby in her arms, singing it to sleep. She seemed to him lovely, in her white skirt and red blouse; the sun glittered on her hair. To his surprise, Ampara pushed past him into the room, snatched up a cushion, clutched it to her breast, and began, in a travesty of Miss Ripoll's graceful walk, to swagger about, singing through her nose. Then she flung the cushion on to the floor and kicked it under the bed.

'Un momento, Señor Norman,' she cried.

She rushed to a drawer, tugged it open, took out a little bunch of keys, went with them to a suitcase in a corner, inserted one in the lock, turned it, and flung up the lid. Throwing underwear on to the floor, she pulled out a handful of leaflets blotchily printed on cheap green paper. She thrust them at Norman, demanding to know what they were. She couldn't read, she said, but she was sure these were things no decent girl would carry about in her suitcase hidden under her pants and brassieres.

She was right, too. One glance was enough to show him what they were, subversive propaganda; they gave an account of the arrest of someone, a communist no doubt, called Jordi Puig. They accused the government of having beaten him up to make him tell who his confederates had been. In hysterical capitals they proclaimed that his only crime had been to love freedom, and called on his fellow Catalans to demand that he and the dozens of other political prisoners be released at once.

He was more shocked than Ampara. No wonder he had felt distrust. The woman was a communist. The crucifix was a typically clever, cynical blind. He wanted to rush downstairs and warn Jonathan, that defenceless sheep. Isabel must be told too; otherwise God knew what might happen to her innocent baby.

'Well, what are they?' Ampara was asking impatiently. 'What do they say? Are they dirty?'

He remembered then a leaflet similarly printed that she had shown him last summer. Her boy-friend Pedro had confiscated it from a youth in a café. It had been crudely pornographic.

'Very dirty,' he said solemnly.

'What does it say? Read me a bit.'

He quoted from memory a paragraph from one of his own short stories. It had been translated into Spanish by a man in Barcelona who had said he could get them published in South America.

Ampara clutched her hair in horror; then she rushed out

on to the terrace and shook her fist. He folded one of the leaflets and slipped it into his pocket.

'She's not fit to be in charge of that poor baby,' cried Ampara, running back in again.

'Certainly not.'

'Look, she even sleeps in his bed.' She punched the dress on the bed several times, with as much venom as if its owner was inside it. 'What she's after is to sleep in it with him.'

'Where did he sleep last night?'

'On the roof. And it rained. She wants to marry him. That's what she's after. He's easy to take in, too. But she won't do it. I'll strangle her first.'

Her rage was exciting and enjoyable, especially when she dashed at the suitcase and pulled out a pair of white briefs that she flung with a snort of disgust on to the floor.

'Look,' he cried, laughing, 'I've brought you a present.' Standing near the bed, he took the necklace out of its tissue paper.

She came over in delight.

'Let me put it on,' he said.

She stepped nearer until he was able to put his arms round her neck. Her hair stank of cheap shampoo, and her breath of onions.

'Where is it from?' she asked.

'Vienna.'

As they fixed the clasp his hands touched the back of her neck; it was surprisingly soft. He had his leg ready behind hers, and when he thought her most off guard he heaved her upon the bed, according to a judo throw he had once been shown. At least that was his intention. Instead he found himself gripped round the chest by arms as hard as iron, and bent slowly sideways until she suddenly let him go and he fell to the floor.

He lay on the cold tiles, looking up at her reproachfully. Even she, obtuse though she was, ought to have seen the difference between this attempt to seduce her and the one last summer. Then she had had a right to be offended, but not this time. He would have been conferring grace on her, and both of them would have been celebrating, as it were, the exclusion from such kindly love of the red-bloused woman in the garden.

Ampara, applying the ethics of a dish-washer and onion-eater, had spoiled that celebration. It was her sort, in millions all over the world, who would in the end make it easy for the communists to prevail. She would never be convinced that to combat communists it wasn't necessary just to have more H-bombs than they, and take care never to believe a word they said; it was even more important for their opponents to keep close together by praising God and loving one another. That was all he had intended to do, demonstrate to Ampara that praise and love.

She bent over him, the necklace tinkling and sparkling. 'If that's the mood you're in,' she whispered, with a wink, 'what about her down in the garden?'

It had already occurred to him. For the saved, the more deadly the sin, the more revivifying the forgiveness. The crucifix too would thicken the odium. Jonathan would be liberated.

Attracted by her hate, Ampara had to hurry out to the terrace again. Getting up, he followed her and was just in time to witness a fascinating little drama down in the garden. Jonathan had come out of the house, carrying what looked like an envelope. He walked straight up to Miss Ripoll who was pushing the pram up and down, and held out the envelope, without speaking. She hesitated, but at last took it; whereupon Jonathan made quickly not for the house, but through the garden and out of the gate.

Ampara and Norman watched as Miss Ripoll stood for a full minute with the envelope in her hand.

'It's a letter,' muttered Ampara, in fury.

'A poem, I think.'

That was worse. 'A poem?' she repeated, choked with jealousy. 'Look, she's going to read it.' Had Miss Ripoll been about to slit the baby's throat, Ampara couldn't have been more shocked.

As she read it, Norman was so intensely interested he could feel the warmth of the sun on the paper. It was her perfume he smelled, not Ampara's. Again he saw the cluster of tiny moles on her right wrist, and the curve of scorn on her lips.

Slowly, with a thoroughness that had Ampara gasping, she crushed the paper in her hand and then, after holding it for a few seconds, threw it among some bushes.

Norman saw it lie on the dry earth, like litter. She hates him, he thought. She really does hate him. Why? Could it possibly be because of his political views? He maintained he had none, but that of course meant he supported the regime in power. Any communist would despise him for that, and look upon him as an enemy. But her hatred did not seem to have a political source.

Beside him Ampara was laughing and jingling her necklace.

Fifteen

Asleep at last, her mouth bunched in a sad little pout, the baby looked so like her uncle that Montserrat, despite her perturbation, could not help smiling. Parking the pram in the shade of the carib tree, she then did something she could not have explained and which had her smiling again. Though there were other chairs, one at least more conveniently placed, she chose the one Jonathan had been sitting on; his book and sun-glasses she moved to another. Then she lay back, with her eyes closed, but opening them now and again to stare, in amazement, at the ball of paper under the bushes, and to remember another like it, three months ago, floating in the pond in the quadrangle at Barcelona University.

A bird kept chirping in the tree above her. Yes, she admitted to it, she was probably blaming Jonathan Broxmead for all the anxieties and despairs of the past few weeks. If she did not have someone to blame, apart from herself, she might not be able to bear them. The trouble was, it meant that that someone must inevitably be involved with everyone and everything that she loved. It was easy enough to imagine Jonathan joining in her mother's lamentations about Jordi and Montserrat's membership of the group.

Moreover, he was such a challenging contrast to Tomas. It wasn't the latter's medium height, black hair, sallow skin, and brown eyes that made him so different; it was above all his fierce air of dedication that, like a sickness, had made his eyes moist and remote, and his face lean and consumed with hate. Tomas did not love freedom; rather he hated those who suppressed it, and those who submitted feebly to that suppression. Similarly, he did not pity or love the poor who lived in hovels and caves; he hated the rich, the corrupt, the inefficient, the indifferent, and the selfish who perpetuated poverty. Among them he included the whole hierarchy of the Church. When Montserrat had once confessed to him that her dearest ambition was to be married in the Abbey of Montserrat, in the presence of the Black Virgin, he had snarled – his lips had actually been drawn back from his teeth, as if the expression had been practised in front of a mirror – that she wouldn't be marrying him in that case.

Like Tomas, Jonathan Broxmead never went to church; but if invited he would go, dip his fingers in the holy water, genuflect before the altar, kneel, and appear to pray, all out of a barren politeness. Thus, too, might he visit the fun-fair at Tibidabo and look at himself in the distorting mirrors. Were Tomas ever to enter a church for her sake, the water would scald his brow, and the wood of the praying board crush the bones of his knees.

Even in their lack of humour they were quite dissimilar. It seemed to her that Jonathan seldom laughed because in every situation his first and instantaneous concern was to protect his dignity. Therefore he was in himself comical, and in other circumstances she would certainly have found a great deal of amusement in observing him. Tomas, on the contrary, never laughed or made others, even those who loved him, laugh. Laughter, he had once cried, was surrender.

Now he had gone, to Russia it was believed. Always an admirer of the communists, and a disparager of his own group of feeble idealists, his desertion had not really surprised her, though it had shocked and disillusioned her almost as much as Jordi's arrest a week ago. For weeks he had missed his university classes, and had not been seen at the bookstall where he worked in the afternoons. Then had come the telephone message, arranging the meeting in the quadrangle, at noon. The clock had been striking as he approached, and still striking as he walked away, leaving her with the letter in her hand. It was strange that both he and Jonathan should be alike in this, that they preferred to express their emotions in writing. Tomas had never told her he loved her; nor did he in the letter. He had merely asked her to go away with him, and ask no questions. While the clock struck, and the pigeons strutted about at their feet, and the goldfish gleamed among the dusty lily leaves, and students behind them and above them on the sunny balcony had chatted and laughed, he had waited for her answer, looking more ill and fanatical than she had ever seen him before. She just said: 'But, Tomas, I can't.' He had turned and hurried away, his shoulders hunched, in some peculiar relief. Going through the pend he had not once turned round, though a swarm of nuns in their wide black gowns had forced him to pause to let them pass. She had crushed the letter and dropped it into the pond. She could still see it floating there.

If she could forget Tomas, and Jordi, and her mother, and Francisco, and the others in the group, now like her in hiding, it would be pleasant enough living here, in this shady spacious garden so close to the sea that the cries of bathers could be heard. She did not write or paint but she loved children, and in looking after three or four of her own she could find more happiness, and certainly more fulfilment, than she had ever done in politics. Her mother, who knew her so well, had told her so often; so, latterly, had Jordi.

She heard someone come out of the house and approach her. She did not need to open her eyes to know it was the American, Ashton. Joking, or perhaps only half joking, Bridie had whispered: 'It's obvious Maddy's finished with him, Montsy. But he's all right, as men go. Consider his advantages: he's American; he's well-off, or will be; he'll take you far enough away from Spain to keep your heart from breaking; he's not a Catholic, but properly handled he could be turned into one, or into anything else, for that matter. Yours for the taking, Montsy: a dutiful, adoring, dollar-ful Yank.'

His rather stealthy self-sufficient walk, physical neatness, pleasure in bright clothes, and air of having performed cruel mysteries, had reminded her of a *torero* she had once met.

As he passed the pram he went on tiptoe, with his fore-finger at his lips.

'Asleep at last?' he murmured.

She smiled.

'It's sure a pity you've got to sit here, while the rest of the world's enjoying itself down on the beach.'

In the silence they heard laughter and shouts and the roar of a speed-boat.

'D'you swim?' he asked.

She nodded. She was, in fact, a keen and expert swimmer.

'Water-ski?'

'No.'

'I didn't think you would. Damned show-off of a sport, I always think. Get out of it, here I come, give me the bay to myself. Do you mind if I sit beside you, Miss . . .? Say, what is your name?'

'Ripoll.'

'Your Christian name, I mean. Mine is Norman.'

She was reluctant to tell him. 'Montserrat.'

'Ah yes, the jagged mountain. You sure look the prettiest jagged mountain ever I saw. I'm going to call you Mont-serrat.'

She tried to be fair. This treating of her as if she was a shy, lonely, not very intelligent child could simply be his usual American way of talking to a foreigner. But there seemed to her something disingenuous about his whole manner.

'It's a pretty village all right,' he said. 'Ruined a bit by all the tourists and painters. You'll have been here before?'

'No.'

'You'll not have seen the church yet?'

'Only from the outside.'

'It's not much from the outside. It needs repainting badly. But it's got a magnificent altar, all gilt and silver. It must have cost a fortune. You'd wonder where a small fishing village found all that money. I'm not a Catholic, Montserrat, but I'm a pretty sincere Christian. I guess, too, you don't wear that crucifix just for show. You're following me? I talk too fast and I slur my words disgracefully, like all Americans. Can you make out most of what I'm saying?'

She nodded.

'Good. You see, it's like this: Protestants go into St Peter's in Rome, into the Vatican, into the church here. And what do they see? Evidence of immense wealth. But what do they remember? Well, they remember having seen in the south of Italy, and in the south of Spain, thousands of peasants living not far above the level of animals, because of age-old poverty. So what do these Protestants with their social consciences say? They say why not spend the money on relieving hunger, eradicating rickets, and spreading education. It's a point of view I have a lot of sympathy with myself. Now what's your answer, Montserrat? Of course, I know this was one of the reasons why the Reds burnt so many churches and slaughtered so many priests during the Civil War. That's a long time ago, though. What's your opinion now, as a progressively minded student who wears a crucifix round your – if I may say so – very beautiful neck?'

He laughed, and stretched out his hand till it hovered over her knee. His face, brought close to, struck her as wearing a mask of synthetic sincerity. His voice was full of gurgles of friendliness.

'But don't give me that old answer about this life on earth

not mattering a scrap of paper, the important thing being a sure front seat in heaven. To tell you the truth, I don't see cardinals and bishops denying themselves much, and nobody's going to convince me they'll not be in the front of the queue outside the golden gates. They'll be there, with their privilege tickets.'

This time, under cover of earnestness, he did lay his hand for a moment on her knee. 'I sure hope what I'm saying's giving no offence? If it is, just say so, and I'll shut my big mouth. It's just that I'm genuinely interested.'

Then he lay back, with legs outstretched; his foot almost touched hers. Hands clasped on his stomach, he waited for her answer. She felt surer than ever there was something about him not only insincere but threatening. She had struck Jonathan; this man she would never strike, even if he were to betray her. As she realized that, she sat amazed and troubled, slowly blushing. Sheltering her had been against all Jonathan's principles and instincts; yet he was doing it, as steadfastly as if it was a duty. He had given up his room for her, and he had resisted his sister Isabel's insistence that she should wash the baby's napkins. She remembered what he had written: 'That you should find it hard to endure my presence, or nearness, does not surprise me, though I regret it a great deal. You will have no reason in the next three or four days to complain.'

'That's right, Montserrat,' murmured Ashton. 'Take time to think about it.'

But she had been thinking about it for years, without ever finding an answer to satisfy herself. For Tomas it had been as simple as it had been for Christ: a society in which children went hungry while bishops prayed in copes sparkling with gems was evil, false, and doomed. But its destruction had to be carried out by men and women, standing proudly on their feet, knowing clearly what they were about, not by mumbling dim-minded petitioners on their knees.

'And don't tell me,' said Norman, laughing, 'that it's a private matter for one's individual conscience. It ain't, you know; it's a matter for the whole world.'

'I can't tell you anything, Mr Ashton.'

'Oh, not Mr Ashton, please; Norman, surely. And why can't you tell me anything?'

'Because I do not know anything.' Because I am a mumbling dim-minded petitioner on my knees.

'Didn't you say you studied philosophy?'

'I think it is wrong for money to be wasted if people, especially children, need it for food. But I think it is right that cathedrals and churches should be grand and beautiful.'

He laughed, again like a patient good-natured teacher dealing with an awkward, diffident child. 'You're trying to get it both ways, just like a woman, I guess. Who, by the way, is Jordi Puig?'

The question was asked without a change of tone; his smile could not have been more benign, nor more venomous.

Against her will almost, her hand crept up her breast to touch the crucifix; her heart turned cold and heavy. She thought, well, if I am taken back to Barcelona, I may see my mother, if I'm lucky or if my captors are merciful.

She could not hate him or those to whom he might betray her; they were not worth it. Was this pride, as destructive as Tomas's, and not humility?

She wondered how he knew about Jordi. On his way from Port Bou had he seen the name chalked up in some remote village? She did not think so; in Barcelona, yes, he might have seen it, though even there it had been blanked out in most cases by the youths of the Falange, who had painted in indelible black their own emblem beside it.

Then she remembered the leaflets in her suitcase. She had noticed Ampara on the terrace outside the bedroom window. The girl had taken a spite against her, and perhaps had expressed it by rummaging contemptuously through her belongings. She had come across the leaflets and had shown them to Ashton.

As if to answer her thoughts he took one neatly folded from his breast pocket, and held it between fingers and thumb as if it was a thousand-dollar bill.

'I thought communists were too cunning,' he drawled, 'to leave incriminating evidence lying about.'

She did not know what to do or say. Trapped, she found herself wishing Jonathan would come.

'Anybody could have *one* of these,' he said. 'They're slipped under doors and pushed into your hand in the street. But hardly a couple of dozen. What's poor old Jonathan going to say when he finds out he's harbouring a seditious female in his house?'

She remembered her mother's weeping when she had heard of Jordi's arrest, and her own sickness of heart when she had been told that he had been beaten up. This teasing light-hearted conscienceless voice treating it all as a joke was the voice of half the world, and of more than half of Spain.

'Now if you and I were going to do a deal, isn't it lucky that communists reject morality as bourgeois nonsense? I advise you to get rid of the rest of these, by burning them. This one I could be persuaded to give back.' Then his voice grew a little more serious. 'I would like to warn you. Burn them quick. It was Ampara gave me this. Apparently she hates your sweet guts. Luckily for you she can't read, but I guess her boy-friend can, or his superiors at least.'

She had never really thought she would be able to escape to Perpignan; she had never convinced herself she wanted to, not while Jordi was in prison, her mother ill, and the others at their posts.

He turned peevish: 'Say, you ain't under torture yet, you know. I'm asking you nothing. I'm interested in helping you.

It happens to be my duty to try and prove to you how wicked and contrary to Christ communism is.'

'I am not a communist,' she said.

His hand was again hovering, small, neat, strong, but somehow callous and stupid, like the mind controlling it. She had met such minds before. Lust was at their core. Disguised as solicitude, as enthusiasm for art, as godliness, as sympathy, it kept giving itself away. In Jonathan Broxmead it was timid, in Norman Ashton hypocritical; timidity was less culpable than hypocrisy. Was that the measure of the difference in her attitude towards the two men? Hardly, for she wished more than ever that Jonathan would come.

The hand descended and clung, almost visibly aching in its effort to pretend to be forgiving, compassionate, and helpful. It was the lust her flesh felt; his face, beaming above the bright blue tie, and his eyes appealing like a dog's, reeked of it. From the soles of her feet to the roots of her hair she shuddered with revulsion. Yet, as Bridie would have said, all that was happening was that a young American, in appearance personable enough, and in morals fairly typical, was trying to blackmail her into allowing him liberties that all over the civilized world were surrendered for a cigarette or glass of champagne or a smile. The trouble was, Montserrat would find it hard to allow her own husband those liberties, even if the Abbot of Montserrat himself had married them.

As his hand shrank back it seemed almost maimed by the virulence of her disgust, though she had not moved an eyelid or uttered as much as a gasp. He fondled it with his other hand, rubbing each finger tenderly. A kind of blankness came over his face. He was like a child that had been refused something on which he had set his heart and to which he felt he had a right; in a few moments he would start yelling with rage.

Then Ampara came into the garden, carrying a basketful

of washed clothes. The clothes-line was near the bushes where Jonathan's letter was lying. As she hung up a napkin, she turned, peg in mouth, and stared at the two sitting side by side like friends. When the basket was empty she looked about her and then began to pick up pieces of litter, among them the crumpled letter. These she put into the basket.

Montserrat jumped up and ran forward. 'Excuse me,' she cried.

Ampara glared at her. 'What do you want?'

'My letter. You've picked it up.'

'I picked up rubbish, that's all.'

'That's it in the basket.' She made to take it but Ampara prevented her.

'What do you mean, it's yours?' shouted the maid. 'So you're for claiming the muck in the garden too? Well, I can't say I'm surprised.'

'I don't know what you're talking about, Ampara.'

'Don't you? So you think you're too pure to wash shitty napkins, do you?'

Flushing, Montserrat heard the American laughing behind her. 'Give me my letter,' she said.

Ampara was as loud, vulgar, and vicious as she could be. 'Come and take it,' she said.

Now the baby was crying.

Why the letter had become important to her Montserrat could not have said. In a burst of anger she seized the smaller woman, pulled her round, and snatched the letter out of the basket.

'You bitch,' screamed Ampara, and with all her force struck Montserrat on the right breast.

Almost fainting with pain Montserrat crept slowly back.

Ampara, tearing her hair, screamed like a madwoman. Ashton's laughter too hardly sounded sane.

Dazed with pain and shame, she found herself at the pram. As she stooped over it, Ashton came up behind her, touched her ever so lightly on the hip, whispered, 'Jordi,' and then, before she could even turn, went off with his *torero*'s swagger.

Ampara, her hair all about her eyes, had gone rushing into the house.

Alone again in the garden, Montserrat, one hand on her breast, pushed the pram with the other, and began to sing softly and agitatedly the Catalan hymn for singing which, a few weeks ago, a number of youths had been attacked by the police in the Palacio de Musica in Barcelona. Only the baby heard, and was neither inspired nor pacified.

It would be a relief to be arrested. When she came out of prison she would be able to give up with honour what Tomas had called the childish whimpering for the too expensive toy, freedom. She would find someone not afraid to marry an ex-jailbird, have children, and, to add Bridie's advice, grow content and fat.

She was weeping before she knew it, and stopped when she knew. One thing she had promised herself: not one of them would ever see her tears.

Sixteen

When he had rushed away after handing her the letter Jonathan had intended to make for the headland four miles away, over the high red cliffs, and brood there in loneliness disturbed by not so much as a gull; but less than two hundred yards from the house, he stopped, stood squirming in the golden dust, and then went hurrying back, to perch on a boulder on the beach not far from the gate. He picked up a piece of wood sticky with salt and held it across his knee as if it was a gun. If he were to see a posse of policemen making for the gate he would not trust himself to sit there quietly and mind his own business. No, he would more than likely charge forward brandishing his weapon and defying them to lay a fascist finger on her. All, including Montserrat, would stare at him as if he was as mad as Quixote.

To hate and fear violence as he did was not necessarily to be civilized; it might merely be a consequence of his pathological squeamishness about being touched by or touching another person. That slap he had given Norman, for instance, had hardly been any more painful than those Isabel gave little Linda in motherly playfulness. Yet every time he thought of it his bowels ached.

The blow Montserrat had given him was different. He had indeed touched her as she bent over the pram, but not mischievously, not in any spurt of lust; in fascination rather, in wonder at her soft beauty, in gratitude to her for existing, but above all in an attempt to lessen the terrifying feeling that though he could speak to her, hear her, eat at the same table with her, look at the same blue sky, bathe in the same sea, and listen to the same bird in the same green bush, nevertheless she was inaccessible. Shattering that remoteness more effectively than his timid nudge had been her blow. When he had got into the house and had seen in a mirror the marks of her fingers on his cheek, he had wished that they would never fade.

Though remote, she was everywhere, and as near as his own hand. This bit of wood slimily green at its end, this boulder, these pebbles and ripples, this whole human village, every leaf of olive and vine, contained her, and were new and glorious. Staring at the church tower, with the clock saying a quarter to twelve, he was aware that a miracle, or succession of miracles, like the continuous ebb and flow in atoms, was happening to him; to him, Jonathan Broxmead, who on his last visit to the church had come out disillusioned afresh because the priest, with only five old women to preach to, had once or twice negligently belched.

It was no use urging his unworthiness. He could not stop that transfiguration which began with himself and spread to the slimy wood, to the boulder, to the pebbles and the ripples, and thence across the ocean embracing all Africa and all Asia and the entire world.

'I only met her last night,' he whispered aloud, 'and in a week or so she will have gone and I shall never see her again. I know nothing about her except that she is beautiful, has a brother in prison, a mother ill, and a dead father who was a lawyer. Perhaps she has a fiancé, though she wears no engagement ring. She despises me, with good cause. Little wonder the three Scottish girls laughed when they heard my name; not it, but I, the whole insignificant ego of me, is ridiculous. What worth am I? She will not be in Perpignan a week before she has forgotten me forever. Why then do I sit here and allow this feeling of unlimited spiritual riches to grow in me, as if I had been given a touch infinitely better than Midas's; what I touch remains itself, but with its beauty revealed as never before.'

Thus the reasons he produced to stop the transfigurations kept them going.

He was in love, and yet, in the letter, he had undertaken never to go near her again. He foresaw ahead of him a week of joy and agony not alternating, but simultaneous.

Then Norman came out of the gate, rather exaltedly, as of course he must if he wanted people to believe in his own peculiar conversion. In everything he did now, even in the coming out of a gate, he must convince the world that God smiled on him particularly, that he had been chosen.

So have I been chosen, thought Jonathan, I too have the world to convince.

'Norman,' he called.

Norman, surprised, turned and came over to the edge of the road. 'What are you doing there?' he asked.

'Listening to the sea.'

'And what have you heard?'

'Wonderful things.'

Norman laughed. 'Had any good slaps lately?' he cried. 'Sorry, Jonathan. I've just been having a chat with the beautiful new nursemaid.'

Thus Norman too became transfigured, atrocious joke, askew bow-tie, and all.

'Interesting girl,' he added.

Jonathan smiled at that so lovable understatement. 'What did you talk about?' he asked.

'Oh, religion mostly.' He put his hand into his breast pocket and half took out what seemed to Jonathan a bank note. Though the gesture appeared to confirm what he had always believed, that those who pressed closest to God's elbows were equally pushing in the scramble for worldly pelf, Jonathan did not this time feel contempt. He felt pity instead. After all, he *had* struck Norman.

'Why don't you join us at lunch?' he said.

Norman glanced at his gold wrist watch. 'I'd like to, Jonathan. But I guess I had better go find out what Maddy says.'

'Norman, I'm sorry I was so rude last night.'

'About God being love, you mean?'

'No, about Maddy.'

'You can make up for it, my friend.'

'How?'

'By helping me.'

'To do what?'

'To carry out God's wishes.'

'That is rather an extraordinary assignment, Norman. Just what is it that God wishes?'

'I told you. I didn't come back here of my own volition. I was sent back. For one purpose only. To marry Maddy. For a start you can help by telling me what sort of a man this Lynedoch is. A Scot, you said?'

'Yes, from Glasgow.'

'He can paint. I'll concede him that. Has he got money?'

'He's very poor.'

'Wealthy connections, though?'

'I doubt it. I believe his father was a plasterer's mate, whatever that may be; and I gather his mother was a charwoman.'

'You're kidding.'

'No, indeed.'

'Then I guess he must be the handsomest guy in the world.'

'Quite undistinguished, I should say.'

'With a personality like a fire-bomb?'

'He may have, but so far he's struck me as rather dull, and commonplace.'

'Then how come Maddy's so sold on him?'

'I'm afraid I can't answer that, Norman.'

'You're her twin, man; you should know.'

'Well, he's rather a remarkable painter. He's got talent, which you and I lack. When she was five Maddy told me she was going to be a great painter. Now she knows she isn't.'

'But she thinks this guy Lynedoch might be?'

'It's possible she thinks so.'

'Of course it's a thousand to one that he'll turn out a flop.'

'Yes, I would say so.'

'In which case she would walk off without the slightest compunction. So you've got to help, Jonathan, not only for my sake, and Maddy's of course, but also for this poor guy Lynedoch's. Put it this way: which of the two, myself or Lynedoch, would you rather have your sister marry?'

'Neither of you,' would have been the truthful answer. Instead he said: 'I don't see things or people with her eyes, Norman.'

'But you'll help me?'

'I'm afraid I'd rather not interfere.'

'Listen, Jonathan, it could be that in a very short time you're going to need my help.'

'What do you mean?'

Norman walked away.

'I object to that remark, Norman.'

But what Jonathan objected to most was that Norman had noticed no difference in him.

Lunch was at half past one. He waited until a quarter to before returning to the house. That Midas touch, or glance, went with him. Even the ants in the garden which previously he had watched with melancholy as illustrating the futility wrapped in enigma that so much of life was, were now seen to have some purpose dear to themselves and even some individuality. One, overburdened, came to a twig over which it painstakingly tried time and again to drag its offering for the community; eventually it failed and scurried away to pick up something else to offer.

He could hardly bear to turn round the corner of the house and come upon her; it would be the joy outdazzling all others, from which indeed they took their source; thus, he imagined humbly, might the mystic enter the presence of God. And it was such a joy, heart-splitting and eye-blinding. Yet all she did was sit in the shade and read. He thought his ecstasy was bound to surge out and infect her; but no, she merely turned a page.

Going into the house, it seemed to him an incredible happiness that she should be sharing it with him for a whole week and perhaps longer. On any of these chairs she might sit, over these tiles she would walk, in this passage she might brush past him, on this towel she would dry her hands, and at this table she would sit and eat.

He had been rejoicing over the table for half a minute before he noticed that only three places were set. Shocked, he stared at the blank cloth where her knife, fork, and spoons should have been; blanker than this would life itself become after she was gone. More alarmed and bewildered than angry, he hurried into the kitchen, to find Ampara standing by the cooker on which sizzled and steamed an array of pots.

'Ampara, why are there only three places set?' he cried, in his stammering Spanish.

She stuck out three short thick fingers. 'You,' she said, 'Señorita Maddy, and Señor Lynedoch. Three.'

'You're forgetting Señorita Ripoll.'

'No, señor, I am not. I tell you this, if she stays in this house then I shall go. I am to make her bed for her. I am to tidy her room, which is your room. I am to wash the napkins, though it is her job. Am I to cook for her too, and wash the dishes she has dirtied?'

'Of course you are. She is a guest.'

'She is not a guest. She is a servant, like me. I shall tell you what she is.' She told him. It was a word he had never heard before, but she made its meaning unmistakable.

He was so shocked he could scarcely breathe.

'All morning she's done nothing except push that pram up and down.' She imitated sarcastically. 'And she's to get a thousand pesetas a month, while I that does all the work get eight hundred. But that's not the important thing.'

'And what is the important thing?'

She stood on her toes to yell it at him. 'The important thing is that a woman like her ought not to be allowed to make a donkey out of you. Where women are concerned, señor, you're a booby. Hasn't she got you writing letters to her already? If you can't look after yourself somebody will have to do it for you. I gave her something she'll nurse for a long time; and if she's not careful I'll give her another just to make the pair.'

He became lost in that welter of furious Spanish. It seemed, however, that she had attacked Montserrat in some way, whether with words or blows he couldn't tell. His scalp tingled with horror.

'Hold your tongue,' he shouted. 'I won't have you speaking like that. I won't, I tell you. What have you done?' In his rage and anguish he lapsed into English.

'It's for your own good, señor. She's a bad woman. Did Señor Norman show it to you?'

'Show what to me?'

'The paper.'

'What paper?'

She fished it up from her bosom and handed it to him. It was warm from contact with her. He did not hide his distaste.

'Yes, it's filthy all right,' she said bitterly.

As he read it he became quiet and perplexed. 'Where did you get this?' he asked at last.

'In your room, that's now her room.'

'Have you been searching through Señorita Ripoll's belongings?'

'I am not a thief, señor. They were in the wastepaper box.'

'They? This is only one. Where are the others?'

'There were two. Señor Norman took the other.'

So that was what Norman had had in his breast pocket?

'Isn't it filthy, señor?'

She had whispered a word that denoted sexual vice. He was amazed that she, however envious, could believe Montserrat capable of such abominations. He was given an insight into not merely her nature but all humanity's. He felt little repugnance, but much wonder and pity.

'How do you know, Ampara?'

'Señor Norman told me. Of course I didn't let him read it all to me. I'm just a servant with rough hands, but I go to church and pray to Our Lady.'

For what purpose had Norman so obscenely deceived her? If it had been to protect Montserrat surely there had been no need to blacken her character. It must be that he was not well mentally: God was lust, not love.

Jonathan read it again. His hands trembled. Joy in Montserrat's presence in his house was deepened by the necessity now of protecting her.

Ampara pressed close, snorting with disgust. Beneath her pale blue uniform dress she wore nothing but pants and brassiere; this was in defiance of his orders, given through Maddy, that she should wear an underskirt, however hot the weather.

Then she giggled; though sound and grimace were horrible they were as feminine as Montserrat's loveliest smile. His old prejudices swirled up in him like heartburn. Wonder and pity were submerged in that sourness; but only for a few seconds. Whatever happened between him and Montserrat, even if nothing did, he would never be the same sour and stunted person again: the long frost was over.

'Women you know are better,' she whispered. 'You can trust them.'

He had to be careful. She must not be antagonized. It was possible she had another leaflet hidden in her room or on her person; she must be prevented from showing it to Pedro. Though oafish he was good-natured and once or twice had revealed surprising Catalan sympathies; but he was ambitious and only too ready to run with information to his *jefe*.

'This is a mistake,' he said.

She drew back. 'What do you mean, a mistake? Didn't I find them in the wastepaper box?'

'Yes. Because I put them there.'

'You, señor?'

'Yes. They were given to me in a café by a fisherman who was drunk.'

She laughed in such a way he knew she hadn't found them in the box at all, but more likely in Montserrat's suitcase.

He wheedled: 'I'm surprised at you, Ampara. I thought you were a good-hearted woman.'

Relish for this flattery struggled in her with jealousy of Montserrat. 'I'm good-hearted to those that deserve it,' she said. 'Think of that poor baby. Will Señora Reeves be pleased when she finds out her little darling is being looked after by a woman who carries a bundle of those about with her? Don't be taken in by the crucifix, señor. All the prostitutes in Barcelona wear them.'

'A bundle?' he repeated. 'You said there were only two.'

She poked him in the ribs. 'You should know, señor. It was you the fisherman gave them to.'

He felt sure there were others. She had been rummaging through Montserrat's things. She deserved dismissal, but instead must be placated. He thought of raising her wages to a thousand pesetas, but such an offer of money made now might insult her. A more personal sacrifice was required.

He approached her. 'I don't know why we're making all

this fuss about her,' he said. 'She's not going to be here for long. When the baby leaves she'll leave.'

'And maybe Señorita Maddy one day will leave too?'

'Yes.'

'Which would leave us in the house alone. What would the old women and the priest say?'

Though she was enjoying every word and every deepening shade of his blush, they would not be enough. Therefore, closing his eyes, he put his finger-tips on her shoulders, and stooping, with an involuntary sigh, touched her brow lightly with his lips.

At the same instant a pot boiled over, with a fierce hissing. There was a smell of Brussels sprouts, and also of onions off Ampara's breath. Then everything in his mind collapsed as she seized him by the head, pulled it down, and was kissing him voraciously on the mouth when after a tap on the door Montserrat came in, carrying the baby under her arm and a teated bottle in her hand.

'I beg your pardons,' she said and hurried out again, after putting the bottle down on the marble with a clink that seemed to Jonathan strangely sad and musical.

The baby, refreshed after her sleep, had been gurgling merrily and clutching at sunlight. She wailed at being whisked away from that interesting scene in the kitchen.

Ampara released him. 'That should cure her,' she cried. 'That should give her something to think about.'

It had certainly given him something to think about, more indeed than he could cope with: implications darted about in his mind like fish in the sea, with sharks among them. That afternoon he must get rid of Ampara so that he could search her room. As for Montserrat, his first impulse was to rush up to her and, on his knees almost, explain how that kiss had come about, but he decided that to do so would be to break the promise he had made in the letter. In any case, he was in love with her, not she with him. For all she cared he could kiss every servant girl in the village, and sleep with them too. Perhaps she thought he did.

Norman did not come back with Maddy and Lynedoch for lunch.

'Yes, we met him,' she said, so curtly that Jonathan asked no more.

She and Lynedoch, indeed, were so intensely irritable with each other they seemed like lovers of long standing. Their knowing the weak spots, to wound precisely there, struck Jonathan as uncanny. Evidently there were more ways than one of falling in love.

At lunch he dared not look higher than Montserrat's hands. Watching them was excitement enough.

In the kitchen Ampara sang with unusual fervour.

'What's the matter with her?' asked Maddy.

'She often sings,' murmured Jonathan, embarrassed.

'Yes, I know, but not as if she was on the stage of the Liceo. Listen to that.'

They listened. Jonathan heard the tinkle of Montserrat's spoon, and also of course Ampara's triumphant bellowing.

'Like a female ape's mating song,' said Maddy.

Did Montserrat chuckle, ever so faintly? He dared not look. Ape-like, he crouched over his plate.

'The woman's enjoying hersel',' said Lynedoch dourly. 'Good luck to her. She's been stuck in all morning, washing and cooking; not like us.'

'I suppose you were enjoying yourself up at the church, trying to talk to those old women?' said Maddy.

'Aye, I was.'

'You didn't look it; but then I'm beginning to think it's true what they say about the Scots, that the next worse thing to enjoying themselves is to look as if they were enjoying themselves.'

'What about yourself? You're still furious.'

Jonathan glanced across at his sister. He had never seen
her more brilliant, or more tender. She was, he realized,
furiously happy. Never had her resemblance to himself been
more disconcerting.

'Small wonder if I am,' she cried. 'He's decided, Jonathan,
not to paint the church after all.'

'That's no' quite true, Maddy. I've said I'll paint it later.'

'There's plenty of time,' murmured Jonathan.

'Yes; yes, there is,' said Maddy, laughing. 'You see,
Jonathan, there's something else he's set his heart on painting.'

'Now, Maddy, I particularly asked you no' to mention it
till I've had an opportunity to discuss it privately.'

With deliberation she turned and gazed at Montserrat.
'He wants to paint you,' she said.

Jonathan had to risk a look. Though smiling, she was, he
felt sure, deeply unhappy. He could see no sign of a blow on
her face, but he imagined he saw her wince as her own arm
brushed against her breast. He yearned and ached to help
her, but had to sit silent and aloof.

'I'm sorry, Miss Ripoll, it's been sprung on you like this,'
said Lynedoch. 'I wanted to talk to you about it first. You've
got a beautiful, very expressive face, but it's no' just that;
you're like what I imagined Spain to be. I canna express it in
words. I think I could in paint.'

'For heaven's sake,' cried Maddy, 'call the girl Montserrat, both of you.'

'If she doesn't mind I'd be pleased to,' said Lynedoch.

Jonathan found Montserrat staring at him. Nothing,
nobody, would ever part him from her, he cried within;
outwardly he put on a stuffy frown.

'I do not mind,' she murmured.

Maddy put her hand on Montserrat's. 'You've not to be
thinking I don't want him to paint you. You'll make a
wonderful picture.'

Jonathan simply had to mutter: 'Indeed.'

'No, what's exasperating me,' explained Maddy, 'is that he's been talking so enthusiastically about painting the church, and now, just like that, he's for postponing it.'

'No, I am not, Maddy. You ought to know that most of a painting is done here, and here.' He touched head and heart.

'No, I didn't know, John. With me it starts when I lift up the brush and stops when I put it down again.'

'I think about a painting for years.'

'But not this one. You've not known Montserrat days, never mind years.'

'Call it inspiration,' he said, laughing. 'But she hasn't said yet she's willing.'

'Yes, I am willing. I am very pleased. But I may not be here long, you know.'

'You'll be here till the baby goes. That should be long enough, though this is a painting I wouldn't want to hurry, or to dally over either. Would you care to start this afternoon?'

'I ought to warn you, Montserrat,' said Maddy. 'He's liable to give you a squint, representing some obliquity in your soul.'

Jonathan had never felt so excluded in his life, not even in his childhood days when Isabel, to discipline him, had shut him out of rooms and games.

'No squint,' promised Lynedoch. 'But it might not be altogether happy.'

'If it is to represent Spain,' said Montserrat, 'it should not be altogether happy.'

They were quiet for a few moments, so movingly had she spoken.

Maddy glanced at her curiously. 'Does the political situation not please you?'

'It does not please me very much.'

'I see. You know, I've wondered about Bridie and Terence

coming here, depositing you, and then fleeing off again. Is your name really Ripoll?'

'Maddy, don't be ridiculous,' cried Jonathan.

'If I remember rightly Terence addressed her as Puig, or something like that.'

'He was drunk.'

Maddy laughed. 'Yes, he was. Don't mistake me, Montserrat. I like mysteries.'

'I would prefer to paint you in the garden, if you don't mind,' said Lynedoch. 'Just for an hour at a time.'

'I'll chaperone you, Montserrat,' said Maddy. 'You know what these painters are. It's not to be a nude, is it?'

'Maddy, please,' murmured Jonathan.

'It's all right, Jonathan. We'd give you fair warning, so that you could sit upstairs in the study with the persianas down, and a bandage round your eyes. Jonathan's a terrible prude, you know, John. He once came home unexpectedly—'

'Maddy!'

'And found Ampara in his shower. Her own was out of order, or so she said. He didn't recover from the shock for months.'

'Maddy, our guests aren't yet accustomed to your sense of humour.'

'That would be a good painting too,' said Lynedoch, 'Ampara as a nude. She's so strong. She represents Spain too. Small breasts and muscular buttocks. Picasso used a model like her once.'

'Muscular buttocks,' repeated Maddy, enchanted. 'A painter's phrase. Jonathan, please corroborate.'

Humiliation rising like a tide now choked him. He had to jump up and rush away, not knowing where to go, and finding himself a minute later in the bathroom.

There he stared desperately at himself in the mirror, not out of the old narcissism, but in amazement and horror that though in love with Montserrat he was evidently still the same person whose limitations and lack of surprises had so often dissatisfied him in the past. The miracle that had turned a spoon in Montserrat's hand into a thing of beauty and wonder, and had given glorious significance to an ant carrying a fragment of fly, had been powerless upon him.

He knew what would redeem him: her love. Yes, if she loved him as he did her, then there would be a metamorphosis to dazzle the world. But how could he expect so beautiful, fastidious, sensitive, and intelligent a woman ever to see a spoon in his hand as the marvel it had been in hers? Every movement of her face and body, every tendril of hair, every particle of her, was precious. Who would ever think so of him? Not even Ampara.

Seventeen

Not even Maddy could be let into the secret. Therefore he had to search Ampara's room by himself, thoroughly, for if any leaflets were there he must not miss them. He went down on his belly to peer under the wardrobe and stood on a chair to examine its top. He ventured into the drawer where she kept her clean if shabby linen, and also into the drawer where she had stuffed her unwashed underclothes. He lifted her pillow and fumbled under her mattress. Her suitcase of cheapest fibre was unlocked, so he did not have to use the assortment of keys he had come prepared with. It contained, among a miscellany of special personal treasures, a holy picture of Christ with bleeding heart exposed, a passport photograph of Jonathan himself, and a small bottle of perfume Maddy had lost months ago. There was another picture on the wall of a pink-faced Madonna with the aurora borealis for a halo; he investigated to see if the leaflets were concealed behind or within it. Then he went into her little bathroom and, after poking among stubs of lipstick, depilatories, and nauseous little wads of cotton wool, lifted the lid of the cistern.

Not a leaflet was to be seen anywhere.

It looked as if only two had been taken from the bundle; he had one, and Norman had the other. Of course Ampara might have another stuffed down her bosom, but he had deliberately stood near her before she went out, listening carefully, and he had heard no crackle of paper. She had obviously been wearing her brassiere with the foam rubber, a type hardly suitable for the insertion of additional extraneous objects. He felt fairly sure that as far as Ampara was concerned all was safe in the meantime. Norman was now the menace. Even if he surrendered the leaflet or had it forcibly taken from him, he could still make a report on it to the police. The old unsaved Norman, guitarist and digger in out-of-the-way sexual sewers, would have wished Montserrat good luck, for the price of a blown kiss; but now that he believed himself appointed to look after the Lord's interests, chief among which was the extermination of communism, he might well consider it his duty to have her arrested.

Jonathan was about to denounce with disgust at so brutal and cowardly a betrayal when it was put to him, by the tart voice of truth, that if Montserrat had been a plain fat woman, with thick ankles and sly conspirator's eyes, he himself would never have let Bridie and Terence persuade him to take her in. Shutting the door in her face might not be quite so heartless as informing on her, but it wasn't very far off it. To the ugly as well as to the beautiful, prison was cruel and degrading.

As he debated thus, in doubt and shame, he could hear them laughing in the garden as John Lynedoch made his first sketches of Montserrat. He wanted to go out and join in, to look at those sketches and, however inspired they might be, find them incomparably inferior to the original. But he could not; as usual in this game of life he was the child forbidden to take part, as a punishment. In vain he tried to read Proust, to listen to Beethoven, to look at an album of famous reproductions, and even to make corrections in the typescript of the few pages of his second novel. In the end he just sat and listened to the laughter, smiling at Maddy's, raising his brow at Lynedoch's, and wondering at Montserrat's. Then, suddenly, someone else's intruded, at which he frowned grimly: Norman's.

He hurried out, to protect her. She sat isolated, with a bushful of yellow roses behind her. She wore a white dress. Lynedoch was working with a rapid assurance, astonishing and impressive. Jonathan was not surprised when, glancing at the canvas, he found those preliminary strokes vivid and magnificent. In drab slacks and shirt Lynedoch was radiant. Maddy, in sky-blue blouse and fawn slacks, was dimmed by comparison; yet she watched his every movement with a strange, shining fondness. Montserrat herself, dearer than ever, her gifts of beauty, dignity, and courage never more conspicuous, was nevertheless seen to be ordinary and therefore attainable, in a way that moved Jonathan to happiness and relief.

Norman, however, was not pleased; he looked let down and disgruntled.

Jonathan lost no time in taking him aside. 'I'd like a word with you, Norman,' he said, quietly.

'Sure. I hope, though, you're not going to show me the door?'

'That depends. Let's stroll about the garden.'

They walked to where the ants marched in long lines like an army campaigning across a desert.

'Depends on what?' Norman kept asking.

'I'll come to the point at once. I want that leaflet.'

Norman grinned and touched his breast pocket. 'What leaflet are you talking about, Jonathan? In our business we get through thousands in a season.'

'Don't prevaricate. Ampara has confessed. I consider it outrageous of you to encourage her to rifle a guest's belongings.'

'Now look here, Jonathan, I encouraged her to do no such thing.'

Jonathan had promised himself to remain composed and to overcome Norman by a display of moral superiority; but a storm of anger began to rise in him.

'You have the leaflet,' he said, in a voice that startled him, so full of hate was it.

Norman too was startled. 'Well, what if I have?'

Jonathan shot out his hand. 'Give it me.'

As if to duck a blow Norman suddenly crouched down, and picking up a stick began to disorganize the ants' supply service. 'I guess God's as far above us in intelligence and purpose as we are above these tiny fellows,' he said. 'I ain't got it, Jonathan. Sorry.'

Jonathan crouched beside him. 'Where is it?'

'I did the decent thing and flushed it down the lavatory.' He noticed some ants wandering off course and clambering up over the hillocks of Jonathan's bare toes. 'That's the truth, Jonathan.'

'There's a Bible in the house. Will you swear to it on the Bible?'

'On a stack of Bibles. Ain't they biting?'

Jonathan became aware of his ant-infested toes. Yes, they were biting. He brushed them off.

'If I'm sceptical,' he said, 'it's because you've not distinguished yourself for truthfulness in this affair. Why did you lie to Ampara about the leaflet?'

Norman laughed. 'Now I thought that was real quick-wittedness. I remember her boy-friend's a civil guard. A man's got to be pretty careful in a situation like this. It could be Miss Ripoll deserved the benefit of whatever doubt there might be.'

'What kind of doubt are you referring to?'

'Grow up, Jonathan. That was a piece of sedition, that leaflet, worth two years in jail.'

'According to Ampara, you led her to believe it contained pornographic filth. Why?'

'Jonathan, you know Ampara better than I. Isn't she like a terrier for persistence? Well, can you think of anything more likely to put her off the scent, and keep her off it?'

They rose at the same time. Norman brushed a few ants off himself, and then off Jonathan.

'Now that I've helped you, Jonathan,' he said, 'in this matter of the leaflet, maybe you'll help me. I got eyes. It's true Maddy's wrapped up in this guy Lynedoch.'

'She appears to be.'

'I'm pleased you like it no more than I do, Jonathan. But here's our hope, is Lynedoch wrapped up in her? I doubt it, I very much doubt it. It's my belief he'll grow tired of her in the end.'

'How far off is the end?'

'Not so far off as you'd think. His father may have been a plasterer's mate, but he's a proud guy.'

'Proud?'

'Wouldn't you be? You said yourself he's got talent, a lot of talent. He'll get tired of us all. We'll be too small for him to waste his time on.'

Jonathan was flabbergasted. To discard a little pride was good for one's soul, but to tear off every scrap was to stand pusillanimously naked. He could not believe Norman was sincere; this was another outcome of his religious eccentricity.

'I don't ask you to take my side or anything like that,' said Norman. 'I know that wouldn't help. I just want you to let me keep coming round.'

'I thought you were returning to America.'

'Sure. I am. But there's such a thing as coming back.'

'Would that be wise?'

'There's one thing you're forgetting, Jonathan. Do you know what that is?'

'What?'

'I'm in love with Maddy. Now don't smirk. You've got a face that's sure suited for smirking, but don't, please, this once. I love her. You said, for a joke I guess, that you love this Spanish dame. Well, I'm not joking. I love her, and I want her. I'm prepared to wait for twenty years, and more.'

Cautiously Jonathan said: 'Isn't it nonsense really to speak of her and Lynedoch in such terms so soon, when they've known each other only a day or so?' Longer, however, than he'd known Montserrat: time might in the end test and defeat love, it had nothing to do with its birth. 'However, I have your word of honour you have disposed of that leaflet?'

'I told you I flushed it down the lavatory.'

'And you promise not to tell anyone about it?'

'No, I haven't said that, Jonathan.'

'Then you must say it.'

'Hold your horses. I've no right to interfere in politics here.'

'Quite so. Therefore you must keep your mouth shut.'

'Sometimes by saying nothing you're interfering.'

'No glib equivocations, please. I must have your sworn promise.'

'What if I can't give it? This is the central problem of our times, Jonathan. You and I can't solve it standing here. Whatever can be said against Spain it's a Christian country. If thugs like Puig get their way it would be handed over to atheistic communism. That must be prevented at all costs. The cost might have to include the handing over of Miss Ripoll and her sort.'

He was so earnest he didn't notice the fury gathering on Jonathan's face. Therefore he was astounded when the front of his shirt was grabbed and hauled up out of his trousers.

Jonathan ground out, between his teeth: 'If you're the means of one hair of her head being harmed I warn you, Norman, I shall pursue you to the ends of the earth if need be, and make you rue it bitterly.'

Annoyed rather than frightened by this ridiculous excess of passion, Norman tried to grab his shirt back without adding to its disarrangement. 'What's she to you, anyway, Jonathan?' he cried. 'As far as politics are concerned, aren't you a eunuch, and proud of it? And as far as lots of other things are concerned too, including, if I may say so, women. Look what happened when you tried to give her a fumble. All you got was a swipe on the face.'

Anger and guilt provoked Jonathan into lies and, more fatally, into truth. 'No more filth, I warn you,' he said. 'Miss Ripoll is the sister of a friend of mine.'

'Even if she is, which I doubt, you still tried it on. I saw you.'

'Her name is not Ripoll, it is Puig.'

Norman was interested. 'Say, Puig was the name on that leaflet. Is she his wife?'

'No.'

'His sister?'

'Yes.'

'So she's one too.'

'One what?'

'A communist.'

'She and her brother are not communists; they are Catalan patriots.'

'Sure, they do wear the most respectable disguises, don't they? You're the kind of sucker they like to get their claws into. You know, I felt there was something about her I didn't trust. The crucifix didn't take me in. The women are worst. You think she's sweet and chaste and holy. I tell you she'd stand by and see torture done, with a smile. You need protection, Jonathan.'

Then they were interrupted by Maddy calling: 'There's tea if anybody's interested.'

'Sure, Maddy, thanks,' shouted Norman.

He made to go but was held back by a frantic clutch at his shoulder.

'There you go again,' he said. 'You've damn near torn it. This a disease you got, Jonathan? Time was you'd as soon have stroked a rattlesnake as touch another person, but now you're for grabbing like a kid at apples. Repression bursting out, I guess. No kidding, Jonathan, you and I have got to get down on our knees and pray together. But now it's tea-time.'

He hurried away to where the clinking of cups could be heard, and laughter, and fussing over Linda; but Jonathan, with a great shudder, turned and went running out of the gate.

Eighteen

Dinner was just over. Maddy and Lynedoch were having coffee and liqueurs out on the terrace, Montserrat had gone upstairs, Linda fed and washed was asleep, Ampara was clearing the table, and Jonathan was moping in the sitting-room, when the telephone rang.

It was Bridie, so hoarse, Irish, and conspiratorial that he could scarcely make her out at first.

'How are things going?' she asked.

He decided to say nothing about the leaflets. 'All right, so far.'

'They aren't here. I daren't say much, for obvious reasons. It doesn't look as if our friend's arrangements will be able to be made from this end after all; you'll have to manage yourselves, as best you can, and the sooner the better. You understand?'

'I think so.' His heart was hopping in his breast like a frog, his hand holding the receiver sweated. He wanted to beg her to reassure him that Norman was wrong, Montserrat was not a communist.

'We can only wish you the best of luck. With a little ingenuity and pluck it shouldn't be so very difficult. Whatever you do, don't let her come back here. It would be useless. F. has gone away.'

She pronounced the last words so that they meant arrested. F. was Francisco, the man who had been going to send the messenger with a passport for her.

'You understand?'

'Yes.'

'It's up to you.' She sounded as if it could have been up to no one she relied on less.

'You don't want to speak to her?'

'No. I can't. I saw her mother this evening, half an hour ago. She seemed to me pretty ill. You'll have to lie. I couldn't. She'd see through me.'

Whereas I, he thought, am as opaque as self-interest, reinforced with callousness.

'Goodbye. Best of luck.'

'Thank you.'

Then she hung up.

'Who was that?' called Maddy.

'Bridie. Just to say they'd got back safely.'

'Good.'

From upstairs Montserrat asked, quietly: 'Did you say it was Bridie?'

'Yes.'

'Did she not want to speak to me?'

Slowly he went up the stairs to where she stood in the passage, wearing her white dress. He stopped a yard or so away.

'She sent you a message,' he said.

She spoke in Spanish: 'About my mother?'

'Yes.' He listened. Ampara was still bustling about from table to kitchen. Maddy and Lynedoch were having another of their rapturous arguments about painting.

'If you don't mind,' he said, in Spanish too, 'I think we should go into your room to talk about it. Or if you prefer we could go for a walk. You haven't been out of the garden all day.'

'Is my mother all right? Bridie promised she would telephone me about her. She must be worse.'

'No, no. She said your mother's a little better.'

'Is it true?'

'Yes, of course.'

She paused. 'If we go out, who will look after the baby?'

'Maddy will. You've not to think you're on duty for the whole twenty-four hours.'

'I'll get my cardigan.'

'One moment, please. In that letter I gave you a solemn promise, which I mean to keep.'

'It doesn't matter,' she said, rather sharply.

Downstairs on the terrace he found Maddy happily teasing Lynedoch, magniloquently tipsy with too much wine. Both of them immediately teased him about Montserrat.

'We've just been talking about the mysterious looks you keep giving her,' said Maddy.

Lynedoch nodded. 'Like young Lochinvar,' he said.

Maddy squealed with delight. Jonathan frowned.

'I committed it to heart,' went on Lynedoch, 'under the torture of the tawse.'

'Let's hear a verse, one that's appropriate,' cried Maddy.

Lynedoch leered with vinous stupidity up at Jonathan. 'The whole poem's appropriate. Listen:

'So stately his form, and so lovely her face,
That never a hall such a galliard did grace.'

Maddy clapped her hands. 'It's true, Jonathan. You and she make a really exciting pair, you know, she dark as Pluto's stallions, you fair as a Viking.'

His vehemence amused them. 'Please understand this,' he said, 'Miss Ripoll is nothing to me now, and never will be.'

Then he noticed that Maddy was staring past him, with a look of startled sympathy. He swung round. Montserrat stood, near enough to have overheard, though, smiling, she pretended not to. In white dress and pale blue cardigan she was so beautiful he could have wept.

'Thank you for looking after Linda,' she said. 'We won't be long.'

'Be as long as you like,' replied Maddy. 'Is there anything the matter?'

'No. Nothing at all.'

'Why should there be anything the matter?' demanded Jonathan fiercely.

'My goodness, why indeed? Sorry I asked. Have a nice time.'

As they left the house and went down the path he kept well apart from her.

The moon shone. It would be pleasant to walk along the cliffs away from the village. He asked her which way she preferred. She answered by making for the quietness of the cliffs.

They had walked in silence about two hundred yards when he drew closer so as to be able to speak with secrecy. There was no knowing what lovers or spies lurked amidst those shadowy olives and pines.

'Shall we speak in Spanish or English?' he asked, in English.

'Your Spanish is better than my English,' she replied, in Spanish.

'I don't think so. However, perhaps it would be safer to talk in English.'

'There's no one here.'

'You never know.'

They walked on for another hundred yards or so, again in silence.

'What did Bridie say about my mother, please?'

'She said she was a little better.'

'Do you think she was telling the truth?'

'Yes, of course. She didn't say very much. She seemed afraid to.'

'Did she say anything about Jordi?'

'No. But I'm afraid she did mention Francisco.'

'What did she say?'

'That he'd gone away. I think she meant he'd been arrested.'

She cried softly, and turning gripped him pretty much as he'd gripped Norman that afternoon. His heart fell as far as the bottom of the cliffs; his blood swished through his veins louder than the sea. This Francisco must be her sweetheart.

He tried to speak calmly: 'She said we've got to make our own arrangements. I understood her to mean about getting you out of the country, over the border, in any way we can.'

'No,' she said slowly, still gripping him. 'I must go back.'

'To Barcelona?'

'Yes.'

'She insisted you must not; and really I cannot allow you.'

'If they are all in prison, why should I not be there too?' She kept forgetting to speak in English.

'It wouldn't do them any good. It would make it all the harder for them, if they knew you were suffering whatever it is they are suffering themselves.' He groaned as he said that. 'Who is Francisco?'

'A friend of my father's.'

'But he must be an old man?'

'Quite old.'

Not therefore her sweetheart. He became resolute, keen-witted, defiant, reckless. Let the whole of Franco's police oppose, he would defy and outwit them.

'You have friends in Perpignan?'

'Yes, my aunt.'

'You would be safe there?'

'Yes.'

'Then we must get you there.'

At last she took her hand away. 'I've no right to let you become involved,' she said.

They had come to a point on the cliffs which was a

favourite of his, high above the moon-dappled sea, with pine woods behind on shadowy hills, and the lights of the village so far away that the music from the cafés could be heard only by straining. The world seemed to him vast and splendid, with innumerable opportunities for happiness, but just as many for disaster.

'Shall we sit down for a minute or two?' he asked.

There was a ledge like a seat with thin grass and flowers. He took off his fawn linen jacket and made it a cushion for her.

For that first minute he forgot everything, except the joy of simply sitting beside her.

'It's not too cold, is it?' he asked.

'No, no.'

He remembered Bridie's taunt about a warm-breasted woman. It was he who shivered.

'Tell me,' he whispered, 'did Ampara strike you?'

He thought she flinched and flushed in the moonlight.

'Did she?'

'Yes, but it doesn't matter.'

'It does, it matters a great deal.'

She was silent.

'Did she actually hit you with her fist?'

Again she was silent.

'I must know.'

'Yes.'

'My God!' Unable to express his horror and grief, he seized his head in his hands, and thereby recalled the strength of Ampara's hard fist.

'I think she was jealous.'

Incredulously he fancied there was a gentle lilt of raillery in her remark. He concluded he must have been mistaken; it was more likely to have been the preliminary to weeping.

'But she should be happy now,' she said. 'You have made it up.'

He was slow to realize she was referring, teasingly too, to that dreadful kiss. 'If you mean I have forgiven her,' he said, 'you are wrong.'

'It looked like it.' It was indisputable now; she really was poking fun at him.

'I had better explain from the beginning,' he said.

'You mean, from the time you found her in your shower?'

Girl, he wanted to cry, remember your situation: your are sought by the police, your brother and friends are in prison, your mother's very ill, you are friendless, your safety, God help you, depends on me. Laugh at me afterwards if you wish, spend the rest of your life in such laughter, but please wait until you are safe. Only then shall I be able to join in.

What he did say was: 'She came across a bundle of leaflets in your suitcase.'

'Yes, I thought so.'

'You knew?'

'It was foolish of me leaving them where they could be found. Mr Ashton had one. I thought that was how he must have got it.'

'How many are missing?'

'I don't know.'

'Well, the important thing is to prevent Ampara from showing one to Pedro. She had one but she gave it to me. I searched her room this afternoon. I couldn't find any.'

'But what is to prevent her telling Pedro about them?'

'She can't read.'

'But Mr Ashton must have told her what they're about.'

'No. For some reason which I haven't yet fathomed – he's an odd fellow, you know, and he's come back with some fantastic claim about being saved, apparently he met Frank Redhall the evangelist in Geneva. He always had a streak of sexual sensationalism in him, but now it's become vindictive through its admixture with religion.'

'What did he tell her?'

'That it was a pornographic joke. I hate to have to tell you this. It's rotten, disgusting.'

She was quietly laughing. 'A pornographic joke!' she repeated, and laughed still louder, until he was afraid she was approaching hysteria.

She controlled herself, and spoke calmly in Spanish. 'It's very funny,' she said. 'If you knew how innocent we've always been, as revolutionaries, if you've ever listened to someone who has been in prison for political reasons, if you have friends there at present, and especially if you knew how apathetic the majority of people are, you'd see how funny it all is. Mr Ashton must have a very subtle sense of humour.'

'No, he didn't say it as a joke. When I demanded the leaflet he said he'd got rid of it. I don't think he was telling the truth. In any case, he knows its contents, and as he thinks you're all communists really, and atheists, it's quite conceivable he will think it his duty to denounce us to the police.'

'Not us; me.'

'While you're here, I'm involved.'

'No.'

'Yes. I want to be. I have a plan.'

She waited.

'There are three Scots girls on holiday in the village. They're coming to tea tomorrow afternoon, so you'll meet them. They were supposed to be going to Perpignan today by coach, but they didn't; I don't think they could afford it. Now my proposal is that we take them, you and I, in my car. We'll borrow my sister Isabel's passport for you. She's dark-haired, and you could wear sun-glasses. It's hardly likely the police will look too closely at a car-load of British girls.'

'What if they do?'

'You can speak very good English.'

'With a Spanish accent.'

'Ah yes, but these Scots girls speak with a Scottish accent, which is a good deal stronger, I assure you. I'm sure it can be done.' Yes, if he kept his nerve and didn't make a mess of it.

'Will your sister be willing to lend her passport?'

'Why not?'

'I don't think she will.'

Neither did he. If necessary he would steal it.

There was a pause. 'You are right to be so anxious to get rid of me,' she said. 'Am I not what you English call the hot potato?'

There was something else; he had not yet made it clear about that kiss in the kitchen. 'You will appreciate I had to keep Ampara well disposed.'

'I hope you succeeded; you tried so hard.'

'I intended merely to look into her eyes and appeal to her decency. It was entirely her idea to grab me the way she did.'

'She is very strong.'

'Like a coal-heaver.' He uttered a long sigh. 'So that's it, I'm afraid. I'm sorry you have to depend on so feckless and unheroic a person as myself. I used to think I might turn out to be a writer, but all I knew was words; what lay behind them I had no idea; even now I've only got the dimmest notion.' Then he remembered he had left something very important unanswered. 'It's not true I'm anxious to get rid of you. The very opposite.' There was a lot more to be said, but this time, though he saw vividly what it was, he could not find the words.

They sat for the next minute or two in silence.

'I wanted to blame you,' she murmured.

He smiled. 'For what?'

'For everything. Jordi. My mother. Francisco. Everything.'

'You were right. Who represented apathy more?'

'No, that was not the reason.'

'What was?'

'I don't know.' She shivered.

He stood up. 'It's getting cold. Perhaps we should get back.'

He held out his hand to assist her. She took it but stumbled over some stones and fell against him, with a gasp of pain. Their bodies met, their faces; they could have kissed.

'What is it?' he cried.

'Nothing.' She laughed.

'You hurt yourself. Is it where Ampara struck you?'

'Yes, but it is nothing.'

He remembered what Ampara had said about a pair. It must be her breast. He had read somewhere that cancer could be caused in a woman's breast by a blow. Yet how could he ask? How could he help? How could he ease the pain and avert the danger? He must consult Maddy, even if it meant letting her into the secret.

As they walked back they heard from the village sardana music.

She stopped, let out a cry, seized his hands, flung them up, and, laughing, began to put one foot forward and then the other, in the steps of the sardana. Startled, he joined cautiously in, not sure what her purpose was: it could have been to demonstrate that her faith in her cause was not lost, or to defy her enemies, or to relieve the unhappiness caused by her brother's imprisonment and her mother's illness, or even to celebrate Jonathan's own absurdity; but when she began to sob too he saw that she was dancing, and making him dance, for all those reasons combined. Nothing he could have said would have comforted her, but the dancing seemed to. Therefore he danced as well as he could, declaring his love with his hesitant, inexpert feet. Her hair brushed against the stars, and beyond her bobbing ear the sea glittered. Perhaps it was making no difference to her who her partner was, but to him it was a joy so cathartic that he did not think he could ever again be arrogant, conceited, or aloof. Not towards her only, but towards everyone, except her persecutors, he would be humble, or would try to be.

Nineteen

At the last minute Katie decided to change the shade of her lipstick as it didn't go well with the big green dots on her dress. There was no hurry anyway, she said; if they never went it would be soon enough.

She had shouted it from the shower, gasped it as she fastened her brassiere across her fat breasts, and now she mumbled it in front of the mirror.

'Say whit you like, in a way we're lowering oorselves. I don't say we actually invited oorselves, but we pretty nearly did. That fellow that wouldna even speak to Peggy, him frae Glesca, why should we go to gie him a chance to apologize? Shouldn't he come to us, if an apology frae him is important; which it isn't? We're no' inferior; but we're different, and I for one am prood to be different. Watch how we talk, Peggy warns us. Why should we? The way we talk to oor folks at hame, no' to mention among oorselves, should be good enough for that shower of snobs.'

Peggy's reply was always the same. 'Speak for yourself, Katie. I'm not going to lower myself. Just the opposite. I'm going to show them, with no disrespect or unpleasantness, that I'm as good as any of them, especially that stuck-up bitch with the spectacles.'

'I don't see whit she's got to be stuck up aboot,' remarked Teresa, 'married to yon walking skeleton with the beard.' She shuddered, and then did it again to hear how opulently her new Spanish bangles and ear-rings jingled. She had on her best dress, with a floral pattern, all blue pansies, little red roses, and buttercups.

'As for watching how we talk,' said Peggy, 'you know fine what I meant.'

'Tell us again,' said Katie.

It was unbelievable, thought Teresa, how this trip abroad had brought Katie out of her shell in so big a hurry. A week ago she had been fat and shy, and afraid of men; yet she had been the only one walked home last night from the café. He had been a Frenchman with sideburns who had been able to speak as much English as she could French, but apparently he had kissed her hand good night. She had come into the room holding it out as if the kiss was sitting on it like a pet budgie. Peggy had tried to give her a row, but she had been too uplifted to hear it.

'Go on, Peggy, tell us again,' she repeated.

Peggy stood where nothing touched her. This wasn't only to indicate her independent spirit, but also to prevent damage to her flared yellow skirt, worn this afternoon for the first time.

'Do you remember old Mr Anderson, our English teacher?' she asked.

'Oh, him!' cried Katie. 'That old boozer. They say he still canna keep his hands aff the lassies.'

'He never laid a hand on me,' said Peggy.

Being Catholic, Teresa had gone to a different school. But she was fair-minded. 'You meet that kind everywhere,' she said.

'Naturally only them that are weel-developed,' said Katie, and laughed. 'Don't mind me, Peggy. I'm just kidding.'

'That Frenchman's gone to your heid, right enough,' said Teresa. 'There's nae need to be insulting.'

'I am far from being insulted,' said Peggy. 'Mr Anderson said we spend lots of money and time on our faces and our bodies, but on our minds, and on our tongues, we were willing to spend nothing. He said it was pathetic to see a girl dressed and groomed nicely, just like us at this minute, and then hear her give herself away the minute she opened her mouth.'

'He had an awfu' cheek saying a thing like that to you,' said Teresa.

'That's what I thought at the time, Teresa, but now I can see it was for our own good.'

'You're doing fine, Peggy,' cried Katie. 'Except maybe for "bitch" you havenae made a mistake yet.'

'And I don't intend to, all this afternoon. What you and Teresa do is your own business.'

'I see your point, Peggy,' said Teresa. 'But you ken me, I'm sure to put my foot in it. A' the same, if yous two can come to an agreement, I'm willing to have a bash.'

'My grannie was a lot aulder and wiser than Mr Anderson,' said Katie, 'and she used to say we should never try to be different frae whit we are.'

'And what, Katie, do you think we are?'

'Markers o' coupons.'

'That's what we do for a living, but surely you don't think it's the sum and substance of what we are?'

'You should hae been a politician, Peggy, like your faither. Do you know, Teresa, he wasnae very willing for Peggy to come to Spain, just because Franco's on the throne.'

'And yours, Katie, wasn't too keen because it's such a Catholic country.'

'Well, I like that!' cried Teresa.

They glared at one another in turn, Katie in her white dress with the green spots rounder than any leaves Peggy had ever seen, Teresa with her floral designs that Katie thought fitter for a girl of fourteen though Teresa was twenty-two with an Irish face into the bargain, and Peggy with her billowy buttercup yellow skirt that in the private opinion of her two friends made her dumpier than ever, particularly her football-player's legs.

Katie was first to giggle, Teresa next, and Peggy last. Then suddenly all three were in stitches and contortions and tears of laughter. That each took care neither dress nor coiffure suffered by no means meant the merriment was feigned or artfully controlled. It had happened often before.

'Let's bamboozle them,' gasped Katie. 'You talk posh, Peggy, I'll talk normal, and Teresa can talk in between.'

'In between's the hardest,' objected Teresa.

That set them off again.

Anyone seeing them cross the plaza arm in arm ten minutes later would have been struck by their determined demureness. Some youths whistled compliments that were properly acknowledged. At the stalls that sold straw hats, scarves, Toledo work, and brooches, the women attendants recognized them and called to them to come and buy, things were cheap that afternoon. Peggy responded with a quick proud smile, Katie with a hearty 'buenas tardes' that corresponded to 'guid afternoon', and Teresa, trying to strike a mean, simpered and flipped her hand in a gesture like a disintegrated crossing of herself. Aware of these deliberately different reactions, they made no comments: the enemy was too near.

Peggy carried the cake they had bought as an offering. She had been proposed for the honour by Katie, with Teresa an eager seconder. Even in the buying of the cake that morning they had differed: Peggy had wanted to buy an expensive one, Katie one no dearer than a cake they would have taken to friends at home, and it had been left to Teresa to suggest one at a compromise price.

'We're making this ridiculous,' Teresa had whispered in the shop.

Now as they entered the gate Katie remarked: 'Needs painting, don't it?'

'It's beautiful ironwork,' said Peggy. 'The Spaniards are famous for their ironwork.'

Like Teresa and Katie, she had been impressed by the iron spiders, beetles, and Don Quixotes in the souvenir shops.

'The whole hoose could do wi' a coat of paint,' said Teresa as, walking slowly, they came in sight of it.

'It must have cost a fortune,' said Peggy.

'Whit we don't know,' said Katie, 'is whether they own it or juist rent it. Maybe they aren't as weel-aff as they make oot.'

'They have a motor-boat and a rowing-boat,' said Peggy, 'as well as a car.'

'Nane of them seem to work,' said Katie. 'I thought you, Peggy, that's a socialist, would die rather than show respect to folk that live in luxury withoot working.'

'Respect's something I show to people,' replied Peggy, grandly, 'not to money, or to the lack of it.'

Tea, they noticed, was to be taken out of doors.

'To keep us oot o' the hoose,' whispered Katie.

Jonathan and Maddy, as host and hostess, were coming to welcome them.

'Don't be ridiculous, Katie,' Peggy whispered back.

Whatever the reason for tea being outside, Teresa was glad. Somehow she felt her shortcomings in the way of table manners and intelligent conversation wouldn't be condemned so much under trees and beside flowers.

Jonathan was dressed with more than usual elegance, in a cream linen suit, white shirt, pale blue tie, and pointed tan shoes. His sister, on the contrary, had on her most casual clothes, silken shirt and trousers to match, in a vivid golden colour.

Their manners corresponded to their dress, she at ease and gay, he grave and curiously anxious. As she shook hands with the tall fair-haired girl Teresa remembered what she had heard about her reputation with men, and of course she had seen her a few days ago going about with the grey-haired wealthy-looking Spaniard. A girl like her in Bridgeton, say, would have been called a tart; apparently if you were going to sin, best do it in style, disguise it in glamour. It was hard to believe she was her brother's twin. In appearance of course they were very much alike, but he was so unsexy as to be almost a pansy. Such anyhow was Peggy's opinion. 'Not that it's any business of ours; he was nice enough to us, or at least he tried.'

Here he was trying again, quite hard. It wouldn't have been so bad, thought Teresa, if they had had only him and his sister to contend with. But here were also the other sister Isabel, dark-haired, thin, tall, in a very short skirt and bikini top, her husband the bearded skeleton in bathing trunks and striped shirt, a handsome Spanish girl in a pale lemon dress, and last and worst of all Lynedoch, their fellow Glaswegian, tidier than at the church but glowering even more dourly. No, he wasn't quite last. There was also the baby Linda sitting up in her pram, so bonny and blonde and friendly that Teresa for one would have been glad to find refuge in prattling to and nursing her.

Peggy, with a nonchalance Teresa marvelled at, presented the cake. Katie, true to her intention, talked louder and more coarsely than Teresa had ever heard her before. Once or twice she hesitated, flushed, and frowned, as she endured the scowls of Lynedoch, the guffaws of Reeves, and squirming of Isabel's nose, but she did not, like Teresa, skulk behind a cautious taciturnity.

Teresa might easily have been miserable. Her ear-rings and bangles, which she had hoped would carry off the situation for her, were soon seen to be mistakes; she hated their every cheap, vulgar tinkle. Her hands too, for all her scrubbing and use of scented creams, were by comparison with Madeleine's and Isabel's, or even with Jonathan's, large and rough like a charwoman's; only Lynedoch's looked as coarse, but his had a recklessness with spoon, cup, and cake that hers, however she forced them, could not achieve. Moreover, though in the shade, she sweated, and was afraid she might smell. To make everything worse, her neighbour was Reeves, with his guffaws, his slappings of his lanky hairy thighs, and his beard into which lumps of cake kept vanishing with a relish that seemed to her quite obscene.

Yet she was not miserable. The baby helped, and the flowers; but what really saved her was her discovery that Jonathan was in love with the Spanish girl. Pansy or no, he could not keep his eyes off her for longer than twenty seconds at a time. Although he kept trying to be courteous, attentive, and affable to his guests, and succeeded pretty well, all the time something seemed to be worrying him, connected with the Spanish girl perhaps, for his frequent glances at her were anxious as well as fond. It could be she didn't return his love. Teresa would have sympathized with him if it hadn't been for his peculiar coldness towards the red-cheeked cheery maid, Ampara; the rest, even the snobby skimpy-breasted Isabel, were more amiable towards her.

Teresa watched the Spanish girl carefully. Ready to dislike and disapprove, she found she couldn't. Teresa herself was bony, with big staring eyes, and bad teeth; this girl had fine shoulders and bosom, white healthy teeth, and lovely brown eyes. So striking a woman, and so clever too, speaking English as well as Teresa herself, better even, had reason to be proud and superior; but she wasn't a bit, and though like the others she smiled as she listened to Peggy and Katie she did it without condescension. Two or three times it seemed to Teresa a stillness came into her eyes, reflective and sad, as if she was thinking about something or someone else.

The conversation turned upon their impressions of Spain. The bearded man asked. He had been inclined to treat their every gesture, sound, and movement as astonishing and amusing; they might have been the chimpanzees having tea at the zoo.

The funny thing was, neither Peggy nor Katie were offended by him.

'Of course,' said Peggy, 'we know it's not the true Spain you see, if you come as a tourist on a fortnight's holiday. For example, before we came, we read it was one of the poorest countries in Europe. Well, we haven't seen much sign of poverty.'

'It's mair likely to be found in the south,' said Katie.

'But surely,' said Isabel, 'you didn't come all the way from Glasgow to see poverty? I should have thought you'd see quite enough of it there.'

They both stared at her.

'Perhaps we need to see it to feel at home,' said Peggy, sweetly.

'Have you ever been to Glesca?' demanded Katie.

'Very briefly, on my way to Skye.'

'So you're juist judging by whit you've read in the newspapers?'

'Yes, I suppose so.' Isabel laughed. 'Are you denying it's a grim, grimy, drab, poverty-stricken place, large parts of it anyway?'

'Such as the parts we come frae?' asked Katie.

'I'm sure I don't know that. There is a belief of course that poverty's picturesque. I'm afraid I don't subscribe to it.'

'Glesca is grim and grimy and drab and poverty-stricken,' said Katie, 'but it's also honest and hard-working and guid-hearted and independent.'

'No doubt it is,' said Isabel, laughing again. 'But there are few places in the world less appealing.'

Again Peggy and Katie glared at her.

Madeleine intervened, bright with mischief. 'Well, John,' she cried, 'let's have your opinion. He's a native of St

Mungo's city, you know.' She spoke in an absurd imitation of a Scottish accent.

Peggy and Katie spoke simultaneously.

'So we were informed.'

'So your brither telt us.'

'Leave me out of it,' said Lynedoch.

Reeves guffawed. 'Spoken like a true, lugubrious Scot,' he cried. He turned to Peggy and Katie. 'Do you know what Jonathan said when I telephoned from Perpignan to say I was bringing a painter from Scotland to visit him? He said he didn't know the Scots ever produced any painters. What was it you said exactly, Jonathan?'

'Like Isabel, David, I was speaking out of ignorance. Therefore I should be obliged if you didn't quote me.'

'Nonsense. Our young friends are tough-minded. He said the Eskimos are more artistic than the Scots.'

'It's true,' said Lynedoch, savagely.

Peggy and Katie sat up, breathing angrily. Teresa, too, felt annoyed. Even if he was right he oughtn't to say it here, in Spain, among conceited English.

'The Glasgow Art Galleries,' said Peggy, 'happen to have one of the best collections of paintings in the world.'

'And it's a mair beautiful building,' added Katie, 'than any we seen in Barcelona, including that collection of sky-scraper tin-openers, the Sagrady Familiar.'

Despite Reeves's bellows of laughter, or because of them rather, Teresa felt she had to support her friends and her native city. 'Thousands queued up to see the famous painting of the Crucifixion by that artist wi' the long moustache, a Spaniard, I think he is. I went three times myself.'

Madeleine was laughing as merrily as her brother-in-law. 'Well, John,' she cried, 'have you anything to add?'

'Doesn't it speak for itself?' he said, as sourly as ever.

Isabel got up. 'So sorry we have to leave just when the

discussion is becoming interesting,' she said. 'But David and I promised ourselves another swim before dinner.'

Her husband rose too. 'Isabel's a regular water-nymph,' he said.

As one nymph to another, Teresa studied her. She did not seem happily married, despite having so adorable a baby. She belonged to a class that often went in for adultery and divorce. Both she and her husband looked as if they had already committed the one and were contemplating the other. She in particular was discontented. Even when she went over to the pram to kiss the baby she could not keep the bitterness out of her face. One thing was certain, with so small a bosom she hadn't nursed the baby herself, and perhaps, at its conception, hadn't loved its father well enough.

As soon as they were gone Peggy and Katie, in defence of Scotland, attacked Lynedoch. Teresa wanted to creep under the table and cover her ears. Maddy, on the contrary, laughed and kept beating time with a spoon on a saucer, as carefree as if she was water-skiing. Jonathan, though, looked as nervous as a football referee. Two or three times he raised his hand as if, indeed, to put a whistle to his mouth and blow for a foul, or whatever it was referees blew for.

'You don't know what you're talking about,' said Lynedoch, rudely. 'As a building the Art Galleries is a monstrosity. As for the paintings in it, how often does any Glaswegian go to see them? One wet Sunday afternoon per year; and even then he's far more likely to spend his time with the model boats and stuffed animals.'

Into Teresa's memory then tumbled the recollection of a visit with hundreds of other schoolchildren to St Andrew's Hall to hear a concert of high-class music played by a big orchestra. It had really been worse than in a dentist's chair. Most of the pieces, with no tunes she could make out, had gone on and on forever, worse than bagpipes. Dozens of children had read comics; those that had forgotten to bring one talked or yawned or put fingers in ears or shouted across to friends to say how awful it was. The conductor had been furious. Teachers had threatened to belt the noisiest when they got them back to school next day. Teresa had always been too timid to be ill-behaved, but all those ceaseless fiddles had been like great needles knitting her stomach and brains into tight knots.

As for the Art Galleries, on the few occasions she had entered them she had spent most of her time giggling at the naked statues in the hall, and at the cuddling going on in quiet corners.

Peggy answered him: 'Surely, Mr Lynedoch, you're not judging by the likes of us? In what country are girls with education and jobs like ours able to appreciate painting and architecture?'

'It's not a country any longer; it's not even a province; it's a parish, with a mentality to suit. Everything's judged by its value in money.'

'We're no more mercenary than any other nation,' said Peggy.

'And even if we were,' added Katie, 'isn't there an excuse? We've always been faur too poor. Noo that we're getting a wee drop prosperity it's grudged us. Whit gave you such a scunner, Mr Lynedoch? Wad naebody buy your paintings?'

'I took a scunner because we're a small country that has never had the humility to admit its smallness, or even to recognize it. We stand on our own midden and try to blow our heads off crowing. Who hears? Who notices? Not even the English. In the past it was a miserably small contribution we made to the world's art. Now we make none, and never will. How can we? We've neither faith nor interest. That's why I for one am never going back.'

'Weel now,' said Katie, 'that'll be a sad blow, but we'll just hae to put up wi' it.'

'So,' said Peggy, 'when you refused to speak to us at the church it was because you were ashamed?'

'That's right, ashamed to the bottom of my heart.'

So anguished his voice, even Peggy and Katie were silent. Teresa noticed he was younger than she'd thought. Perhaps he had some justification for his disgust; she supposed it might be difficult to earn a living in Scotland as an artist; and if she was one herself she would prefer to paint here in Spain where the sun shone and everything was bright and it was easy to relax. Certainly the altar in the little village church was more magnificent than any she'd seen in the biggest Glasgow chapels. She recalled having learned in history how, at the time of the Reformation, mobs, maddened by John Knox's furious heresies, had broken into churches and destroyed everything that was artistic and beautiful.

Ten minutes later, after some tepid conversation about various things, Peggy rose: 'We'll have to go now, Miss Broxmead. We would like to thank you and your brother for your hospitality.'

He had jumped up, strangely alarmed. 'No, you mustn't go yet,' he cried. 'Must they, Maddy?'

His sister smiled as if she didn't mind at all if they went. 'Perhaps they would like to see some of John's pictures?' she asked.

'Some ither time, thank you,' said Katie.

Peggy nodded.

Teresa was disappointed: she would have liked very much to see them, but was too cowardly to speak up.

'When do you return home?' asked Jonathan.

'On Monday,' said Peggy.

'You weren't able to get to Perpignan, after all. What a pity!'

'There are other years. Well, goodbye again, and thank you for the tea.'

She made a good departure, not too haughty, but not too meek either. Katie backed her up well.

Teresa lingered. She wanted to say the word that would sweeten all bitterness but did not know what it was. She could just grin, stupidly she felt sure. All her life she had been warned about that stupid grin, at home and at school. Nobody ever suspected it was caused by her good nature being in excess of her intelligence.

She made a point of shaking Lynedoch's hand. 'I hope you hae success wi' your painting,' she said.

To the Spanish girl she wanted to give her blessing. All she could think of to say was: 'I'm a Catholic too, you know.'

Then off she went after her friends, rocking on her high heels.

'Just a moment, please!'

She turned. It was Jonathan running after her. He looked as if he'd just discovered she had picked his pocket. But why should I think that, because he's so eager and anxious? Maybe I was wrong in thinking he's in love with the Spanish girl; maybe it's with me, Teresa McGuire. She could not help hinnying at the fantasy. A honeymoon with him, even in sunny hot-blooded Spain, might be the bluest of blue dos.

'There's something I want to ask you,' he gasped.

She giggled coyly. 'Me just?'

'No. All of you.'

Peggy stepped forward with aggressive friendliness. 'If you've come to apologize on behalf of your guest, Mr Broxmead, there's no need. We know you are not responsible.'

He dabbed his face nervously with his handkerchief.

'You mustn't mind poor Lynedoch,' he said.

They looked suspicious, ready to feel ashamed.

'Whit do you mean, poor?' asked Katie. 'Is there onything the maitter wi' him?'

Aye, that's it, thought Teresa, tears in her eyes already,

like all great young artists Lynedoch is dying from some
incurable disease, and his only spite against his native land is
that he'll never be able to return to it again.

'A few months ago his fiancée died.'

Peggy stared sternly at the sea, Katie puffed out her
cheeks, while Teresa let the tears slide.

'In Glasgow?' asked Peggy.

'Yes.'

They stood in silence, paying homage not only to the
dead girl but to their native city in which she had died, just as
their own husbands some day might die in it.

'What I really wanted to say was this: Miss Ripoll and I
are going to Perpignan in a day or so by car, and we would
be very pleased if you would come with us.'

'If this is just another way of apologizing,' said Peggy,
gently, 'I told you it's not necessary.'

'It's kind of you,' said Katie, 'but it wouldnae be convenient. Thanks all the same.'

Teresa would have liked to go, but she nodded loyally.

They were all taken aback by the desperation that came
into his face and voice. 'You must come with us,' he said.

Teresa wondered if it could be an attack of sunstroke.

'Must's a funny word to use,' said Katie.

'Yes, I know. I beg your pardons. Let me put it this way:
you would oblige me, and Miss Ripoll, very much indeed, by
accompanying us.'

'You'll admit,' said Peggy, laughing, 'that's a mysterious
statement, in the circumstances. I mean, how would we
oblige you?'

Did he want the three of them as chaperones, wondered
Teresa. Maybe Miss Ripoll's parents would never allow
their daughter to go on a journey alone with a young
man, even one like Jonathan, in whom all thought of sex
could be easily paralysed by one well-aimed dig of knee or
elbow.

'Yes, I agree it is rather mysterious. There is an explanation. I'm sorry I can't give it to you now. When we get to Perpignan I will.'

'Mair and mair mysterious,' said Katie.

Perhaps they're going to elope, thought Teresa.

'You're not smuggling, are you?' demanded Peggy.

He gave a sad frightened smile. 'Not really.'

'Not really? What does that mean exactly?'

'I can't explain.'

'In any case, Mr Broxmead, as Katie said, it isn't convenient. We've other things to do. Buenas tardes. Come on, girls.'

As she left him Teresa unobtrusively made the sign of the cross among the pansies and buttercups.

'Why was he so anxious for us to go wi' them?' she asked, eager to put forward her own theory.

'Don't you know?' cried Peggy.

They got ready to laugh.

'All girls together!' she said.

'What do you mean, Peggy?' asked Teresa.

'Surely you see?' She lowered her voice. 'He's a pansy, isn't he?'

Teresa shook her head. 'You've no right to say it, Peggy.'

'You said it yourself this morning.'

'But I hadn't seen Miss What's-her-name then, the Spanish girl.'

'What's she got to do with it?'

'He's in love with her, Peggy.'

Peggy and Katie laughed shrilly and clutched at each other. Teresa often came away with remarks like that.

'Laugh if you like,' said Teresa. 'I'm sure of it. Don't you see, he wants to elope wi' her?'

'And take us along?' cried Peggy.

'As far as Perpignan.'

'But, Teresa,' said Katie, when she'd stopped laughing,

'that one's too fond of himself ever to be fond enough of anybody else to such an extent you could say he was in love. Did you notice his finger-nails? They were manicured like a model's.'

'Maybe you're right, Katie.' But Teresa didn't really think she was right. It could be said about everybody in the world that he, or she for that matter, was too fond of himself to love someone else perfectly. You loved as much as you could, that was all.

'Cheer up, Teresa,' cried Katie.

She put one arm through Teresa's and the other through Peggy's. Droning through her nose like bagpipes, she swept them forward down towards the village.

The result was that within ten minutes they'd been invited into a café by three young Spaniards who had just arrived from Barcelona on scooters.

Twenty

In brassiere and pants, Maddy was brushing her hair in front of her dressing-table, and now and then glancing past her own enigmatically happy reflection to that of the dead girl in the portrait behind her, when a knock came to the door. She smiled, in affectionate derision, so easy it was to picture Jonathan's forefinger as cautious as if it had a boil on its tip. Once before he had blundered in and found her wearing nothing at all.

'Come in,' she called, at the same time, in that inventory of comparisons, putting down her own hair as more beautiful than the dark shopgirl's.

In he came, recoiling a little with an involuntary tut when he saw how little she had on. 'Really, Maddy,' he murmured, and picking up her green dressing-gown from the bed dropped it over her shoulders. Then he sat down where he could not see her still uncovered front in the mirror. 'I need your help, Maddy,' he said.

Margaret's eyes, she admitted, were more honest; but for that very reason less resourceful, less brilliant, and less interesting. She preferred her own.

'Is it Montserrat?' she asked, intending to tease.

'Why do you think that?' he cried, in alarm.

'I've got eyes, Jonathan.'

So had Montserrat: very dark, very lively, subtle, calm, but hinting at passion.

'And what,' he asked, 'have your eyes observed?'

'Well, to begin with, yours glued on her. But don't look so

appalled. Properly handled, she's just what you need to waken you up; though she may not be so easy to handle.'

'Please don't talk about her like that, Maddy. Don't talk about her at all.'

She decided she didn't approve of the humble, desperate quality in his voice; it sounded profoundly false.

'How can I help you with her if I'm not to talk about her? You can't kiss a woman, you know, without touching her. You can't eat a cherry without putting it into your mouth.'

'She has hurt herself.'

Maddy waited for the rest.

'I want you to go and find out how badly; if you think she should see a doctor.'

'When did this happen? I saw no sign of it ten minutes ago.'

'Don't ask. Don't ask anything. Just go and find out, please. She's in her room.'

'Why don't you go yourself?'

'Please go, Maddy.'

'Heavens, Jonathan, what a fuss! Now, do you mean?'

'Yes, now. I'll wait here.'

What in heaven's name could it be about? Had he, clumsily and voraciously, assaulted the girl? Less than an hour ago Isabel had been confiding to Maddy how disgusted she was with him for never showing any signs of normal sexuality. It had struck Maddy as odd, considering Isabel was herself embittered and almost demented about the effect on her of the most normal sexuality there was.

She stood up and wrapped the dressing-gown round her. 'Do I just walk in and announce: Jonathan says you've hurt yourself; how bad is it? Don't be silly. If you've gone this far, you can go a little further and tell me what it is she's hurt.'

He whispered.

It had been so low, strangled in modesty or shame, that she couldn't make it out. 'I didn't hear,' she said.

'Her breast.'

So he had been mauling her. It must have happened during their stroll last night. Yet when they had come in Montserrat had seemed happier than at any time since her arrival. She did not strike Maddy as the kind to cherish a manhandled and bruised breast.

She stared at him, in revulsion and love. Poor Jonathan, so over-civilized, pawing like an ape.

'For God's sake, Jonathan,' she said, and hurried out.

As she passed Isabel and David's room she heard them squabbling again. No doubt Jonathan had panicked too. There were more ways than one of mauling. In most cases fear was the cause. When she remembered John Lynedoch's painter's hands she felt safe herself.

She tapped on the door.

'Who is it?' Montserrat spoke in Spanish.

'Maddy. May I talk to you, Montserrat?'

Half a minute later the door was unlocked and opened just enough to let Maddy slip in. Montserrat, too, was wearing a dressing-gown, and seemed as sparsely dressed beneath it. Convenient, thought Maddy, for investigating injuries. On the dressing-table she noticed something new: a photograph holder containing two photographs, one of a smiling young man with piled-up wavy hair, and the other of a stout, middle-aged sad-eyed woman.

Linda, asleep, snuffled in her cot.

'Sorry to disturb you,' whispered Maddy. 'I won't keep you long.'

'It is all right. Will you sit down?'

'Thanks.' Maddy sat on the bed. 'I'd better go straight to the point. I understand you've hurt yourself?'

Montserrat blushed, all the way down to the sore breast itself. 'Who told you?'

Maddy rose. Sympathy was called for here, as well as

explanation; and perhaps some advice too. She went over to Montserrat. 'Jonathan,' she said. 'He's very anxious and, I suppose, repentant. He asked me to find out how bad it is.'

To her surprise, Montserrat, though still crimson, smiled. 'It is nothing,' she said.

'I must say you don't look very much hurt.' And thank God too, she added to herself; he made it sound as if you'd been the victim of savage rape. Now it was her own turn to blush. 'Your breast, he said.'

It would have been difficult to say whose face was redder; Maddy's perhaps, since it was fairer to begin with.

'Yes,' murmured Montserrat, and touched her right breast.

'Is it painful?'

'Not too much.'

'Do you mind if I have a look at it, just to be able to reassure him?'

With a gesture that, though as modest as could be, still suggested exciting potentialities, Montserrat untied the cord, and pulled aside the gown. The bruise was vivid. The breasts themselves, beneath the sleek fine tanned shoulders, were very pale, and on the right one the dark purple yellowish bruise was startling. There could be no doubt what had caused it. A fist. Fastidious though Jonathan might be about his hands, he had the authentic gorilla instincts in them too. Isabel need not worry. But all the same surely the fool could have found some other woman than this proud, intelligent, probably virginal girl to practise on?

'I'm very sorry,' she said. 'Are you sure it isn't painful? It looks it.'

The dressing-gown hid it again. 'A little. Not much.'

'It won't happen again, you can be sure of that.'

'Yes.'

They stood smiling at each other. There's a lot more in

her, thought Maddy, than any of us, especially Jonathan, knows. Can you, she wondered, in the end marry a woman whose breast you've bruised in the first caress?

For the sake of saying something she pointed to the photographs. 'Friends of yours?' she asked.

'Yes. My mother, and my brother.'

Your mother, yes; there's a resemblance. But your brother? An English girl would scarcely carry her brother's picture about with her. Did a Spanish girl?

'Are they still in Barcelona?'

'Yes.'

Again they smiled.

'Well, I had better go and let you get dressed,' said Maddy. 'You can be sure it won't happen again. He's really very contrite, as he certainly ought to be. You don't think you should see a doctor?'

'It's not necessary.'

'Well, we'll keep an eye on it.' She turned in relief to the door, but something about the other woman, she couldn't have said what, some very appealing quality, made her feel this parting was too cold and inadequate. It might be she would become Jonathan's wife. Therefore Maddy came back impulsively and embraced her.

The result was disconcerting. Montserrat, a moment before so composed and proud, burst into a passion of weeping.

For God's sake, Jonathan, what have you done? thought Maddy. No wonder you looked so humble and scared. First time out as it were you land yourself with this complex and lovely bundle of trouble.

'Now it's not as bad as that,' she said firmly.

But this was not weeping merely for virginity insulted. There was more to it than that. The poor girl, God help her, was perhaps in love with Jonathan.

Slowly Montserrat quietened.

'This job as nursemaid,' whispered Maddy, 'it's not all that important, is it? I mean, wouldn't it be better, in case of further complications, if you were to give it up? We'd all be sorry to see you go, Linda especially, but in the circumstances it might be the sensible thing to do. You could say' – she caught sight of the photographs – 'your mother's been taken ill.'

She felt her shudder.

'But if you like we'll leave it for tonight.'

'Yes, please.'

Back in her own room, Maddy grimly closed the door behind her. 'You're a brute,' she said.

'Is it very bad?'

'Bad enough.'

'Have you told her she must see a doctor? Isn't cancer sometimes started by a blow there?'

Their mother had died of cancer.

'That's an old wife's tale. Is it really her you're concerned about, or the possible consequences to yourself? I've advised her to go back to Barcelona.'

'But she can't do that, Maddy!'

'Yes, she can, and bloody well should. Either that or carry a cosh. How did you come to hurt her like that? You must have pawed her like an ape.'

'Do you think *I* did it?'

'Didn't you?'

'Maddy, I wouldn't hurt a fly that had landed on her.'

'Have I got this all wrong? I was sure you'd done it.'

'I?'

'For heaven's sake, Jonathan, you looked as if you had. And she didn't tell me otherwise. If you didn't, who did? It was done by a blow, and it looks very recent.'

'Is it very painful, Maddy?'

'It's by no means the most insensitive part of a woman's

body, Jonathan. There's a piece of information for future use. Well, who did it?'

'All right. I suppose I ought to tell you.'

'I should damn well think so, after deceiving me like this. She must have thought I was a half-wit.'

'Ampara.'

'What about Ampara?'

'She did it.'

'Don't be ridiculous? Why should she?'

'Absurd as it may seem, out of jealousy. It's nothing to laugh at, Maddy.'

'No, it certainly isn't. We ought to get rid of her. But she must have taken leave of her senses.'

'At the moment there are more important things to deal with. Maddy, I want you and John Lynedoch to do me a favour.'

'What kind of favour?'

'I want you to come with me and Montserrat to Perpignan, perhaps on Sunday.'

'To Perpignan? I don't in the least want to go to Perpignan; neither will John. He's just come from there. And, Jonathan dear, nobody will want to go with you driving.'

'You can drive, or John. That doesn't matter.'

'There *is* a mystery. I knew it. Out with it. Who is this girl? I've thought from the beginning it was just too convenient her turning up with Bridie and Terence the way she did.'

'If I tell you, will you give me your solemn promise to keep it to yourself?'

'That depends.'

'I hope I can trust you, Maddy. She is wanted by the police.'

'Good heavens! Whatever for?'

'Why should you smile, Maddy? Need you be so callous?

This is not a joke, I assure you. Montserrat belongs to a group of Catalans; they call themselves patriots, I suppose, print leaflets and distribute them, and chalk on walls. I told you it isn't a joke. Last week her brother was arrested. He'll get six years in jail. Is that a joke?'

'No, it isn't. So he is her brother?'

'What do you mean?'

'She's got the photograph of a young man on your dressing-table. She said he was her brother, but I didn't know whether I should believe her. After all, Jonathan, I don't think I'd carry your photograph about with me. Her mother's, too.'

'Her mother's?'

'Yes. Looks what Montserrat will become herself at fifty, fat and sad-eyed.'

'Does that matter?'

'Calm down. They'll hear you all over the house.'

'Her mother is ill, very ill.'

'Oh.'

'She doesn't know just how ill. Bridie warned me not to tell her.'

'Why?'

'Because if she goes back to Barcelona to see her mother she'll be arrested herself.'

'I see.'

'She's got friends in Perpignan. She must be taken there.'

'Suppose she was arrested, what would happen to her?'

'Surely what you saw a few minutes ago should give you an idea?'

'Yes. How horrible. But, Jonathan, what can we do? We daren't become involved.'

'There's something else. Foolishly, I admit foolishly, she brought with her a bundle of leaflets, dealing with her brother's case. Ampara got her hands on them.'

'Don't tell me she left them lying around?'

'They were locked up.'

'Most certainly we'll have to get rid of Ampara.'

'The minute Montserrat's safe. You know Ampara can't read. So she showed one of these leaflets to Norman Ashton. For some reason of his own, he misled her about its contents. But yesterday afternoon he more or less threatened to hand it over to the police. He said he might consider it his duty to do so, in his crusade against communism.'

'So she's a communist?'

'No, she is not. But let me warn you, Maddy, it would make no difference to me if she were.'

'What did he tell Ampara was in the leaflet?'

'He led her to believe it was one of those pornographic sheets. Yes, I thought that would appeal to your sense of humour, Maddy.'

'So you haven't learned yet, Jonathan, that something can be funny and heart-breaking at the same time? I think you'll learn it before this thing's finished.'

'You still have influence over Norman. I want you to persuade him to say nothing to the police.'

'If it was to save myself from going to prison, Jonathan, I'd refuse to ask any favour from him.'

'To save someone else we may do things we wouldn't do to save ourselves.'

'Doesn't it depend on who the someone else is? Montserrat's an interesting woman. I rather admire her, I think I could come to like her a lot, but at this moment I don't see why either I, or you, should risk going to jail for her.'

'I love her, Maddy.'

'You'll be having me laugh again. You're hysterical; God knows why, but you are. You've known her only a couple of days.'

'As long as you've known John Lynedoch.'

'Have I said I love him?'

'No, not said it. It's seldom said, Maddy. But you've let

him kiss you, make love to you, and most brazen of all you've not tried to hide from me the fact he's made love to you. Are you so depraved you cannot believe love can be innocent?'

'Not depraved, Jonathan; experienced. I'm afraid we can't allow you to get involved in this; it's too dangerous.'

'Who cannot allow me?'

'Not so loud. Isabel and I.'

'I used to have faith in your humanity, Maddy; I never had any in Isabel's.'

'Look how wildly you talk. She's your sister. You've known her all your life. She's in trouble too, you know. I was right. She's pregnant again.'

'How dare you compare them? Isabel is a denier of life, Montserrat welcomes and honours it.'

'I'm not going to argue with you, Jonathan, at any rate not here. Let's discuss the whole thing after dinner, with Isabel and David. I'm sorry for the girl, Jonathan. Anyone would be who saw her weeping as I've just done, anyone, that is, but a fascist bully.'

'Weeping? My God, was she weeping?'

'I'm afraid so. But for all that she is not our business.'

'She is my business, Maddy.'

'You don't make a human being your business just by saying so, Jonathan. She's got to acknowledge it, surely. And I'm certain she hasn't, not to you.'

'You're wrong, Maddy. She has; but not in words.'

'How then?'

'Laugh if you like. But she did acknowledge it.'

'Well, tell me how.'

'Last night, in the moonlight, we danced the sardana together.'

Maddy suddenly covered her face with her hands. He did not know whether she was weeping or laughing behind them. When he pulled them away, to find out, he saw that her face was streaming with the most genuine of tears; yet she was smiling.

Then they were interrupted by Isabel who came proudly in to get Maddy to admire her new dress.

Twenty-One

In his autobiography Frank had written:

> In those dark lonely days before I put my hand into
> that of the Eternal Father I found myself all too often
> stumbling into ditches of despair, into swamps of
> inertia, yea, even into those aforesaid pits of sinfulness;
> but from the blessed moment when I felt that life-
> giving clasp my vision was made as bright as the
> noonday sun, so that in every crisis of my life thereafter
> there were guiding signs, although in those first few
> months my eyes, dulled and sluggish so long with
> selfishness, were not quick to see them.

Norman was still at that stage; he knew the signs were there,
he kept proving they were, but his eyes were as yet not quick
enough to see them straight away. This was not necessarily a
disadvantage; it meant that most of the time expectancy,
naked and golden-haired, waited round every corner.
According to the experiences of most mystics and saints,
this period of promise was often more joyous than later
when the assurance of heaven was reflected in a plethora of
little daily earthly certainties. Then indeed the soul might
grow pampered and smug, requiring, according to some
authorities, a dose of sin to jolt it back into humility and
gratitude. As Frank had said, though not in the published
version, when the world sneered at a man of God because of
some backsliding it was demonstrating its impercipience;

only the enlightened and unprejudiced realized that the deed of worldliness, which more often than not took the form of some venial sexual transgression, was salutary, and at bottom in the Lord's service. Without it a man might well get to commit the most diabolical of all presumptions; which was to imagine he was purer than God Himself.

All those doctrines Norman appreciated and accepted. He rather looked forward to that exciting maturity when he might have to seduce some girl or consort with a miscellany of whores in order to refresh and consolidate his godliness; but he preferred not to hurry this development, and therefore was content at present to take for granted that signs were always prepared for him, even if he was not able to detect them at once. Meanwhile the uncertainty was delicious; it was as if he was standing, say, in the centre of Plaza Catalunya in Barcelona, surrounded by hundreds of strutting pigeons, one of which, apparently indistinguishable from the rest, was the divine messenger.

In this matter of Señorita Puig, the pulchritudinous communist, not knowing whether he was to denounce her or not, he waited, with an almost sexual expectation, for the sign. It was not of course a matter of passive waiting; no, he had to be on the alert, ready to use, as relentlessly as a bloodhound, his newly acquired sense of God to scent out the likeliest places. It was like one of those childhood games of hide-and-seek which you always won through cheating, but, just as in those games, much of the pleasure was in deliberately seeking at first in places where you knew the thimble, or in this case the sign of divine favour, was not to be found. In the end, at the ripe moment, when further putting off would spoil the fun of finding, you made straight for the spot, and there it was, surer and safer than money in a bank.

How rich that leisurely assured seeking made the simplest and commonest of experiences, and also the dullest and

most commonplace people. To sit at the café table, for
instance, and study every person at the other tables or
passing outside, as the possible conveyor of God's message,
was to appreciate the importance, from God's point of view,
of every human being, however ugly, lewd-minded, obese
and greedy by human standards.

This great-bellied bald old man in the white shorts who
crouched at the table nearest the beach was obviously in a
perpetual thin slaver of lust as he gawked at the women in
bathing costumes, particularly at those with bulging glittering bosoms and buttocks that, like masses of quicksilver,
kept having to be shoved in, only to ooze out elsewhere. His
own thighs were gross and hairy; he kept clawing them with
hands pudgy as paws. He clawed the right thigh with the
right paw, and the left with the left; never once, in the half-
hour Norman watched him, did he do otherwise. If, thought
Norman, the next time he scratches he breaks the sequence,
then it will be the sign, it will mean – well, what will it mean?
That I really do flush the leaflet down the lavatory, or that I
pass it on to Pedro, Ampara's boy-friend, thus appointing
him the Lord's agent? For of course this being allowed to
interpret the sign when given was the climax of the pleasure.
An atheistic intellectual like Jonathan Broxmead would
despise and condemn the whole process as characteristic
self-deception, carried to the point of corruption. But then
did not Jonathan and his like revile prayer in the same way?
Denying God, they denied not only the magnificent mysteries of God but also His innumerable little jests, of which
this attribution of divine purpose to a fat old lecher's
scratching of his thighs might well be an example.

Away from the sunbathers a father, grey-haired, sharp-
nosed, round-shouldered, and bespectacled, competed with
his twelve-year-old son at throwing stones into the sea. The
man strove to regain his childhood, the boy to celebrate his
coming manhood. Whose victory would provide the sign?

Half a dozen throws and the man was tired, his arm jerked in its socket, his body discouraged by the puny distance of those splashes. The boy mercilessly persevered; at last one of his throws fell beyond his father's furthest; he yelled and danced in triumph. His father, conceding victory not to his son only but to time that narrowed horizons, stiffened muscles, and reduced a stone's throw, slunk along the beach to where his wife sat, clad in a bright blue bathing costume. Not being so foolish as to challenge time, but rather being wise enough to reach an accommodation with it, she looked happier and younger than her husband.

Meanwhile their son kept throwing. Victory over the decaying generation was not enough; he wanted mastery over earth, sea, and sky. Among its other devilishnesses communism corrupted youth on earth and threatened to sully the glory of the stars. Therefore the boy's victory might well be an indication.

When he returned to the hotel there was a letter waiting for him. It was from his mother. As he went outside to read it on the terrace among the potted orange trees and palms, above the swimming-pool, he told himself that if she called him honey, say, five times, this would be the sign. But, before he had opened the envelope, he reproved himself for cheating: he knew only too well she would use the word a dozen times at least. Well then, what would be fairer, less obvious, more of a gamble? No, he decided, there couldn't be any sign in this letter.

He read it. Honeys were in every sentence, used not only as endearments, but as expressions of dismay, grief, worry, fear, and appeal. His father was dying. The doctor had given him no more than another year. And what, wondered Norman, glancing up to watch a tall dark girl in a red costume about to plunge into the pool, was so strange, or alarming, or even sad, about a doctor's warning that an old man of seventy-three might not make seventy-five? He had never

forgiven his father for being forty-seven when he himself
was born, or his mother for being forty-two. Between them
they had devoured his childhood. Dragging him about
Europe for years, from city to city, from hotel to hotel,
they had also deprived him of what even nigger kids had,
memories of home. If, as Frank had warned, he sometimes
presumed too far on his rights in relation to God the Father,
it was as a reaction against being done out of his earthly filial
rights, or at least of those that mattered most once childhood was past. Now in their old age his parents thought by
lavishing money on him – another cheque for five hundred
dollars was enclosed – to compensate for those early
depredations. His mother was really begging for forgiveness. She pleaded with him to come home as quickly as
possible, and if he brought with him as his wife or his
intended the fair-haired English girl he had written about,
she would be more than welcome too. Wouldn't it be
wonderful if, before his poor father passed on, he was able
to look on his grandchild? As for Norman's conversion, this,
as before, she mentioned briefly and evasively; it was as if
he'd taken to wearing a beard, an eccentricity not repre-
hensible but not to be rejoiced over either.

The tall girl had come dripping out of the pool. Her hair
lay across her face like seaweed. She tugged at her costume
in a contemptuous French way. Neither in her, nor in the
letter, nor in the cheque, was there a sign.

Remembering the crucifix round Miss Puig's neck, he
gazed over the bay at the church. The sun glittered on the
gilt hands of its clock, reminding him that even for those
seeking signs time laid traps. If he did not act soon she might
escape. Perhaps while he sat there she had already gone,
either back to Barcelona, to hide in some dark flat in a street
off the Ramblas, where rats, whores, and communists
lurked, or across the border into France. He felt sure that
if he were to know her, in the biblical sense of the word, he

would be the first man to do so; and it was a knowledge that every fibre of his brain, every member of his body, now began to ache to attain. Together they could expiate her sin, and expiation would be all the more complete if before it he had betrayed her to Pedro or his superiors.

It was the privilege of the saved to be allowed to use evil to drive out evil. Just so, to exterminate communism, hundreds of H-bombs might one day have to be dropped on Russia, and perhaps on China too. As Frank had said, only the hallowed thumb of one protected and guided by prayer could press without guilt. Here was the same problem on the individual level. Communism not only corrupted men's souls, it annihilated in them belief in God; therefore millions of lives might have to be sacrificed to wipe it out. Similarly to destroy it in Miss Puig would necessitate the despoiling and humbling of a proud, beautiful woman.

He became aware he was anticipating the interpretation of the sign before he had been given it. That could ruin everything. As a punishment, or warning, he began to do what he had been afraid of doing: think about Madeleine Broxmead.

He could not bear to think of her. Now when she began to slither into his mind and his desires, past all his defences, like the sea past the dam of loose stones he had watched some children make that morning, he had to jump up, hurry into the bar, gulp down cognac after cognac, conjure up the lewdest visions he could, and finally dash up to his room, where he kicked the cushion on to the floor, dropped to his knees, held his hands together as if manacled, and tried to pray. It was no use: Maddy, gay, splendid, laughing, loving, blasphemous Maddy, could not be exorcized. He sobbed recriminations at God, threatened to divulge His secrets, to blackmail Him, to disown Him, and expose Him as the Illusion that had mocked the ages.

This was the mood of blackest despair and treachery that

Frank had described so well. With courageous humour he had likened it to the rage felt by a child when it first discovers candies are not free for the taking, and the world is inhabited by a multitude of creatures as selfish and grasping as himself. In the old days, and indeed today in remote and medievally minded monasteries, holy men flogged themselves with whips to subdue that filthiest of rebellions. The peace that had finally come to the scourged and bloodied body must have been very like that which followed on sexual fulfilment. Therefore Frank had advised his Voices to get married as soon as possible, to enticing and kind-bosomed women so that, if ever that snarling beast of rebellion should seize the soul, loosening its grip would be less painful, and more legitimate, than by knotted cords. What though, Norman had inquired, if a Voice or someone aspiring to be a Voice should be overwhelmed while still single? Prayer under a cold shower, Frank replied, had been his method; others might have to devise their own.

After dinner he succumbed and telephoned Maddy, or tried to. It was Ampara who answered. In his disappointment he could almost smell onions.

'Señorita Maddy has gone out,' she said. 'With Señor Lynedoch.'

She laughed. His rage grew.

'And Señores Reeves?'

'They've not come back yet.'

He wondered if she was alone in the house, save for the baby. To go there and take her on Jonathan's bed might well give him all the purification he sought.

She seemed to read his thoughts. 'Señor Jonathan is here.'

'And the other señorita, she you attacked, Ampara? Has she gone back to Barcelona?'

She was surprised. 'No. She is on the terrace reading; with Señor Jonathan.' Then she became indignant. 'Pedro does not believe me, señor; about those papers, I mean. He says she is too well-bred a woman to have such things as you said. He says you must have been making a joke, but not a nice one, since you were speaking to a woman.'

Were there not many signs, all pointing to the one act? Let Ampara and Pedro work for God.

'Why not show one of them to Pedro?' asked Norman.

'I haven't got one. I gave it to Señor Jonathan.'

'Aren't there many others?'

'Pedro says I mustn't. He says it would be stealing. Besides, they're hidden away. He says something else too.'

'What else?'

'He says you are one of those with only one kind of thought in your head. When you see a cloud in the sky, or a flower in the ground, or writing on a piece of paper, that is what you always think of.'

Quietly, in English, he said: 'You ignorant bastard of a lousy servant woman, go to hell.'

'I don't understand, señor.'

To alienate her, he knew, was foolish and mischievous. God had probably arranged parts for her and Pedro. Nevertheless he found himself saying, in slow, faulty but intelligible Spanish: 'If you were the last woman left on earth, I wouldn't dirty myself with you.'

Her reply was cheerful. It was a word considered to be one of the filthiest in the language. Then she hung up.

He was left with the feeling that he had done something naughty, like a small boy in his parents' absence from home, and was waiting until they returned to find out and punish. Neither prayer nor reading the Bible eased his ache of guilt, with the result that by the time he fell asleep part of his anger had again been directed against the Lord who, like a neglectful parent, had stayed away too long and left him to get into mischief.

Next morning, after a successful prayer, he went back to waiting gladly for the sign. The forenoon he spent like any wealthy holiday-maker, swimming in the pool, drinking, and chatting with other guests, on whom he took care to make a good impression; indeed, he practised on them as a Voice, because as Frank had pointed out Voices were like ambassadors, who did as much of their most useful work over cocktails as at conference tables. He was earnest and jocular, talkative and attentive, courteous and tolerant. It was not an act, though he did now and then stand apart to inspect his performance. After all, the qualities he displayed were genuine, and would be his stock-in-trade as a Voice.

During the afternoon he watched the three Scots girls pay their visit to the Broxmeads. He knew they were Scots because afterwards in a café he heard them talking to three young Spaniards, students, apparently, of the British Institute in Barcelona, where it seemed the English they learned hardly helped them to cope with the peculiarities of the Scottish accent. The misunderstandings were numerous and hilarious; the chief one, though, was very quickly and capably cleared up, especially by the smallest of the three girls, who left the youths in no doubt that after the Coca-Colas would not come passion among the pines. No ill-will was felt on either side. More Coca-Colas were ordered, and further hilarity ensued.

After dinner, dressed all in white except for a blood-red bow-tie, Norman strolled through the village to where he could keep a vigil on the Broxmeads' house. Half an hour passed. He felt utterly alone; not even the Lord was with him. Then Pedro, in uniform, with his gun, slunk up from the village keeping to the shadows, and went through the gate. Five minutes later out came Lynedoch and yes, Miss Puig herself, glimmering in a white dress. They began to walk towards where Norman stood.

To hide from them he had to clamber up the bank and stand still among the pines. He did not venture far in, as he hoped to overhear what they were saying as they passed.

Lynedoch was speaking, with that loud careful self-important articulateness that Britishers, and Scotsmen in particular, used when talking to foreigners. He seemed to be apologizing, with a quite unusual fervency.

'Mind ye, it's no' just arrogant to say you're ashamed o' your country, it's daft as well.'

That was all Norman heard distinctly. Lynedoch went on to explain what daft meant, and she, quietly, appeared prepared to contest his statement; but these were just guesses. As Norman lingered among the pine trees, feeling excluded from the group in the house that contained Maddy, from those two who had just passed, from the Scots girls and the Spanish youths, from Ampara and Pedro, and from his parents grown old in America, he felt a hatred seething up in him against them all, and at the very same moment, as if it rose from that hatred, he smelled human ordure. These trees would of course be used as a lavatory. Disgust at all humanity fed his hatred. He almost gave way to weeping. In a frenzy he searched through his pockets and found a peseta. As he flipped it into the air, saying tails I do nothing, I stay excluded, heads I give the leaflet to Pedro, the stench grew stronger so that he could scarcely bear it. Down came the coin. He caught it as he would have a moth. Opening his hand he saw, not the plump dictator's face, but the shield. With a sob he tried again; again it fell tails. The third time it fell as he wished.

As he climbed down the bank again and hurried along the road to the village, panting as if he'd been wrestling with evil for hours, he became aware he was carrying the stink with him, and perhaps would always, for the rest of his life.

Madly he shuffled his feet in the dust and scuffed them among some thick plants; but he could not get rid of the abomination. Limping, he ran on towards the lights of the village, where he staggered down to the water's edge and began to scour his soles with wet sand and scrape them with flat stones. Searching through his pocket for paper, the only pieces he could find were the cheque and the leaflet. He used the latter and then tossed it, soiled, into the sea as far as he could.

Sobbing, and pleading with someone, he did not know whom, to commend him for what he had done, he washed his hands amidst the green, yellow, and red reflections.

Twenty-Two

It was Maddy who packed Lynedoch off with Montserrat, with orders not to return for at least half an hour.

'What's up?' he asked.

'I'll tell you about it later.'

'Don't fash,' he said, with a grin. 'It'll be a pleasure, and business too. I've got to learn what fury it is she's got caged up in her.'

'Fury?'

'Aye. You're a pet poodle by comparison, you know, Maddy, for all your temper.'

A little jealous and sad, she went out to watch them go down the path to the gate. For some reason they seemed inevitably intimate. Could it be because both of them cared passionately about their respective countries, whereas she, like Jonathan, had always taken England's superiority for granted, an attitude in which there could be little love?

She noticed Ampara and Pedro talking in the garden.

Isabel and David were sitting out on the terrace. He read yesterday's air edition of *The Times*. She, tight-lipped, kept turning her wedding ring; in ten more turns, or twelve, or twenty, the truce would end.

It isn't Montserrat we should be consulting about, thought Maddy, it's you two. Cheerfully she asked them in.

Isabel jumped up and went in grimly. David sat and grumbled. 'It's cooler out here, Maddy,' he said.

'Don't be a fool,' called his wife. 'It wasn't a request. It was an order.'

Maddy and he looked at each other. He sighed and shook his head.

'It's just something I think we ought to discuss in private,' she said.

'I hope,' he murmured, as he got up and went into the sitting-room, taking the newspaper with him, 'it's not too private.'

'It's really about Jonathan.'

'Has he got troubles? Don't shatter my last illusion, Maddy. Sometimes, you know, when things get rather much, I manage to escape from them by imagining I've crept in beside Jonathan in his womb within a womb. Don't tell me the silly fellow's gone and got himself born after all, and the rest of us with him.'

They were seated in silence, smoking, when Jonathan came in, pale, nervous, and strange.

'Is the inquisition already convened?' he asked.

'Ampara's got Pedro in the garden,' said Maddy, quietly.

Isabel recognized it as a warning. 'What is this?' she demanded. 'What's going on? Ever since we've arrived I've felt it. If we're not welcome, for God's sake be honest enough to say so and we'll not trouble you one minute longer.'

'Be sure, Isabel,' he replied shrilly, 'I shall have that amount of honesty if you make it necessary.'

'Good God, Jonathan,' cried David, 'what are you saying?'

Down Isabel's cheeks tears fell sparsely. 'Whatever you do, Jonathan,' she said, 'whatever's happened, don't blame the rest of us if you've suddenly found yourself inadequate. Even as a child you planted nothing. How did you ever expect anything to grow?'

True enough, thought Maddy, loving them both; but surely you can see, Isabel, something's growing in him at last; otherwise why do you think he's so sick and strange? Isn't it up to us to help it grow?

'Stop it, both of you,' she said. 'Being spiteful's not going to help.'

'Did I start it, Maddy?' Down Isabel's cheeks two or three tears, like concessions, trickled.

Maddy turned to Jonathan. 'Are you going to explain, or do you want me to?'

'I shall, Maddy. David, is that yesterday's *Times*? May I have it, please?'

Surprised, David picked it up from the floor and handed it over.

Jonathan knew where to look. In his shaking hands the thin paper crackled, but did not drown the hoarse sigh which prefaced his reading.

Isabel, brows up, smiled at David and Maddy as if they were all in a box at the opera and something on the stage had gone wrong.

A Barcelona military tribunal yesterday sentenced three men and one woman to prison terms ranging from eight to ten years on charges of subversive activities and offences against the Spanish head of state, General Franco.

After he had finished reading, his fists went on, forcing the paper to express the horror he evidently felt, to Isabel's indignation and David's astonishment.

Maddy shared his horror a little. She had not known about those prison sentences. She seldom read the newspaper.

'Well, for heaven's sake, Jonathan,' said Isabel, with a laugh, 'is that all? Why trouble to read such stuff to us? We know it goes on. We don't cross ourselves exactly, but we do hasten to assure ourselves and everybody else who's interested, that we don't approve but also that it's none of our business. Do we not?'

'To our shame, Isabel.'

'To our credit, I should say.'

'Not this time.'

'Why?' asked David. 'You don't happen to know any of these people, do you?'

'Better, David, than I shall ever know you. Yet I have never met him.'

'Well,' said David, huffed, 'if you and I haven't exactly swopped confidences, whose fault's it been?'

'Mine, no doubt, David. I apologize. You see, I have just been given a glimpse of what is called the human situation.'

'It's been there all the time, you know, not exactly skulking either in recent years.'

'I realize that. Yes, Isabel, I have also become aware of my utter inadequacy.'

'Some of us have been aware of ours for years,' said David. 'In no one's case does it amount to a revelation.'

'This man you know so well whom you've never met,' asked Isabel, 'are we to be told who he is?'

'He is Montserrat's brother.'

'Montserrat? Oh, you mean the nanny. Well, I can't say I'm surprised to hear it. I thought there was something odd about her. But I was under the impression you hadn't met her before.'

'Nor had I.'

'Well, of course it isn't at all remarkable that you should know him better than you do David whom you've known for years.'

'I love Montserrat.'

'And you despise me?'

Sometimes he did; he could not disguise it. 'Often I despise myself,' he muttered.

'So I should think myself in good company? So, Jonathan, at last you're in love?'

'And what is so incredible about that?'

'Yes, it is incredible. I always thought you quite incapable of loving anyone, apart from yourself. That was why I was so anxious to see you with Linda in your arms. But it didn't work, Jonathan. If you have ever despised yourself, I think it must have been for the pleasure of forgiving yourself. Do you think I'll ever forget watching you sit by Mother's bedside, with your hands clasped, as if you were waiting politely for permission to leave? That's how I'll always see you.'

'You did not understand, Isabel, then, nor do you now. If a child of twelve is waiting for death to enter, how else should he sit? Politeness is his only defence.'

But those were Broxmead ghosts that David refused to let haunt him. 'I don't think this is going to get us anywhere,' he said, 'supposing, that is, we do have somewhere to get to. Very well, Jonathan, you're in love with Montserrat, and her brother whom you therefore know better than me has been sentenced to eight years for subversive activities. Now that we've got over the initial shocks, what then?'

Jonathan could scarcely speak; his whole face seemed crushed by sorrow. 'She is wanted by the police,' he whispered. 'She too will be imprisoned for eight years.'

David rubbed his nose with his beard. 'Eight years is a very long time,' he admitted, 'for offences probably no more heinous than those of the Scottish Nationalists. Remember, Isabel, that rock at Sligachan, in Skye? It had painted on it, in letters of red: Make Scotland Free. Miles from anywhere, too; not even the sheep were interested.'

'Surely,' said Isabel, 'if you are rash enough, brave enough, if you like, to work illegally against a dictatorship, you must be prepared to suffer the consequences if you are caught.'

'She has not been caught yet,' whispered Jonathan.

'No. Not yet. Under the circumstances, I consider her

presence in the house an indiscretion, to say the least. She must go. While she's here we're all in danger.'

'Not you, Isabel.'

'Well, you then. Heaven knows, Jonathan, you've had to be looked after all your life. What you call your inadequacy has had to be hidden from you, you know.'

'You called it that, Isabel. And if she goes, who then will look after your child? Ampara? Maddy? Anyone but you.'

She gasped and turned pale.

'That's below the belt,' cried David. 'Isabel's here for a holiday; she needs one, and she's going to get one. I hope you don't grudge her it, Jonathan.'

'It seems, David, she grudges Montserrat her liberty.'

'Nonsense. To be blunt, Jonathan, with all due respect to your feelings for the girl, isn't it simply true she ought not to be here, sheltering in a foreigner's house?'

'What is simply true is this, David: I will do anything, anything at all, to save her.'

'But surely you didn't know she was involved in these activities?'

'Yes, I knew. Terence told me. She told me herself.'

Isabel laughed, and kept on laughing.

Maddy felt sorry for David, now stretching out a thin swordless hand, and for Jonathan finding that in a heart not prepared by pity suffering could not be contained, but especially for Isabel revealing, in laughter, an unpleasantness that she had spent long patient years in trying to conceal or even to overcome.

'It must certainly have been love at first sight,' Isabel cried. 'You know, I did wonder how it had come about that you, Jonathan, whom I've seen spurning an old woman begging in the street, should give up your room, your very bed, to this stranger who, whatever else she may be, is in unmistakable female shape. David has even wondered if by some marvellous chance you slip down to share the bed with her after we're all asleep.'

'For God's sake, Isabel!' muttered David. That had been a joke murmured in the sanctuary of the marriage bed.

Isabel still laughed. That very night, she thought, *she'd* slip along and let Miss Puig have a few home truths.

Jonathan had his face covered with his hands. Maddy was afraid that behind them he was shedding tears, not, forgivably, of sorrow at Montserrat imperilled, but of hatred of Isabel. But when he took his hands away his eyes were quite dry.

'Insult me as much as you like,' he said. 'Only help her to escape. Please.'

'Out of the country, you mean?' asked David.

'Yes. She has friends in Perpignan; as you know, it's a Catalan town too, although it's French. She has an aunt living there.'

'Has she got a passport or exit permit or whatever it is Spanish nationals need to leave the country?'

'No.'

'I thought people in that line of business could always lay their hands on forged documents.'

'The man who was to have sent those to her has himself been arrested.'

'Then she's in a fix all right, and I don't see there's anything we can do. Well, is there?' He glared round at the three of them.

'I think there is, David,' said Jonathan eagerly. 'Isabel's black-haired, like her; about the same height, too. If Montserrat wore sun-glasses she might, in the interior of a car, with a baby on her lap, say, be taken for Isabel, especially by a passport officer sitting in an office.'

'If that's what you're thinking,' said Isabel promptly, 'forget it.'

'Maddy and David could come too,' said Jonathan. 'We would be a family party. There would be very little risk.'

'There would be one very damnable risk,' said David, warmly. 'And if they did find us out, my God wouldn't we be in a pickle?'

'Wouldn't it be awkward,' asked Maddy, 'if Isabel's passport was stamped for exit but not for re-entry? Wouldn't they ask a lot of questions when she was leaving the country herself?'

'The page could be torn out.'

'The number of pages is stated,' said David.

'But never counted.'

'You can't depend on that, Jonathan.'

'Isn't all this discussion rather futile?' asked Isabel. 'I utterly refuse to allow either my passport, or my child, to be used for such a purpose.'

'I must agree,' said David. 'Really, Jonathan, it's out of the question.'

'Is it?' murmured Maddy.

'Of course it is, Maddy.'

But her eyes were shining. 'I've got a passport too,' she said, 'which I don't regard as a sacred document. But I'm blonde, and she's as dark as midnight.'

Jonathan stared at her with hope and love. She could almost see that exciting growth in him. It was her duty, and would be her pleasure, to foster it.

'There was a time when you were dark yourself, Maddy,' he said.

'Oh yes, and auburn too, and purple; but on the passport it says blonde.'

'She could become blonde for the time being, could she not?'

'No, Jonathan, she could not.'

'But Spanish girls often dye their hair, Maddy.'

Yes, indeed. Every day on the Diagonale in Barcelona they could be seen, blondes of all kinds, fair and ash and strawberry. Chic to their finger-tips, they always looked spurious. It was just not possible to picture Montserrat as one of them.

'You see, Jonathan, we just don't know her. I'm sure, though, she'd never agree to it.'

David butted in pompously: 'She can't alter the colour of her eyes, you know.'

But neither of them heeded him. That uncanny resemblance to each other excluded everybody else; except perhaps Linda, his offspring, whose hair and eyes were the same as theirs. He had a feeling of complicity, killed instantly by his wife's sneer.

'That's the trouble,' Maddy was insisting, 'we don't know her. She's a mystery. Yes, I know she danced that sardana with you, and it may have meant something of what you imagine it did. But she's still a mystery. She won't dye her hair, not even to keep her out of prison. She'd as soon betray her religion.'

'Are you sure that's genuine?' asked Isabel.

Maddy remembered John's remark about the fury caged up in Montserrat. It might be that poor Jonathan, lamb-like in spite of the intellectuality of his bleats, was yoking himself to a panther.

'Maddy, is it impossible for me to love her, knowing her imperfectly?'

'No, I wouldn't say that, Jonathan.'

'Who would?' muttered David. He resented being excluded from their conspiracy whose purpose was not merely to smuggle a girl out of the country, but also to widen the horizons of love.

'I do love her, Maddy.'

'Well, something has happened to you. It might as well be love.'

'You will lend your passport, if it is necessary?'

'Yes.'

'I'll persuade the Scots girls to go with us. They said they wouldn't, but I believe if I explained they would agree to come.'

Then he became aware that Isabel was weeping, and David was timidly and uselessly trying to comfort her.

'Perhaps I do not love her at all,' he said, in dismay. 'You see, I promised her – no, I promised myself in her presence, out of gratitude – I promised to be humble, or at least to try and be, to everyone.'

'You're raw all right,' grumbled David, 'if you think love works miracles as swiftly as that.'

'But it does, it does,' murmured Maddy.

'I'm sorry, Isabel,' said Jonathan.

'If you're apologizing just because of some idiotic promise you made to that woman, then don't bother. I'm not so dependent on your goodwill, Jonathan, that I'll humbly accept what little of it you have to spare.'

I hope, thought Maddy, John was right and Montserrat does have a fury caged in her. Jonathan must have a wife who will claw and pummel and astonish out of him the qualities he has been hoarding up. That sardana may well have been the first pounce.

Twenty-Three

There were times, in art galleries for instance, when Isabel felt proud of David's beard and thought it gave authority to his opinions. Once when he had appeared in a television series on the appreciation of great paintings she had been gratified by the dozens of letters he had received, mostly from women, ecstatic not about his exposition or knowledge or taste or wit, but about his prophetic and virile beard. There were other times, however, such as when he supped soup in public, when she felt embarrassed and exasperated; but the worst time was usually when he was getting ready for bed. Then all his long skinniness, of rib, haunch, neck, leg, and arm, was revealed, with the beard like some absurd rudimentary contrivance of concealment. Few men could stand, clad in pyjama jacket only, yawn, scratch some quarter of their meagreness, and retain dignity; no man at all could, wearing a beard that came down below the third button and looked fitter for John the Baptist. These were the occasions too when he liked to try out on her the most glittering of the phrases in his latest article. If she was feeling like a lover she found funny and endearing the contrast between his intellectual conceit and his appearance of a castaway searching anxiously for coconuts; but if she was feeling merely wifely, or as nowadays motherly, she saw that contrast as exasperating, in a way she had never yet quite defined.

That night, as she waited until Jonathan had gone up to the roof to roost, she sat in her bedroom, with her hands clasped over her stomach which, after Linda's birth, she had got flat again through diligent and perspiring exercise. Now, if nothing was done, it would inevitably swell once more, with all the attendant discomfort and ugliness. Montserrat, with the crucifix round her neck, represented not Catalan nationalism or democracy or temptation to Jonathan or danger to Maddy; no, she represented not the immaculacy of conception so much as its sacredness. Maddy had thought that the Spanish girl would never dye her hair, because even that innocent kind of falseness was distasteful to her. Isabel had thought, from the moment she had first seen her, that Montserrat would never countenance what she herself had been trying to make up her mind to do. Unlike Jonathan and Maddy, Isabel believed in God. During the past few weeks she had been driving herself to the point of accepting that, in these days when over-population was threatening to starve millions of His human creatures, He must, however reluctantly, be giving His sanction to birth control, and even, where this had by accident failed, to judicious abortion. She had collected articles by progressive clergymen putting forward that point of view, and had avoided others rejecting it. Now when action was urgent in her own case, when it would have to be done very soon if it was to be done successfully at all, she had had to meet this girl who, without ever saying a word, without even knowing Isabel's predicament, had condemned the doing of anything that would relieve it. That Montserrat was also a revolutionary, plotting to overthrow a dictatorship, ought to have invalidated her attitude to so feminine and private a thing as birth, but somehow it did not, if anything it strengthened it. Therefore Isabel prayed she would be caught and imprisoned; indeed, as she sat waiting, with her hands so prescient on her belly, she wondered if she ought, before Maddy and Jonathan got any further with their ridiculous scheme, to inform the police herself. One of the most useful roles in the tragedy of Christ had been that of Judas.

'Mind you,' David was saying as he at last drew on his pyjama trousers, 'it would be a pity if she went before John got a chance to finish her portrait. I think he's going to make a wonderful thing of it. I agree, of course, she hasn't really got a face that represents the true, historical Spain. I much prefer those long lean ascetic Castilian faces of Velasquez. Whereas she, whatever Maddy may say, and whatever the crucifix may stand for, is damn near voluptuous.' He laughed as he tied the cords. 'Not at all the sort I'd have thought Jonathan being infatuated with.' Then he performed his nightly ritual of touching his toes six times without bending his knees. But for the beard he would have resembled a giraffe drinking. 'Yet why not?' he gasped, when he was straight again. 'As a compensation for the thin dreams he must have had, poor fellow. As you know, my dear, I've never agreed with you that he is – well, queerish; but I grant you he never scribbled a single obscenity on any lavatory wall. Curious. Well, my queen of Aragon, shall I switch off the light?'

'I'm going along to speak to her.'

'To whom? Maddy?'

'No.'

'Not Montserrat?'

'Yes. And why not?'

'Do you think it's wise to interfere, Isabel? For one thing, if anything went wrong I wouldn't put it past Jonathan throwing us all out. Besides, what can you usefully say to her?'

'I can tell her to clear out and leave us all in peace.'

'Comparative peace,' he murmured, to himself. Aloud he said: 'Yes, I suppose you're entitled to tell her that. The true villains of the piece are Terence and Bridie. We can't blame the poor girl for seizing any breathing-space she can, but they ought to have had more sense of responsibility. Only, my dear, don't say anything to her that might inflame our host.'

'You have already given me that warning.'

'Yes, because you don't seem to be taking it seriously. It is possible, you know, that he is in love with her.'

'You haven't known him as long as I have.'

It was his opinion that her knowledge of Jonathan as a child obscured her view of him now. 'You can't deny he's prepared to go to jail for her. Not to mention risk sending all of us there with him. These dreamers of bleak dreams are apt, when they break out, to demand from life the most luscious compensations.'

'And what precisely is that supposed to mean?' Thus in certain moods she demanded prose in place of poetry.

'If policemen came here to arrest her he'd attack them.'

She laughed. 'You know as well as I do how squeamish he is about violence.'

'Yes.' He had himself seen Jonathan almost faint when in a café one drunk man had swiped another, bloodying his nose. 'But he wasn't in love then.'

'Don't use that word,' she whispered, turning on him with her face twisted with revulsion. 'Don't. You keep using it to torment me. Don't.'

She got up, gathered her dressing-gown about her, and was out of the room before he could say or do anything to prevent her.

As he sat staring at his long wincing toes, into his empty mind tumbled, clown-like, envy of Jonathan. Yes, however enigmatic the latter's love might be, and however much of a bungler he proved as a man of action, nevertheless how lucky he was to be given this opportunity to try and rescue a beautiful girl from the clutches of tyranny. Often David had maintained that the most contemporary of all experiences wasn't to suffer at the hands of communism or fascism, but rather to contemplate a truly modern painting, such as this portrait of Montserrat by John Lynedoch might well be; but over the years had been accumulating a respect for action. To Jonathan, fumbler with passports, erratic driver, boor to officials, this chance of adventure had fallen. He would fail, or worse still succeed bathetically. Heroism would be mocked, tragedy kept at bay, like a neutered tabby.

Exercising his toes, David felt them growing more and more prehensile, and the hair on his chin appeared, as he stared down, to clothe his chest. Despite art the jungle was never far away. He did not know whether to be pleased or appalled. In the room where his tiny gibbering offspring lay, a conversation might well have started that, despite the perfumed bodies and civilized voices of the two women taking part, would to the subtle veracious listener be hardly distinguishable from the shrieking of female monkeys, incensed by jealousy, in the top of a tree.

On her way to Montserrat's room Isabel paused and leant over the rail. The glass door into the sitting-room was closed, and the light was out; but Maddy was still there with Lynedoch. God knew, and Isabel guessed, what they were up to. It wasn't that she wanted Maddy punished, by remorse even; no, she just wanted to be able to understand, and so be able to accept, the pattern of life that included among its complexities Maddy's carefree wantonness and her own anguished scruples.

Moments later, when she had knocked at Montserrat's door and the Spanish girl had come from her bed to unlock it, dressed from throat to toes in a white nightgown, the incomprehensibleness thickened. Here, in substantial flesh and blood, full-bosomed, black-haired, alien, was the object of her brother's love. It was like watching a miracle that kept unfolding, with a smile, a hand to the mouth to cover a little yawn, a murmured apology in Spanish, a row of pink-painted toenails, a wrist with a cluster of tiny moles, ankles calloused at the back, and above all eyes in which frankness, intelligence, courage, and humour were luminous and brown.

'Were you in bed?' asked Isabel, entering. 'I'm so sorry. I just had to see Linda before I went to sleep. I thought this evening she looked a little flushed, as if she was fevered.'

'No, she is not fevered, Mrs Reeves. She is quite cool.'

Isabel had her hand on her daughter's brow. 'Yes, so she is, thank God. Mothers are such anxious creatures, aren't they, especially when they have only one child. You Spanish women,' she added, as casually as she could, 'are very wise in having several. So many women in northern Europe nowadays stop at one, for reasons which I'm sure you wouldn't approve of.'

Montserrat's brows were up. She seemed as much amused as surprised at thus being got out of bed to have her tenderest feelings and deepest religious beliefs prodded so sharply.

Isabel laughed, making no effort to disguise its falseness. 'I'm sure you intend to have half a dozen at least,' she said.

Those fine black brows went up a little higher still. 'I should be pleased.'

'Provided of course you marry someone with enough money to give each of them a decent chance in life. It may be impolite for a guest to pass remarks, but really one can't help noticing how in so many Spanish villages there are far more children than there can possibly be sufficient food for. Isn't that true?'

'Yes. I have not been to England, but it is also true, I believe, that there much food is wasted, by greedy people, that could remove the hunger of these Spanish children.'

Well, thought Isabel, this one can stand up for herself all right. Better let her have it straight and to the point.

'Miss Puig,' she said, 'my brother has told me about you. I have come to ask you to leave. Tomorrow morning, please, as soon as is convenient. You had no right to come in the first place.'

Montserrat flushed, but by no means cringed. 'Your brother asked me to come,' she said.

'He didn't know what you were.'

Isabel found herself confronted by a dignity, quiet but menacing.

'And what am I, Mrs Reeves?'

'You know very well what I mean. You're wanted by the police. You will bring trouble to this house, so don't put on that air of soulful innocence. Jonathan might be easy to deceive. I'm not.'

'I am deceiving no one. Yes, it is true I have been wishing to bring liberty and democracy—'

'Oh, my God!' cried Isabel, affronted by being offered, at this intimate level, those soiled and public words.

Then she was overwhelmed by a flow of Spanish, quiet for the sake of the baby and also for the sake of dignity again, but eloquent, passionate, and more than a little scornful.

As she listened, Isabel was made to recognize that for any human being to be dragged off to prison was a degradation of humanity in general; but particularly that if this girl, so lovely, fearless, and sincere, was thus degraded, Isabel herself would never afterwards feel clean in her soul.

Her share of guilt made her harsh. 'Please talk English,' she said. 'I don't understand Spanish.'

'But I cannot say in English how I feel in my heart.'

Isabel began to feel that her own falseness must be showing. She tried to cover it up. 'I don't really care how you feel,' she said. 'Nobody in this house is interested in politics, though I must say that I personally would rather have Franco than communism. However, that's none of my business. But my brother and sister are.'

'Your sister?'

'Yes. They've both got some mad scheme to smuggle you

out of the country, using her passport. You would have to
dye your hair. I can't agree to it, and I hope you won't agree
to it either.'

'I do not want to leave Spain.'

'I wouldn't think so, if you're so anxious to bring liberty
and democracy here. How can you do that if you run away?
However, that isn't my business, as I said.'

'Please. You will wake up the baby.'

Faced with that candid, smiling scrutiny Isabel realized
her solicitude wasn't really for Jonathan or Maddy; it was for
– for no one. She just wanted to interfere. Thus had she
spoiled their schemes and stratagems long ago.

She lowered her voice. 'I want you to promise you'll leave
the house in the morning, go away, and stay away. That's all,
and I think I'm entitled to ask you to do it.'

As if defeated Montserrat sat down on the bed and looked
at her hands. Magnanimous in victory, Isabel sat beside her,
near enough for their shoulders to touch. She was about to
put her arm round the other woman's shoulders, but shrank
from that half-sincerity.

'You mustn't think,' she whispered, 'I don't feel sorry,
especially as your brother's in prison; but I've got my own
brother to keep out of prison.'

'Does he know you are speaking to me?'

Surprised by the question, which seemed an impertin-
ence, Isabel said carefully: 'No, he doesn't.' She felt
Montserrat shiver. 'Perhaps I ought to explain to you about
Jonathan, though I don't much want to.'

Montserrat turned and stared, almost sternly.

'I expect you know he thinks he's in love with you?'

Montserrat stared more sternly still.

'It's awkward explaining, especially to you, a Catholic.
Our parents were divorced when we were very young. My
mother ran off with another man. We visited her sometimes.
We saw her before her death; she died of cancer. Jonathan

was in the room when she actually died, although I don't think he's aware of that even now. What I'm trying to say is this, that partly because of those circumstances, and partly because of his nature, my brother's development, emotionally, has been rather peculiar. I hope you understand what I'm hinting at, because I really can't do more than hint at it. Intellectually he's clever, but emotionally he's abnormal.'

'Because he thinks he is in love with me?'

Was that softness genuine, or was it mockery veiled? Isabel could not tell, and so was provoked into saying what she had no right to say, on earth or in heaven, whether it was true or not.

'He can't be in love with you, don't you see, because he's not capable of being in love with any woman. I said peculiar. Good God, are you so simple I've got to spell it out in words of one syllable?' Then she hissed a word of five.

To her indignation and horror Montserrat laughed, no mere hysterical titter either, but the merry confident laughter of a woman who, having been shown proof of her lover's virility, is able to take as a joke any assertion that he is incapable of it.

Isabel leapt up and shrank back. How dare this Spaniard, in the white nightdress tied with ribbon at the neck and wearing a crucifix, pretend to a chastity she no more possessed than Maddy! Surrounded by deceit and carnality, Isabel retreated to the cot in which her daughter, innocent herself, but representing something of that very deceit and carnality, lay asleep.

Montserrat rose. 'I am not laughing at you. But you are wrong. Your brother, he is so shy, that is all.'

'You seem to have helped him to get over it, call it what you like.'

'No. Have you not noticed? He will not look at me.'

'I thought you had him dancing the sardana in the moonlight?'

'But he did not look at me even then. He looked at the stars above my head and at his feet trying to dance. No, I do not think he loves me.'

'He says so, and he's prepared to stick at nothing to get you to France.'

'He is very kind.'

'You're the only one I've ever heard call him that. He's monumentally selfish.'

'No.'

Isabel advanced again, leaving the protection of her baby. She came so close to Montserrat she felt she could hear her heart beating, in an alien Spanish way.

'Are you in love with him?' she asked.

Montserrat stared back bravely, and then, stricken by humour rather than by modesty, turned and looked towards the dressing-table.

'Well?' demanded Isabel. 'Because if you are, even if you just feel you might be, then don't you think you ought not to let him get mixed up with things that don't concern him, and might get him into a lot of trouble?' Even as she gasped out the words she knew how lying, feeble, and false they were. If he did love her, why then he must joyously venture his very life to help her.

To her amazement, after a few moments' numbness, what she felt was an envy. Discoveries lay ahead of them.

'We have danced only one sardana,' said Montserrat, smiling.

'What's going to happen,' said Isabel, with sobs of rage, of foreboding, of envy, and of goodwill, 'is that you're going to dance yourselves, both of you, into the hands of the police.'

As she returned, half weeping, half laughing, to her own room she thought she would have the child after all, love it, call it Jonathan or Montserrat, and never feel ashamed of it because its father had a beard.

David was supine in bed, with his feet far from him protruding like separate living creatures. His beard lay over the sheet, like seaweed on white sand; his nose thrust up like a kind of limpet. Whatever submarine trance he was playing at, he was reluctant to come up out of it at his wife's entry, arresting though this was because of her sobs.

'Well?' he murmured, as if from a great depth.

'Well?' was all she could reply, as she went down on her knees by the bedside.

Slowly and hesitantly out came his long arm, to wave about, before descending to touch her head.

'It's all right,' she sobbed. 'I don't mind any more. I'm glad. I really am.'

Eyes on the ceiling, he had been rehearsing what he would write in his first article about John Lynedoch. Now, catching the new note in his wife's voice, he switched his mind on to her. 'What's happened?'

'Linda's sweet, isn't she?'

'None sweeter.'

'And lovely?'

'An authentic Broxmead golden girl.'

'And healthy?'

'Chubby as butter.'

'And intelligent?'

'Considering her parentage, why wonder?'

'So what's so horrible about another like her?'

'Nothing in the wide world, my darling.'

He raised his head, glad for her sake, a little disappointed for his own. Though he had left it to her, either to go on and have the child, or else get rid of it if this could be done decently and safely, still he had kept hoping that nature, which had done the trick, as it were, might, like the consummate conjurer she was, undo it again with similar magic before their very eyes.

'Why should we worry?' cried Isabel, laughing.

'Montserrat says she's going to have half a dozen. Can you imagine Jonathan surrounded by so many?'

Though she wept as well as laughed, it was somehow gladly. He dared not now, lest he should break this spell of joyful weeping, which was evidently cleansing her soul of the past few weeks' bitter frustrations, ask her how it was that, having gone to apprise Montserrat of Jonathan's dearth of masculinity, she had returned with this fantasy of their over-fruitful alliance.

Far, far away he heard laughter. It was scarcely from Jonathan on the roof, gazing at the stars; it was too vulgarly uproarious for him. Nor was it from the puny-hearted myrmidons of authority waiting to ensnare the two lovers; it was much too rich with appreciation of the human comedy. It must therefore be from God Himself. He stood, bearded like David, on the hill above the village, leaning His elbow on the dome of the radar station, and nodding His head among the stars. And so He laughed.

'What are you laughing at?' asked Isabel, but not crossly, as she would have done half an hour ago; fondly rather, as if, shown how, she would laugh herself. 'You'll wake the whole house.'

'The whole world,' he cried.

It was up to him to show her how.

Twenty-Four

Next morning it seemed to Jonathan that Isabel's self-pity had put off its drab irritableness in favour of a bright shoddy gaiety; underneath it was still the same. In so much as it probably represented an effort on her part to spare others, and recover some of the respect she had tossed away, he tried to do what she wanted, that was, regard it not as self-pity at all but as genuine happiness, expressing itself in a desire to atone, inspire, and infect. He winced a little when at breakfast she went out of her way to be quite sisterly towards Montserrat, frowned when she insisted on helping Ampara in the kitchen, where she was seldom welcome, but smiled when she let everyone know she was going to bath Linda herself, and ordered them all to come and see.

Like him they went hoping by humouring her really to transmute the flashy self-pity into true joy. At least that was Jonathan's motive, and surely David's too. Maddy and Montserrat, though, were as enthusiastic as small girls as they knelt by the bath, tickling the baby, crying nonsensical endearments, and shrieking into raptures when she banged the water with her fists and splashed them. Lynedoch peeped amiably in, but soon went away. David had to remain and found room by sitting on the lavatory, thus confusing Jonathan who did not know whether to be offended by so vulgar a gesture or grateful to it because it helped to obscure what, in Montserrat's presence, had been troubling him.

Isabel would not let him be aloof. She demanded that he

too must bow down and adore the infant. He had to indulge her, and since Maddy slipped out of the way he found himself side by side with Montserrat whose face, hair, and hands were dappled with pink suds. As the baby held him by his finger and splashed him with her other hand, to everyone's delight, he kept warning himself that this inter-lude of jocund domesticity was not for him: he ought to be at the hotel stifling Norman, and at the pension cajoling the Scots girls.

Two or three times he nudged against Montserrat, and made it plain it wasn't his fault, that the general jostling was to blame, of which she was doing more than her share. But she seemed not a bit annoyed, and once, quite intentionally, flicked a sud on to his ear. She laughed as she did it, and he could not help remembering, gloomily, what had worried him for hours last night on the roof, that in Barcelona her mother might at that moment be dying, or dead. He felt then for her a love so overwhelming and responsible it could only be expressed by a scowl, as if her teasing was bother-some. Luckily, or miraculously, she again seemed not to mind; indeed, in her playing with the baby she at times was the more gleeful.

Half an hour later, as he was about to set out to look for Norman and the Scots girls, he was accosted by Isabel with Linda in her arms.

'I must say this, Jonathan,' she said. 'I wish you, and Montserrat, all the luck there is. I can't let you have my passport or Linda, but I shall pray that you get her over the border safely. As Maddy said, we don't know her; but I'm sure you're right, she's worth knowing. If you like, you and she can go bathing this morning, when the sitting's over. I'll look after my pet. Won't I, darling?'

'Thank you, Isabel,' he said, cautiously, not sure what her purpose could be.

'What will you do after you've got to Perpignan?'

'Return here of course. What else?'

'I thought you might be staying with her for a while.'

'Isabel, I doubt if in Miss Puig's eyes there could be anything more incongruous in Perpignan than my prolonged presence.'

She laughed. 'Do you hear him, Linda? He must think we're daft, as John Lynedoch would say. We know, don't we, if Uncle Jonathan doesn't, what a sardana in the moonlight means to a señorita from Catalonia.'

'In this instance it meant, I am afraid, simply that she was recognizing the fact that a fool, albeit well-intentioned, was in her company. She is devout, Isabel; she believes God made us all, including me; and since she has a sense of humour herself she sees no reason to suppose He does not enjoy His own joke occasionally.'

Linda went into a fit of chuckles so ecstatic as to be divinely prompted.

Isabel too could not help laughing, though when she spoke her tone was very fond: 'What's the matter, Jonathan?'

'Good heavens, Isabel, do you ask that, you who have known me all my life? Linda is more percipient. Last night when I said I loved her you laughed, most justifiably.'

'I wasn't justified at all. It was dreadful of me.'

'If you are considering my feelings, Isabel, scorn is more endurable than sympathy. Yes, I do love her. It is a joy to me to look to see what dress she has on, what shoes. I envy the ear-rings in her ears. It is, I agree, a matter for laughter. Linda laughs. David laughs, too. Listen.'

They heard him, bellowing, out in the garden where he was watching Lynedoch at work on his portrait of Montserrat.

'But, Jonathan, he's not laughing at you.'

'The nature of laughter has puzzled philosophers for

centuries, Isabel. There is, it seems, a zone of incongruity; this when we glimpse we laugh.'

The four of them in the garden must have got a good look then, for they all laughed heartily.

'Most people,' said Jonathan, 'at some time or other find themselves inhabiting that zone. A few dwell there permanently. Among them am I.'

As if to show he was facing that truth about himself without bitterness, he stroked the baby's cheek with his finger. The gesture did not satisfy him, and he changed it for a sudden, gasping kiss on her brow. Then he strode away.

As Isabel stared after him, she murmured to the child in her arms: 'Never be sorry for yourself, darling; it makes you too vulnerable.' But the warning was itself an expression of self-pity. In any case, should one not recommend rather than warn? What recommendation was there that contained in itself every other? Was there any so comprehensive? If there was it had to do with love. 'Cherish love,' she murmured, 'especially if it's maimed or ashamed or comic.'

When Maddy saw Jonathan making for the gate she shouted and ran after him. Behind her he noticed the others gazing in amusement. Lynedoch wisely wasted only a second or two, and returned to his painting. David, exuberant that morning, waved hugely with both hands, thereby making all the more conspicuous the slightness of Montsterrat's gesture; she merely lifted her hand from her lap, waggled her fingers, and dropped it again.

'Where are you going?' asked Maddy.

'To see Norman. He's got to be silenced.'

Startled, she looked at him as if for gun or knife.

'It's not a joke, Maddy,' he said, passionately.

'No, it isn't.' Often he refused to laugh at humorous remarks or situations, not because he couldn't see them, but because their laughableness did not pass his own peculiar tests. She had sometimes been surprised by what he rejected, but not this time. 'Would you like me to go with you?' she asked.

'There's another thing, Maddy. She wants to telephone to find out how her mother is.'

'Well, isn't that natural?'

'It's also dangerous. She mustn't. I want her to wait till she's safe in Perpignan.'

'But, Jonathan, if her mother's really ill, in danger of dying, perhaps Montserrat would rather go and see her, even if it meant running the risk of being caught. She might think a year, two years, three years even, in prison, worth enduring for the sake of seeing her mother before she died.'

'It isn't only the length of a prison sentence that matters, Maddy.'

'No, but it does matter.'

'You're still smiling! What do you find to smile at, in what we're discussing? Tell me, Maddy. I would like to know.'

'If you see a sad thing in your mind, Jonathan, do you never smile at it? I often do.'

'So you admit three years in prison is a sad thing?'

'One day. Particularly for Montserrat. You're lucky, Jonathan. You've found a treasure.'

'I have found only one thing, Maddy: I love her, and as a consequence even this leaf, look' – he plucked it from the tree in whose shade they stood – 'is to me precious and beautiful. Yes, all right. I have found a treasure, but one I can hardly claim.'

'I wouldn't be so sure. Never mind what Isabel said last night. She's saying different things today.'

'She still refuses to lend her passport.'

'Most people would.'

'You haven't, Maddy.'

She smiled. 'With us it's different. I couldn't refuse. Now, do you want me to go with you and talk to Norman?'

'No.' He had considered it; Norman might impose some insulting condition, dug up out of the Old Testament.

'I admit,' she said, 'I'd rather not. I've got nothing to say to him, on my own account. I doubt if he'd pay any heed to anything I said. Perhaps if Montserrat herself spoke to him?'

'I'd kill him first.'

She almost smiled. 'Well, that's out,' she said.

'I don't know if he told you he's been saved, has seen the light.'

This time she could smile. 'I'm not surprised. That was a side of him you didn't see. He was morbidly concerned about his soul.'

'He is concerned no longer. It nestles in the hand of God.'

She turned and looked to where Lynedoch went on painting. 'Don't you see now why John's so wonderful?' she asked. 'The rest of us are so ordinary, artificial, petty, so feebly sane; by comparison he's gigantic, and marvellously sane.'

He was amazed and disquieted. In one respect only did Lynedoch rise above the commonplace: he could paint fairly well.

'You haven't had a look at what he's done already of Montserrat's portrait. You'll be astonished. If you ever want to know what you love her for, it will tell you.'

Her insinuation was worse than any of Isabel's.

It will also tell you, she added to herself, that there's a fire in her from which you may run screaming away, or worse still may wish to extinguish with squirts of tepid timidity.

'Isabel's all right now,' she said.

After a blink or two of reflection, he thought she must mean that Isabel's body had shown proof she was not pregnant after all. About to be shocked by that menstruous inference, and displeased with Maddy for being so indelicate as to mention it, with Montserrat in view if he turned his head three inches, suddenly he felt, like a change of tide in

him, reverence instead, reverence for the human body, male
and female, and all its miraculous processes.

'I mean,' said Maddy, 'she's decided to go ahead and have
the baby. That's why she's glad.'

So he had been unjust to Isabel. He had learnt very little.
Love that illumined a leaf left a sister darkened. He saw he
could not leave everything to it; unaided, it must tire and
fail.

'I had better go,' he said.

For he had seen in his imagination Norman at that very
moment approaching the police station, with the leaflet in
his hand, and on his breast the tie sprinkled with 'God is
Love'.

He dashed out of the gate and down the road.

The leaf was still in his hand, like some talisman of myth
that conferred on him not invisibility or invulnerability or
prodigious speed, but simply the desire, no, more than the
desire, the need to know and love some at least of these
village people among whom he had lived for three years, and
whom all that time he had regarded with no more affection
than if they had been the heaps of rubbish they vexed him by
dumping on the shore or on the tracks behind their houses.
Almost every day he had passed them; sometimes he had
greeted them, sometimes not, and never cordially. It had not
mattered, they meant nothing to him, they were con-
veniences who supplied him with fish, vegetables, milk,
bread, cheese, and wine. He knew none of them as a friend,
had been a guest in none of their homes, and had shaken
none of their hands. Where, after September, did these
women go who tended the summer stalls? Where the waiters? Where the fat ice-seller? For all he cared they could
have been wrapped in straw and laid on shelves. This cripple
too, who sat outside the chemist's and polished shoes, was
he married, had he children, did he make enough to keep his
family in food, in which of the small houses up which of the

dark narrow streets around the church did he live? These old women in black, with faces like scrolls on which fragments of scripture were imprinted, why did they pant up every day to kneel on hard boards and pray, for what, with what expectations, and with what gleams of paradise?

Every country, every town, every village, every street, every house even, in which people lived had its own dis- tinctive flavour, compounded of innumerable ingredients, such as love and hate, pride and humility, laughter and tears, pity and arrogance, and others, not human at all, given by the earth, sea, and sky. Enjoyment of life consisted in being capable of relishing these flavours, which could never be done unless one's own contribution, however paltry, was freely added. And no one could add anything unless he had learned beforehand the value of what he had to contribute. That self-knowledge, never easy, was impossible if one kept repairing the barriers between oneself and everybody else. In that maze of selfishness even the taste of self grew quickly insipid, and became a poison. He had thought that the only way out might be through art; now he knew that love was the thread leading to the gateway.

The way to the hotel lay past a small pebbly beach, speckled that morning with the vivid colours of bathing costumes. Wearing three of the smartest and brightest of these were the Scots girls; they also wore wide-brimmed straw hats, and lay, shining with oil, two on their stomachs, and one, she called Teresa, on her back. Like sausages in a frying pan, at various stages of cooking, he thought. Then he realized the similitude was characteristically unkind, a sour bleat from the maze of self, all the more shameful since he had come to ask a favour, upon their granting of which Montserrat's liberty, and his own peace of mind for years, might well depend. Therefore, with an effort of charity, he made himself see them as young girls who, living in grimy Glasgow streets, and working in a dull office at the dullest of tasks imaginable, had courageously come here to Spain for a new flavour and also to absorb as much sunshine as they could during a brief and expensive holiday. As he went down towards them the pebbles under his sandals crunched out a warning not to step out of one maze into another, this time of self-deceit.

He was almost upon them before he saw that they had company. Three young Spaniards, clad in red trunks, with hairy tanned torsos and legs, were chatting to them in broken English. The youths wore saints' emblems round their necks and on their wrists watches with big faces. Their hair was as black as Montserrat's, their eyes as brown. Perhaps they were students and knew her.

He stopped and was about to slink off among the sun-baskers when Teresa rose, turned, and caught sight of him. Skinny in green, she called and beckoned. Peggy and Katie, the latter plumper in her sky-blue than he had supposed, raised their heads and stared. They did not call. It was evident from their socially prim mouths that they believed they had taken proper farewell of him yesterday, and so this approach of his, unless accidental, was an intrusion.

The youths gazed politely, but one of them at least could not help sneering a little as he compared his own dark muscularity with Jonathan's pale flabbiness. Nevertheless, as Jonathan himself noticed, and as he saw Peggy and Katie noticing too, there were not a few women, dark-haired, French and Spanish, in two cases very handsome, staring at him with a quite competitive admiration. That this gave him pleasure was not, some newly awakened instinct told him, the old selfishness of the maze; it was not only pardonable, it was essential, part of his contribution to the flavour of life on the beach that sunny morning.

'Friends o' ours frae Barcelona,' said Teresa. 'Celestino, Andres, and Enrique. I can never mind their other names.'

To them she said: 'Mr Broxmead who lives here; he's English.'

On their feet, restless as boxers, they shook hands.

'Do you speak Spanish, señor?' asked Celestino, in that language.

'A little.'

'Are you a painter?' asked Andres.

'No. I try to be a writer.'

'He's got a sister who's a twin,' said Teresa.

They had to have that explained to them. It increased their interest in Jonathan.

'Do you write about Spain?' asked Enrique. 'I hope not.'

His friends laughed. 'Enrique's a nationalist,' they said.

'Do you think I should portray you unfairly?' asked Jonathan.

Enrique gave a shrug. 'Unfairly does not matter. What is important is that you portray us truthfully. That is not possible for you, a foreigner.'

'Sometimes, they say, the spectator sees most of the game.'

'What is happening in Spain, señor, is not a game.'

'I suppose not. But does this mean that if I were to marry a Spanish girl we would not be able to understand each other?'

Celestino laughed. 'Love makes everything clear.'

Then he and Andres with whoops went running down to the sea and plunged in.

Jonathan stood smiling at Enrique. There were two ways of being a nationalist in Franco's country. On the walls of Barcelona University Jonathan had seen painted in letters of black *Fe en Franco*, Faith in Franco, and also, in much larger letters, *Protesto*. Which of these had Enrique saluted? Did he look on Montserrat and her kind as heroines or as troublesome bitches?

Jonathan could not resist saying: 'Have you heard of Jordi Puig?'

Enrique turned inscrutable, to an Englishman anyway. 'Why do you ask?'

'When I was in Barcelona recently I saw his name painted on walls.'

'If you do not know why, señor, you do not understand us. Go back to England. Do not marry a Spanish girl.' Then he too raced down into the sea.

The girls were greatly huffed that he had chased away their boy-friends. They were also of the opinion that he had been rude in not speaking English. Therefore they were cool.

It was Teresa who spoke; she could not keep up a grudge more than a minute. 'And whit was all that about, Mr Broxmead?'

'Teresa,' said Katie, 'don't you know it's manners to wait till you're told?'

'I used to know two girls,' said Peggy, as if to her friends. 'Dolina McCutcheon and Catriona McGlashan. From the Highlands, and very clannish. They could speak Gaelic, and sometimes did, in company.'

'I beg your pardons,' said Jonathan.

'Granted,' cried Katie. 'Now what can we do for you, Mr Broxmead?'

'That's no way to talk, Katie,' said Teresa. 'She's bad-tempered, Mr Broxmead, because instead of turning brown she's peeling.'

Katie's blush, indeed, was spread over several layers. 'Discreet, aren't you, Teresa?'

'There is something you can do for me,' said Jonathan, sitting so as to be able to speak more privately. The leaf, he noticed, was still clutched in his hand.

They waited, but both Peggy and Katie pretended to be more interested in the Spaniards now swimming like seals. Ashamed of them, Teresa showed an interest keen enough for three.

'Yesterday I asked if you would accompany me to Perpignan on Sunday,' he said. 'I want to ask you again. There's a special reason that I'm prepared to tell you, but not here; this is too public.'

They looked interested, but Peggy said at once: 'It so happens we've been invited by our friends to go with them to Tossa del Mar on Sunday.'

'On their pillions,' explained Teresa. 'They've got scooters. I'm no' keen.'

'What's the special reason?' demanded Katie. 'We're no' children, you know, to be enticed wi' talk aboot special reasons, secret ones at that.'

'Very well,' he whispered, 'I shall tell you. You met Miss Ripoll at my house?'

'Is she the Spanish girl?' asked Teresa.

'Yes.'

'Your girl-friend, according to Teresa,' said Katie. She knew it was cheeky and said it cheekily.

'Yes, my girl-friend.'

They stared.

'Is she really?' asked Peggy.

Katie giggled.

Teresa said: 'I told them. She's beautiful.'

'She must be got out of the country.'

'Say that again,' said Katie, after a pause.

He did, hoarsely.

'Well, what's to hinder her?' asked Peggy.

'It's easy,' said Katie. 'All you do is buy a ticket and show your passport to the man.'

'It's not as easy as that, I'm afraid.'

'Why not?' asked Peggy. 'What's the mystery?'

'She has no passport.'

Another pause. 'Well, in Glasgow they cost thirty shillings,' said Katie. 'Here two hundred pesetas maybe.'

'She cannot get one. She's wanted by the police, for political reasons.'

'My God!' muttered Teresa. 'And me thinking she was a good Catholic.'

'Is she a communist or something?' asked Katie.

'Quiet, Katie,' said Peggy. 'You don't need to be a communist to get into trouble in Spain.'

'This is your faither's talk, Peggy. Communist or no, we should hae nothing to do wi' it. It's no' our business.'

Sadly, for she wanted very much to oblige, Teresa said: 'Whit does the priest say? It would be different if he approved.'

'Why should he be consulted?' asked Peggy. 'The Church supports Franco.'

'It's not unlikely the priest would approve,' said Jonathan, 'but he wouldn't dare say so.'

'Are you trying to tell us,' asked Teresa, 'that a priest says one thing and thinks anither?'

'Be your age, Teresa,' said Katie. 'They a' do, Protestant and Catholic alike.'

'Miss Ripoll is as devout a Catholic as there is in the whole of Spain.'

He said it with a pride he had no right to, and was accordingly punished.

'You're no' one yourself?' asked Teresa.

'No.'

'But if she's as devout as you say she'll want to be married in church.'

'Yes, of course.'

'And to be married in a church you'd have to become a Catholic yourself?'

'I suppose so.'

'Nae supposing about it; you would.'

The two others had been lying in wait; now they sprang.

'Would you?' demanded Peggy.

'If onybody's got to turn,' said Katie, 'it should surely be the woman.'

'Why should it be?' asked Teresa. 'A woman wants her children to have the faith she kens to be the true one. It stands to reason.'

'What doesn't stand to reason,' said Peggy, 'is that it is the true faith.'

'But, Peggy, you and Katie hardly ever go to church.'

'That's our business, Teresa.'

'But it makes a difference.'

'If we never went at all it would make no difference.'

A few days ago their argument would have been to Jonathan the senseless yapping of dogs. Now, again exercising charity, he saw it as tedious and academic, not merely because marriage between Montserrat and himself was extremely unlikely, but also because, if it ever came to such a marriage, he would certainly not let a genuflection or two hold him back. In these Scots, bigotry was rooted in centuries of ignorance, murder, treachery, and hatred.

The Spanish youths had come out of the water, flexing their muscles and shedding silvery drops like scales.

'All right,' said Peggy. 'We'll discuss it among us, and let you know.'

'Just a minute, Peggy,' said Katie. 'Let's get this clear. What are we expected to do? I mean, are we actually being asked to commit a crime?'

'Use your imagination, Katie. We're wanted to make a crowd so that maybe she'll not be noticed.'

'Aye, maybe. Whit if she is? And, wi' due respect to Mr Broxmead, what about his sisters, and his brither-in-law wi' the beard, no' to mention that scunner o' a painter? Hae they refused? It looks like it. Why? We're entitled to know.'

There was no time to tell her. The Spaniards arrived, proud and wet. They had swum very well, showing off like boys, and looked for compliments. Jonathan congratulated them. Andres mentioned that Celestino was a champion diver, Celestino that Andres had been third in the university four hundred metres backstroke championship. All this in Spanish. Jonathan left them trying to turn it into English.

The leaf was still in his hand. He felt like a hero of legend, only the efficacy of his amulet had not been guaranteed by the gods, nor was the end of the story known or the fate of the heroine to whose rescue he was now hastening, not through an enchanted wood where every tree writhed and impeded, but among men and women, most of them as terrifyingly indifferent as real trees, some more pertinaciously evil than any tree of myth, and a few brave, generous, and reassuring as leaves in spring.

'Un momento, señor.'

He turned. Enrique was pursuing him.

'Yes?'

'I want to tell you that Jordi Puig is a hero of Spain.' As he said it, in a whisper, he looked about him quickly; his holy medal tinkled on his neck. 'I am not a hero.'

'Few of us are. Has Jordi Puig got a sister?'

He looked surprised. 'Yes, Montserrat Puig. She is a very brave woman.' But he did not sound as if he altogether approved of her bravery. 'Thank God she has escaped.'

'Do you know her?'

'No, but I have seen her often at the university.'

'Is she well known there?'

'Very well known. She studied English. Do you know her yourself?'

'I have heard of her.'

Jonathan imagined her walking across the sunny quadrangles, discussing politics in the cool arcades, in the dark lecture rooms studying Beowulf and E. M. Forster. He saw her waiting for a tram in Plaza Universidad, or taking a yellow and black taxi. She walked along Pelayo, past the shop that advertised 'Helos Calientes' towards the Ramblas.

Always she was alone in the midst of crowds. Surely she must have had companions, friends, a lover? Why did his imagination exclude them?

'Are she and her brother communists?' he asked, just for the sake of speaking about her.

Enrique was indignant. 'That's just like you foreigners. If a man demands freedom in Spain he is thought to be a communist. It is unfortunate, because often in the end, fed up, he becomes one, like Tomas Balaguer.'

'Who is he?'

'Montserrat Puig's friend.'

The leaf dropped from his hand. 'Her friend?'

Enrique noticed it, made to stoop to pick it up, saw what it was, and left it. 'Yes. They were to be married, I think.'

'And where is he? In prison, too?'

'No. In Russia, they say.'

'So he's a communist?'

'He became one. He is very clever, and an atheist. That is a pity. Perhaps now that she has escaped she will join him in Russia. She has a very passionate mind.'

Jonathan smiled. 'You don't seem to approve of women with very passionate minds?'

'No. For women politics are not good. They turn their breasts to stone. Better for them children and a home. Do you not agree? Goodbye, señor.'

He held out his hand. Jonathan took it with a firmness that surprised them both. Then Enrique, with a bow, returned to his friends.

Jonathan picked up the leaf, now withering, and continued on his way to the hotel.

His mind was strangely clear, compassionate, and un-jealous, as he thought of Tomas Balaguer, Montserrat's sweetheart.

By fleeing to Russia he had shown he placed – what? – before his love for her. In the light of that tremendous

decision, it was seen that no young man became a communist in order to wrest from people their free minds and
give them in return packages of obedience, torturing if need
be any that opposed. Why then did he? Surely because, in
the face of much hatred, persecution, and contumely, he
believed that he was helping to bring about, with humani-
tarian speed, the end of hunger and ignorance, and all the
injustices inherent in them. Intelligent and truthful, he had
read accounts of how so many young men like himself had
grown disillusioned, after discovering the necessity, in a
brutal and sordid world, of brutal and sordid methods, how
the best of them had withdrawn into private silence, and
how others had turned like wolves upon their own dying
ideals. Young, and with hope like a passion, he had vowed
that no such disillusionment would ever demoralize him. On
the contrary, by his example he would show how brutality
and sordidness could be overcome. To achieve this millen-
nium, as glorious as Christ's, he had given up Montserrat.
But even if he were to succeed and became another saviour
of mankind, whose name would be remembered with
reverence for two thousand years, Jonathan would not wish
to take his place.

'I'd rather have her in the world as it is, than not have her
in the world remade,' he said to himself, aloud, as he began
the climb of the long flight of steps, between bushes of
purple flowers, up to the great white hotel. 'But of course I
shall not have her in any world. Why should I? How have I
deserved her? What is there in me for her to love? What
have I ever risked?'

Pausing, he looked back down on the beach and saw
the Scots girls dwindled to beetles. Two or three days ago
he would have described their existence as literally hellish,
rotting in a near slum in a grimy Glasgow side street, and
condemned to check football coupons. He had read that
fortunes of over a hundred thousand pounds could be

won in those pools for a stake of twopence, but that the odds were millions to one against. Well, his chances of winning Montserrat were hardly any greater, and ought not to be, since he had never all his life ventured even twopenceworth. For those who tried those coupons he had felt contempt, seeing them as degraders of life; now he was able, without humbug, and without any feeling of having to propitiate any revengeful god, to sympathize with them.

A surprise awaited him at the hotel reception desk. There he was told Señor Ashton had left by the early bus that morning.

'Didn't he leave any message?'

'What is your name, sir?'

When Jonathan gave it he was handed an envelope addressed to him.

He took it out on to the wide terrace above the swimming pool. It did not feel thick enough to contain the leaflet, but then half a sheet of thinnest notepaper would do to say the leaflet had already been handed in at or posted to the police station, and to explain why so godly a betrayal had been necessary.

It could well be that at that very moment Montserrat was being arrested.

He had to sit down, so heavy had the envelope become. His fingers were so apprehensive they couldn't tear it open. He looked about him piteously at all these carefree well-to-do holidaymakers.

At last he got it open. The message, whatever it was, was very brief. Slowly he unfolded the sheet, and, about to read, closed his eyes.

If Montserrat was still in the house when he got back he would tell her he loved her, taking every precaution that the manner of his telling would not insult her, whatever the disclosure itself might do. He would try to announce it with discretion, consideration, and dignity; wit he would eschew; eloquence and passion could be left till later if, that was, she did not dismiss him out of hand. Incongruity of course would do its best to stultify the announcement, and in all likelihood would succeed.

He opened his eyes and read Norman's message. Expecting anything from pornographic snarls to maudlin vicious piety, he was astonished.

> I have decided to return home to the States to see my parents. In a month or so I shall fly back and find out if Maddy still prefers her painter, or if, as I expect, he has packed up his easel and left her.

That was all. No mention of God; worse still, no mention of Montserrat or the leaflet, or even of Jonathan; only of Norman himself, and Maddy in terms of Norman. Egotism could go no further.

Yet the small curt words, with their massive conceit, reminded Jonathan of someone he knew. For a minute or so he wondered who it could be, and then found the truth leering him in the face; yes, it was himself. He too had emptied the world of everything but self; or, God pity him, he had been content to do so until he had fallen in love with Montserrat Puig.

Could love then be, not the conquest of self, but rather self's ultimate triumph?

Ransacking Norman's note again, and his own heart, he saw what was missing: humility. Without it love was an aggression of the spirit; with it, a surrender without shame. Like Norman, he had none; and like him too, despite that tie, he did not know how it could be cultivated. Montserrat must instinctively detect the flawed nature of his love. This would not necessarily mean she would reject it; her acceptance indeed might be as passionate as he could cope with;

but there would remain this deficiency that through time must bring inevitable deterioration.

He became aware he might be asking from himself, and so from Montserrat too, what was seldom, if ever, achieved. He was no different from those coupon fillers who, in avaricious dreams, spent the hundred thousand pounds they had one chance in millions of winning.

Twenty-Five

Posing for Lynedoch, and listening to Reeves's faintly lewd reminiscences of artists, Montserrat found herself comparing both of them with Jonathan, to their infinite disadvantage. At the same time she kept watching for him with an eagerness that she tried, several times, to subdue. When he did at last appear her perfunctory wave deceived them all; but she herself realized it meant more than if she had jumped up and run laughing to be clasped in his arms. He was too far away to see the blush that followed, and the smile.

Lynedoch she sympathized with and admired; but he seemed to her to stand at the centre, watching, appreciating, absorbing, but never letting himself be involved. She saw how he was prepared to use Maddy, and ruthlessly discard her once her usefulness was exhausted, which might be in a week, a month, or twenty years. He had spoken to Montserrat about his dead sweetheart, with sorrow, but also with a curious reconcilement, as if those experiences, of love and loss, had been undergone simply for his advancement as a painter. She had watched him hold Linda in his arms as capably as any woman, and he had told her how as a boy of ten he had looked after the babies of neighbours in return for pennies to buy paper and coloured pencils. Yet not for a moment had he given the impression that he would ever be interested in children of his own, whereas Jonathan had, for all his diffidence and awkwardness, his slightly outraged elegance, his use of

articulate endearments, and his embarrassment when
Linda made plain her fondness for him.

Reeves seemed to her basically selfish and casual in his
emotions. Part of his beard's purpose, she thought, was to
hide the effort he had to make to keep his love for his wife
and child alert. His intellectuality reminded her of Tomas's:
for him people were for drawing, or for the appreciation of
clever criticism such as his own, just as for Tomas they were
for the satisfaction of a passion for justice.

Jonathan was the handsomest man she had ever seen.
From the minute she had set eyes on him she had been
wanting to stroke his fair silken hair; which was why in the
garden she had so promptly slapped his face. What had
irritated Bridie, his calm-browed dignity, she found moving;
it seemed to her promise of a maturity in which the sadness
of so much of human life would be recognized, without
cynicism or despair. Despite what Isabel had said, she
thought him kind; and what the rest, himself included,
considered conceit and self-love, she saw as innocence.
Sometimes, troubling his fine face, it gave him a resemblance to a saint she had seen in one of the fourteenth-
century paintings in Montjuich Museum. He might not
admit it, but he was very religious; otherwise why should
he struggle so hard to get rid of what obscured God in him?

Without answering her own question as to whether she
was falling in love with him, she let herself dream of
marriage to him, living in the south of France in sight of
her beloved Pyrenees, or in the fogs and rain of England,
and having children one of whom at least would be fair-
haired, and one called Jordi. She would take her mother to
live with them, and Jordi too after he was released.

Smiling, she would hardly have noticed the tears running
down her cheeks had not Lynedoch stopped painting and
stood staring at her.

He came closer. 'I'm sorry,' he said.

'It is nothing. I'm very foolish. Please go on. I am so sorry.'

'No. That's enough for one day. I've been told I'd want to keep on painting if the world was ending about me.'

It must have been his dead Margaret who had said it.

'You'll be feeling yours is pretty near an end,' he said. 'Your brother in prison, your mother ill. Maddy told me.'

She shook her head. 'She'll get better, he will be free.'

'Aye, that's right; and Jonathan will get you to Perpignan.'

David had dozed off. Now he awoke. Out shot his long neck and twitching nose to inspect her exciting tears.

'So you saw it after all?' he cried. 'Jonathan said no, but it seemed to me you had a right to.'

'I do not understand,' she said.

'Yesterday's *Times*. There's a report in it about your brother. You haven't seen it? Just a sec, and I'll go and see if Ampara hasn't used it to wrap up fish heads.'

He got up and went skipping in.

Lynedoch scowled after him. 'He knows where it is all right. I saw him slip it behind the books. He wanted you to see it.'

'But Jonathan did not?'

'He was passionate about it; that's to say, as far as he can be passionate about anything. I know it'll show my inferior upbringing if I'm rude about my host behind his back; but he's such a phoney.'

'A phoney?'

'False, you know; insincere to his finger-tips, or should I say to his toe-nails? Don't depend on him too much, if you can help it.'

'Who else am I to depend on?'

Lynedoch sneered at his own thoughts, and also at her predicament. 'Well, just be careful,' he said. 'My mother was a small woman, about this height. She worked at scrubbing office floors. Sometimes when she came in at night her back

was so sore and bent she couldn't straighten it. Her hands
were as rough as paws.'

He glared at Montserrat's own hands, soft and well cared
for, and appeared, from his frown, to be suggesting that,
compared with his mother's lifelong servitude, her brother's
and her own imprisonment, if that befell, were hardly worth
the world's sympathy and headlines. He was like Tomas,
with one difference: he did not seem prepared to risk a finger
to alleviate the poverty he was so bitter about; on the
contrary, he seemed in a curious way pleased with it, as
something to reveal in paint.

Reeves came hurrying out with the newspaper. 'I was just
in time to save it from the fish heads,' he cried. He handed it
to her, folded neatly, the paragraph marked with red ink.
'Maddy and Isabel are ready,' he said to Lynedoch. 'You're
ordered in to wash the paint off your hands and change your
clothes.'

They were all going down to the beach.

Montserrat read proudly. Lynedoch and Reeves were for
the moment hateful, especially the latter, whose sympathy,
like his curiosity, was too sexual. She wished Jonathan would
come.

'It's not so bad as it looks,' said Reeves, with bright
English fatuousness. 'Under Spanish law, I believe, a sentence of eight years is usually reduced to about three.'

'I've just been saying,' said Lynedoch dourly, 'my mother,
and multitudes like her, served life sentences of hard labour,
for no other crime than poverty. Nobody ever called her a
martyr.'

'Don't heed him,' cried Reeves. 'He's a sour Scot.' He
tried to take her hand, but she did not let him. 'Cheer up.
Come with us to the beach. After all, isn't tonight the fiesta
of San Juan?'

Yes, it was; and she had vowed to put up the leaflets all
over the village, as her contribution to the festivities.

'Let's rejoice,' said Reeves. 'Let us for one day forget our troubles. Tonight we're having a party. What the hell if the lava's flowing down on us?'

'I shall wait here,' she said.

'For Jonathan?' In that hairy leer were amazement and envy.

'Porque no?' she asked, smiling.

He shook his head. 'I wouldn't, in your position, depend too much on him.'

'Just what I've been telling her,' said Lynedoch.

She was alone in the garden, with a view of the gate, when Jonathan returned. He entered, long-striding with purpose, but when he saw her seated in that unusual place, he stopped, under a tree whose flowers were almost the same shade as his mauve shorts. The sun, piercing the screen of leaves, shone on his yellow hair. Thus had meditated the saint in the painting, oblivious of his denigrators.

Slowly he came forward, on sandals like the saint's, over earth as Catalan as that the saint had trod, hundreds of years ago. His hands, as empty, were as full of glory, as he held them out towards her.

She had never felt anything like this at any other man's approach. Jordi in prison was safe; her mother was recovered; Spain had her freedom.

He stood looking down at her. Demurely, laughing within, she tugged her skirt another fraction of an inch over her knees, which were still revealed, and were, she was glad to see, as attractive as such knobbly pieces of bone could be.

Suddenly he dropped on his beside her, and laid his hand on the arm of her chair.

'I have something to say to you,' he said, in agitated, ungrammatical Spanish.

She waited, knowing what it was. Her scalp tingled, her

knees, her very toes; her sore breast ached, with joy. She had
a great desire to put out her hand and stroke his hair.

'I have no right to have you here,' he said, 'and not say
this. But let me make it clear. It puts you under no obli-
gation whatever. I gave you a promise which I intend to
keep. Please don't be insulted. I must say it, for the sake of
my own peace of mind, and of your protection. It will make
no difference, at least as far as I am concerned, to your
staying here, or to our journey to Perpignan on Sunday.'

She wanted to laugh now, to celebrate his innocence. She
felt rather as she did when Linda was in her arms. His own
child would have fair hair and blue eyes.

'Te quiero,' he said.

This time, her face like a rose, she did laugh.

He repeated it in English: 'I love you.'

'No.' What she was denying she didn't know. Certainly
not his right to say he loved her.

He assumed it was. His face was stricken. The saint had
lost sight of God. He could not speak. An ant that had taken
his leg for a tree now discovered its mistake and hurried back
down. She seemed to know that ant, and loved it, and all its
fellows in the grass.

'I'm sorry,' said Jonathan. 'I shan't ever say it again. I
shall try not to let it show, either when we're alone, or
when we're in company. I'll try, though I may not be able
to prevent it. Perhaps you think I haven't known you long
enough. That's true; but there's a kind of knowing that in
an hour can find out more than other kinds can in a
lifetime.'

Yes, it was true. Did she not know even that ant, still
descending his knee? She knew him better than his sisters
did, better even than Madeleine, who had been with him in
their mother's womb.

She was about to confess that she might be in love with
him; instead, to her own surprise, though not to his, she

found herself saying, harshly and arrogantly: 'I want to telephone to find out how my mother is.'

His hand travelled, hesitant as the ant, up past his face to his hair. 'Yes. But Bridie said you mustn't, not until you're safe.'

'My mother is more important to me than my own safety.'

Words and tone were provocatively cruel. She could not understand why, unless it was, as Tomas had said, that she, like all Spanish women, kissers of crucifixes, needed a daily sacrifice. Whatever the reason, wishing with all her heart to surrender and weep with joy in his arms, she felt her face turn hard.

'Your safety is important to me,' he stammered.

'If you're afraid that telephoning from your house may get you into trouble, then I'll do it from a café.'

'I am afraid, for your sake.'

'Many people hide behind that plea. If they were not afraid for their wives, their husbands, their children, their parents, how brave they would be, how they would suffer pain and persecution, how they would give their lives, to oppose injustice.'

'In many cases they may be speaking the truth.'

She knew he was right. Yet she said, scornfully: 'Easy for them to say so, since it's never likely to be put to the test.'

With a sigh like a groan he rose. She saw the impression of the grass on his knees, and fragments adhering. The ant had gone.

'Very well,' he said. 'Telephone if you wish.'

She jumped up. 'I do wish. Now.' She ran towards the house.

Ampara looked out of the kitchen, saw who it was in the hall, snorted, and withdrew.

Montserrat lifted the telephone and recklessly asked for her own number in Barcelona.

Jonathan appeared in the sitting-room. In the kitchen Ampara banged pots together.

The telephone crackled in her ear.

Jonathan came forward shyly. 'Sometimes it takes half an hour to get through to Barcelona,' he said.

She stared at him insolently. 'Of course. We Spaniards are so inefficient.'

'I didn't mean that.'

'It's true. We aren't even fit to govern ourselves. But you are not interested in politics.'

'Not really. I'd rather be interested in people.'

'Good heavens, weren't you, like everybody else, born with such an interest?'

'Interested in them for their own sakes, I mean. No, I wasn't born with such an interest, I'm afraid. I lack humility.'

Not altogether, she thought; but she said: 'Only God is interested in us for our own sakes.'

He smiled and nodded. 'I met a student this morning who said he knew of you. He told me about Tomas Balaguer. I can understand, having known a man like Tomas, you must find most other men, and me especially, trivial, ineffectual, and selfish.'

I think you have for me, she thought, far happier potentialities than Tomas ever could have. Yet she kept staring insolently at him. Some protective instinct seemed to be at work in her; Lynedoch's and Reeves's warnings had nothing to do with it.

Then she was through to Barcelona. It was her aunt who spoke, astonished and frightened. 'Yes, yes,' she gasped, in a great hurry, 'your mother wishes you not to come, not to telephone. She is well enough.' That was all. The telephone went quiet again. Hardly ten seconds had passed.

Jonathan came closer. 'What is it? Montserrat, what is it?'

'I don't think it's true.'

'For God's sake, she's not—?'

'Dead? No, on the contrary, she's well. So my aunt says. But it is not true. I think someone was there.'

'Bridie said there would be. That's why it's dangerous to phone.'

She put down the telephone. 'Today's San Juan,' she said.

'Yes. I keep forgetting. I'm not in a festive mood, I'm afraid. Maddy's having a party here tonight. I'm sorry.'

'Why be sorry? I shall have a party myself, after everyone has gone.'

'What do you mean?'

'I am going to put up leaflets about Jordi outside the police station, and all over the village.'

She went so close that her breasts touched him. He shrank back.

'But what good will that do?' he asked.

'Are you afraid?' Again she pressed forward, again he retreated, this time into the sitting-room. She followed. 'This isn't a game, Jonathan.' It was the first time she had called him by his Christian name.

'I know that, Montserrat.'

'In a battle, if your comrades are captured or killed, do you lie down in the mud and shut your eyes, or creep away on your knees?'

'It's people I want to believe in, not causes.'

'Causes are people.'

'I don't quite see that.'

They were so close she felt him trembling. She trembled herself. Let her smile, and they would embrace. She would then at last have set out on the retreat from the cause in which she had grown up; but retreat ought not to be joyful.

'I believe in freedom for the people of Spain.'

'Yes, but so many of them are not interested. Perhaps, like myself, they are not sure what it means. To be able to vote for this or that party is hardly freedom.'

'You are from England where there is freedom; but you prefer to live in Spain, where there is none.'

'There is a good deal, Montserrat.'

'Tell me. Tell me about this wonderful freedom which I, and my brother, and my friends, have been such fools as not to have noticed.' She was in tears of indignation.

Wishing to console her, he still persisted, his face pale: 'Freedom to fall in love.'

'You might as well say, freedom to breathe the air.'

'That, too. To marry; to have children; to sit in the sun; to drink wine; to swim in the sea; to listen to music.'

She stared at him. 'You are a coward,' she said, and repeated it in English. It was not an accusation so much as a discovery.

'It's possible I am, according to any one of a dozen definitions.'

'According to mine. I could never marry a man who is a coward.'

For a few seconds, her breast heaving, she stared at him in an angry sadness. Then she ran upstairs to her room.

He heard the door shut, not with the slam of transient anger, but with the quietness of permanent renunciation.

Minutes later, as he sat bewildered, Ampara appeared in the dining alcove and began to lay the table for lunch. She set down each plate, spoon, and glass with deliberation, as if sending him a message. He knew what it was.

'Why worry about her, the insolent stranger? Even if you are a coward, what right has she, a guest in your house, to accuse you? You do not need courage, you who do not have to work for your living and associate with people you do not like. As for a woman to love, why, there are any number made the same way she is. Yes, she's better-looking than most, but is not her chastity a form of pride in her beautiful body, which neither you nor any other man is ever going to be allowed to caress, even in love?'

A knife clinked against a glass. It said: 'You were furious with me for striking her. Aren't you grateful now?'

Before he knew what he was doing he was over at the table and had seized Ampara, as if trying to hurt her as she had hurt Montserrat.

She yelled out, snatched up a knife, and struck his wrist with the blunt edge. She was laughing. His grip of the foam rubber was not very painful; indeed, it was quite pleasurable.

'You struck her,' he said, so enraged he might have been drunk. 'I'm warning you, if anyone hurts her again, I'll kill him. Tell Pedro that.'

Then he fled into the garden.

Stroking her breast, she went out on to the terrace to watch him pacing up and down as if, she thought with a grin, he was nursing a baby that wouldn't sleep.

What he was nursing were the twins cowardice and shame.

Twenty-Six

Maddy was indignant when he asked her either to cancel or moderate the party she had arranged in honour of John Lynedoch's saint's day. The whole village, she cried, indeed the whole country, would be celebrating. It would do Montserrat more good to join in the fun rather than sulk in her room sticking pins into Franco's image or, more likely considering her recent attitude, into Jonathan's. Loftily and mendaciously he replied he had been thinking of Linda. Was the unfortunate infant to be kept awake in terror, by the fireworks and music from the village, and also by drunken revellers in the garden and house? If the parents didn't object, Maddy snapped, why should the uncle? Then, relenting, she had patted his cheek and whispered: 'She's Spanish, after all. We may know the language well enough, but not, God help us, the soul.'

Since lunchtime they had all noticed that Montserrat had become closer to him but also more hostile. David had wondered if Jonathan, miscalculating as only Jonathan could, had made a pass at her; and Isabel had answered tartly she hoped so, for though she had nothing against the girl, except perhaps her air of possessing the most precious virginity in Christendom, still she would much rather Jonathan didn't get entangled with her and her politics.

'Look at what's happened to him already, because of her influence,' she said. 'Didn't he more or less tell us that if he had to choose between us and her, we're the ones he'd throw out, his own sister and his own niece?'

'Not to mention his own brother-in-law. What he ought to have done, Isabel, with our connivance, with our assistance even, was to take one of those little Scots creatures – he could have spun a coin to decide which – and practised on her. What I mean is, now that he's condescended to step down into the mud beside us, he's got to learn that it's not only one's trousers one removes, it's also one's dignity. No man, not even our Jonathan, can make love, or even dream of making it, with dignity. The trouble is he's apparently got it into his Apollo-like head that with this black-haired Spanish beauty he may be able to achieve it. But, I fear, most certainly not with her. They tell me these Spanish girls, once the priest has blessed the unions, are the most exuberant of partners.'

'Need you be so coarse?'

'Coarseness, my dear, is like salt. Without a pinch of it how unappetizing the choicest of flesh.'

'You of course have fistfuls to spare.'

These accusations were on their reverse side compliments to his virility, in his own estimation well enough deserved. Therefore he received them with appreciative cackles.

'As you know, my love, it is a belief of mine that all women, even revolutionary Catalan virgins, abhor the dignified approach even more than nature abhors a vacuum. Therefore I can't say I'm surprised she has gone sour on him. Consider it yourself, darling. How would you like to have a dignified pass made at you? Lust in a top hat?'

'I might welcome it for a change.' But she could not help smiling at what really was the most ludicrous of contemplations.

Jonathan confided in Maddy. 'She thinks I'm a coward.'

Maddy was furious. 'Well, she's got a damned cheek. Doesn't she realize that for you to try and smuggle her over the frontier, with your equipment if you see what I mean, is nothing short of heroism?'

'Yes, I see what you mean, Maddy. So apparently does she. We all know I'm more than likely to bungle it out of sheer funk, and land us all in jail.'

For which reason Isabel and David were still opposed to his attempting it.

'If she thinks that,' said Maddy, 'then let her find someone else to save her. She's surrounded by Catalans, isn't she?'

'Be fair, Maddy. As an Englishman I have a better chance, and if I'm caught I doubt if I would get anything like the punishment they would.'

'The fact remains, they'll all be celebrating tonight, while you're worrying yourself sick about her.'

'I love her.'

'I wish you didn't.'

'You said yourself she was a treasure.'

'So she is, but somehow not for you.'

'For someone with courage?'

So the party went on, from ten till half past three, wilder and gayer than last year's, for Maddy this time had a John of her own to fête. The garden was hung with Japanese lanterns, the record player was brought out on to the terrace, there was dancing among the trees and upon the ants, and beer bottles accumulated in the flower beds.

Montserrat was invited to come down and join in; she declined. An hour or so later David staggered whiskily up the stairs to ask her again, and found her door locked; he pleaded, talking a great deal about the discarding of dignity, but in the end had to be content with a visit to the bathroom.

Jonathan, keeping a vigil under her window, found himself molested by a small long-haired toothy woman, a middle-aged painter of nudes, who made him dance with her and broke her promise not to do anything indiscreet. He noticed, as she clung round his neck, her feet off the ground, that Montserrat was looking down. He hoped she realized that his forbearance, in the face of the shrieks of the other guests, was a sort of courage.

About one o'clock an opportunity to show more orthodox courage presented itself. Pedro, in civil guard uniform, and carrying a gun, appeared in the garden. He did not immediately, as was his custom, slink along the side of the house to enter by the back door and dally with Ampara in the kitchen. Instead, he stood watching the merriment. No doubt his feet were tired and he thought he deserved half an hour's solace from his sweetheart. But his purpose could be altogether more sinister; he could have come to prepare the way for his colleagues now waiting outside to rush in at his signal and drag Montserrat off to prison.

That he yawned, was unshaven, reeked of cheap wine, picked his nose, and was subservient in no way disproved sinisterness. Brutalities and injustices were inflicted by ordinary men of one class at the orders of ordinary men of another. Men remained themselves when committing evil.

Towards Jonathan, Pedro was always respectful, but also very awkward. This, Jonathan knew, was because he was jealous. Ampara tormented him by hinting, or by saying openly, that he, Jonathan, slept with her. Even a moron would have known that to be absurdly untrue, but Pedro was in love with her and so capable of submoronic suspicions. To reassure the fellow, Jonathan had, without ever uttering a word on the subject, made it clear he considered her as far beneath him sexually as socially. Pedro may or may not have been reassured, but he had certainly never shown himself grateful.

He saluted amiably when Jonathan stood beside him.

'I hope we're not disturbing any of the neighbours,' said Jonathan.

Pedro laughed. 'All the world is enjoying itself tonight.'
He pointed to the sky.

Rockets exploded into blue, green, and red stars. In the
plaza a sardana band played as if for dancers on distant cliff
tops.

'Señorita Maddy is very happy,' said the policeman. He
liked Maddy, and as he watched her dance with Lynedoch
his small eyes under the tricorn hat glittered. His neck
seemed to grow thicker, a sign, Jonathan had read, of lust.

Then Pedro added: 'I don't see Señorita Ripoll, the
nursemaid. Does she not dance?'

Whatever else, it was an impertinent question; and it
could be a great deal else.

'The baby is disturbed by the noise,' said Jonathan. He
had caught sight of a beer bottle lying on the grass; against a
gun, or half a dozen guns, it would make a poor weapon, but
he would use it.

'Ah yes,' said Pedro, like all his race considerate of
children. 'For the little ones it is not good. For dogs,
too. All over the village they howl.'

More rockets burst above them. Beyond shone the stars of
eternity.

'Are your guests all English, señor?'

Jonathan glanced again towards the bottle. Were the ants
reconnoitring it? Did they sleep at night? Would the smell
of beer sicken them, as it did him? How little he knew, after
all.

'No. There are French, German, Swiss, and Spaniards.'

'No Americans?'

'I don't think so.' They were Maddy's friends, not his; she
had invited them.

'Señor Ashton, he is not here tonight?'

'No. He left this morning to return home to America.'

Pedro's eyes became smaller. He scratched his thick neck.
'He is very rich?' he asked.

It was unexpected, but still sinister.

'I believe so.'

'I ask, señor, because last night I met him in the village, and he gave me this.'

He took longer to get it out of his pocket than was surely necessary. It wasn't a leaflet, but something almost as ominous, a thousand-peseta note. Pedro laughed. 'Half of it is for Ampara. She will put it with the rest of her savings. She says I want to marry her for her money. She says too she won't because my hair is black.' He laughed again. 'I tell her I shall be like the ladies of Barcelona and dye it.'

Was that a hint he knew about the plot to smuggle Montserrat over the border? What traitor had told him? It could not have been Ampara who, eavesdropper though she was, did not know English. Isabel perhaps, advised by David?

Maddy was arranging a sardana. She called to Jonathan to come and join in; he paid no heed. She called to Pedro, who apologized and said his feet were too tired. About a dozen formed the ring. Only she and three Spaniards knew the dance, the rest relied on high spirits and agility. The result was hardly as dedicated or progressive as a good sardana should be. Montserrat would have been offended by those antics, but not her fellow Catalan Pedro, who enjoyed them hugely.

It was a shock therefore when he asked: 'Excuse me, señor, but what do you know about Miss Ripoll?'

The coward in Jonathan stammered, and wished to run away; the lover kept him where he was, determined to protect her; the Englishman bristled at the impertinence.

'Why do you ask that?' he demanded, shrilly.

'It's really my duty, sir. You see, Señor Ashton told me she was a communist, wanted by the police in Barcelona.'

'Was he drunk? He must have been, handing out thousand-peseta notes and saying absurd things like that.'

'Is she a friend of yours, sir?'

'As a matter of fact, I am going to marry her.'

Pedro's face beamed then, like a fellow lover's, not a policeman's.

'Let me tell you this, about Mr Ashton,' whispered Jonathan into that hairy ear. 'He came here hoping my sister would marry him. She refused, therefore he began to molest Miss Ripoll. He was that kind of man.'

Pedro nodded. 'I warned Ampara about him.'

'And I had to warn Miss Ripoll. So for spite he spreads this ridiculous lie about her.'

'It is a pity; otherwise he's a fine gentleman, very merry, and generous.' He picked reflectively at his nose. 'He said another thing about her.'

'About Miss Ripoll?'

'Yes.'

'I'm afraid I don't want to hear it, Pedro.'

'He said her name wasn't Ripoll at all, but Puig.'

Jonathan hated Norman then, but felt pity for him too. What desperation, what lack of faith in man and God, had provoked him into this denunciation of a woman who had done him no harm and whose devoutness he had coveted?

Pedro went on dourly: 'He said her brother, Jordi, was arrested in Barcelona a week or so ago, for activities against the government.'

All this time Pedro appeared to be still enjoying the jumps and prancings of the dancers. But there was a stink of policeman off him, ranker than that of cheap wine, of sweat, of garlic, or of the polish with which he'd burnished his hat, or of the oil on his gun.

'I've investigated,' he said. 'It's all true. She has got some leaflets. Tell her to burn them. Do it yourself, señor, for all our sakes. Do you understand?'

'Yes.'

'May I wish you both, sir, good luck? By the way, I

wouldn't tell anyone, not even Ampara. Will it be all right if
I go in and have a chat with her for a few minutes?'

'Ampara?'

Pedro nodded.

'Certainly you may. And thank you for your good wishes.'

Jonathan watched him as he discreetly made his way
round to the back door. It seemed incredible that Montserrat's liberty, and his own happiness, should depend on so
commonplace a man, with his eyes close together and hair in
his ears. But then surely one of the lessons of history was
that evil in evil men was conquerable, it was the evil in the
commonplace men, that was to say, in the vast majority, that
by its very cumulative bulk poisoned so much of life and
kept the race's moral stature from growing.

Slowly he admitted that such a judgment was unjust and
showed no growth in him. The truth was that Pedro,
representative of that majority, was taking as big a risk as
Jonathan himself. In commonplace men was a willingness to
defy or at least attempt to frustrate evil.

One thing was certain, Montserrat must now be made to
give up her own wild defiance; for Pedro's sake, if not for her
own, the leaflets must be destroyed.

At last, with the approach of dawn, and the running out of
the drink, the guests went off. The painter of nudes wanted
to sleep with Jonathan, and announced it in a series of cries
like a cock crowing. She was hurried away by friends while
Jonathan, hiding on the roof, hoped Montserrat had not
heard.

Maddy, drunk herself, dragged Lynedoch to her bed,
where he indulged in a long morose self-exculpation.

Isabel and David retired to their room, he so drunk he did
not reach the bed and collapsed on the floor, she so annoyed
by his behaviour during the party when he'd kissed at least
half a dozen women, that she seized his beard and used it as a

rope to haul him to his feet and into bed. Failing, she left
him to wake up next day with a chill in the bladder and
aching shoulders.

Leaving the empty bottles and dirty glasses, Ampara
climbed into the lower bunk and wished Jonathan was in
it with her.

Jonathan kept watch on the roof. Now that the rockets
had ceased the stars were bigger and brighter. After the din
of celebrations the village slept. Far off a guitar played
wearily, but it too soon went quiet. Looking about him at
the shining roofs, Jonathan tried to adopt a godlike view,
not out of vainglory, or contempt for the littleness of his
fellows, but from a desire to be fairer to them than he had
ever been before, and also, above all, to keep away
thoughts about Montserrat which in any other man he
would have called lascivious and which in himself deserved
no better name. Yes, despite the danger by which she was
surrounded, he yearned to seize her in his arms, kiss her,
and enjoy with his body the softness and beauty of hers.
Therefore in a kind of flight, he tried to imagine himself
a disinterested, disembodied, universally compassionate
spirit; but he could not possibly succeed, with that
fiery-blooded intruder within growing more and more
earthy and urgent in his desires.

Afraid lest she should escape him, he slipped downstairs,
and sat waiting, amidst the litter of the party and the stench
of spilt beer. Less than ten minutes later, before he had time
to fall asleep, he heard her door open and then the third top
step creak under her cautious weight. Soon she was in the
sitting-room. In her hand she held the leaflets.

She did not notice him in his corner, and was out of the
house half-way to the gate before he made up on her. She
refused to stop. He took her by the arm; she flung off his
grip, and hurried still faster. Almost at the gate he threw
both arms about her; part embrace, part arrest, it succeeded

as neither. She kept on, pulling him with her and trampling on his bare toes.

Then suddenly, their heads amidst an odorous bush, she stopped struggling, went quiet and still in his arms, save for gasps and shivers. He remembered her sore breast which he must have hurt. He quaked with tenderness and compunction.

'I'm sorry,' he said. 'If I've hurt you I'm sorry.' He became aware his toes were smarting where her heels seemed to have lifted off the skin. 'I'd rather I was torn to pieces than have you hurt.'

'What do you mean, attacking me like this?'

'I've got you now, and I'm never going to let you go.'

'No one's got me. Didn't I say you were a coward?'

Yes, she had. But at that moment, with her in his arms, reminding him he was a coward, he felt happy and brave. When he stared down at her in the grey light she stared up at him so boldly that kissing her, on the nose more than the mouth, was the gladdest and certainly the bravest thing he had ever done. She did not kiss him back but neither did she draw away or trample on his toes again.

There was silence. It lasted five seconds, but during it he made the most exciting discovery of his life, not that she loved him but that she was prepared to consider the possibility of loving him. It seemed so tremendous a concession on her part he felt he ought to warn her against it.

'I could never love a coward,' she murmured.

He would have kissed her again, but she stopped him with a question that tore at his heart: 'Am I to do nothing to help my brother?'

'What can we do?'

Both of them noticed his use of the plural.

'We can put these where people will see them,' she said.

'No, no. These will have to be burnt.'

'Burnt?' She tried to push him off.

'Yes. You see, Pedro knows about them. He knows you're Montserrat Puig, he knows about Jordi.'

'Who told him?'

'Norman Ashton.' Again, with rage and hatred in his heart, and in his voice, he wondered at the barrenness of faith that had produced such treachery. 'He's gone now, but he told Pedro before he went. For some reason, for some marvellous reason, Pedro's willing to say nothing.' He had never felt more grateful to any man.

'He is a Catalan.'

Yes, but Judas had been a Jew. 'That could be it, partly. I'm afraid I owe him an apology. I used to think of him as stupid and ordinary.'

'Don't apologize,' she said, intensely. 'Most of them *are* stupid and ordinary.'

He paused, disconcerted. That she had a reason to condemn them showed all the more clearly he had none.

'Still,' he said, his lips against her hair, 'he's going to say nothing to his superiors.'

'If I burn these?'

'Yes. He's afraid, I suppose, of being accused of all kinds of complicity.'

'Stupid and ordinary and afraid.'

He bent down until his head was touching hers, so that he could feel the passion of protest in her. It was an ingredient in her own whole wonderful strangeness. Yes, she was a treasure, to be spent for the rest of his life, if not here in Catalonia, then across in Rossignol in France, where her beloved Catalan was spoken. Done in her company the smallest things in life, like entering a shop to buy bread, would bring delight, and there would be an endless consecution of them.

Her fingers were digging into his arm. 'Take me to see my mother,' she whispered.

His heart again went so swiftly cold with fear he knew he

must indeed be a coward. Filthy-handed, filthier-minded men were waiting to seize her, and her mother was dying. He could not bear to watch her suffer or be ill-treated.

'Don't you want to see her yourself?' she asked.

Of course. Love had duties, which it ought to have known instinctively. Loving Montserrat, he must also attempt at least to love her people. 'Yes, yes,' he said.

'If I didn't see her myself, and you did, I should be satisfied.'

'I would like very much to see her, and tell her about us.'

After a pause, she said: 'What about these?'

She meant the leaflets. He knew now they could never be burnt. At the same time they must not be allowed to destroy her and Pedro.

'There are places between here and Barcelona where they could be used.' On the door of the cathedral at Gerona, for instance, at the top of the immense flight of steps.

At that moment the sun began to sparkle on the roof-tops. A cock crowed. Within a minute the earth was as young and fresh and golden as in his expectations. Somewhere a pail clattered. The human day was beginning.

Twenty-Seven

By ten o'clock they were ready to leave. Ampara, blear-eyed with sleep and suspicion, got out of bed to make breakfast for them, though they had been happy enough to make it for themselves. Though it was obvious Pedro had said nothing to her about Montserrat's true identity, she distrusted their happiness and kept asking obliquely what they were up to, to be reminded politely by Jonathan that it was none of her business. Thereupon she inquired sarcastically if they intended to be back for lunch. No, she was told. For dinner? Another firm but courteous negative. She knew he was treating her with such magnanimity not because she was herself, Ampara, red-cheeked, with hair as black as Montserrat's if not quite so expensively shampooed, but because she was a member of the same sex as his sweetheart. She would have been better pleased had he been rude.

He did not want to go without telling Maddy; after all, it was possible he might spend the next month or two in a Spanish jail. But he could not bear to knock on the door of her room while she lay within beside Lynedoch. That was an ignominy on her part, a degradation, an indulgence to what in her was cheap, vulgar, and despairing. Bright-minded though she usually was, Maddy had in her a core of darkness. He, who knew and loved her so well, could detect it at the heart of her merriest laughter and in the tilt of her head as she skied across the bay. Her present enthusiasm for Lynedoch's work was genuine enough, for she admired adventurous and original painting; but it was also partly a revenge upon herself, and perhaps upon Jonathan too, for their unmitigatable mediocrity. Last night when Jonathan had appealed to her she had called him an archaic, sterile, and cowardly prude. He had tried in desperation to explain that her drunken fornication with Lynedoch was all the more hateful to him in that it inevitably depreciated his own feelings for Montserrat. Love, like peace, seemed to him indivisible; those who made it sordid for themselves made it so for everyone; the redeemers were those who honoured it for the glory it was.

He was determined to be such a redeemer.

Among the legacies left him by his aunt had been some valuable jewellery, most of which he had passed on to Maddy and Isabel. His aunt had requested that he should keep her engagement ring and give it some day to his own fiancée. Now this morning he took it out of the safe in his bedroom while Montserrat was packing some clothes into her suitcase. The door was open. The cot with Linda asleep in it had been carried out on to the terrace.

'I'd like you to have this,' he said.

She stared at it in his palm, shook her head, smiled, and blushed. 'No.' But she stopped packing and sat down on the bed, making the movement of slipping a ring on to her finger.

He knelt beside her. 'It will commit you to nothing, unless you wish to be committed.'

'But we have known each other so short a time.' She counted the days on her fingers.

'Does that matter? I know you well enough to love you. I don't want to know you completely, all at once. I just want to know you more and more. Nothing, I think, could be more wonderful.'

He gazed at her: face, hands, knees, body, feet, all were beautiful, cherished, and strange. He bent and kissed her

knee. She put her hand on his head. Passion surged
through him: it might have been expressed by sliding
his hand up her thigh, or by pushing her back upon the
bed – after a detour to shut the door; what he did was to
take her hand gently and slip the ring over her third finger.
It was a good fit.

She glanced from ring to him with a mixture of pride,
humbleness, amazement, amusement, and affection. 'Innocent,' she whispered.

She meant him, and she was not being contemptuous
either, although he saw in her eyes that she was aware of the
fleshly thoughts that had been, indeed still were, turgid in
his mind.

'Perhaps if they think we are engaged,' he said, 'it may
help.'

'They?'

'The police.'

She wanted to kiss him for his innocence, and did so, on
the brow.

He could not speak, so dry with fear had his mouth
become at the utterance of the word. Holding her hand
tightly he was about to plead with her not to risk their visit
to Barcelona when something stopped him; it was simply an
understanding of how necessary it was for her to see her
mother.

'Will you tell your mother?' he asked instead.

'Tell her what?'

'That we are engaged.'

'Are we?' She touched the ring with her lips. 'It's very
beautiful.'

'It could never be beautiful enough for you. I want to
explain.'

'There's nothing to explain, Jonathan.'

'Yes, Montserrat, there is. You called me an innocent. I
suppose in many ways I am.'

'I meant it as a compliment.'

'I know you did. But others have used the word opprobriously; that's what I want to explain. It concerns my attitude to women, or sex. I'm afraid I've always regarded them with some disdain. Their laughter I used to call vulgar and immodest. To be frank, I still find it so, in many instances. So many of them cheapen love; my own sister, I am sorry to say, is one. I love Maddy, but she does seem to me to take a dreadful pleasure out of cheapening love, as if it could only be made bearable by being made a little sordid.'

She tried to calm him, but he went on, more impassioned than ever: 'The result was, I retired behind fastidiousness, and cynicism. Many think therefore that I'm devoid of passion and normal desires. It is not true. I find this very difficult to express in Spanish – with so many mistakes and a ludicrous misuse of the subjunctive – but what I really mean is this: I'd rather the police arrested you in my sight than that I should dishonour my love for you.'

She had listened with acute concentration, like a language tutor, and once or twice helped him out with a word or expression when he got stuck; but at the end, when he looked for grave appreciation, she laughed. Two or three shocked blinks later he saw such laughter was the right, the cleansing response. He joined in, a little shakily. The ring on her left hand sparkled with happier promise than the sun had on the roof-tops at dawn.

Thus they were, he still kneeling, she on the bed, both laughing, when Isabel, yawning and haggard in a yellow dressing-gown, looked in on them.

'What's this?' she asked, with sour humour. 'Don Quixote wooing his Dulcinea?'

She came in, saw the ring, and was angry. More than once she had hinted it ought to be given to her; her own was so less splendid. Now she was being proved right; no more than a child, or a monkey, was Jonathan fit to have the disposal of so valuable a gift. Here he was playing at lovers, as embarrassingly as she had imagined he would, and handing over to a stranger a ring worth five hundred pounds. As Isabel had suspected all along, this Spanish girl wasn't wanted by the police for nothing; the truth more likely was that she and her brother were malcontents, unscrupulous, out to grab whatever they could, under the guise of political martyrs. What decent girl of any nationality would take advantage of so obvious a sexual simpleton as Jonathan, by first enticing him into offering and then by brazenly accepting this ring worth eighty thousand pesetas? That was shameful enough, but still worse was her claim, made in every look, in every twinkle of her crucifix, that to her love, marriage, conception, and birth were sacred. If Jonathan wanted to find out the truth about her, let him take a glance at John Lynedoch's unfinished portrait. At first Isabel had thought it unfair and uncouth. That beauty of gleaming black hair, firm red mouth, strong but elegant nose, creamy skin, and strong graceful body, was recognized, as Isabel was recognizing it now; but the degeneration into dominance, fat, and religiosity were also powerfully hinted at. As her husband, and the father of her half dozen or more diminutive solemn-faced sardana dancers, Jonathan would no doubt have fulfilled the promise of his early absurdity. Still, it was Isabel's duty as his elder sister and self-appointed guardian to save him for the fate which she saw as his proper one; which was to remain safely and dignifiedly single, and to mellow into a harmless intellectual fop, popular with and indulgent to his niece and nephew.

'Are you playing games?' she asked.

Jonathan took Montserrat's hand, and held it under his sister's covetous eyes. 'Montserrat and I are engaged,' he said, 'and we are going to Barcelona to tell her mother.'

Isabel gave him a glance, decided he was in truth like a small conceited boy playing games, and then turned her attention upon the Spanish girl, to be confronted by a gaze not indignant nor shifty nor even haughty, as she expected, but amused, in a peculiarly feminine, quite un-English, way. Disconcerted, she asked: 'Is this true?'

Slowly Montserrat nodded.

They were, Isabel had to admit, an impressive couple. She could be wrong in her forecast as to how their marriage might turn out. That portrait was a malicious exaggeration, as any by Lynedoch was bound to be, considering the number of grievances he had imbibed with his charwoman mother's milk.

'You hardly know each other,' she said. It sounded feeble, and was: there were shortcuts to knowing, just as there were wearisome detours; love inspired took the former, love humdrum and seeking its own ends, the latter. 'Well,' she added, reluctantly, 'I suppose I ought to congratulate you and wish you both well.'

'Thank you, Isabel,' said Jonathan.

Montserrat murmured it in Spanish.

Then Maddy appeared in the corridor, with no dressing-gown to cover her very brief white pink-dotted pyjamas, the jacket of which was fastened with only one button, so that her navel could be seen. Her hair, already tousled, she made worse by rumpling it with both hands. She yawned with deliberate grossness, making a hole in her face and also a noise which ended with a groaned: 'Oh, my God!' Evidently she had a headache, but not an upset conscience. Like Jonathan, Isabel had detested her sleeping with Lynedoch in the house; she had prophesied to David it would happen sooner or later, but found only the tartest of pleasures in having her prophecy come true so quickly. She foresaw that Maddy, if not taken in hand, would end up as a middle-aged baggy-eyed tramp, pathetic with decayed laughter. The signs were there already, as Lynedoch, that ruthless inspector, knew better than anyone. They might get married, for they needed each other; but their marriage was more likely to end in sordid muddle than Jonathan's in dreary comedy.

'Maddy,' she called, 'come and hear what this pair have done, and intend to do.'

Maddy came in, scratching her bare stomach. 'Not, I hope,' she said, 'without benefit of clergy?'

Isabel cut off a giggle; she mustn't encourage Maddy, though Montserrat certainly deserved the insinuation. 'They've got engaged,' she said, 'and they're off to Barcelona to announce it.'

'Bold deeds, for a coward.' Laughing, Maddy took Montserrat's hand and stared at the ring. She was very like Jonathan, borrowing his most aloof sneer; so that she surprised them all by suddenly kissing Montserrat on the cheek, with affection, goodwill, and pity. 'God help you both,' she said, 'but it's worth trying.' Turning to Jonathan she seized his hands. 'I think you're lucky.'

'I know that.'

'Luckier than you deserve.'

'I know that too.'

'So you're going to Barcelona?'

'Yes.'

'You may be arrested.'

'I hope not, but it's possible.'

'Good. Montserrat may be.'

'I am aware of that, Maddy.'

'You may get married.'

'That's possible too.' He could not keep annoyance out of his voice. Being arrested could never be good. Yet he had wished to sound glad at the prospect of marriage. Maddy had a knack of muddling one's reactions.

'Good again. But you may not.'

'That of course is possible too.'

'Yes. But the wonderful thing is you've at last stopped dipping in your toes only. In you've plunged, head-first, deeper than you know. I wouldn't be surprised if you were to come up with lumps on your forehead, bruises on your knees, and a book worth reading. What are your plans? You still intend to cross the border, after you've returned from Barcelona?'

'Yes.'

'When will you be back?'

'Tomorrow night perhaps, if all goes well.'

'And if not?'

He shook his head.

'In that case John may have to finish the portrait from memory?'

'I'm afraid so.'

'Perhaps,' said Isabel, irritated by the smug way Maddy had spoken about Lynedoch, 'it would be better left unfinished.'

'What do you mean, Isabel?'

'It's not a likeness at all, it's a spiteful caricature, like that other portrait, the one of his dead girl. He uses us all to get his own back; especially you, Maddy.'

Maddy smiled sweetly. 'You'd prefer something suitable for a sherry advertisement?' she asked. 'Is that your mother in the photograph, Montserrat?' Before she could be stopped she went over and snatched it up off the dressing-table. 'John's never seen this, but nobody that's going to be fair will deny there's a strong resemblance between it and the painting. Isn't there, Jonathan?'

Gazing at the stout, weary, and anxious face in the photograph, Jonathan shook his head coldly. 'I have not seen the portrait.'

'That's right. You've refused to look.'

'I always prefer to wait till a work is finished.'

'The girl John's painting looks capable of handing out illegal leaflets; of prayer in church; and of being the enthusiastic mother of a bundle of niños. I don't know, Jonathan, if that's the girl you think you've fallen in love with. I suspect not.'

Isabel decided to attack her sister, but not in defence of their brother. 'No one's ever going to portray you as an enthusiastic mother, Maddy.'

Maddy smiled. 'Yesterday you were short on enthusiasm yourself, Isabel.'

'I'll tell you this, John Lynedoch will never paint me.'

'I'm sure he won't. I doubt if you stimulate his imagination.'

'One minute, please.' Jonathan stepped between them and held up his hand. Isabel's own fist was clenched and half raised. Montserrat, too, looked fierce; she had taken her mother's photograph from Maddy, kissed it, and now held it close. Out on the terrace Linda, wakened by the angry voices, added her own to them.

'What's important,' said Jonathan, 'is not what any of us is likely to become in twenty years, or five, or one; but what we are now, at this very moment. How grotesque to portray Linda as a woman of thirty, cancerous from radioactive fall-out.'

'Or Maddy as a middle-aged tart,' said Isabel.

'Or Isabel as the doting mother of six,' said Maddy.

'Or myself as tired and ill as my mother,' murmured Montserrat.

Jonathan looked round at them all. 'Whatever happens, I shall always remember this as a moment of supreme happiness.'

Envious of an innocence which they themselves couldn't afford, and which they thought neither could he, the three women looked at him with exasperation softening into pity that softened still more into their respective kinds of fondness; but on each of their faces traces of the original exasperation lingered.

Then Montserrat, followed by Isabel, hurried out to the terrace to solace Linda, whose howls at being neglected were being reinforced by furious rattlings of her cot.

Twenty-Eight

The car stopped at the petrol pump in the plaza. As usual the attendant wasn't about, but contrary to custom Jonathan saw nothing disgraceful in any sane man's preferring to chat in the shade with friends rather than stand and fry in the sun simply in order to save impatient motorists a minute or so's delay. Therefore his sounding of the horn was almost musical and amiable, and his greeting of the shirted attendant when he came hurrying was so urbane and considerate that the man, who knew him, was more put out and flustered than he would have been by the expected asperities.

Jonathan was a little downcast. 'Isn't it curious,' he observed, in English, 'how even our slightest acquaintances seem to be in a conspiracy to prevent our development? We become a part of their lives; any change in us is apt to make them lose faith in their entire cartography. They lose their way. But surely losing one's way often leads to interesting self-discoveries. Don't you agree?'

Montserrat, in sun-glasses, had the map of Catalonia open on her lap. She had been appointed navigator. 'Few people ever change so much,' she said cautiously.

He laughed, like one in whom earthquakes of change had occurred, and still were occurring. To prove it he gave the attendant a tip that, two days ago, he would have considered an insult to them both; now it produced smiles of respect.

Before he could drive on again, he saw the Scottish girls bearing down on him; not all three, the plump one lingered behind, in a tartan dress.

Peggy stared in at him, and ignored Montserrat. Teresa's smile, at each in turn, was a kind of blessing.

'Well,' said Peggy, 'we've considered it; about going to Perpignan with you on Sunday. Are you still interested in us going?'

'Very much so,' said Jonathan.

'I'm willing, Teresa here's half willing, but Katie there's not willing at all.'

He glared at the recalcitrant Katie, and saw, with satisfaction, how like an eczema was the peeling of her skin.

'She's got a right to refuse,' said Peggy sharply.

A car behind hooted imperiously. A German wanted petrol.

Jonathan drove out of the way, with Peggy and Teresa walking after. He got a chance to say to Montserrat: 'Two will be enough. Speak to Teresa; she's the thin one with the big eyes. She's a Catholic. Probably she's afraid she'll be committing a mortal sin if she helps us. She's got a naive belief that the Church in Spain is on Franco's side.'

Before Montserrat could protest against his irony, Peggy was staring in again. 'Teresa's got something she'd like to ask.'

Teresa laughed sadly. 'You've no' to be offended.'

'Say it,' snapped her friend. 'You've got a right to.'

Teresa looked shyly in. 'I really want to help,' she said. 'But, you see, I'm ignorant about politics. I wouldn't want to do something the priest wouldn't approve of, especially since I'm in a foreign country.'

Peggy gave a presbyterian snort.

'To tell you the truth, miss,' said Teresa, to Montserrat, 'I'm ashamed to look you in the face, seeing that you're in trouble and here I am swithering about helping you; but I've always tried to be a good Catholic – you have to be, in Glasgow, if you want your faith to be respected, which it isn't much, notwithstanding – and, to cut a long story short, if you can gie me an assurance you've done nothing the priest wouldn't approve of—'

'Teresa,' said Peggy sternly, 'you're going too far.'

'I just meant,' said Teresa blushing, 'as far as politics are concerned.'

'What has a priest to do wi' politics?'

Montserrat, who had removed her sun-glasses, put her hand on Teresa's. 'Some priests would not approve, others would.'

'For heaven's sake,' muttered Peggy, 'why all the fuss? They're just men under their black skirts. Isn't the Church rich at the expense of the poor?'

'You're a Catholic of course?' said Teresa.

Montserrat nodded.

Teresa blushed again as she avoided looking at Jonathan. 'And you always will be?'

'Isn't there such a thing as freedom of conscience?' muttered Peggy.

'Always,' replied Montserrat.

'So you can't be a communist?'

'I'm not a communist.'

'And you'll be married according to the rites of the Church?'

'If I am ever married, yes.'

'And your children, they'll be brought up Catholics?'

'Teresa,' said Peggy, 'this is ridiculous. Do you think you've got a saint in front of your name?'

'My children will be brought up Catholics,' said Montserrat.

'Then my conscience is clear,' said Teresa, in triumph. 'I'll go with you on Sunday.'

'Mine isn't,' said Peggy, 'not now. I didn't mean to give my reasons for going with you, but Teresa's forced me to. I'm going because I consider it my duty, as a human being, mind, not as a Christian or a Protestant or a democrat or a fearer of priests. Like Teresa, Katie's prejudiced. Don't tell her it's none of her business. If she goes, she says, she'll feel responsible for you. Teresa's pleased you're going to get married and have a scattering of wee Catholics; well, it just so happens Katie's not a bit pleased at that prospect.'

'In Scotland,' said Jonathan, 'you seem to be still waging the Reformation.'

'Maybe there's reason for it. It's been calculated that at their present rate of increase there'll be a majority of them in Glasgow by the year 2000. That's something I could live to regret. Where will you pick us up on Sunday?'

'If you wish, at your hotel.'

'At what time?'

'About ten o'clock.'

'That should give Teresa time to go to church first. Well, that's it fixed then. We'll detain you no longer.' As grim as a passport bureaucrat she waved them on.

Teresa waved far more cordially. She had seen the ring.

'Did you see the ring, Peggy?' she said. 'They must be engaged.'

'What I saw was this, Teresa: between the pair of us we've managed to convince them we must be a crowd of barbarians that come from Scotland.'

Teresa looked from her friend's dour intense sun-darkened face to Katie's nose up in huff, and then around her at the people drinking and laughing under the striped awnings. She remembered on the visit to Barcelona last Sunday seeing sardanas being danced by hundreds of young people in the great square in front of the cathedral.

'Well,' she said, timid but resolute, 'maybe we are.'

Twenty-Nine

In the train coming from Barcelona, Bridie had described him as young, tall, intelligent, fastidious, and handsome if you didn't object to a trace of blonde effeminacy; comfortably off; with good teeth; proficient at Spanish; and possessing British nationality to confer on his wife. Obviously therefore, in any country, highly eligible. Many women too, especially in Spain, would consider creditable his insistence on purity. Any woman with beauty, brains, and resolution could easily have him. If she was Spanish her chances would be all the better.

She had ended by saying bluntly he could be Montserrat's for the taking.

At first, not noticing his wife's intention, Terence had added to her praises, and even had hinted at potentialities in Jonathan waiting to be fulfilled; but when he had realized she was trying to interest Montserrat into making a bid for him, he had at once turned from casual commendation to quite fervent abuse. Jonathan was the kind of man whose house you stayed in and whose whisky you drank without compunction, whose elegance in an era of jeans you admired, whose opinions and attitudes you amiably despised if you were sober, but whom, if you were a woman in your right mind and with your passions sane, you just did not contemplate marrying. In every courtship, surely to God, if not in every marriage, there ought to be at least one spasm of abandon; Jonathan, wooing or wedded, would take a pride in remaining calm and dignified, like a penguin. Granted most men, especially in their relations with women, were conceited; still, it was more or less a biological and therefore sufferable sort of conceit; in Jonathan's case God knew what bizarre form it might take. The only kind of woman likely to make a success out of marriage to him was one as mannish as he was effeminate, who would systematically replace his books in their wrong places, leave lip-sticked cigarette stubs on the tablecloth and in the soap-box, and hand him out his ration of sex with his clean pyjamas.

Thus prepared, Montserrat had been sure she would hate him, and at first she had, all the more because she had soon found herself being attracted by that quality in him which she had called innocence. She had never met anyone, not even Jordi or Tomas, who spoke the truth so uncompromisingly to himself. What others, including his sisters, called conceit or callousness, had struck her as true humility; this she had never believed would show itself in cringing or abasement. It would mind its own business, without self-advertisement; it would passionately hate violence and cruelty, and distrust those who provoked them. As for his purity, she, who had danced the sardana with him on the cliff top, would certainly grant him that.

At the same time she had to be sure she was not letting herself be persuaded by Bridie's reasons. For years, true to her Spanish nature, she had in the depths of her being wished for marriage, not to some revolutionary like Tomas but to someone as remote as possible from that life of furtive meetings, refrigerated ideals, foolish slogans, pretentious hopes, smudged leaflets, and brutal arrests. From her first sight of him Jonathan had been that someone, so much so that nursing Linda had become a peculiarly poignant pleasure because the baby was so like him he could have been her father. Several times Montserrat, in a kind of rehearsal, had pretended the child was his and hers, and this house by the sea was theirs. When he had, as it were, taken part, first with looks of affection, then with touches, and finally with words, it had confused her into, well, striking him and accepting his ring. Lying in bed she would, without blushing, put out her hand to take his as he lay beside her. Yes, she had imagined him and her in every circumstance and posture of married life, and none had struck her as impossible or repellent or ludicrous. When she had called him a coward she had really been warning him she was falling in love with him. When he had put the ring on her finger she had almost let herself feel the betrothal was genuine.

In Gerona they stopped for lunch. As they were about to get out of the car he took some of the leaflets from under his seat.

'We might as well take the opportunity of disposing of a few of these,' he said.

She snatched them from him. 'No.'

'Why not? Wasn't Gerona the scene of a famous resistance to Napoleon?'

She crushed them in her fist.

'What's the matter?' he asked.

She stared out at the sunny town. Jordi, she thought, I shall help you more if I make use of this visit to Gerona to encourage Jonathan to want to marry me. When you come out of prison you will have a place to go to; and if by that time I have a child, half-English, with your name, perhaps you too will be persuaded that in human love, in family, happiness lies, not in the pursuit of illusions.

Jonathan poked her in the ribs. 'Well?'

She answered by taking the ring from the shelf and putting it back on her finger.

How, she wondered, did one recognize genuine love in oneself, and in another? Her insides quaked, and his face shone with a happiness she had never inspired before.

'But it isn't a choice, you know,' he said, gently. 'If you mean what I hope you do by putting on the ring, it doesn't follow you've to give up helping your brother.'

She shook her head. 'I think it does,' she said.

He became very earnest. 'Not on my account. You've got a right to help Jordi, and your country. Only those who hate you want to take that right away. I love you.'

'I think,' she whispered, staring through the windscreen at an old man sweeping the street, 'I love you.' Quickly, her face as red as the old sweeper's neckband, she turned to him. 'I want you to come with me to the cathedral. I'll give you my promise there.'

He smiled. 'As a matter of fact I'd intended to stick one of the leaflets to the cathedral door.'

'No, no.'

'I didn't think you'd consider that sacrilegious.'

'No, I would not.'

'Why not then?'

'Because I want Gerona to be just for us. I want us to celebrate our engagement here.'

It was not done in Gerona, or in any Spanish town, for a man to kiss a woman, whether his wife or sweetheart, in a car in a public street in bright sunlight; but Jonathan, hitherto approving of the ban, now contravened it boldly; and was startled when Montserrat kissed him back with a fervour that made his own effort half-hearted, so that he had to try again, to outdo her, as was proper for the male partner.

Lips bruised, breath panting, eyes shy, they drew apart. Jonathan it was who squinted defiantly out to see if the glory of that kiss was being misinterpreted by prudish civilians or prurient police. Luckily, it was not. If the street sweeper had seen, it had not taken away his attention from the fallen leaves and scraps of greasy paper.

'We must get married now,' gasped Jonathan.

It was surely proof of his innocence. That first passionate kiss had committed him, as love-makings and even pregnancy itself did not commit so many others. She laughed, but not altogether in derision; mostly indeed because she felt secure with him, and happy, despite Jordi and her mother.

Though not instantly, he understood her laughter and joined in.

'There's one thing, my dear,' he said, gripping her hand. 'I'm willing to get married in any church you like, and for our children to be brought up as Catholics, particularly if they're living in Spain, as I hope they will be. But I ought to warn you that I have no religious beliefs, or at any rate am unable to accept most Christian dogmas. I cannot believe, for instance, in Christ as the Son of God, or in the Immaculate Conception, or in any after-life.'

Her father had died holding those same blasphemous opinions, to her mother's still inconsolable grief. Jordi, if he was honest, would have to admit he held them too.

'I'm sorry,' said Jonathan.

She had to smile at that apology, so earnest and yet so inadequate.

'But you mustn't hold my views against me. As a Christian, it's your duty to try and convert me.'

'I shall convert you, if it takes me forty years.'

'Bueno! Begin then by taking me to the cathedral.'

Hand-in-hand they set off, and soon stopped on the bridge over the river to watch the reflections of the houses that rose out of the water, giving the town its name of the Catalan Venice. In a lane near the cathedral steps they stopped again, to kiss.

Going up the great flight of steps, Montserrat imagined it was to their wedding, and so she felt, and recklessly displayed, a lightness of heart, a vivacity, and a sureness of faith, such as she had not shown for years.

Laughing, he held her back. 'We've got all our lives in front of us. There's no hurry.'

Some tourists, Americans, came down from the cathedral, with cameras at the ready. Montserrat, in her pink dress, attracted them, as being so splendidly and joyously Spanish. Their hands itched to photograph her, and they asked courteously if she would mind. She cried she wouldn't, but perhaps her fiancé might. She looked at him as if this decision, like every other decision concerning her, was now his. Proudly he gave his consent, and was repaid by being included in some of the snaps.

'But you're not Spanish yourself?' said one of the tourists. 'You sound English.'

'And if you'll pardon me saying it,' said another, with a jolly laugh, 'you sure look it.'

Whether it was intended as a compliment or reproof was not clear.

At the cathedral door Montserrat asked for his handkerchief to put on her head. As he gently tied it on, knotting it under her chin, she wondered if Jordi would approve of him, and thought, with anger, he would not. Jordi would accuse her of using Jonathan to escape from obligations of which she had grown weary. Jonathan was not the coward, he would say; she was.

Be careful, Jordi, she whispered to herself, be very careful. If I have to choose between you and him, don't think I shall instantly choose you, don't think I shall in the end choose you at all.

Though it was Jonathan's fingers which were busy under her chin, it was Jordi's she felt angrily gripping her shoulders, as he replied: 'Choose him if you like, Montsy. But be honest about it. If you're using him as an excuse to run away, say so. I won't condemn you; you know that.

Tomas would, and others; but how could I, your brother, who's loved you all your life? Here in prison, all I ask is that you be honest. We know many Spanish girls marry not because they're in love, but because marriage is an escape from various things, from parental domination, from the disgrace of spinsterdom, from the fear of never having children, and, in your case, Montsy, from the political struggle in which you have for a long time been losing faith. This Englishman is a godsend to you. That's why you minimize or ignore the shortcomings that exasperated Bridie and Terence, and even his sisters; and that's why you persist in calling his crass selfish unawareness of other people innocence. You've got it worked out in that feminine head of yours that if you were to marry him you could easily, with your superiority of passion, subdue him into whatever shape suited you. You do not really love him, Montsy; what you see in him is simply an opportunity to escape into the kind of life that appeals to the coward in you: a comfortable house, especially by the sea; a good safe income; a manageable husband; children. Tomas was the kind of man the heroine and the patriot in you wanted to marry, a man with passion to match your own, and with a willingness to risk his liberty or even his life to get rid of this cynical acceptance of injustice that is stifling our country.'

'There,' said Jonathan, 'that should hold. You look very pretty.'

'You don't have to come in, if you don't want to.'

He was surprised by her harshness. 'But I do want to.'

'So that you can sneer at all the ridiculous mumbo-jumbo?'

He flushed a little. 'I'll not deny I have sneered in the past.'

'And what has happened to stop you?'

'Surely you know that? I have met you.'

She sneered. For a moment she was minded to pull off the ring, throw it at his feet, and shout to him to pick it up and go and never come near her again; it was Tomas Balaguer she loved, not he.

'Besides,' he said, 'you've to give me your promise in the church.'

Whatever Jordi said, or rather her own conscience using Jordi's voice, she did have a warm feeling for the tall fair-haired Englishman. Perhaps it was not love and never could be; but many women married men towards whom their hearts were much colder. If she were to send him away, the cathedral for all its magnificence and holiness might seem empty.

Together they went into the vast cool dark vault. Inside were more tourists than worshippers; a party, chatting reverentially, came out of the side door that led to the cloisters and the rooms where the centuries-old tapestries were on display. When Montserrat crossed herself with finger dipped in holy water, Jonathan did likewise, despite her sharp shake of the head. He genuflected with her as they crossed in front of the altar. Then she angrily wriggled her fingers free of his and, going into one of the rows of benches, knelt among the handful of worshippers. Jonathan, again in spite of her scowl of disapproval, followed and knelt beside her.

Prayer did not come easy to her. As she waited, minute by despairing minute, she began to weep.

She wept for Tomas, whom she had hoped to marry; for her father miserably dead after so much useless suffering; for her mother, now dying, martyred by politics which she had not understood and in which she had had no interest; for Jordi humiliated and tormented into wishing for another war in which a million more Spaniards would kill one another; and for herself, now on her knees seeking God's permission to desert her comrades.

Jonathan, though so close that their elbows touched, had no place in her weeping, so that when she did become aware of him, as concerned as God Himself on her behalf, she was for a second or two bewildered, wondering who he was and why he was there.

'Weep if you like,' he whispered in anguish. 'Weep if you need to.'

Soon, no longer weeping, hands calmly clasped, she gazed for minutes on the peacefulness and splendour of the great altar, and waited for the decision she had made to be ratified. She imagined she saw Christ on His cross smile and nod.

'I shall marry you,' she whispered, 'whenever you wish.'

He said nothing.

She had to add, 'If you still want to.'

'Yes, Montserrat, I want to, more than anything.'

'What's wrong then? You don't seem so sure now.'

An old woman turned round, saw them, and instead of frowning them to silence as they expected, smiled, and returned to her own prayers.

'Yes, I'm sure,' he whispered. 'I want you to be sure too.'

'Am I not saying it here, in this place where it's holy for me and where I must speak the truth?'

'Yes. But there's Tomas Balaguer, isn't there?'

'What about him?'

'Isn't it about him you keep worrying, as well as of course about your mother and brother?'

'No.'

'Weren't you in love with him once?'

'Not any more than I am with you now.'

'That's all I want to know. I wouldn't like to take advantage, in his absence, while you're so troubled, but if it's a matter of my chance being as good as his, or anyone else's, then I certainly would never withdraw. This place is holy for me, too; any place is where you are.'

A minute later she whispered: 'Shall we go?'

Had she been dying or pregnant or decrepit with age he could not have been more attentive as he walked with her over the worn slabs out into the heat and radiance of the afternoon.

Before giving him back his handkerchief she wiped off the marks of tears with it.

'You think it's foolish, to weep while praying?' she asked.

'No, not really. I think I understand.'

'You think, why weep if God is about to grant you what you ask? Or if He in His wisdom decides it is better for you not to have it granted?'

'No. What I think is this: she's weeping, Montserrat's weeping, and I cannot comfort her. I felt jealous of God.'

As they stood there, at the top of the cathedral steps, two other tourists passed them, white-haired, elderly, a man and woman, she in a pale lilac dress, he in a linen suit and Panama hat.

'Sure it's grand, Bert,' said the woman intensely, in an accent that reminded Montserrat of Norman Ashton, 'but I still say religion ought to be kept new, not let get old and dusty.'

'I guess you're right, honey,' replied her husband, fat and complaisant.

'Sure I'm right. The older it's allowed to get, the more it gets covered up with superstitions—'

'You're hitting the nail on the head, Emily.'

'—until you just can't tell where superstition begins and religion ends.'

'Sure, sure, sure.'

Then they were out of hearing.

Montserrat looked after them, not with annoyance or

contempt, but with wonder. They must have been married at least forty years; in the States they would have grand-children. Now even the Mother of God in Her glory was not so important to them as they were to each other, despite his big belly and her shrivelled neck.

Thirty

Calle de Manresa, where Montserrat lived, was below the Diagonale not far from the port, therefore in summer very hot and humid, and no longer fashionable. The flats in it had been built for wealthy people more than fifty years before, and even today, dilapidated, inhabited by the poor, they kept a sullen dignity. In those days it had been thought prudent to keep out the sun, and so every street was narrow. Here and there were open spaces, with gardens, a consequence of the Civil War when warships had shelled the city. The church of San Sebastian had been destroyed too, with dozens of worshippers inside praying to God to avert that very disaster. It had since been rebuilt, grander than ever.

All along the street, narrow though the pavements were, people sat out on them, at the entrances to cafés and flats. Their flesh, that laughed and relaxed, showed more than the solid stone the ravages of poverty and hardship.

'I warned you,' said Montserrat, more than once.

'Who's being snobbish now?'

'They're good people.'

'I'm sure they are.'

'Don't say it like that, to soothe me as if I was a child. They *are* good people.'

He gazed out at them, seeking in their workworn ordinariness that goodness. Almost he saw it in their need of one another's company, and then he did see it, without any doubt, in their making of that simple human environment, so necessary to the fruition of his love.

'They're my people,' she said.

'And therefore mine too.'

'There it is,' she said, 'Number one hundred and ninety.'

'Where the two women are sitting outside?'

'Yes.'

He drove past slowly. 'The fourth floor, you said?'

'Yes.'

It wasn't possible to see the windows from the car. Montserrat, though, her fists clenched on her lap, was, in imagination, in the house, by her mother's bedside. Jonathan tried to be there too. At the same time he kept a look-out for policemen.

'Who were the women?' he asked.

'The portera, and a friend, I suppose.'

'Is she to be trusted?'

'What do you mean? She knows none of my business.'

'I meant, if she were to see you, would she report you?'

'Why should she?'

'To protect herself, I suppose. Better not trust her, better in the end to trust no one.'

'Do that, and you put trust itself out of existence.'

He was about to suggest that it didn't exist already, when he realized that he was willing to trust her, in some respects still a stranger, with his very life, and she was prepared to trust him. Maddy too he trusted; Isabel and David, if the occasion was important; Bridie and Terence, for if they failed it would never be out of malevolence; and surely Pedro, who could have won favour in the eyes of his superiors by betraying Montserrat. Yes, trust did exist, and somehow irradiated out into the world.

They came out into the small pleasant plaza of San Sebastian, where, besides the great church, were trees, a plot of grass bordered with flowers, a fountain, old men dozing on seats, and pigeons.

Jonathan parked the car up a quiet side-street. Then resolutely he walked with Montserrat to the church.

As he stood beside her on the steps, in silence, he felt growing in him, hard and bitter, resentment against the evil forces by which she was threatened. With poignant honesty he saw he had in the past contributed to them, and perhaps, at this very moment, still did. He had known that persecution went on, all over the world, as well as here in Spain. Beyond deprecating it, as something apt to sully his own aspirations, he had done nothing to prevent it, and even had been reluctant to sympathize with its victims.

She touched his hand. 'Cheer up,' she whispered. 'I'm still here.'

'Yes, but for how long?'

'For as long as you wish.'

'Go into the church, Montsy. Stay there. Don't come out for any reason. I'll be back within an hour.'

'You're not going to make it a long visit.'

'Just in case, here are the car keys. If I'm not back in an hour, drive to the Hotel Lerida. You know where it is, near the top of Balmes.'

'I told you I've never learned to drive a car.'

'Take a taxi then. You'd better have this too.' It was his wallet. 'If I'm held back for any reason, I want you to promise me you'll return to Cabo Creus tomorrow. Maddy will help you to get out of the country. I'll join you as soon as I can. Promise.'

She was silent.

'You must promise, Montsy. They can do nothing to me, except hold me for a day or two.'

'All right. But for God's sake, be careful. If there's anyone there, come away again. Don't get mixed up.'

'Don't worry. I've got it planned. My main concern is not to lead them back here. That's just the sort of thing I'm likely to do,' he went on, bitterly, 'and I'd regret it to the end of my life.'

'Hardly as long as that, Jonathan. Whatever happens, we'll meet again.' She clutched his arm. 'Bring me back good news about my mother.'

He was greatly agitated. 'I hope I can.'

'Tell her, if you manage to see her, tell her I'm well, and happy, that I'll write to her as often as I can. Tell her not to worry too much about Jordi, time will pass, he'll come back to her again.'

She was at last in tears.

He gazed at her, dismayed, helpless, almost in tears himself.

'Be very careful,' she said. 'I'll pray for you.'

She turned and hurried up the steps.

He looked after her. For a moment or two all of her was strange, from her feet to her scarfed head. Avidly he looked, and recognized nothing, except her loveliness; and then, moments later, more lovely than ever, she was more famil- iar, dearer, and closer, than his own body. He remembered her bruised breast, and it, with the fallen leaves, the pigeons, the water glinting out of the fishes' mouths in the fountain, the old men dozing, the blue sky, and the stone effigy of Christ above the church door, were suddenly all com- mingled, in a way he could not have explained, but which made the chances of life seem inexhaustible and glorious.

At the door she turned.

For a few moments they stared at each other, making no sign of love or even of recognition. Then she gave one wave, and not waiting for him to wave back went into the church.

She was gone, and he tortured himself by imagining it was for good, that never again would he see her. Almost he called upon Christ, with His stone arm uplifted in blessing, to descend and help him. Then, resisting that profoundest pessimism, he thought of her, not two minutes away, kneeling in prayer. Perhaps she was weeping again, as she had done in Gerona Cathedral. Like him she suspected her mother was much more seriously ill than either of them had pretended; but unlike him she believed her prayers could help, could persuade God to intervene and cure. He wondered at that belief, which, far more than their difference of nationality, of political beliefs, and of upbringing, set them apart from each other. Aureoled in it, she became strange and unknowable. Yet, as he left the church, he found himself hoping that her tears did not mean her faith in prayer was weakening.

More cautious than a cat that knew where all the dogs lived, he advanced along the street. Almost visibly, he carried Montserrat's safety in his hands. Carefree, he would still have been conspicuous, with his height, fair hair, and patrician handsomeness; burdened and cat-footed, he attracted glances and provoked smiles. Aware at last of some of these, he had to sit down at a café table on the pavement and order cognac, in an attempt to steady his nerves. Yet so far he had not seen one policeman in uniform and since he saw every second man as one in disguise he knew he must be wrong, and there were none.

The two women still sat outside the entrance to Montserrat's flat. In that calm warm humid air they looked content to sit and chat all night. Across the street from them a young man, big and beefy as a policeman, talked to a girl, who reminded Jonathan of Lynedoch's dead girl-friend in the portrait. An old man waited by the pillar-box outside a tobacconist's; perhaps it was pain or illness that made him so vigilant.

Suddenly impetuous, anxious to get it over with and return to Montserrat, Jonathan almost ran forward, up to the two women.

They stopped chatting when he halted beside them, and stared up at him with an interest that developed on their shrewd wrinkled faces from curiosity through amusement into suspicion.

'Excuse me, please,' he said, 'I'm looking for an empty flat in this district. Can you tell me if there is any available?'

They now examined, from this new point of view, his air of superiority, his expensive clothes, and, in spite of his good Spanish, his haughty Englishness.

'I heard there was a flat vacant in this building,' he said.

'Mother of God,' whispered the portera's friend, crossing herself. She was a small thin woman of about fifty, with a sharp nose and a habit of showing the tip of her tongue at the corner of her mouth. 'And the poor woman hardly settled in her coffin.'

The portera was stout, with a thick strong warted face and bushy grey hair. She held up a big hand, fingers outspread, in a powerful crude gesture that Jonathan did not understand.

It was incredible to him that Montserrat could have lived here most of her life and associated with women like these. Looking more closely at the entrance to the flat, through which she must have passed so often, he saw how shabby it was, and at the same time he made out on the wall her brother's name, Jordi Puig, the arrogance of the white paint dimmed but not extinguished by much scrubbing.

For all its inspirations love had to keep struggling against disillusionment. As the two women stared up at him, the one scowling and the other sighing, he wondered for a few craven moments if he had not after all been too precipitate in his relationship with Montserrat. Yes, he loved her; the thought of her waiting for him in the church almost stopped his heart with a shock of gladness. But there was another unavoidable view, that represented by Isabel and all the other possessors of the earth; it acknowledged love and most of its miracles, but nevertheless often advised rejection, on the grounds that these very shocks of gladness alternating with spasms of disillusionment burnt the heart out too soon. Better be true to one's own limited needs and accept only as much of love as one could safely accommodate.

Montserrat's mother was dead. So much the tip of the woman's tongue and the portera's plump pink hand kept telling him. Would his love for Montserrat, and hers for him, not yet deeply enough rooted, be able to withstand so brutal a blow?

'The administrator for these flats is Señor Bruch,' said the portera. 'His office is in Calle de Aragon. Apply to him, señor. I'm only the portera.'

Suddenly he needed their sympathy, their help, and their trust. 'Is it Señora Puig who has died?' he asked.

'I should have thought,' said the portera scornfully, 'all Barcelona knows that by this time.'

'Though you'll not find it mentioned in the newspapers,' whispered her friend.

'Adela!' said the portera sternly.

Adela sighed, a little rebelliously. 'A woman's not responsible for her family's actions,' she murmured, 'especially if she's dead.'

'When did it happen?' asked Jonathan.

They were surprised by the trembling of his voice.

'Perhaps I should tell you,' he went on desperately, 'I am a friend of Señorita Puig's. I've come for news of her mother.'

'You're a foreigner!' said Adela accusingly.

'English,' added the portera.

'Yes.'

'Where is she? Señorita Puig?'

'Better not ask that, Juanita,' muttered Adela.

'What kind of daughter is it that doesn't come to see her dying mother?'

'For God's sake, Juanita, what else could the girl do?'

'A daughter's place is by her mother's side.'

'How could she be by her mother's side if she was in prison?'

'Well, I wouldn't like to have on my conscience what she'll have on hers the rest of her life.'

They hadn't forgotten Jonathan. Not sympathy, however, kept him in mind, but distrust.

'When did it happen?' he asked again.

'She was buried this morning,' said Adela, after a pause.

'If I was you, Adela, I wouldn't say another word. Señor, we can do nothing for you. Goodbye.'

'Is Miss Puig's aunt in the house?'

'She's gone. She didn't say where.'

Then they sat in a silence that grew more and more remote and impenetrable. Yet, faced with the ordeal of having to go back to Montserrat with such bleak news, he needed their sympathy or at least their understanding. But he did not know how to appeal to them. He had more than enough Spanish, what he lacked was a common humanity, and it could not be acquired at a minute's notice, not even by feeling as humble and desolate at he did then. With hardly a word of Spanish John Lynedoch would have convinced these women he was one of them; the more Jonathan tried the less he would succeed.

'Thank you,' he said, and walked away.

When he glanced round they were staring after him, but when they saw him looking they looked away. They had passed a sentence of excommunication on him and now were carrying it out. He felt frightened. Everybody he saw, and would see, would similarly ostracize him. No one would be interested in his denial that he was a police agent. Had he not admitted on the church steps that in a way he was such an agent, and had been, for many years? Throughout this city, and throughout the country, millions would be saying about Montserrat what he had said himself about other revolutionaries imprisoned or hunted: that, unfortunately ruthless though their methods might be, nevertheless the police would hardly persecute the completely innocent. If

Montserrat's activities with handbills and secret meetings had been trivial and scarcely a danger to a regime so thoroughly established, still had she not defied the advice of her Church, and had she not helped to break her mother's heart? Thus he would himself have argued had he not known and loved her.

This discovery, that most of mankind were as hypocritical and resolutely selfish as himself, was not new, but never before had it overwhelmed him as it did now. No wonder Christ was turned to stone and would not descend. No wonder Montserrat, wishing to pray, wept instead. No wonder John Lynedoch, appalled by his artist's insight into his own and other people's natures, sought refuge in a personal mediocrity, out of which Maddy, with such misguided ambition, was scheming to bully and shame him. No wonder Tomas Balaguer's pity had turned into an unrelenting principle.

Keeping looking about him to make sure he wasn't being followed, he walked quickly in the twilight through several narrow streets until he came upon a taxi.

'Plaza Catalunya,' he said.

First he made sure no police car was following; then, ignoring the garrulous driver's remarks about a football match being played that evening, he sat back and tried to prepare for the ordeal of telling Montserrat about her mother's death. Into his mind kept creeping, from what source he hardly knew, the consolation that Montserrat, once she had got over her grief, would be more readily and completely his. He tried to keep it out, as shameful; but he could not.

I think, he said to himself, she would be happier without me. What can I possibly bring to her? If she were to go to prison, like her brother, there would at least be this gain: she would be able to forget me.

The taxi-driver went on meditating aloud about the Barcelona team's lapse from glory.

And when she came out, reflected Jonathan, perhaps Tomas Balaguer would be waiting for her. With him she could lead a life of purpose.

'Forty million pesetas for a forward who can score goals,' said the driver. 'Madness, my wife says; but if you want the best you've got to pay for it. Here's the plaza. Where do you want put down?'

'Anywhere.'

'Anywhere's easily reached.' He drew in at the kerb. Then he turned and gave Jonathan a long grin. 'Foreigner, aren't you? If it's a bit of excitement you're looking for I'll take you to the very place; on the expensive side maybe, but worth it, they tell me.'

'No, thank you.' The charge on the meter was twelve pesetas. As Jonathan handed over fifteen he almost wished he was free to go to the high-class brothel, rather than to the church of San Sebastian.

The driver noticed his hesitation. 'It's not far; and if it's the law you're worried about, forget it. This place has very important clients.'

Such as policemen of high rank. Shaking his head, Jonathan began to walk across the great square in the direction of the Ramblas. As he passed the tall statues of naked women at the fountains he did not think of Montserrat's mother newly dead, or of his own dead long ago, or of Montserrat waiting for him, or of Maddy; he thought of, or tried hard to think of, the women in the place the taxi-driver had spoken of; and decided that in their naked perfumed flesh there could be as little comfort for him as in this massive marble. Among flowers, chastely floodlit, crouched one statue by herself, naked too, with one arm across her breasts. He walked slowly past her. No doubt the sculptor had meant to portray a lovely modest woman, as innocent as the flowers, and in her marmoreal blindness immune to lust. But to Jonathan then she seemed to be crouching in fear or shame.

The noises of the city, particularly of tram-cars screeching by, prevented her screams from being heard; but they could be as easily imagined as those of the picador's horse at the bull-fight, its vocal cords severed.

He had meant to go in a taxi to, say, Plaza España, and there take another taxi back to Plaza de San Sebastian; but the hour was now up, and in any case he had sunk into a dumb, unhappy anxiety to return to Montserrat. He remembered how, not so long ago, before he had even heard of Montserrat, he had pointed his finger at the horned cloud and imagined himself arrived at the moment of truth. How full of theatrical trivialities his life had been! And like a coward he was tempted to wish to go back to it.

The Plaza de San Sebastian was very quiet. He stood under the trees, listening to the taxi drive away. The lamp-light gleamed on the wet noses of the fish in the fountain, and on the stone face of Christ above the church door. The pigeons had gone, and the old men; the day's debate was over; the world's did not concern them. In the distance could be heard the throb of the city, and the stars were lost in its upflung radiance. Lovers were strolling along the Ramblas, or by the coloured fountains of Montjuich, or in front of the cinemas, talking of trivialities. He, so good at such exchanges, had instead to go into this church and talk of death.

Keeping in shadow, he hurried to the steps and slunk up them into the church, to find it darker and quieter than the plaza outside. Standing at the back, he counted only three worshippers. At first he could not see Montserrat and thought, in terror, she had gone; then he caught sight of her seated alone at a bench near the front, in an attitude of peculiar weariness, as if she had exhausted her soul in prayer, and God's patience. For two or three minutes he stood and watched her. Here in this large silent beautiful church, with the main altar bright among the many shadows, she was at her most strange, so much so he felt he would not have to try very hard to convince himself and her that they owed each other nothing and so could part without injustice or much hurt to either. Here, in this church of the pierced saint, he had to decide, and also to make his decision known, to her, and, for want of a better, to the great white gold-bearded Christ above the altar. Unworthy himself, in so many proved ways, he still had to be convinced she was worthy of him: he had seen where she lived, he knew she associated with political malcontents, at this very moment he was being warned her devotion might as she grew older degenerate into bigotry and idolatory. These were faults that, a week ago, he would have abhorred in any woman, and, indeed, still did. Yet he loved her, so completely that if he were to go away it would be into annihilation: without her there would be nothing. Therefore there was really no decision for him to make; his every heart-beat was making it for him. When he looked towards her a tenderness flowed through him such as, he thought, the saint himself, lover of God, had never experienced. He wanted to shout out his exultation in the great church.

As he went forward his footsteps, despite his wish to convey pity and love, rang out triumphantly on the stone floor. She turned and gave him a look in which recognition itself almost seemed stifled. Love blazed up in him and shrivelled all those mean cowardly doubts and reservations.

Her hands were cold. They were so tightly clasped he had to give up trying to take one. But he must tell her about her mother. Seeking help, he fixed his eyes on the pink, blue, and gold Christ above the main altar. The sculptor had allowed too much sweetness to seep into the meekness and love. The result was an expression of simpering guile that the gilt beard and hair accentuated. Jonathan wondered whether a believer, like Montserrat, could find in it comfort and strength. He himself could not; he had therefore to depend upon his own human resources, which never before had seemed so paltry.

Scalp icy, he blurted out what he had intended to say so reverently: 'I'm sorry. Your mother's dead.'

Again he tried to snatch her hand, and again she would not let him.

'She was buried this morning.' Then he dared say no more, could only try to share her suffering.

After what seemed a long time she asked, with a curious calmness: 'Who told you?'

'The portera.'

'Did you see my aunt?'

'No. She's gone. Tomorrow we'll try to get into touch with her.'

She said nothing, yet he could not have felt more excluded if she had been screaming at him to go, that she, her mother, and her aunt were none of his business and never could be. Her face was as tightly clasped as her hands. She kept shivering.

'I'm sorry,' he whispered.

'I'd like to pray.'

'Of course.'

But she waited, remotely, until at last he understood she either would not or could not pray for her mother's soul while he, who disbelieved, sat beside her. Whether he ached with sympathy or gloated with malice made little difference: his disbelief turned him into a nullity.

'I'll be waiting,' he said, and slipped away to sit at a bench at the back.

She prayed or grieved for over half an hour. When at last she came slowly up the aisle he noticed she held something in her hand. It was his wallet. As she gave it to him he saw she was not wearing the ring. She made sure their hands did not touch. Her face, marked with weeping, was tense and distant; and a little cruel.

Outside, as she went down the church steps, she said: 'I shall get my case out of the car, and then I shall take a taxi.'

'Where to?' he cried, in anguish. Not even the death of her mother explained or justified this cruelty.

'I shall go to a friend.'

He felt like crying, You had no friends to go to when you came to Cabo Creus, to my house. What he did say was, as gently as he could: 'But, Montsy, wasn't it arranged we should keep together? You heard me telephone the hotel.'

She didn't reply.

'What is it, my dear? What's gone wrong? I know you loved your mother, but I thought you loved me too, a little. Didn't you promise, at Gerona? I love you a great deal.'

Again she refused to answer, and walked on to where the car was parked. He could have wept in pity for them both. Never had she been so dear, so necessary. What she was condemning him to was a lifetime of paralysing loss. He remembered how the leaf in his hand, the ants under his feet, and the stars in the sky had been transfigured by her presence. If he lost her he would lose a glory that extended to the smallest crevice in the loneliest shore. He could not believe it possible.

'God knows I'm not worthy,' he said, 'but I want you, I need you.'

He strove to control himself. Her mother's death had stunned her. At this moment she felt a revulsion against the whole world, himself included. He must be patient.

Yet somehow she did not look repelled; on the contrary, when he stared into her face beside the car, he thought he had never seen her so dedicated. Fanatical was really the word that occurred to him. He sweated in terror.

'My case, please,' she said.

'No, Montsy. Just one hour ago when I left you in the church it was understood we were to keep together, return to Cabo Creus tomorrow, and on Sunday cross the border into France. It was even agreed we were to get married. Now you won't even talk to me. I know your mother's death is a terrible blow. I want to help you bear it. Please, you must let me.'

Eyes closed, she was shaking her head in a gesture as much of disdain as of denial, when suddenly they were joined by three men who came striding out of the shadows.

They were policemen, in plain clothes.

'Señorita Puig?' asked one, the leader.

Jonathan furiously pushed him away. 'You're wrong,' he cried. 'Her name is Ripoll. She's my fiancée. I'm an Englishman. You daren't lay a finger on her.'

'My name is Puig,' she said proudly.

'Yes, señorita, we know. We have a warrant for your arrest.'

'No,' cried Jonathan. 'I won't allow you. It's ridiculous. What has she done?'

'If you'll take my advice, señor, you'll lower your voice, and not attract attention. Better keep out of it.'

'He never was in it,' said Montserrat, turning away.

She was not trying to defend him; no, she was denying him. In his despair and fear he could have struck her.

The two other policemen took firm hold of him.

'We have a car along here, señorita,' said the one in command.

'Where are you taking her?' panted Jonathan. 'What are you going to do with her? She's just learned her mother's dead. Have some pity.'

'We have our duty to do.'

'My case is in the boot of the car,' said Montserrat. 'Am I allowed to take it with me?'

'Yes, of course. Get it, Miguel.'

Jonathan refused to hand over the key. 'You'll have to take it from me by force.'

'Then Señorita Puig will have to do without her case.'

'If she asks for it I'll give it to her.'

The policeman holding Jonathan laughed.

She would not ask.

'Here it is,' said Jonathan, sobbing.

Miguel took it, opened the boot, and pulled out the case.

'Well, shall we go, señorita?' asked the leader.

'One minute, please,' begged Jonathan. 'Just give us one minute, alone.'

As the policeman hesitated, Montserrat said: 'There's no need,' and walked away.

The policeman holding Jonathan let him go. There was a smell of garlic off his breath. 'No point in making a fuss,' he said. 'This is more or less routine. With luck she might get off with a fine. At the worst she'll get no more than a year. Plucky of her trying to convince us you weren't one of her crowd. But we knew that already. All the same, if I was you I'd be careful. Good luck.'

He hurried to join his colleagues. In another minute their car drove off.

Jonathan was left alone, his mind in pieces. As he closed his eyes, trying to recall her face as it had been before this desertion, it was the ants in the garden he remembered. They were protected by their single obscure purpose, and for those two or three minutes of utter desolation he envied them.

Thirty-One

After the car had gone bumping down the road out of sight Maddy remained on the terrace, murmuring, over and over again, 'Best of luck, Jonathan.' What she was expressing, though, was really her own confidence in her possession of John Lynedoch. It was almost as good, in some ways it was even better, than her discovering this sunny morning that she had been miraculously granted the power to paint well. To nurture his gift was more exciting. Perhaps she would go with him to Paris, so that he could study there. But more necessary than any perfecting of his technique was of course the ridding him of those absurd personal and national shames which at present coarsened his work. Yes, good luck to Jonathan and Montserrat on their foray into the guarded city; but the preparing of John Lynedoch for the painting of masterpieces was more important than the liberation of the whole of Spain.

She was joined by a peevish Isabel nursing a fretful Linda.

'So they've actually gone?' said Isabel.

'Yes. Good luck to them.'

Isabel sniffed, and then burst out: 'Heaven knows what'll happen to it.'

'To what?'

'Aunt Edith's ring. Go on, say I'm mercenary; I don't care. It ought to have been mine in the first place. Now it'll be sold to provide funds for a lot of half-baked revolutionaries.'

Linda, frightened by her mother's shrillness, fretted more pitifully.

'What's the matter with the little darling?' asked Maddy.

'I think she's got dysentery again. Her stool was horribly loose, and it stank. Need you look so smug, Maddy?'

'Was I looking smug?'

'Insufferably so.'

'I'm sorry. May I take her?'

Isabel, glad of a respite, handed the baby over; but a minute later snatched her back again.

'No,' she said, hugging the child. 'No. There's something else stinks.'

'What do you mean, Isabel?'

'My God, for months, all during the winter, I looked forward to this holiday: relaxing in the sunshine, I thought; dancing under the stars; drinking wine in the moonlight. Instead of which here's Linda with dysentery, Jonathan gone mad with a scheming bitch of a Spaniard, and you making a fool of yourself with a scruffy little Scotsman.'

She was almost hysterical.

'And now David's got a chill in the kidneys; or so he says. He was too drunk to get into bed last night, so he slept on the floor. I'm glad you're amused, Maddy. I suppose your paramour's got a pain in his back too, for different reasons. Linda darling, heaven knows what lies I'll have to tell you about your Aunt Maddy by the time you're old enough to inquire.'

'Just tell her I'm married to a wonderful painter.'

'No, Maddy. A man that lets you dominate him the way you do hasn't the guts to be a good painter. He'll end up painting the way you want him to paint. He'll paint like you, only with more skill. You've said yourself the better your kind of painting is done the falser it is.'

Maddy laughed. 'You can all go to hell.'

'Even as a child of five you were an unscrupulous little bitch, Maddy, always using your blue eyes and fair hair to get your own way. Be careful, though, Lynedoch's not quite as guileless as he seems.'

'She needs changing again,' said Maddy.

Isabel took it as the grossest of insults. Hugging her child, so innocently noisome, she rushed away.

When Maddy a few minutes later went back to her room she found Lynedoch had gone, taking the portrait of Margaret with him. As she made for his room she noticed that other paintings had been removed from the walls. His door was locked. She knocked indignantly.

'Who is it?' he asked, his voice at its surliest.

'Maddy. What have you done with the paintings? Come on, let me in.'

'Are you decently dressed?'

She smiled, suddenly relieved. 'They've gone. Jonathan and Montserrat have gone.' It seemed to her their adventure was not unlike hers and John's.

'To Perpignan?'

'No. To Barcelona.'

'I thought the police were waiting for her there.'

'Probably so they are. But she wanted to see her mother, who's ill; so Jonathan's taken her. I think it's marvellous.'

'He's a fool.'

'A fool?' She was astonished.

'Aye. If he wants to create anything worth while he should never let himself be used.'

'But he's in love with her.'

'What difference should that make?'

Alarmed, she again rattled the handle. 'Let me in.'

'Maybe. When you've got your clothes on.'

Furious but anxious she ran to her room, dragged on slacks and a blouse, and hurried back, hair dishevelled and feet bare.

'You can't have put much on in such a short time.'

'Please, John, let me in.'

He opened the door. She saw instantly he was packed, ready to go. More ominous than his battered bulging suitcases was his smile, arrogant, cruel, resentful, determined, and plebeian.

'You're still no' quite decent,' he said, and buttoned her blouse for her.

She clutched him. 'What are you all packed for?'

'I'm leaving.'

'Leaving?' Incredulity made her squeal. Surely he must realize that his success as a painter, his chances of adding grace to his strength and originality, depended upon her help. By himself, the labourer's son from Glasgow, he would never be more than a kind of primitive, powerful but crude. 'I thought it was understood you were to stay here and hold an exhibition?'

'By you, Maddy, no' by me. I'm not going to be used.'

'Used?'

'That's what you do with people, Maddy, just use them. You were disgusted with Ashton for praying after copulation.'

'You put it so elegantly.'

'I put it truthfully. You would be so far away, you know, he probably thought he had a better chance of getting into touch wi' God. You take everything, and give nothing.'

'I thought I'd given you more than you were able to take.'

He grinned. 'I'm sorry if I've disappointed you.'

'You've got a bloody nerve,' she cried. 'How much of yourself do you give? You're ten times more ruthless than I could ever be.'

'I've got a purpose.'

She knew he meant his painting, and she agreed with him. All of him should be saved for his painting. 'All right. I want to help you to achieve that purpose.'

'Then you'll not mind me going.'

'But I do, I can't help it,' she cried, in dismay.

'That's right, you can't help it; it's your nature to dominate all the men you meet. I can't let you dominate me. So I'll have to go. I'm not taking this. You can give it to Jonathan if he wants it.'

It was the unfinished portrait of Montserrat.

'Aren't you going to finish it?'

'No. It turned out she wasn't all that interesting.'

'And you have the nerve to call me ruthless.' Then she faced him, as humbly as she could. She felt strange, as if her whole nature was about to yield to humility. 'Please stay. I promise I won't ever interfere. I'll leave you absolutely alone.'

'But I wouldn't want you to.'

'What do you mean?'

'You're a beautiful woman, Maddy. If I stayed, do you think I'd want to have nothing to do with you? Surely you see I must go?'

Suddenly she did see it; she also saw him, somewhere out of her reach, making, with indomitable patience, for that superb assurance out of which grew masterpieces. She would have given her life to be able to be with him.

Shaken and trembling, she sat down on the bed.

In the silence they heard Linda cry, Isabel shout, and Ampara angrily sing.

'Where will you go?'

He shrugged.

'Will you leave Spain?'

'Not for a while.'

'Have you got money?'

'Enough.'

She could not bear to think of him without her. 'Aren't you going to leave me something to remember you by?'

'I've got nothing.'

'You've got everything.' So he had: sunshine, oranges, faces, churches, sky and sea, all were his. 'What about one of your paintings?'

'If you like. Take your pick.'

'Any one?'

'Aye.'

She looked through them till she came to the portrait of Margaret. 'This one too?'

He nodded.

Then she was in tears. 'I want them all,' she murmured. 'I want all those that aren't painted yet.' She snatched one up at random and ran to her own room where she flung herself on the bed, laughing and sobbing.

About fifteen minutes later she heard him drive away.

The Captain of Police, accompanied by a yellow-faced Pedro, called after lunch; and just before dinner Jonathan telephoned from Barcelona.

Thirty-Two

Jonathan found he needed human company, as much as he needed air to breathe. On his way to the hotel, therefore, he stopped outside a bar so popular that at other times he had avoided it. When he went in, the hubbub struck him at first as a concerted derision; these men and women, like Montserrat, were Spanish, and cruel. It took him almost five minutes, standing in the crush, to realize that not one of them was concerned about him, and that, indeed, most of them, laughing and talking and arguing, had troubles which they regarded as more important than his. Everyone believed himself betrayed. Who, not in this bar only but in the whole wide world, believed that the promises of life had been granted or ever would be?

Prostitutes of middle price frequented that bar. One, black-haired, not unlike Montserrat though coarser and more vulgarly made up, kept staring at him, and smiling in a way that reminded him of his rejection. All he had to do was smile back, and then she would come over, to take him away and sell him what solace and oblivion were in her plump body. He did not smile, and soon, giving him up with an unresentful shrug, she tried someone else, a small, furtive, obviously married man, who crept over, bought her a drink, and soon went trotting out after her. As she went she revealed a trick of walking not unlike Montserrat's, a proud swaying of the shoulders, so that Jonathan gazed out of the window after her, feeling betrayed for the second time that night.

Every woman in the bar, however meretricious, reminded him in some way of Montserrat.

Then it occurred to him that Maddy who could comfort him was only as far away as the telephone at the end of the long counter. At present it was being used by a man so Spanish in appearance, with swarthy face and thin black moustache, and so gleaming with pleased arrogance, that Jonathan, twitching with impatience, had seldom before hated a human face so much. It was the face of self-satisfaction, of impenetrable indifference; the face therefore that Montserrat must have seen when she had looked at him.

He's never been in it, she had said. Yes, and even now, in this bar, was he not proving her verdict just, even if her sentence remained savage and unpardonable? Only he, of a hundred people, kept aloof, speaking to no one. Smiles, winks, nudges, gestures with glasses, remarks, all these he ignored, as he had always done. Yet he had come in here for their company.

At last the telephone was his. He guarded it during the few minutes it took to get through.

Unfortunately it was Isabel who answered. He could scarcely hear her, because of the din around him, and the faraway faintness of her voice; but in any case he had nothing to say to her, she was chief among the many who would find neither surprise nor tragedy in what had happened to him.

She sounded tired and hoarse, and made an effort to be loving. 'Well, thank goodness you've at last decided to let us know what's happened to you. We've been sick with worry. Where are you speaking from?'

'A bar.'

She laughed. 'It sounds like it. What a rabble. It's almost as bad here. Those eternal sardanas have started. It's a wonder you can't hear them.'

'Is Maddy there?'

'Yes, she is. Well, what did happen? We've had a lot of

excitement here today, I can tell you. The police were here, as you'll probably know.'

'Yes. Who told them where we were? Who betrayed us?'

'Pedro brought them.'

'The treacherous, lying bastard.'

'Jonathan, please.'

'But he didn't know we were coming to Barcelona, to visit her mother. You did, Isabel, and you didn't approve of her.'

'So that's what you think of me, Jonathan? No one told them. They told us. They were expecting it. We couldn't warn you. Have they arrested her?'

'Yes, Isabel, they have.'

'I'm sorry, Jonathan, I truly am. Is she in prison?'

'Where else?'

'She'll have the ring to remember you by.'

'Don't worry about the ring, Isabel. She gave it back. You can have it after all.'

'Won't you be giving it to her when she comes out again?'

'Please, Isabel, I would like to speak to Maddy.'

She did not answer.

'And hurry, for God's sake. This isn't a private phone, you know. There's somebody breathing down my neck waiting for it.'

Content to wait, the man had a hairy finger with a big gold ring on it. He kept grinning at Jonathan, to let him know there was no hurry.

'I ought to warn you, Jonathan.'

'What about?'

'Maddy. You see, Lynedoch's gone.'

'Well, what's surprising about that? I didn't expect him to stay.'

'No, but Maddy did. To tell you the truth, if I didn't know her, I'd say she's breaking her heart for him; which would be ridiculous.'

'Yes, wouldn't it, Isabel? Do you know me well enough to be sure I'm not breaking mine?'

'Yes, Jonathan, I think I do. You and Maddy have always had each other, you've never wanted and never needed anyone else.'

'Please ask her to come to the telephone, Isabel.'

'Very well. Be as tactful as you can.'

He could have wept. 'Tactful?'

'Yes. She's really upset. I don't know if they quarrelled, but she certainly didn't want him to go. Of course it's the best thing that could have happened, but she can't see that yet. Just a moment.'

He heard her put the telephone down on the little table in the hall. Seeing it, he saw the whole house that during the past few days had grown so much dearer because of Montserrat's presence in it. The sense of loss overwhelmed him again.

Then Maddy's voice, wild and warm with sympathy and love, brought him back from that terrible blankness. 'Oh Jonathan darling, I'm so terribly sorry.'

Tears came into his eyes. 'Isabel's told you?'

'Yes. It's awful, I know, but it's not unbearable. A year's a long time, two years, three years, but in the end, what joy!'

'But, Maddy, she's given me up, thrown me over, denied me. I don't know why, Maddy. I came back from visiting her mother, and she was in the church waiting for me. I wasn't away more than an hour, but she had changed, completely. She gave me back the ring. She kept looking at me as if she didn't know me. Why, Maddy, why? You're a woman. You ought to know.'

'Well, Jonathan, they say, don't they, that it's the lady's privilege to change her mind?'

'Don't make a joke of it, Maddy. I love her. I love her so much that being without her is more than I think I'll be able to bear. I could have waited for ten years, but now I'm waiting, you see, for nothing, nothing at all.'

'Yes, Jonathan, I see. What about her mother?'

'She's dead. She was buried this morning.'

'Poor Montserrat. How awful for her.'

'Yes, but it wasn't that either. Even if I had brought back good news she'd still have denied me. She had prayed herself into it. Yet in Gerona Cathedral she promised so solemnly to marry me. I asked her not to commit herself, but she said she wanted to. She even kissed me, of her own accord. Whatever happens, she said, we'll meet again. Yet half an hour ago she turned her back on me. Why did she do it, Maddy?'

'Was this when she was arrested?'

'Yes.'

'Wasn't she trying to protect you?'

'No, Maddy. She'd decided before they appeared. My God, she was more friendly to them than she was to me. You haven't been able to suggest any reason, Maddy, that I can understand.'

'She's Spanish. As I've said before, we know their language but not their minds.'

'You mean they're cruel?'

'You and I know lots of kind ones.'

'Could it be, Maddy, that she acknowledged them, the police, I mean, as being involved, even though on the wrong side, whereas I've never been involved at all?'

'Involved in what? I'm sorry, Jonathan, if I sound awfully obtuse, but it's so hard to make you out, you're so upset, and the line's so bad, and I'm so miserable myself, and it's so noisy with sardanas down in the plaza. I suppose you mean, involved in their struggle for political rights?'

'Yes, but it's wider than that, much wider.'

'Yes. Yes, it is. Really, Jonathan, you and I have ventured far out of our depths. Luckily it was the Captain of Police I know who called. I hope we won't be flung out, but it's in the balance.'

'Pedro betrayed us.'

'Yes. He looked very dejected about it. I'm afraid we've betrayed ourselves. You'll be home tomorrow?'

'I haven't thought about tomorrow. I'm afraid to. I can't think one minute ahead; you see, it's empty of her, that minute, and oh God, there are millions and millions of them.'

'You must come home.'

'No.'

'But what can you do in Barcelona?'

'I can try to see her. I can write to her. I can get a lawyer to fight her case. I can send her food and books. I can see her at her trial. Laugh if you like, Maddy, but the very fork she put to her mouth was sacred.'

'I'm not laughing, Jonathan; far from it. But you've known her such a short time.'

'As long as you've known John Lynedoch. I'm sorry, Maddy. I shouldn't have said that. Isabel told me he's gone. Too bad. I mean, you wanted him to stay, didn't you?'

'Yes, I wanted him to stay. But, darling, hasn't it occurred to you that all the time she's been in love with someone else? She told me about a Spaniard she evidently liked and admired.'

'But that's over long ago. He became a communist.'

'If she loved him, he could have become a leper, and it would have made no difference.'

'Maddy, no one could have made a more solemn promise than the one she made to me this morning in Gerona Cathedral.'

Maddy paused. 'Perhaps it wasn't really to you.'

'To whom, then?'

'To this Spaniard.'

He was indignant. 'I may be as ineffectual and transparent as innocence denotes, Maddy, but I do have some little individuality, some modicum of personal flavour. I believe Tomas Balaguer's as black as a gipsy.'

'Poor girl.'

For an instant he thought that her pity ought more justly to be for him. Then he remembered Montserrat in prison, mourning her mother; and he caught a glimpse of why he had been rejected.

He became aware Maddy was crying.

'Are you crying, Maddy?' he asked.

'I'm afraid I am. You see, I've lost someone too.'

'You mean Lynedoch?'

'Yes. Good night, Jonathan.'

'Good night, Maddy.'

He put down the telephone, and the fellow waiting, before picking it up, patted him on the shoulder with that hairy gold-ringed hand, and whispered, with tipsy, facetious solicitude: 'Courage, friend.'

Yet what use was courage? If she had only been arrested, and therefore at that moment further from him than if she had been at the other side of the world, he could still have made in his soul preparations to journey to her, and at their meeting, no matter how long delayed, what joy, as Maddy had said. But by her denial of him she had put herself as far beyond his reach as if she were dead, and every bright reaching towards her, every foretaste of that immense joy of seeing her again, had instantly to be extinguished.

MORE TITLES BY ROBIN JENKINS

The Missionaries

Set on the remote Scottish island of Sollas, this complex and thought-provoking novel explores the themes of social and moral conflict. When a group of Christian sectarians invade the island to live and worship at its ancient shrine, the island's owner Mr Vontin and his daughter take steps to have them removed.

Caught in the middle is Andrew Doig, proud of his moral integrity and passionate in his defence of the sectarians. But his uncle is in charge of the eviction and also demands his allegiance. *The Missionaries* charts Andrew's voyage of self-discovery and his realisation that ahead of him still lies 'a whole lifetime of searching'.

Many people can produce a novel, but very few are authentic writers whose sentences and paragraphs give intrinsic pleasure. Jenkins is one of them.
J. B. Pick

198 x 129mm paperback
229 pages
£6.99
ISBN 1 904598 59 5
2005

A Very Scotch Affair

'The trouble with you Mungo, is that you're too Scotch.
You enjoy letting your conscience torment you. You're out-
of-date.'

Robin Jenkins' novel is set in Glasgow and tells the tale of
Mungo Niven, a man who feels trapped in a drab and
unfulfilling existence. Mungo's wife is the extroverted and
excessively cheerful Bess, who dismisses Mungo's vague
intellectual and amorous ambitions as pointless dreams.
When Bess is stricken with cancer, Mungo sees an opportunity to escape his loveless marriage and tyrannical conscience.

Readers are pulled into a story which has well-drawn
characters, a strong sense of place and real people involved
in real situations. The complex themes of betrayal and
conscience are explored with precision and a delightfully
wicked sense of humour.

Quite simply a major contemporary Scottish writer.
The Herald

198 x 129mm paperback
192 pages
£6.99
ISBN 1 904598 44 7
2005

Some Kind of Grace
Introduction by James Meek

Two British travellers, Donald Kemp and Margaret Duncan, have disappeared in the wild and mountainous region of northern Afghanistan; a terrain into which western Europeans seldom penetrate. The authorities in Kabul say that they have been murdered by the inhabitants of a small and primitive village and that retribution has already been exacted in the form of wholesale reprisals. John McLeod, a friend of the missing couple who has spent some years in Afghanistan as a diplomat, is deeply suspicious of these explanations. He returns to Kabul and starts his own enquiries, but everywhere he is met with obstruction and evasion.

[Jenkins] finds another rare spot, that place of honesty where multiple contradictory truths reside, where men and women can be both wicked and brave, vengeful and remorseful, bigoted and generous; where, when they go looking for absolute truths they fail to find them.
James Meek

198 x 129mm paperback
256 pages
£6.99
ISBN 1 904598 19 6
2006

The Thistle and the Grail
Introduction by Harry Reid

The Thistle is the unlucky football team of Drumsagart, a drab industrial town in Lanarkshire. Cursed with poverty, an ineffectual president and a string of defeats, they are running low on morale. Everyone seems to be against them, including the devious local policemen. The sanctimonious new minister and, even, their very own wives.

When they actually start winning, a momentum grows in the community, and they come to represent ambition and hope.

Easily the best book written on the relation between football and society in Scotland.
John Cairney

198 x 129mm paperback
304 pages
£6.99
ISBN 1 904598 76 5
2006

Dust on the Paw
Introduction by David Pratt

Abdul Wahab, an Afghan science teacher, is eagerly anticipating he arrival of his British fiancée, Laura Johnstone, in
the capital of his home country. After meeting while Abdul
was a student at Manchester University, the couple are eager
to settle down in Isban. However, Abdul is not the only one
interested in Miss Johnstone's arrival. Prince Naim, one of
the sons of the king, sees the marriage as symbolic of the
successful union between East and West, and, in his hurry to
cement this union, promotes Abdul to a position of power
he is far from ready for.

*Jenkins [is] a remarkable writer whose gentlest touch induces the
greatest of pleasures.*
The Times

198 x 129mm paperback
288 pages
£7.99
ISBN 1 904598 84 6
2006